Roxana's Revolution

To my friend Tracy

Farin

Roxana's Revolution

Farin Powell

iUniverse, Inc.
Bloomington

Roxana's Revolution

iUniverse books may be ordered through booksellers or by contacting:

iUniverse
1663 Liberty Drive
Bloomington, IN 47403
www.iuniverse.com
1-800-Authors (1-800-288-4677)

ISBN: 978-1-4759-8062-2 (sc)
ISBN: 978-1-4759-8063-9 (hc)
ISBN: 978-1-4759-8064-6 (ebk)

Library of Congress Control Number: 2013904798

Printed in the United States of America

iUniverse rev. date: 04/16/2013

To Reza, Hamid, Nahid, Nadi, and all those whose lives were changed because of the Iranian Revolution

Acknowledgment

I would like to thank Richard, and Bobby for being my first readers and critics. I'm grateful to Jimmy, Judith and Feri for their enthusiasm about my work. Special thanks to Soraya for her book club reading efforts, and finally, many thanks to Ambassador John Limbert for being a class act. Despite his 444—day experience in Tehran, he still believes that there should be dialogue between Iran and the United States. The world would be a better place if we had more diplomats with John Limbert's depth of knowledge and cultural understanding.

Prologue

June 1990—Paris

Having touched death several times in her life, Roxana Ramsy has never been afraid of her own death. She fears instead for the life of her childhood friend, Lili, who's returning to Tehran without her Iranian passport, having forfeited it after leaving a sensitive government job many years ago. Using her British passport, Lili is trying to enter Iran and free her father from jail. She is ready to endure any political consequences. Or she believes she is.

After an emotional farewell to Lili, Roxana doesn't feel like going back to her hotel room. She walks by the Seine until she finds a quiet area. She sits on the riverbank facing Notre Dame Cathedral. She cannot enjoy the scenes around her when Lili is facing danger.

Staring into the water, she calculates the approximate time Lili's plane will land in Tehran. Can Lili survive in prison? Will she ever see Lili again? She wonders.

Anxiety crawls under Roxana's skin like millions of invisible creatures. She hates the feeling, the numbness of her brain and the rapid heartbeats. She imagines that she should be used to fear by now. She gripped its hands every time Saddam Hussein bombed Tehran, and every time her husband abused her.

She raises her gaze to the towering spires of Notre Dame and the picturesque scene across the river. Sitting on the bank, with her heart halfway across the world, she expects to hear sad music, the kind played during rainy funeral scenes in movies. Instead, she hears the thunderous cry of *Allahu Akbar,* God is great—the same chant she heard so many times during her years in Tehran.

The passage of a large Bateau Mouche and the cheerful buzz of its passengers interrupt her thoughts. *Lili is in danger, and carefree tourists enjoy their boat ride on the Seine River. What's wrong with this picture?* She is in Paris, her favorite of all European cities, but she doesn't feel the city is there.

Roxana's friends often tease her for considering Paris a mistress—a thrilling diversion from her problems. Since her first trip at the age of seventeen, she believed she owned a small piece of that city.

Now, after living through the Iranian Revolution, Saddam's cruel war, and a stormy divorce, she finds that Paris can't remove the bitter taste in her mouth. No, this isn't the city she used to know, the mistress she used to have.

She has known for some time that the city doesn't belong to her anymore, the same way she doesn't belong to Paris, or any other city for that matter. The question, though, the one that has haunted her throughout the day, is how can she save Lili?

All her life, Roxana has solved her friends' problems. Why does she feel so helpless now?

She starts walking alongside the river, remembering her life, Lili's, and the lives of those she has left behind. She doesn't know that by the end of the day, her own life will change forever.

PART 1

Chapter 1

November 1979—New York City

On Monday, November 18, 1979, Roxana read the deportation notice once more. She took a deep breath to digest what she had read. The letter had the official seal of the Immigration Office; it was real. For a moment she felt she had been pushed off a cliff and was tumbling down with no one around to help her. What was she supposed to do? She had heard about immigration jails and forced deportation. Fighting tears, she wondered about her future. Her American dream had just been shattered, like a house of cards blown away in the wind.

* * *

Sunday, November 4, 1979. Roxana finished the final draft of her pleadings in an antitrust law case that her law firm was handling in Geneva. She felt tired. She put her legal pad down and took a ten-minute break. She fixed herself a cup of coffee and returned to her Queen Ann desk chair. Huddled over the steaming cup, she pressed her spine into the quilted leather of her chair and let out a deep breath. She looked out the window, taking in the beauty of the sunset reflected in the Hudson. A white charter boat drifted out of sight behind the Merrill Lynch building, which obstructed the left angle of her view.

Occasionally, Roxana sat there and wondered what it would be like to work for a big company like Merrill Lynch but knew she had a long way to go before such a job could be within her reach. She needed a few years of corporate law experience.

She finished her coffee and realized that she should be grateful for the job she had—especially as she'd been so close to giving up on the idea of a job in New York City before Rubin & Stein—a small Wall Street law firm—hired her. If she'd heard, "You have a doctoral degree; you should be teaching law," one more time during those lean months, she thought she'd scream.

Yet the partners at Rubin & Stein seemed more than impressed by her expertise in international law, her awards, and the long list of law review publications—the exact things that had worked against her in previous interviews.

Luckily for her, Rubin & Stein's clients transacted their business in Europe, mostly in Switzerland. Her knowledge of several foreign languages and her ability to write pleadings for European courts landed her the job after only a thirty-minute interview.

After reviewing her brief for a last time, she piled the legal pads—with instructions—on the secretary's desk. Rubin and Stein were both in Geneva waiting to receive the materials.

She was too tired to take the subway home. She called the firm's limousine company and ordered a car—a reward her bosses allowed anytime she worked late or during the weekends.

The limousine driver dropped her in front of her apartment building on East Seventy-Ninth Street. She remembered she had nothing to prepare for dinner, so she walked into the small convenience store near the building and bought a TV dinner, a can of Pepsi, and one vanilla ice cream cone.

Back in her apartment, she ate her dinner by the light of a small lamp on the table next to the sofa and listened to her answering machine. After the first lengthy message, something about a New York Bar Association event, her friend Lili Cohan's panicked voice crackled across the line.

"Roxana, I don't have your new office number. I've been trying to reach you all afternoon. Some students have taken hostages at the American Embassy in Tehran. Please call me."

Roxana's fork fell to the floor. She put her unfinished TV dinner on the table, turned the TV on, and switched from channel to channel, watching the story unfold.

She couldn't believe what she was seeing. She turned the TV off, stared at her melting ice cream, and muttered, "Oh my God."

Chapter 2

As it was 3:00 a.m. where Lili was in London, Roxana didn't call her, assuming she'd be asleep. Instead, she called her younger brother and sister, both of whom lived in New Hampshire.

Her first call was to Bahram, who didn't have much to say about the matter. He was busy at work and was preoccupied with a project he had to finish.

So she called her sister, Neghar, to find out her take on the situation.

Neghar had more time to chat with her sister and talk about the hostage crisis. After they hung up the phone, Roxana checked her call list. Nina had called too. She marveled that Lili and Nina, whom she'd known since childhood—and who, along with Roxana, had been dubbed "The Three Musketeers"—still kept in such close contact. She felt grateful every day to have them in her life, though circumstances kept them apart geographically.

When Roxana dialed Nina's number, she got her answering machine.

Probably at the hospital, she thought.

Although she was shocked about the seizure of the US Embassy in Tehran, Roxana slipped under the covers that night, confident that the American hostages would be released within the next few days.

* * *

Amrika Held Hostage: Iran Crisis was the title of a TV news program Roxana hated to watch. Every day, she promised herself that she would not watch the program anymore, but every night she found herself glued to the TV set, watching Ted Koppel's powerful coverage of the crisis.

A few days after the US Embassy's seizure in Tehran, President Carter boycotted the importation of Iranian oil. Then, on November 13 and 14, 1979, he ordered the freezing of about $12 billion of Iranian assets in the United States. The next order was the deportation of Iranian students whose visas had expired or who were not enrolled in school. At the time, Iran had over fifty-one thousand students in the United States, more than any foreign country except Japan.

Roxana and other Iranians felt floored, as though everything they'd known and counted on had disappeared in a puff of smoke. In the seventies, they were used to first-class treatment in the United States, mostly due to the celebrity status of the Shah of Iran and his relations with Israel and the States. The February 11, 1979, revolution did not cause any anti-Iranian sentiments in the United States. But after the hostage taking on November 4, 1979, Iranians turned into savage, hostage-taking barbarians in the eyes of many Americans. At least that's how it felt to Roxana, as she continued to conduct the normal business of her life.

She began to feel as though she and all Iranians had been blamed for the hostage taking. Friends came to her with stories of attacks on Iranian students and businesses. Anti-Iranian bumper stickers and T-shirts cropped up everywhere. Some compared the treatment of the Iranians to that of the Japanese after Pearl Harbor. It felt as though she moved through her life under the constant angry eye of her community, and she wasn't sure she had the strength to shrug that feeling off for long.

She reluctantly watched every TV news channel, read each newspaper article about Iran, and kept praying the crisis would be over soon. She was surprised when certain political pundits ignored the reasons behind the Iranian Revolution and only analyzed its impact on the Soviet-US relationship. She felt the urge to question the pundits. *What about the impact of the revolution on the Iranian people?*

Her question didn't echo anywhere.

* * *

One evening, Roxana went to the law library at NYU to do some research. By the time she finished, it was after 11:00 p.m. She found Washington Square Park completely empty. She took a deep breath, surprised at the feelings of apprehension that rose in her. To her, the sight was surreal. The park and the surrounding streets were always crowded. What had happened to the Russian and Ukrainian chess players? They were like permanent fixtures in the park.

As she began walking toward the First Avenue bus stop, she became aware of a black limousine, with dark tinted windows, gliding quietly behind her. She pulled her jacket more tightly around her body and started walking fast.

The limousine continued to trail her slowly, keeping pace. A sudden fear crawled under her skin. Her heart pounded violently in her throat. She looked around desperately, hoping to spot someone else on the street, but saw no one. Choked with fright, she hastened across the street, but before she reached the curb, two men wearing black suits, like gangsters from the '40s, jumped out of the car and grabbed her.

Her scream died in her throat as one of the men shoved a rough piece of cloth into her mouth. The other one pulled a hood over her head, covering her face. Everything went dark. Her only thought was, *Oh God, let me live.* A pair of hands shoved her into the limousine, and then one of the men lifted the hood and pressed a strip of tape over her mouth.

The limousine took off with a screech and sped through the streets of Manhattan. Roxana's hands were tied behind her back, and fear and desperation created a violent hammering in her chest that she felt sure would kill her any second. Who were those people? What did they want? She tried to grab onto any bit of logic she could muster, but her world and her thoughts were too dark. *Let me live*, she thought again, and that one thought filled every part of her being.

After a long drive, the limousine stopped. Roxana's body trembled. The men grabbed her and lifted her out of the vehicle, and someone fastened a heavy bag around her neck. The next thing she felt was a strong push, her body falling through the air, and then the chill of water rushing around her. The sound of the splash echoed in her head.

Then she was drowning.

Chapter 3

Roxana bolted out of bed, her trembling body soaked with sweat. Her heart beat so loudly that her ears pulsated to its rhythm. She stumbled from her bed and ran toward the kitchen. Her shaky hands reached for a towel lying on the counter, and she dabbed the sweat from her forehead and neck. She poured herself a glass of cold water and downed it in one gulp. Setting the glass down on the counter, she leaned back against the adjacent wall and slid down to the floor. She held her head in both hands. *It was only a dream, only a dream.*

She didn't have any appetite for breakfast, so she took a shower and left for work. Upon her return, she found a letter from Immigration and Naturalization Services in her mailbox.

"What now?" she asked, tearing it open.

The note ordered her to contact the agency for a deportation hearing. It acknowledged that her student visa was valid until June 1980. However, since she had already received her degree, she could no longer be categorized a student. The notice didn't mention the pending application for permanent residency that Rubin & Stein had filed on her behalf.

She sat down and took her head with both hands, trying to squeeze the shocking news out of her brain. She felt numb, her body weak as it had been in her dream. Why was she being punished for the actions of some students thousands of miles away?

She decided to see an immigration attorney before the partners returned from Switzerland. She knew all too well about the horrors of the deportation cases.

A day later, she found herself in the office of Brett Klein, an immigration attorney.

Mr. Klein, a man in his fifties with impeccable posture, reviewed all of Roxana's immigration documents. "I know a wonderful immigration judge in New York City. He may not get your case, but I am going to talk to him about you."

"Mr. Klein, I don't want to go through deportation procedure; can we expedite the process of getting my green card?"

"Not with this hostage hysteria going on."

"Please do whatever you can to stop this deportation."

"Let me see what I can do. In the meantime, be patient; this crisis won't be resolved soon."

* * *

Roxana anxiously followed the news about the lawsuit that a group of Iranian students had filed in the District Court of Washington, DC. They had challenged the legality of President Carter's order. The court ruled that it was unconstitutional to single out Iranian students and not other foreign students. But the attorney general appealed the decision.

The Court of Appeals agreed with the government that the actions of the hostage-takers had posed "an extraordinary threat to the national security, foreign policy, and economy of the United States," as declared in President Carter's orders.

Roxana, tired of the media frenzy, accepted an invitation for a night out with her friend Judith. Although a busy literary agent, Judith—an attractive brunette—usually dressed up like a New York model. She was also the only friend who managed to coax Roxana out of a funk or away from her obligations.

"You have to give yourself a break. Have a little fun," Judith said.

She picked out a nice Italian restaurant on the West Side, telling Roxana it was impossible to be in a bad mood there. The restaurant was crowded, but a table waited for them when they arrived. As soon as they sat down, Roxana heard a heated debate among three men at the adjacent table.

"Carter should send the marines and set the Iranian oil wells on fire," one man said.

"No. We should close the Persian Gulf to stop the flow of their oil. That would really choke them up."

But the third man, who appeared to be the youngest of the group, shook his head and said, "That will jeopardize the lives of the hostages. Carter should ask the Israeli commandos to rescue them."

Roxana did not need to hear any more to know where this was headed. She had published a law review article about Entebbe, where Israeli commandos raided Uganda and rescued over a hundred Israeli hostages. She shuddered at the thought of such a bloodbath. She wondered how the three men would react had they known that she was Iranian.

When the waiter came to take their order, Judith stood and said, "Sorry, we have to go. It's too noisy here."

They left the restaurant and searched for another.

"You see, there's no escape," Roxana said. "The TV coverage, the newspapers, people riding the subway. Everywhere I go people are talking about the hostages. All of a sudden Iranians are barbaric. Iranians living in the States had nothing to do with the hostage taking."

"How did Rubin & Stein react to the news?"

"Since their return from Geneva, they've tried to expedite my green-card process, but the government has suspended all applications for Iranians. You know, it blows my mind when I really think about it. There were hundreds of thousands of Americans in Iran before the revolution, and no one ever displayed any hostility toward them. We had many Americans in my neighborhood in the '60s. The number increased ten times more in the '70s."

"Well, that was during the shah."

"It had nothing to do with him. I'm talking about the people, the culture. We're the most hospitable nation in the world."

"Don't worry; the crisis will be over soon."

"It's getting worse. Sometimes, when I'm walking, I'm afraid that someone will point to me and say, 'Arrest her; she's an Iranian.'"

"It's not that bad."

"Yes, it is, trust me. I can't get the images of the protestors on TV, and their signs, which read, 'Deport all Iranians,' or, 'Iranians, get the hell out of the US,' out of my mind."

"Why don't you come and spend the weekend in our place in South Hampton? It's cold, but it's more relaxing than the city."

Roxana had shied away from all of Judith's previous invitations for Thanksgiving, Christmas, and New Year's Eve parties. "I can't promise, but I'll try."

She hugged Judith, thanked her for the dinner, and headed home. It was raining, so she ran to the subway entrance.

When she transferred to the Lexington Avenue train, she noticed a charming man standing a few feet away. He was watching her while pretending to read the *New York Times*.

The ride was short. It was still pouring outside when she exited the subway.

She had walked less than a few feet when she heard a voice behind her.

"Miss, would you like to share my umbrella?"

She turned around and met the man from the train face-to-face. She wondered whether the man was an Immigration or FBI agent following her. She looked at him again. His heavy attaché suggested to her he could be an attorney or an accountant. After a brief hesitation, she decided to take shelter from the storm. She ducked her head underneath the stream of water pouring from the umbrella's edges and pulled her body under the large umbrella as much as she could. It felt good in that moment to be protected from the rain.

"Thanks. Where are you heading?" she asked.

"Second Avenue."

"Me too."

"Can you believe a tropical rain in January?"

"It's rather unusual."

"I'm a patent lawyer; I work on Lexington Avenue. Do you work in midtown?"

"No, I work on Wall Street."

When the two arrived at Second Avenue, she turned to the man to thank him. He spoke before she could.

"I was hoping we could have lunch sometime."

"Thanks, but I'm very busy these days."

The man looked disappointed but didn't put up a fight. When they reached Second Avenue, he spoke again. "You don't have any accent, but your beautiful reddish hair and the European look—where are you from?"

She smiled and waved at him. "You don't want to know." She ran toward her building.

Before heading to her apartment, she stopped at the convenience store to buy a *Time* magazine. The old female cashier gave her a worried look when she approached the counter. "You'd better go and dry that long hair immediately. You're gonna catch a cold," she said.

Roxana smiled at her concern, which was uncharacteristic for the usually dour woman who'd barely spoken to her before.

She handed her a five-dollar bill and the magazine. On impulse, she asked, "Do you follow the hostage crisis?"

"No," the cashier replied. "When I go home, I like to watch something that makes me laugh, like *Lucy*." She handed Roxana the change.

"I'm an Iranian, you know," she blurted for reasons she herself didn't understand.

"So? You're here. You didn't take no hostages."

Roxana smiled at the woman and left the store.

Chapter 4

When she saw Brett Klein's face, she knew he had bad news.

"Well, there's a moratorium on immigrant applications of Iranians," he told her, as soon as pleasantries had been exchanged. "And because you've finished your education your student visa is no longer valid."

"So what are my options?"

"The good news is that the judge was very impressed with your resume. In fact, he said, 'How can I deport a woman who has three law degrees more than I have?' He's willing to delay the deportation hearing until things cool down."

Roxana felt an icy calm descend over her, and she stood, as if automatically. She picked up her coat and purse, extended her hand toward her attorney, and said, "Thank you, Mr. Klein. There is no need to delay the hearing. I'm going home. I'll leave New York as soon as I settle my lease with my landlord."

"What about your job? You told me that the firm was merging with Baron & Rosendorf, and your bosses want to take you with them. Why give that all up?"

"Because of anti-Iranian sentiments, the big law firm can only offer me a paralegal job."

"Ouch!"

"I have some pride, and I'm not going to hide as an illegal alien. Thanks for everything you've done for me. I'll send you a check for the remaining—"

"That won't be necessary. The retainer fee you paid is enough. I'm still shocked you're leaving, though. I have several clients who stop by my office every day, trying to get their relatives out of Iran. They say life is so miserable there."

"Life is no paradise here, either."

* * *

Her landlord allowed her to terminate her lease after Roxana found a new tenant for him—the firm's new secretary, newly arrived from Minnesota and looking for an apartment in New York.

"You don't rent apartments in Manhattan," she jokingly told the woman. "You inherit them. You're lucky my landlord accepted you."

She *burned* all of her belongings, as her friends put it, by selling the secretary everything she had in that apartment for only $500.

On the last day of her work, the two partners took her to an expensive restaurant. Though they'd given up trying to persuade her not to leave the country, they asked her again. She gave them the same response she had given to Attorney Klein.

After the lunch, she walked to Battery Park and sat on a bench facing the Statue of Liberty.

"If only you knew what's going on in the world these days," she said to the statue, thinking about all that it symbolized to her, and especially all that it stood for when she'd first arrived in the States.

On the long walk home, she felt pierced by nostalgia, as though she had started missing New York City before she'd even left. She wanted to capture the images of Madison Avenue antique shops, the Fifth Avenue stores, Central Park, and the East River ferries. She felt sure she'd never see New York City again.

She arrived home exhausted. Two messages waited on her answering machine.

First Lili: "I've decided to go back home too. And guess what, Nina is also heading for Tehran. Call me."

Roxana jumped for joy. She didn't hear the rest of the message, dialing Lili immediately. "When did you make that decision?"

"When I lost my job," Lili said, "and please don't ask whether it was hostage related. I'm so sick and tired of the media coverage."

"You're a British citizen. Do you think you can get a visa to go back?"

"Do you think they're gonna take me hostage too?" Lili laughed. "I can get an Iranian passport. My father is still an Iranian citizen. That should be good enough."

"Why's Nina going back?"

"She'll tell you herself. She was up to get a position at the hospital, but they gave it to someone else."

"But, she's a US citizen!"

"It doesn't matter. She's from Iran."

"Listen, Lili, I want to spend some time in a neutral land. I want to go to Paris first. Would you come to Paris?"

"I'll think about it."

Roxana hung up the phone and stared at a picture on top of her dresser. The picture, taken at a high school event, showed the teenage Roxana, Lili, Nina, and a few other high school classmates. Lili was the only blue-eyed blonde in the group. Roxana sighed, realizing how much she had missed her two childhood friends.

* * *

Roxana listened to the second message on her answering machine—a dinner invitation from one of her NYU law professors. He wanted to chat about Iran. The idea carried absolutely no appeal to Roxana, but she called him and accepted the invitation.

Professor Haldane had a beautiful home in Greenwich Village. Roxana was surprised to find three other male guests. The men wore three-piece suits, which made them look like government officials. Ironically, they were from the State Department. Roxana chuckled to herself but greeted everyone politely.

Professor Haldane introduced Roxana. "This young lady made history in our law school by not only getting our most prestigious award in international law, but also finishing her doctoral degree in only eighteen months."

"Professor, no one is interested in hearing that," Roxana said, feeling her face redden with embarrassment.

"She's too modest!" Professor Haldane commented.

While the professor bundled about with the preparation of dinner, the three men cornered Roxana to share their knowledge of all the significant events of the Iranian Revolution.

They knew about "Black Friday," September 8, 1978, when the army opened fire and killed many people who had demonstrated in the area near the Iranian Parliament. They knew about the August 1978 burning of Cinema Rex in Abadan that killed several hundred people, and they knew about the strikes and demonstrations by millions of Iranians that had paralyzed the country.

What they didn't know, or pretended not to know, was the fact that the 1979 Iranian Revolution was not religious in nature, nor was it the "ayatollahs' revolution." All opponents of the shah participated. This included the National Front, the Freedom Movement of Iran, the Constitutionalists, liberals and intellectuals, the Bazaaris, the reformists, the Islamic Marxists, and the Communist Party.

Roxana explained the specific grievances of each antishah group, but emphasized that the core of dissatisfaction was the lack of political freedom.

After dinner and after spending hours in kind but tedious conversation, Roxana thanked Professor Haldane and left his home. It was a cold January night, but she decided to walk in the Village area one last time. She knew she wouldn't have time to come back to this part of the city before her departure.

She sat on a bench in Washington Square Park and looked at the illuminated Etoile, which always reminded her of Paris.

For a moment, she closed her eyes and heard the cheers of thousands of students and their families who had filled Washington Square on the graduation date. She remembered the proud faces of her family members and friends when the dean handed her the JSD diploma, adding that the degree was rarely awarded.

Leaving the park, she passed the Ukrainians and Russians, playing chess.

At least some things will stay the same, she thought.

Chapter 5

She called her parents to tell them she'd decided to go to Paris for a while before flying to Tehran.

Her father was excited, but her mother kept saying, "They're trying to put women under *chador* again like fifty years ago."

Her father assured her that women still enjoyed their own fashionable clothes and didn't even have to wear scarves, much less the head-to-toe *chador.*

"Why Paris?" he asked.

"I need a neutral territory for a while. I can't hear anti-Iranian propaganda one day and '*Death to Amrika*' the next."

As she gathered clothes and other items for charity, she called her friends to say good-bye. As expected, they didn't understand her decision.

"You'll regret this," Judith said. "You'll find out even your best friends in Tehran have changed. You'll have culture shock."

"I love you, Judith, but I've no choice. I helped a lot of illegal aliens on a pro bono basis, to get work permits or green cards. For some I was successful; for the others I was not. I know how they felt when the Immigration Office sent them deportation notices. I'm not going to be an illegal alien in this country."

She spent a weekend in Westhampton with Judith and her family, but the minute some of Judith's guests found out she was an Iranian, the topic of Iran's revolution and the hostage crisis dominated every conversation.

Exhausted and tired of the discussion, Roxana excused herself to go to bed.

As she climbed the stairs, Judith's husband called up after her. "You don't have to carry the weight of every crisis on your shoulder. I promise you, the world won't collapse while you're asleep."

She waved good night without turning around or saying a word.

* * *

Three days before her departure, Roxana received two interesting phone calls. The first came from a staff member at the New York office of one of the shah's relatives.

"We would like to hire you as a legal advisor." Politely, she declined the offer.

"Most people would consider this a great honor," said the man, obviously shocked.

The second came from the office of the Language Services of the State Department. Secretary of State Cyrus Vance needed her to translate some legal documents.

She liked Secretary Vance, but she declined that request too. She had made up her mind to return to Iran.

Bahram came to help her, picking up all of her boxes and delivering them to various charities. In the end, she was left with just one suitcase.

She made sandwiches, and while they ate, she found her gaze drawn to it—one lone suitcase, resting on the floor of her apartment.

"Something's wrong?" Bahram asked.

"No, I was just thinking—ten years of life here, and that suitcase is my only possession."

"Your asset is in your brain," Bahram said, "not in that suitcase."

It hurt more than she imagined it would to say good-bye to her brother. She rejected his offer of a ride to the airport. She hated airport good-byes and couldn't imagine parting from him in the midst of harried passengers.

She decided to walk down Broadway on her last evening, to soak up the sights of the Theater District. The area was as illuminated and as crowded as ever. She had seen all the movies on the marquees: *Kramer v. Kramer, Apocalypse Now, Being There, Norma Rae.* But she hadn't seen *Manhattan* yet.

She had lived there for five years, yet the last movie she chose to see was about Manhattan. She bought a ticket and went inside.

* * *

On the morning of her departure, she listened as a Diana Ross song filled the narrow confines of her taxicab.

"Do you know where you're going to? Do you like what life is showing you? Where are you going to? Do you know?"

Roxana smiled sadly at the irony. The lyrics echoed in her head. Did she know what she was doing?

During the ride to JFK Airport, Roxana looked out the window, watching the streets and skyscrapers pass with the sense of awe a first-time tourist might feel. Her brain became a camera, taking snapshots of every street the cab drove down.

You may never see your favorite city in Amrika again.

She thought back to the last day of September 1976 and her arrival in Manhattan. After she gave her hotel's address to the cab driver, he asked in his thick Brooklyn accent, "Who're you gonna vote for mayor? Ed Koch or the other guy, what's his name?"

She smiled. No wonder she loved the city so much. The minute she entered New York City, she became a New Yorker, despite the fact that her suitcase and hotel destination revealed that she was an out-of-towner.

Now she was leaving the city and forfeiting her New York citizenship—she was no longer a New Yorker.

She left the city on a cold, gloomy day while, in most American cities, yellow ribbons were tied around trees to show support for the return of the hostages.

Chapter 6

January 1980—Paris

When the taxicab entered Rue de Sevigne, Roxana saw Lili already outside her building, waiting for her and waving. Lili's blonde hair in its usual ponytail, and her childlike enthusiasm, reassured Roxana that her childhood friend had not changed a bit. She leapt from the cab, and the two friends, tearful but happy, hugged and held on to each other for a long time.

"*Mademoiselle, je suis presse,*" the cab driver complained.

"Pardon, Monsieur," Roxana said as she paid her fare and carried her suitcase. "*Gardez la monnaie.*" The driver smiled at his big tip and drove off.

The third-floor apartment Lili had rented in the *Le Marais* area was small but had everything they needed: two beds, a large sofa, a kitchenette, a TV set, and a small dining area.

"This is the best place I could find," Lili said.

"It's perfect. We just need a place to sleep and shower."

"Let me look at you," Lili said as she stepped back, staring at Roxana. "I thought the hostage crisis had given you some grayish hair and wrinkles. You still look stunning—very chic, very New York."

"I can't wear jeans like you all the time. I'm in a stuffy profession. I have to wear a business suit most of the time."

"Even when you're traveling?"

"Some lawyer friends came to the airport to say good-bye."

The two friends talked for a long time about their families back in Tehran, their respective lives in London and New York, the revolution, and the hostages. As Lili talked, Roxana couldn't help staring at her friend's youthful, round face. She was still the same carefree, cheerful Lili she had known since age six. For a moment Roxana felt she was in Tehran visiting her family.

* * *

It grew dark in no time, and Lili realized she was hungry. Despite many good restaurants in *Le Marais,* she decided to take her friend to Quartier Latin. She chose a nice sidewalk café not too far from the *Sorbonne.* It was cold, so they sat inside at a table by the window.

While engaged in animated conversation, Lili saw how delighted Roxana was in the clusters of people passing by on the street. She also noticed Roxana's divided attention. "You lived in Paris before. This is your sixth trip. Why are you acting like a first-time tourist?"

"You have no idea how good it feels," Roxana took a long, deep breath before she finished her sentence, "to sit in a restaurant without hearing a debate on the hostage crisis. I feel like thanking Paris!"

"Well, Paris has always been your *mistress*. She has never disappointed you."

"You and Nina never let me forget my joke. These days, I agree with Thomas Jefferson and his description of Paris as 'everyone's second home.' That's how I feel right now."

"Do you remember the first time we visited Paris? Instead of visiting the tourist attraction areas, we followed the path of Jake Barnes from *The Sun Also Rises.*"

"I remember. We walked to the Avenue de l'Opera, then through Rue des Pyramides and Rue de Rivoli, the direction that Jake's horse-cab had taken."

The two friends reminisced about their first trip to Paris, the silly things they did together, and the portrait drawn of the two of them by a Montmartre artist.

After dinner they didn't feel like going back to their apartment. They wrapped their woolen scarves around their necks and walked through the streets of Quartier Latin. They walked and talked until their toes felt numb.

* * *

Despite the cold weather, Roxana and Lili toured Paris on foot every day. At night, they took their friends or relatives up on invitations to parties or political gatherings.

The subject of discussion was always the revolution.

"The ayatollahs will take Iran back fifty years," said one of those gathered. "Khomeini will turn Qom into a Vatican-like city and rule as a Moslem pope."

Someone else hoped that the revolution would bring back the democratic era of Prime Minister Mossadegh before the 1953 CIA *coup d'etat.*

"What do you think?" a voice asked Roxana. She turned. The voice belonged to a tall, good-looking man who resembled the British actor Lawrence Harvey.

"About what?"

"Your revolution?"

"I came here only to listen."

"Can I buy you dinner tomorrow night and hear your point of view?"

"No, thanks. I don't go out with strangers."

"Oh, forgive me. My name is Steve Radcliff. I'm a journalist working for the *Washington Post*. I plan to go to Tehran soon. Your friend Lili tells me that you know a lot about the revolution."

"She exaggerates. I need to learn about this revolution myself."

"You've an American accent. Were you born in the United States?"

"No, I have this gift of imitating accents. Put me in Alabama for one month. I'll speak like Alabamians."

"Well, this is my card, in case you change your mind about the dinner." Steve handed Roxana his card. "I am staying at a hotel in *Mont Parnasse*."

Roxana took the card, put it in her purse without looking at it, and said good-bye. She found Lili and admonished her for sending the American reporter to her.

"He said he was very attracted to you." Her eyes twinkled with mischief. "He must have dated a lot of blondes, because he wasn't interested in me. He must love your mysterious brown eyes and the sexy red hair."

"Lili, I said good-bye to the Americans and America because I wanted to forget that part of my life."

"He's so handsome."

"So what?"

* * *

Nina, her husband Bijan, and their two children arrived in Paris on February 15, 1980. Nina, a tall, slender woman with curly, short black hair, towered over Lili, a blonde, and Roxana, a redhead, who both stood at five feet five. It had been years since Nina had visited her childhood friends. They jumped up and down and hugged each other several times before finally settling down.

"Let me look at you two," Nina said. "I don't see any ring on anyone's finger."

"The fact that you are six months older than us doesn't make you our mother!" Roxana said.

"But you guys are pushing thirty soon. Aren't your biological clocks ticking?"

"No," Lili and Roxana responded simultaneously.

"We met a good-looking guy on the plane from Boston to here. He looks like Marcello Mastroianni. He's thirty-five with a PhD in economics just like you," Nina told Lili. "I invited him to have dinner with us when we go to my cousin's party. You're going to like him."

"How come you didn't choose him for Roxana?" Lili objected.

"Because he has majored in business and banking. He's more your type. And listen to this. He wants to advise the Iranian government how to unfreeze billions of their assets."

* * *

The three girlfriends were exhausted after spending half a day in Montmartre and climbing so many steps to reach the *Sacré Coeur* Basilica. They sat on top of the steps and watched Paris under their feet. While having their lunch near *Place du Tertre,* they watched the portrait painters for a while.

The next stop was the Notre Dame Cathedral. Nina had never been inside.

"Do you know you have taken us to three churches today?" Lili complained. "You are Christian. We're not."

"Jesus was a Jew, closer to your religion than Roxana's. She's not complaining."

The trio went inside the church. Nina made the sign of the cross and sat on one of the benches. Roxana sat behind her, deep in thought, while Lili stood on the side and watched the tourists taking pictures.

When they came out, Lili asked Roxana, "What were *you* praying for?"

"For the release of the hostages."

During the last day of her stay in Paris, Nina wanted to visit *Les Tuileries* and *Le Jardin du Luxembourg*. Roxana and Lili indulged her. The three sat around the Medici Fountain in the Luxembourg Gardens and talked about their future.

"We're acting like three soldiers heading for a battlefield," Lili said.

"You two are lucky; you're single," Nina said. "I have to worry about the future of my kids."

"I think we are afraid to lose control over our lives," Roxana said. She knew that was true for herself, at least.

Chapter 7

Roxana attended the party thrown by Nina's cousins.

"I've invited the man I met on the plane," Nina said.

"Why?" said Lili. "I'm not interested in a setup, and I already invited Steve Radcliff."

"Why did you do that?" Roxana complained. Lili gave her a naughty smile.

At the party, Steve, who obviously did not understand Farsi, flashed a smile at Roxana and went to the bar to get a drink. There were at least thirty people there—half French, half Iranians. Steve Radcliff was the only American.

Nina helped her cousin serve their guests coffee and cake, but when she spotted the man on the plane, she rushed to him and pulled him away from some of the French guests. She apologized, took him by the arm, and led him to Lili.

Roxana chuckled to herself as she watched it unfold. She'd recognized Kayvan the minute she spotted him but amused herself with watching the inevitable revelation to Nina.

"Lili, this is Mr. Kayvan Panahi I was telling you about," Nina said.

Lili and Mr. Panahi froze for a moment, but both their faces revealed the softness of being pleasantly surprised. After a few more awkward silent moments, Mr. Panahi said, "Lili and I have known each other for several years."

"We both attended the London School of Economics," Lili said.

"Oh no … oh … no …"

Nina ran up to Roxana, as expected. "Guess who the passenger was?"

"What passenger?" asked Roxana, although she already knew.

"The PhD guy I was trying to introduce to Lili. Look over there." Nina motioned to the corner of the room.

"All right, I confess that I already knew Kayvan," Roxana said. "I met him in London when I visited Lili four years ago."

"How come Lili shares more with you than with me?"

"You're married, you're a mother, and you're a surgeon. Lili can't reach you on the phone the way she can reach me."

"So what happened?"

"He decided to go back to Iran. Lili was happy with her life in London. So he left and got married."

"He's married? Oh my God, poor Lili! What a stupid mistake I made inviting him here tonight."

Steve Radcliff approached with a martini in his hand.

"We haven't been introduced," Steve said to Nina. He put his drink on the table, extended his hand, and said, "My name is Steve Radcliff. I'm a journalist. Could you please ask your beautiful friend to have dinner with me? I'm writing about your revolution, and I really need her help."

Nina sized up Steve. "You're not a CIA agent, are you?"

"No," Steve snapped. "What is this paranoia with you Iranians? Three people have already asked me the same questions. Okay, the CIA staged a coup in Iran decades ago. We didn't try to reinstall the shah this time."

"Okay, Roxana, you can have dinner with him. He seems harmless," Nina said with a smile.

* * *

Lili and Kayvan moved to a quiet corner in the living room; they spoke of their interrupted romance. He talked about his dying father and the fact that his father died shortly after his arrival in Tehran. He talked about his job with Bank Markazi and about his PhD at Harvard.

"I saw the revolution; I was part of it. It was so exciting. It felt so beautiful."

"Why did you have to get married?" Lili sighed.

"I asked you to marry me, remember? You didn't want to come back to Tehran. What was I supposed to do?"

"Maybe you should have tried harder to convince me."

Lili covered her face for a long time, then stood and went to the window. She stared at the illuminated streets of Paris for a while.

Kayvan stood behind her.

"You're still a big part of my life. The part that I can never forget," Kayvan said. He softly touched Lili's hair. "I haven't stopped loving you."

A storm of tears filled Lili's eyes. The lights in the streets of Paris seemed distorted now, as if the city was soaked under the rain.

* * *

Steve's effort to get Roxana to meet with him and talk about the revolution failed, so he moved on to Kayvan, who was not only pleasant to chat with but also knowledgeable on the subject.

Kayvan agreed to answer Steve's questions about the revolution, but his first question, "Are you a CIA agent?" annoyed Steve.

"Hey, man, don't get mad. I have a job with this government," Kayvan said. "I don't want some picture of us talking to show up in a document suggesting that I'm selling you government secrets."

"Listen, my name is Steve Radcliff. This is my driver's license." Steve pulled out his driver's license and showed it to Kayvan. "I'm from Ohio, but I've lived in DC, New York City, Cairo, London, and Tokyo. I work for the *Washington Post*."

"I've never seen your name anywhere!" Kayvan looked at him suspiciously.

"I gather the information and send it to my boss. He assigns someone to analyze the information and write the article. I keep my name out of it so that people can feel comfortable talking to me." Steve handed his correspondent ID card to Kayvan.

"That ID card is not enough. I'll talk to you only because in my culture we tend to trust people until we're proven wrong."

They met for lunch.

"Before I ask you about the revolution, I need to know Roxana's story. I can't even get near her."

"She's a scholar, an intellectual, someone you probably meet once in your lifetime."

"Why is she avoiding me?"

"According to Lili, she almost married a lawyer from Texas in 1978. Her fiancé was supposed to relocate and live with her in New York City, but he got a good job offer from a big law firm in Dallas. So he decided to stay there. Roxana refused to go to Dallas. She loved Texans but didn't want to live in Texas. She had a job offer to teach at Berkeley, but she didn't want to live on the West Coast, either."

"A true New Yorker, huh?"

"Yes. You could say that. Lili tells me she left America so that she wouldn't have to deal with *hostages* or Americans anymore. She didn't expect to meet you here."

"But she's a beautiful single woman. Why can't she accept a simple dinner invitation?"

"You remind her of the life she left behind. Wait a minute. You told me you're married. Why are you pursuing her?"

"My marriage is dead. My wife is a real estate agent and lives in Dayton, Ohio. She makes so much money that she doesn't need me, and I travel all around the world."

"Why not divorce, then?"

"I don't have enough time to go back to Ohio and get a divorce. We have an open marriage that's like being divorced."

The two men had their lunch and some beers. Steve took his pad and pen out of his briefcase, and took a lot of notes as Kayvan talked.

After a long discussion, Kayvan gave a pamphlet to Steve and encouraged him to read it. "This is a summary of what happened in Iran," he said.

Back at his hotel room, Steve immersed himself in the information Kayvan provided. He read the literature and took notes, but from time to time his thoughts would leave his reading to settle on the mysterious Roxana Ramsy. He couldn't get her out of his mind.

* * *

Nina and her family flew back to Tehran, taking a bit of Roxana's heart with them. Paris grew colder every day. The rainy, gray city forced Roxana and Lili to visit every museum and art exhibit in town.

After they finished their tour of the museums, there was nothing else to do but walk the streets of Paris like *flaneurs*.

The Paris trip was the longest vacation Roxana had given herself in a decade. Although she still had anxiety about her unforeseeable future in Tehran, Paris had washed away her bad memories of the painful days in New York.

She avoided Steve, who was still in Paris and who would still show up from time to time, somewhere unexpected, to try to coax her into a date. He claimed that their Paris Bureau needed information about European reactions to the Iranian Revolution and the hostages.

Kayvan changed his plan and decided to go back to Tehran with Lili after the second week of March.

Roxana did not approve of Lili and Kayvan spending so much time together and often felt she was serving as unwitting chaperone.

One night, though, when Lili came back to the hotel late, her cheeks flushed and a satisfied glint in her eyes, Roxana couldn't hold her tongue.

"Which part of you doesn't understand the meaning of the word *married*?" she asked. "Is it your British part or the Jewish part?"

"Don't be so self-righteous," Lili said calmly. "We're just friends."

"Why don't you forget about him and come to Rome with me?"

"When did you decide to go to Rome?"

"When the weather got colder, and I counted my money."

"That's fine with me."

* * *

That evening, at a dinner party thrown for Kayvan by one of his friends in Paris, Roxana ran into Steve yet again. Apparently, Kayvan liked the man. He seemed to invite him everywhere.

When Steve heard about the trip to Rome, he suggested that the four of them travel together. "We should rent a car and drive there."

"Excuse me! Who said you're invited." Roxana felt her cheeks warm with indignation. "The trip is for me and Lili."

"Have a heart," Kayvan said, grinning and exchanging a look with Lili. "Rome is big enough for the four of us."

"Besides, two attractive young women alone in Rome. You'll need our protection," Steve added.

Roxana gave up when Lili also favored a group trip. But deep down, she agreed with Steve. During her last trip to Rome, men had followed her everywhere. She, however, suggested traveling by train so that they could sleep at night.

Chapter 8

Contrary to what Roxana had expected, the trip started well. Kayvan and Steve stayed in their sitting car until dinnertime. It became clear that Steve was genuinely gathering information about the Iranian Revolution.

In the evening, the foursome settled around a small table in the dining car.

Once they ordered their food, Steve said. "I've been dying to ask you about a lot of things. First of all, what's this obsession with a PhD? Is there any Iranian who doesn't have a PhD?"

"Iranians you meet abroad are mostly there for education. I promise you, the cab drivers in Tehran don't have PhDs," Kayvan said, laughing.

"Also, why are you all such Francophiles?"

Kayvan motioned to Roxana. "I believe she can answer that question better."

Lili nodded.

"It's funny you're asking me," Roxana said. "Most of my friends went to Paris to continue their educations. I was the only one who chose the United States. I suppose they were the real Francophiles."

"Why the United States instead of Paris?" Steve asked.

"Maybe there is a little *Yankee Doodle Dandy* in me," Roxana said with a smile.

"No, seriously. Why did you choose the United States?"

"I can answer that," Lili volunteered. "In seventh grade, English is compulsory in Iran. I loved our teacher's British accent, but Roxana thought it was funny. She continued talking with an American accent, which made our teacher very upset."

"How could you imitate an American accent if you had never lived in the United States?"

"We had an American TV channel in Iran. We had American neighbors. I also studied at the Iran American Society for three years. But accent wasn't the only thing. I fell in love with America when I was a teenager, mostly because of the movies. Once, when I was about twelve, I went to see a movie with my family. There was some problem, so the projectionist showed a ten-minute film about Halloween. I didn't care that much about the costumes or the trick-or-treat part, but I fell in love with the scene that showed a field with hundreds of pumpkins. A big carved pumpkin served as a cashier box, and a scarecrow posed as a cashier. People would pick up their pumpkin and drop their money in the big pumpkin. That was the day I fell in love with America."

"Amazing!" Steve said. "Now, let's go back to my Francophile question."

"It has something to do with history and the culture of the two nations," Roxana said. "France was the first country that established a diplomatic relationship with Persia in the sixteenth century. Politically speaking, unlike the British and the Russians, France never occupied Iran and never attempted to make Persia a French colony."

"And it also goes back to the number of Iranian students who went to Paris over the past fifty years and got a French education," Kayvan added. "When they returned home, they brought their love of the culture with them. They even had an impact on the language. In Farsi, all the technical words are borrowed from French. We routinely say, 'Merci' instead of *Motshakeram* or *Mamnoonam*."

"Some of our intellectuals call this admiration for French or other Western cultures 'Westoxification,'" Lili said.

"Jalal-e-Al Ahmad, our famous writer, used the title *Gharbzadegi,* or 'Westoxification,' for his book," Roxana said. "But as much as I adore the man and his writing, I totally disagree with him. I think different cultures can and should learn from each other. We love our great poets, Sa'di, Hafez, Omar Khayam, Molavi, and also our philosophers, such as Attar, but that doesn't mean we should ignore the literary giants that existed in France, Russia, and other European countries."

"I agree," Kayvan said. "How can you possibly not read Dostoyevsky, Tolstoy, or Chekhov? Or Nabokov?"

"My favorite French philosopher is Voltaire," Lili said. "He could scandalize a party by declaring, 'Jesus committed suicide,' hinting that if he were really God, he could have prevented his own crucifixion."

"I love his famous quotation," Roxana said, "'If God did not exist, it would be necessary to invent him.'"

* * *

The next morning, Roxana got out of her bed quietly and left the sleeping coach without waking Lili. She stood by the large window between the two cars and looked outside. The train roared along. It seemed as if the trees in the distance ran alongside.

She stood there wishing for a moment that the train would never stop. She longed to see her family. She wanted to take part in the exciting revolution. But she didn't have a job waiting for her in Tehran. She had never been without a job, even as a student.

And what if she couldn't live in revolutionary Iran? Was that the reason she needed to stay in Paris so long? Was that the reason she had to visit Rome too? Why did she have this feeling that once in Tehran she might never leave again? For the first time she wondered whether she had made the right decision. She could have simply called Craig in Dallas and said, "I've changed my mind. I'll marry you now."

Why did she have to leave? Was it because of President Carter's warning of a military attack against Iran? Was she scared that she would never see her family alive again?

The train rocked, jarring her body. She felt her life had turned into a runaway train.

"You're lost in your thoughts." Steve appeared in the passageway. "What are you thinking about?"

"Do you always have to get into people's heads?"

"No. I'm only interested in knowing what's going on in your beautiful head."

Lili joined them, announcing she was hungry. When the three of them entered the restaurant car, they saw Kayvan at a table with his half-eaten breakfast hovering over dozens of papers.

"Salam. Sobh be kheir," Good morning. Kayvan said when he saw them. He and Steve pulled back two chairs for Roxana and Lili.

"You guys have to teach me a little Farsi before I go to Tehran," Steve said.

"Ask Roxana," Lili said. "Among the three of us, she is the best and the most patient one."

"I don't know about the best," Roxana said. "Okay, Steve, I'll teach you some basic Farsi."

They had a few more hours before they'd reach Rome. Kayvan stayed at the restaurant to share some of his banking theories with Lili. Roxana moved to the next table to teach Steve some basic Farsi. She started with Farsi alphabets, emphasizing the letters that didn't exist in English, like kh, gh, jh, and zh. Steve was alarmed when he learned that there were two *t*-sounding, three *s*-sounding, and four *z*-sounding letters in the Farsi alphabet.

Roxana told Steve that one of the first things he should learn about the Persian culture was to understand *Ta' arouf.*

"What's that?" he asked impatiently.

"It's not edible," Roxana laughed, "but it's a sweet form of exaggerated etiquette, or you might call it extreme Persian hospitality. When someone says *chakeram*, it means 'I'm your servant,' but it doesn't really mean that he is your servant. A taxi driver or a street vendor may tell you *Ghabeli nadareh*, meaning it's unworthy. That doesn't really mean the cab driver's service to you or the sold item is for free. Or when they say *Pish kesh,* meaning 'it's yours,' it doesn't really mean it's yours."

"Suppose someone takes those words literally."

"Well, *Ta' arouf* is a back-and-forth pleasant exchange among Persians. The recipient of *Ta' arouf* knows that nothing is free."

After a few hours, Roxana grew tired. She promised Steve that when they went back to Tehran, she would find him a book or cassette tapes to teach him Farsi.

"I have one question before we end our session," Steve said.

"What's that?"

"How do you say in Farsi, you have the most beautiful face I've ever seen?"

"That comes in the advanced courses," Roxana said with a smile. "I'm sure a gorgeous Tehranian woman will teach you that someday."

Chapter 9

Their hotel was located on *Via Villono Veneto,* one of the most elegant streets in Rome. After taking a shower and resting for a while, the foursome was ready to explore the city. This was Roxana's third visit in Rome, so she assumed the role of a tour guide.

Everyone wanted to see the Roman Coliseum first. Roxana informed her friends that the Coliseum was build around 72 AD by Emperor Vespasian. It was Rome's primary stage for combat among gladiators for four centuries. It had the capacity of accommodating up to fifty-five thousand spectators. "The Coliseum has seventy-six numbered entrances, each designed in such a way that the entire audience could exit the amphitheater in only five minutes," Roxana said.

"Wow," Steve said. "Maybe some of the architects who design our football stadiums should come here and study this ancient building!"

Everyone laughed.

The next stop was the Roman Forum—the center for political, business, and social activities before the fall of the Roman Empire. The columns and arches of the ruined Forum reminded Roxana of Persepolis and Iran. Lili and Kayvan made similar comments.

"You guys have to give me a special tour of Persepolis," Steve demanded.

"Of course," Lili said.

The next day, the four travelers visited the Victor Emmanuel's Monument and the Temple of Julius Caesar. Steve took a lot of pictures and would sometimes ask Roxana and Lili to pose in front of the monuments. But he noticed that Kayvan would shy away from being photographed, so that night when they were back in their room, he asked him what was troubling him.

"Man, it's so hard. I'm falling in love with her all over again, and I have no right to do that. I'm a married man."

"Well, at least you're having some good times with the woman you love. Look at me and the Ice Princess."

"I resent that term. You don't know her. She's one of the most caring people I've ever met. Did you know she's a poet?"

"No."

"She's even published some of her work. I don't know much about poetry, but the experts say her poems remind them of Forugh Farrokhzad's."

"Who?"

"Forugh is a legendary female poet who's worshipped by women in Iran. She died in a car accident. To Iranian women, she's like Evita or Joan of Arc. She revolutionized modern poetry. She wrote about her lover and sexual desires—something unheard of in Persian culture."

"If she's a poet, what's with that cold exterior?"

"Well, she's anxious about this revolution, the hostages, and her future."

"I'm concerned about the hostages too. But here I'm a full-blooded American boy, in Rome, with a gorgeous woman I adore. I can't even ask her out. I feel like I'm traveling with a nun."

"Persian girls don't sleep around. They believe they should be in love with the men they are dating. Maybe you should warn President Carter that if he is planning to attack Iran, he should know that the American soldiers wouldn't have fun there. Iran is not Korea or Vietnam."

"Boy, I really miss having a girl from back home right now. They know how to have a good time."

"If you can't make her fall in love with you, just be happy to have a platonic relationship with her."

"You Persians are nuts! You know that?"

* * *

The foursome spent most of their last days in Rome visiting the Vatican City. They took some pictures of St. Peter's Square in front of the most famous Christian church in the world. They visited the Sistine Chapel, with the paintings that depicted lives of Moses and the Christ. Kayvan and Lili searched for a long time before they located Michelangelo's *Creation of Adam* and *The Last Judgment* in the ceiling. Kayvan, who had gotten a little stiff neck, complained, "Couldn't Michelangelo paint these things on the walls rather than on a ceiling?"

"Maybe he was scared that a French king would capture them and place them in the Louvre," Roxana said, laughing.

That evening they visited some of Rome's famous piazzas and their fountains. When they arrived at Fontana di Trevi, Rome's most beautiful fountain, the girls couldn't resist following the tradition.

"If you throw a coin into the fountain, you return to Rome," Lili said to Steve.

She then turned around and tossed her coin over her shoulder with her back to the fountain. Roxana repeated Lili's action.

"You've been here several times. You want to come back again?" Kayvan asked Roxana.

"I didn't wish for my return."

"So what did you wish?"

"It's silly. You're going to laugh. I wished for the safe return of the hostages."

Steve stood near Roxana, listening. At that moment he loved that woman so much he wanted to grab her and give her a big kiss on the mouth. Instead, he muttered, "No wonder Alexander the Great was defeated!"

"What?" Roxana asked, further undoing him with one look from her soulful brown eyes.

"Alexander the Great conquered Persia, but everyone knows he was defeated when he fell in love with a Persian princess named Roxana. He stayed in Persia for so long that the Greeks thought he had betrayed them. You see, I know a little history too!"

"I'm impressed."

* * *

After dinner, the four friends walked in Piazza del Paradiso. Despite the nightfall, the weather still felt pleasantly warm.

Roxana turned to Lili and said, "I wish *Cinecittà* had a tour like the Universal Studio. This trip would be perfect if we could see where Fellini made his masterpieces."

"I agree," Lili said. "I still remember his famous movie—*8½*."

"Do you remember Kasra Movie Theatre?" Roxana asked Kayvan.

"Yes, I do."

"You've got to hear this story. One afternoon I had administrative law for two hours—the only boring subject in law—with a boring professor. So I decided to go and see *8½*." I slipped in just as the previews had started. During the movie, I noticed that every few minutes, some people would leave. By intermission I counted thirteen people had remained in the theater. One of them was a woman with blonde hair who had her back to me. When she turned around, it was Lili. I almost screamed; I was so surprised and happy to see her."

"That was a tough film for me to follow," Kayvan said. "You two were members of what was the name—? Oh, I remember—the Iranian-Italian Cultural Society. Not everybody had your brochure to understand why Fellini hanged the man in his studio."

"I loved Marcello Mastroianni in that movie," Lili said.

"Was that the reason you dated Kayvan, because he looks a little bit like Marcello?" Steve asked.

A sudden silence ended their discussion. Roxana started walking fast; Steve followed her. "What did I say to cause the dreadful silence?" he asked.

"You don't talk about people's love relationships," Roxana said. "You should learn this if you're planning to live in Tehran."

"Why is everybody pretending not to see the huge elephant in the room?"

"If people talk about their relationship, then you can comment on it. If they don't, you should respect their privacy. I've known Lili since we were six years old, and you don't see me talking about her love life in front of people."

* * *

During the train ride back to Paris, before going to bed, Roxana noticed Lili's red and puffed up eyelids. She had not spoken more than a few words all day. "Are you going to tell me what's happening with you?"

"We said our good-byes. He's going back to his wife."

"Lili, you know if he continued with you, the guilt would kill him. The problem with a Persian man is that he is in love with the concept of love, not the person he's supposed to be in love with."

"I was the one who said no to his proposal years ago, remember?"

"I remember."

"So, you think American men know more about love than Persian men?"

"No, but when they fall in love, nothing can stop them."

"If American men are that wonderful, why did you dump Craig, and why are you ignoring Steve?"

"I thought we were talking about you, not me."

"I can lecture you too," Lili said while pressing her head with both hands. "Why did he have to reappear in my life? I had almost forgotten about him."

* * *

Back in Paris, Steve changed his plan and decided to go to Tehran on the same flight with Kayvan. Although all his credentials and Iranian visa were in order, he felt he might run into trouble at the airport.

The four friends had one last dinner in Paris. When they left the restaurant, Roxana wished Steve success and a good time in Tehran.

"You owe me a dinner date!" Steve said. "I asked you out on February 7, 1980. You said no. I'll have that date in Tehran."

Roxana smiled.

The weather had turned warm in Paris even though spring was still two weeks away. Again, Roxana and Lili walked the streets of Paris every day and dined with friends or relatives in the evening.

During their last few days in Paris, they did some shopping. They bought souvenirs for family members and friends back home. Roxana bought some of Adamo's new music, adding to the box of music records and tapes she was taking with her to Tehran.

* * *

When their taxicab was heading for the Charles de Gaulle Airport, Roxana noticed several signs in different parts of Paris reflecting the Parisians' preoccupations: "Jacques Chirac for Mayor," and "Afghanistan, the Soviets' Vietnam."

PART 2

Chapter 10

March 1980—Mehrabad Airport, Tehran

The Air France pilot announced their descent into Tehran in approximately twenty minutes.

Roxana looked at Lili. "We're almost there!"

Lili nodded and flashed a big smile. They'd both last been in Tehran in 1973 when Lili was visiting her family, and Roxana was interpreting for a US-sponsored conference in Tehran.

Roxana's heart pounded in her chest. She pretended to be calm like Lili, but anxiety pulsed within her. She hadn't seen her siblings for seven years. Even though she had spent a month with her parents during the Bicentennial visit in Washington, DC, she still missed them.

"Look, there's the illuminated Tehran," Lili said, pointing out the window.

Roxana leaned over her to look outside. The plane reduced its altitude, and for a moment, it seemed as if the ground had turned into a stunning sky full of sparkling stars. She fought back tears. This was the Tehran the Americans couldn't see. During her last three months in New York, the only images she saw of Tehran were those of angry mobs chanting, "*Marg bar Amrika*," "Death to America."

The plane landed. Roxana and Lili unbuckled their seat belts, gathered their carry-ons and waited impatiently for the flight attendant to come and lead them out.

Roxana and Lili were the only two passengers on the upper level of the plane. They heard some commotion in the lower level of the plane, followed by hurried footsteps. Roxana looked at Lili, wondering what was going on. Finally, two men in military fatigues climbed up and approached them. They carried machine guns.

"*Chi darid?*" one of the men asked.

"Nothing," Roxana volunteered. "We have some personal items, some souvenirs."

Before Roxana could finish her sentence, the two men came to their seats. One grabbed Roxana's carry-on bag, the other Lili's. Lili had some books and T-shirts.

The man let Lili zip her bag. "You can go."

She hurried from the cabin.

The second man went through Roxana's bag, pulling everything out and spreading the items on the seat before him. He ignored the books, but Roxana's ten long players and three music cassettes got his attention.

"What are these?" he asked.

She explained that the long players were a collection of Beethoven, Tchaikovsky, and Bach. The cassette tapes were modern music. The man returned the classical music but kept the three cassettes of Adamo. She almost pleaded, "Please don't," but she realized it was unwise to argue with someone who carried a weapon.

Back on the bus, which headed for Mehrabad's main terminal, Lili asked Roxana why the man detained her for so long.

"He took my cassettes," Roxana said, trying not to let feelings of disappointment and trepidation overwhelm her. "Apparently, the modern music is *corrupt*."

* * *

At the terminal, as they waited in a long line for passport inspection, Roxana couldn't recognize the Mahrabad Airport. Everywhere, large portraits of Ayatollah Khomeini and Ayatollah Montazeri, his potential successor, hung on the walls. Slogans spread across banners: *Death to Amrika! Down with Imperialism and Zionism!*

Roxana's skin crawled. She didn't want to read any more. This was what she had dreaded in New York, and this was the reason she had stayed in Paris for so long. She thought her long vacation would prepare her for those images, or slogans, but she knew she'd never get used to, *Death to Amrika.*

There was no sign of Mehrabad's beautiful restaurants and chic Iranian women. Many women wore scarves. Roxana, with her red hair and milky skin, and Lili, with her blonde hair and blue eyes, looked like foreigners. The two friends said "Good-bye," and tried to find their suitcases.

Roxana was losing her patience with the airport security when she heard a familiar voice, "Roxana *Jaan*, Salam." It was her uncle Parviz. She threw herself into his arms.

She was surprised her uncle had gotten into the arrival area. Every time she traveled through Mehrabad Airport, it was her uncle who made everything smooth for her. He knew everybody in town. But Parviz, a monarchy loyalist, had recently resigned as the head of the Budget Division of the Ministry of Interior because he couldn't stand being ordered around by some inexperienced *Hezbollahis*, as he called them. Despite disparagement by the government that a necktie was a Christian symbol of the cross, he still wore different expensive ties every day.

"Who is your connection with this government?" Roxana whispered in her uncle's ear.

"Don't worry, I can deal with them," Parviz said, "We're all Persians; only a few of us wear *amameh,* turban."

As they reached the exit, Roxana saw the smiling faces of her family members behind the large window, and her heart lifted. Far away from them stood Lili's relatives.

The two friends waved at each other and walked in opposite directions to greet their family members.

"Where's Grandma?" Roxana asked, scanning the faces of those waiting for her.

"She's visiting friends in Mashhad," said Parviz.

Outside the airport, a huge crowd had gathered to welcome the passengers. Before the revolution, well-wishing crowds could go to a balcony and watch their loved ones' departure or arrival, but after the revolution, only the ticketed passengers could enter the terminal.

Roxana looked from one relative to the next, wanting to hold and hug each of them for hours. Her father had a patch of white hair now. Her mother looked thin and aggrieved, her brows knit together in a fixed expression of anxiety. Even though she was clearly excited and happy to see Roxana, her unspoken words rang out loud and clear: "Why did you come back?"

Roxana's brother and sister, teenagers when she'd last seen them, had transformed into young adults.

Parviz, who had disappeared with Roxana's suitcase, appeared in his car. Roxana and her mother slid into the backseat, and she expected her father to sit in front, but he climbed into her brother's car.

"Why isn't Father coming with us?"

"Because your uncle constantly criticizes the revolution and the government. Your father cannot stand it anymore."

"Puri *Jaan*, I keep telling you these *akhoonds,* clergies, are going to destroy our country! You didn't believe me when I told you they're going to bring back *hejab.* Now you see they have already started. I promise you in one year they're going to put women under *chador.*"

"Parviz, could you please not ruin my daughter's arrival?" Puri asked. "I want to talk to her."

Against her mother's advice, Roxana asked her uncle to change the route and drive by the American Embassy, forgoing the highway that would take them directly to Zarfar Avenue, in the northern suburb of Tehran.

Parviz alerted Roxana that they were approaching the American Embassy, or as it was renamed by the revolutionary government, *Laney-e-Jasusi,* the Den of Spies.

Several Revolutionary Guards stood outside the embassy. The walls around it were too tall to see anything inside. They were covered by slogans such as, "America Can't Do a Damn Thing against Us," one of Ayatollah Khomeini's famous quotations.

While her uncle provided more information about activities outside the embassy, Roxana thought about the fifty-two hostages and their families.

"God, please help them go home," she prayed.

"Are you paying attention to anything I'm saying?" Parviz asked.

"Oh, what were you saying?"

"They have turned this area into a revolutionary picnic site. They bus in people who have been given food and money and make them chant 'Death to Amrika.'"

Roxana's mother interrupted again. "Would you please leave her alone? She just got here, for crying out loud."

* * *

After a few hours of feasting and talking to her family, exhaustion overtook Roxana. She took a shower and went to bed. Her mother had prepared her old room for her. It felt strange being there—the same paintings on the walls, the same curtains on the window. She stared at her favorite Persian miniature, and then at an imitation of Van Gogh's *Starry Night*, painted by an unknown Persian artist. She closed her eyes and remembered the cheerful teenager who had lived in that room. She tried to fall asleep and forget the images of the fatigue-clad individuals who had confiscated her music cassettes at the airport.

Chapter 11

Roxana woke to the rhythm and sounds of Tehran. Although their house was in a suburb, she could hear the sounds of cars traveling on the nearby highway. She always bragged about the fact that if someone blindfolded her and took her to any of her three favorite cities, she would know instantly which it was from the sound of the city's traffic. Yes, this was the unique sound of Tehran, not that of Paris or New York City.

She sprang from bed and hastened to the window to see Damavand. The highest mountain peak in Iran or "the Middle East's roof," as some called it, still stood there majestically.

In the short period she had spent in Tehran, she had seen many changes. But Damavand Peak remained unchanged. Maybe the mountain was one of the reasons she loved Tehran so much.

She tried to figure out what so enraptured her about Tehran. Was it its attractive, hilly areas, its rivers and large boulevards, or its tree-covered roads? After mulling it over for a long while, she realized that aside from geographical attractiveness, she adored Tehran for two reasons. First, she felt she owned every inch of Tehran, as if every mayor of Tehran since her birth had given her the golden key to the city.

The second reason was the Tehranians. They were kind and generous. They were color-blind and religion-blind. Although they joked about other people's dialects, they were not biased. Moreover, Tehranians had a great sense of humor. They would start their mornings with a joke or two at their workplace.

"Where are the Tehranians?" she kept asking her family after spending a day walking and shopping in Tehran.

"Many Tehranians have left the country," Roxana's mother said. "Those who've stayed here can be found in their homes or at private parties."

"But Tehranians are outdoor people."

"Women don't feel safe dressing up, and men cannot use alcohol in restaurants. So, a lot of Tehranians don't feel like going out," said Syrus, Roxana's brother.

"There are no nightclubs, no good movies anymore," Elli, Roxana's sister, added. "So people find entertainment at home."

Roxana noticed that anytime she asked questions, only her mother and her siblings answered. Her father was quiet. This was a man who was known to be a walking encyclopedia. Yet he steadfastly held his tongue during every political discussion.

So one day, she asked him why he didn't engage in their conversations.

He looked at her with fatherly love. "This revolution is only one year old, and no one is patient enough to give it a chance."

"So you think things will get better?"

"I'm certain. People should be patient."

"Do you still believe this is the best country in the world?"

"America is best for Americans, Germany for Germans, but this is still the best country for me."

* * *

When Syrus heard that the Revolutionary Guard at the airport had confiscated his sister's music cassettes, he reassured her he could purchase every one of them in Tehran. Roxana was doubtful at first, but after she visited a special new shopping area near Queen Elizabeth Boulevard, she believed him.

There, she found cassette tapes of the most recent music recorded by Elton John and Rod Stewart, as well as by European artists. She felt lucky when she learned that her mother had saved all of her Adamo records.

"There are economic sanctions against Iran. Where do you get these music cassettes?" she asked Syrus.

"Everything we need comes from Turkey, Dubai, and other Persian Gulf states."

"The Europeans haven't boycotted us," Ellie said. "They still sell us items we need."

She saw abundant foreign goods in Tehran the next day when she shopped with her mother at Zafar's supermarket. For a moment she felt she was in a store in the United States.

As she was putting a box of cereal into her cart, a chic Tehranian woman approached her and asked in Farsi, "Are you coming from *Amrika*?"

"Yes," she responded in Farsi.

"Everybody's dying to go to there. Why did you come back?"

Roxana didn't expect that personal question, so she tried to use a little humor, "I came back to live *zir-e-sayey-emam,* under the shadow of *imam*."

The woman looked shocked. "Has he brainwashed you too?" She didn't wait for an answer. "You know he is *Hendi*. His ancestors came from *Hend*, India. He lives and survives by drinking the blood of young boys—"

The woman was still talking when Roxana's mother pulled her arm and dragged her off to another section of the store.

"What line was that—'under the shadow of imam'?" she mocked her daughter. "Wait until they put you under *chador.*"

"I'm still wearing what I wore in Paris."

"The day will come soon. Wait."

* * *

That afternoon, Lili came to Roxana's home with her cousin, Iraj. They decided to go to Chattanooga, a famous café on Pahlavi Road where the three had spent a lot of time in the late sixties.

"I have to tell you. There is no music, no alcohol. It's just a place to sit," Iraj said.

"That's okay," Roxana said. "I just need to sit there and watch the road."

In order to drive to Chattanooga, Iraj had to pass the neighborhood's *Komiteh* on Zafar Avenue.

"Please lower your gaze," Iraj said. "Sometimes they stop people and question them for no reason."

Roxana had heard similar comments from her brother before, every time they passed the *Komiteh.* A nice Bee Gees song played on the car's cassette player. Roxana and Lili both loved the song. They had danced to it at many parties. As they approached the *Komiteh*, they moved their upper bodies in an approximation of the Hustle.

"Are you two nuts?" Iraj shouted as he pushed the gas pedal and accelerated the car. "I hope they didn't see you."

"Relax, Iraj. We didn't do anything illegal," Lili said, laughing.

"Didn't you just tell me that they confiscated Roxana's music cassettes at the airport?"

"Yes, they did, but here the car windows were up. They couldn't hear anything."

"These days, they're looking suspiciously when they see a man and a woman in the street or in a car."

"Exactly what's the role of a *Komiteh*?" Roxana asked.

"They are like the Islamic moral police."

"What happened to the police precincts?"

"They are still around, but they are also supervised by the *Komiteh* members or the Revolutionary Guard."

"I think it's true when they say, 'power corrupts.' Remember how the shah's constable put you in jail?" Lili asked Iraj.

"How can I forget? I was lucky Roxana was with us," Iraj said.

Roxana remembered the incident. One late afternoon in 1973, the three of them had been walking in one of the beautiful areas of *Saltanat Abad,* when they noticed a constable hitting a ten-year-old boy with his baton.

Iraj jumped to the child's rescue. "*Sarkar,* please let him go. I'm sure he'll apologize for whatever he did."

"It's none of your business. Step back," the constable ordered. When Iraj refused, he turned around and handcuffed him. "You're insulting the shah," he said.

It was Friday night, the Iranian weekend. The precinct's captain, who had authority to make decisions about Iraj's release, had already left. The police sergeant on duty had no power to release a detainee.

Roxana insisted on seeing the captain. The sergeant reluctantly called the captain at home and told him that the suspect had an attorney. Roxana and Lili waited for two hours in the precinct before the captain arrived. Iraj stood handcuffed in a cell facing them.

"Send the attorney to my office," the captain ordered when he walked in.

Roxana went inside the office, introduced herself, and gave the captain details about the incident. "The officer didn't arrest him for disorderly conduct, or for any other real offense," Roxana emphasized.

"Why is he here then?"

"According to your constable, Iraj insulted him; therefore, he insulted the shah."

"Did he actually say that?"

"Yes. I have three witnesses who can testify in court."

The captain came out, ordered the sergeant to release Iraj, and then left without talking to anyone.

When the trio arrived at Chattanooga, they chose a table near the road and ordered three espressos. There were only a few people there—no music, no happy faces, and no sound of laughter. Chattanooga's ambiance had vanished.

Roxana stared at the road and watched people pass. The voice in her head nagged again, "Where are the Tehranians?"

That night, she struggled to fall asleep. She had forgotten about Iraj's unjustified arrest, but their conversation reminded her of the political atmosphere in Iran during the shah, of the power given to a constable on the street, and of how that power was abused to silence people.

But now, those who were running the *Komiteh* acted just like the shah's constables, only the antishah label had changed to *Zed-e-Enghelab*, antirevolution. Maybe history had proven again that revolutions didn't bring victory; they only replaced the old masters with the new ones.

Chapter 12

Roxana realized she couldn't be chauffeured around in Tehran all the time. She had to strike out on her own. Driving in the congested Tehran was next to impossible; fortunately, taxicabs were available everywhere. The cabs, however, only ran in one direction. Quickly, she learned how to use different taxi lines to get to her destination, but she still felt like a tourist in her hometown. She had to learn the new names of the streets—the former streets such as Queen Elizabeth, Eisenhower, Churchill, and Kennedy. Even some of the streets with regular names had been changed to commemorate those killed during the course of the revolution.

She made a list of the people she knew before she left Tehran. She hoped they could advise her on how to find a job. The first name on the list was Dr. Hatefi, a prominent lawyer who used to be the legal advisor to the Judiciary Committee of Iran's Senate, where Roxana did her internship.

In the '60s, women were allowed to become judges in Iran after an exam and a period of internship with a judge. During her second year in law school, Roxana was the only female accepted for an internship with the Senate's Judiciary Committee. But when a new law allowed female law graduates to become judges, she decided to talk with the dean of the law school and get his advice on her career.

The dean explained that in order to become a judge, first of all one had to be twenty-five years old. She was only nineteen.

"You're not going to like the environment in the Ministry of Justice," the dean said. "It's a very male-dominated place."

Roxana's father was disappointed when he learned she had chosen internship with the Senate over that of the Ministry of Justice. "Your great-grandfather was a well-known jurist of his time," he said. "He was always called upon to act as an arbitrator. I thought you would follow his path."

Despite her earlier uncertainty, Roxana found the internship with the Senate's Judiciary Committee highly challenging and equally rewarding.

Under Dr. Hatefi's supervision, she worked with famous appellate judges, who advised the committee. During her years of internship, she had to divide her time researching for three judges who worked in different fields of law. The outcome was impressive: three digests of laws on commercial, civil, and criminal codes of Iran.

* * *

Dr. Hatefi was full of smiles when he first saw Roxana, but he immediately asked, "What are you doing back in Iran?"

"I've come to live under the shadow of the imam," Roxana said, knowing that the naughty remark would always raise some eyebrows.

"Well, that's admirable!" Dr. Hatefi smiled. "But you should know that I spent time in jail before the revolution. As the president of Tehran's Bar Association, I had prepared a report enumerating human rights violations in Iran. We had the revolution, so we thought from then on we'd enjoy freedom of speech, but we cannot criticize this government either. So what's the difference?"

"I believe things are going to change."

"I admire your optimism."

After talking to several other lawyers, Roxana realized there was no corporate law practice left in Iran. All the big Iranian companies were nationalized and run by the government.

She talked to one of her female friends, a former law school classmate who had been a judge for several years. She learned that female judges were given administrative work, sometimes writing legal opinions for the male judges.

"They're really trying to use the Koran to justify that a woman cannot be a judge in Islam," she said.

That afternoon, Roxana took a walk on Enghelab Avenue, where Tehran University was located. Tears filled her eyes at the sight of the entrance gates. She'd heard that the government had turned a large area of the university's campus into a mosque for Friday prayer. Every Friday, an important ayatollah assumed the role of the imam and delivered a political speech.

The entrance of the university, with all its guards, resembled a military compound. The familiar bookstores and restaurants, though, still looked the same across the street. They brought back old memories—like the day when Roxana and her friends were practically kicked out of one of those restaurants. The voice of the owner still rang in her head, "You come here, order a coffee, and talk about *Jhanehepole-Sart* (Jean Paul Sartre) for three hours," he had said. "You plan to bankrupt me?"

Roxana smiled and kept walking. The newsstands around the university sold all kinds of newspapers, magazines, and books. People were engaged in political discussions everywhere. Some criticized the government while others defended its actions. No one was afraid of being arrested. There was an excitement in the air.

As Roxana started walking away from the university gate, she heard a commotion. She turned back. Two Revolutionary Guards were holding a young man and arguing with him. She walked closer to the area. As the man was shouting, "What have I done?" a military jeep stopped in front of the gate. More Revolutionary Guards jumped out of the jeep. In a split second, one of them put handcuffs on the young man and pushed him inside the jeep. On an impulse, Roxana ran toward the jeep. "*Sarcar*, Officer," she addressed one of the men who seemed to have more authority, doubting whether that was the proper title for a Revolutionary Guard. "What has he done?" she asked.

"It doesn't concern you; move back."

"I am an attorney; maybe he needs one."

"He can call his family from the *Komiteh*."

Roxana took a business card out of her purse and dropped it in the jeep before it took off. "Call me if you need an attorney," she said to the young man in handcuffs.

The man flashed a thankful smile but didn't say anything. None of the onlookers who had gathered around the jeep questioned the arrest.

They were more interested in staring at Roxana, a foreign-looking woman who had no scarf. Roxana noticed women who entered the university; all wore large headscarves.

She moved away from the gates and walked toward a park close to the northern part of Tehran University. She needed to sit down on a bench and try to make sense out of what she had witnessed. She didn't know why the man was arrested. She remembered *The Gulag Archipelago* and Solzhenytsin's stories about the arrests in the Soviet Union. He had described how people were pulled from their beds in the middle of the night, or in the street—or even from a hospital bed. He wondered why nobody objected, nobody cried, and nobody resisted. The young Iranian man questioned the arresting Revolutionary Guard, but it didn't make any difference.

When she got closer to the park, she saw a group of people listening to a speaker. The speaker belonged to Iran's National Front Movement. He was criticizing the government. For a moment, she felt the place resembled Hyde Park in London where anyone could climb on top of a bench and criticize the government or even the queen. It also resembled Berkeley's campus during the Vietnam War era. Was it possible for Iran to have another democratic system, like the pre-1953 CIA coup d'etat? But why had the Revolutionary Guards arrested the young man without charging him with any crime?

Chapter 13

A week after her arrival, Roxana finally received a phone call from Nina. She and her husband had rented a large two-story townhouse in a rich neighborhood in Tehran. She had found a job in a nearby hospital, and they planned to turn the first level of their home into a clinic for their practice. The mass departure of doctors and dentists from Iran had created a huge shortage in the medical field.

Roxana was not surprised that Nina, a surgeon, was the first to find a job. Lili had applied to several banks, but she hadn't heard back. The country's judicial system had changed so drastically that there was not a great deal of work left for lawyers. Still, Roxana made phone calls and visited law offices, hoping that she'd find a position. It made her anxious to be idle for too long.

* * *

Roxana noticed there was only one week left before the Persian New Year, and there was no tray of sprouting seeds, no *Haft Siin* (seven *S*s) table, and no pots of hyacinth, daffodils, or tulips. She asked her mother what had happened to their *Noruz* tradition.

"We've gone through a tough revolution; a lot of people have died," her mother said. "This year, I really don't feel like celebrating."

"We've always followed our tradition. I was looking forward to helping you out this year."

"Okay, if you want, go ahead and start. I'll get you the stuff you need."

With the help of her younger sister, Elli, Roxana set a small but a fancy *Haft Siin* table at the top corner of their living room—next to the red and golden Louis XVI sofa. The table looked a bit awkward in a room that resembled a tourist attraction area in Versailles. She arranged all of the items that started with the letter *S* and thought of their special meanings: *Samanu,* a sweet pudding, symbolized affluence; *Senjed,* a dried fruit, meant love; *Sir,* garlic, symbolized medicine; *Sib*, apple, meant beauty and health; *Somaq,* herb, reflected the color of sunrise; and *Serkeh*, vinegar, symbolized age and patience. The last item was *Sabzeh*, the green.

Roxana had planted wheat and lentil seeds in two separate casserole dishes, hoping that at least one would sprout before *Noruz*, enabling her to complete her *Haft Siin*'s table.

* * *

Although a fascinating place in the spring, Tehran sometimes grew cold during the *Noruz* celebrations. So those Tehranians who longed for warmer weather would pack and leave for Shiraz, Abadan, or Ahavaz—the warmer Iranian cities in the south.

Nina planned to spend her *Noruz* vacation in Shiraz, where her in-laws lived.

Before her trip, she planned a big *Chahar Shanbeh Suri* party, and invited some twenty high school friends.

Roxana enjoyed *Chahar Shanbeh Suri*, a Zoroastrian tradition where Persians jumped over fire on the eve of the last Wednesday before the Persian New Year. With each jump, they would say, "*Zardi-e-man az to, Sorkhi-e-to az man*," literally translated as, "my yellowness to you, your redness to me."

But the real meaning behind the ritual was to rid oneself of the old year's illnesses and to have a healthy, rosy new year.

After the revolution, the government tried to mock the unique Zoroastrian tradition, as well as the whole thirteen-day *Noruz* celebrations, by saying that not only was *Noruz* not a Moslem tradition, but it also belonged to the era of the kings—a custom that should be abandoned in an Islamic republic.

But the public reaction surprised the government. More people participated in the *Chahar Shanbeh Suri* than ever. This was the second year that the Islamic government had tried to dissuade Iranians from celebrating *Noruz*. Roxana had heard that the anti-Persian sentiments of some government authorities were so high that they were ready to eliminate anything related to Persian kings, even destroying the Persepolis.

One of the first stories she heard related to the Statue of Ferdowsi, a tenth-century Persian poet revered in the Eastern hemisphere the way Shakespeare is in the Western hemisphere. One day, the Moslem revolutionaries tried to bring down the statue of Ferdowsi in Ferdowsi Square in Tehran. Regular people in the street attacked the revolutionaries and stopped them from touching the statue.

The poet's sin was that his poems were all about the Persian kings. Iranians had enjoyed reading *Shahnameh* (*The Book of Kings*), for hundreds of years. Even illiterate people could recite some of the poems from Ferdowsi's popular epic.

Roxana witnessed firsthand how the Islamic government attempted to change the mentality of the people. However, at the end, they realized that this was still a Persian nation with a little Zoroastrian living in every Iranian's soul.

* * *

Nina had chosen the small park behind her townhouse and gathered some dry bushes and thin logs in preparation for *Chahar Shanbeh Suri*. By the time Roxana arrived, it had grown dark enough for Nina's husband to strike the match and start the fire.

Lili jumped over the fire first.

Roxana taught her godson, Yerem, Nina's younger son, how to jump over the fire, but he was scared. So she took him in her arms, and they both jumped over the fire.

"Boy, that was fun," Roxana said as she led Yerem away from the fire.

"It sure was," Lili said.

"I'm glad Nina invited us tonight. I don't know what's wrong with my mother. She's not in a mood to do anything this *Noruz*!"

As Roxana watched other guests lining up to jump over the fire, she spotted Kayvan and Steve coming toward them. She froze, but Lili walked right over to greet them.

Roxana found Nina near the fire, grabbed her arm, and whispered in Farsi, "What the hell are they doing here?"

"Relax, it's *Noruz*. I wanted Steve to see our tradition."

Nina stopped talking as Kayvan and Steve approached. Kayvan said a quick hello to Roxana and then took Lili with him to jump over the fire.

"Where have you been hiding all these days?" asked Steve, looking down at her with an expression of uncontained excitement.

"I thought we said our good-byes in Paris."

"You promised to find a book and some cassette tapes for me to learn Farsi."

"Oh, that. Well, you can buy them from bookstores around Tehran University."

"Kayvan took me there and bought the tapes for me. So when are you going to have dinner with me?"

"Maybe I don't like the idea of having dinner with a married man."

"You have to come up with a better reason. You know that my marriage is dead."

"Okay, what about the fact that I have no control over my life? I left Iran ten years ago because the political oppression was choking me. I longed for a revolution. I'm back now, but I'm having a hard time understanding this revolution."

"What's that got to do with having dinner with me?"

"My mind is on so many things—the future of Iran, the Soviet invasion of Afghanistan next door, the hundreds of thousands of Afghani refugees here—"

"You can't fix all the problems in the world."

"I know, but I can't ignore them, either. I can't think of dating when there's a war going on next door, and people get arrested before my eyes."

Nina gathered her guests and led them inside her townhouse, up to their residence on the second floor. She had a huge round living room with large windows overlooking the park. Unlike Roxana's parental home, which was decorated with classic French style furniture, Nina's townhouse looked more like a modern American home—large sofas, comfortable chairs, and recliners.

After serving dinner, which consisted of famous skewered Persian kabob, rice, and different *khoroshts,* Nina put some Persian music on and invited everyone to dance. Roxana was surprised there was no foreign music. One of her high school friends explained to her that over the last decade, Persians had started appreciating their own modern music and their own traditional dances.

At least six female guests started dancing in the middle of the living room. Some women danced together, trying to coordinate their hand movements. There were a lot of quivering bodies, swaying waistlines, and seductive looks in the women's eyes. The men danced the male version, extending their arms wide in the air, around and above their bodies, trying to follow the women's moves.

"Boy, this is more exotic than the belly dance!" Steve said. "Can you teach me how to do this?" he asked Roxana.

"This style of dance is so coquettish, so flirtatious, that I don't think I can even dare to do it alone in my room."

"Well, some women seduce a man with their bodies, some with their brains, like you."

"I've never heard that a woman's brain can seduce a man."

"I am experiencing it this very moment!"

Roxana was rescued when two of her former high school friends came over to talk with her. She introduced them to Steve.

One of the girls said, "We owe a lot to this woman. We were bothered a lot in high school because we were Bahaii, but Roxana was our advocate."

When Nina put on some new music and encouraged people to dance, the two women excused themselves, jumped over to the dance area, and started dancing again.

"So the non-Moslem kids were bothered in school?" Steve asked.

"Not really. In every school, you ran into some kids coming from fanatic families. Iranians are very tolerant. Look at the guests here. We have Jews, Christians, Zoroastrians, even Bahaiis."

"I hear that the Bahaiis are having a hard time after the revolution."

"I hope not. I don't know. I've just arrived here trying to learn about this revolution."

Lili came and took Roxana away. Steve joined Kayvan and Bijan, who were watching the female guests dance.

After the music stopped, Bijan got everyone's attention and said, "I have an announcement to make. We have some entertainers from America to perform for you."

He put on the "Boogie Woogie Bugle Boys" record, dimmed the lights, and said, "May I introduce to you the Andrews Sisters."

From behind the dining room curtains, Steve could see the backs of three women dressed in long-sleeve male shirts and skirts of the forties. The women started singing:

> "*He was a famous trumpet man from out Chicago way.*
> *He had a boogie style that no one else could play.*"

Then the three singers turned. Steve and Kayvan could not stop clapping and laughing. The three Andrews Sisters were none other than Roxana, Lili, and Nina.

> "*He was the top man at his craft, but then his number came up, and he was gone with the draft. He's in the army now, a-blowin' reveille; he's the boogie woogie bugle boy of Company B.*"

When the long song finished, there was a roar of applause, whistling, and bravos.

"Where did you guys learn that?" Steve asked. "Next to Bette Midler's version, this was the best performance I've ever seen."

"We performed this in our high school graduation celebration," Nina said.

"The all-talented trio," Bijan added.

Kayvan looked at Lili affectionately but didn't comment. The guests asked for an encore, a request that was granted. The second time around, the trio had a lot of fun themselves, singing and dancing.

Back in Kayvan's car, Steve posed a question to his friends. "Tonight I saw some Iranians who looked like our African Americans, and some looked Chinese to me. Where do they come from?"

"Leave it to an American to do racial profiling as soon as he sees different people!" Kayvan said jokingly.

"What am I supposed to think when I see an African or a Chinese woman speaking in Farsi?" Steve asked.

"The African-looking one was from Ahvaz, a city in the Persian Gulf area," Lili said.

"You know something, I have known Simin since elementary school," Roxana said. "I saw the slanted eyes, but I never questioned it in my mind."

"Because we don't categorize people like some people we know," Kayvan said.

"You are too sensitive about this," Steve said. "I'm curious. I'm a journalist. I should know these things."

"Wait a minute," Roxana said. "I just thought of something. Simin's family comes from the Caspian Sea area. Maybe her ancestors are *Torkaman.* I read that when Genghis Khan attacked Iran, a lot of members of his army married local girls."

"So Iranians don't care about one's race, religion, or ethnicity unless he or she is Bahaii," Steve commented.

"People don't have any problem with the Bahaiis; the government does," Lili said.

Chapter 14

Roxana's lentil seeds had sprouted in the casserole dish and looked groomed, but the wheat seeds were just sprouting. She placed the *sabzeh* in the middle of the *Haft Siin* table. Now she had completed her list.

The *Noruz* tradition was to visit each family for short periods—between thirty and forty-five minutes—but this became impossible for Roxana when some relatives insisted that she should stay for lunch or dinner.

On the third day of *Noruz*, Roxana had two surprise visitors: Batool and her daughter, Adeleh. Batool was the family's part-time maid. Adeleh, who was two years older than Roxana, practically had lived with Roxana's family.

In high school, Roxana played the role of Adeleh's teacher. She forced her to stay up every night and finish her homework. Eventually, though, Adeleh dropped out of high school and disappeared into thin air with her mother. Puri gave up on the search, but Roxana persisted until she found them. She negotiated with her high school principal and got Adeleh reenrolled in school again. When Roxana left for the United States, Adeleh was in college.

Batool was an amazing woman. Despite her difficult life raising her daughter as a single mother, she always had a cheerful disposition. If it weren't for the financial help of Roxana's family, she wouldn't have survived.

The minute she saw Roxana, she started crying.

She hugged her and said in Turkish, "Let me sacrifice myself for you! You and your family helped me and Adeleh survive."

Roxana hugged her back and tried to calm her down, but she was too emotional. Then it was Adeleh's turn for a long, emotional hug.

She was married now, had two kids, and was the principal of the same high school she had attended with Roxana, Lili, and Nina. It was the same high school she had dropped out of as a young girl. *What poetic justice!* Every principal of that famous high school came from a well-known Iranian family and had a PhD in education from abroad.

Bravo the revolution! Roxana smiled.

Batool mumbled something in Turkish but couldn't finish. She became tearful again.

"Adeleh, is there something wrong with your mother?" asked Roxana, growing a bit alarmed.

"It's because of your grandmother. She was my mother's only friend in this world, and when she died—"

Roxana's body went cold. "What? Who died?"

"You don't know? Your grandma died a few months ago."

"No, no. It can't be true. Please tell me that it's not true."

She ran to the kitchen and found her mother tearful, talking to someone on the phone.

"For months you kept this from me?" Roxana cried.

"We couldn't tell you." Puri handed the telephone to Roxana, picked up a tissue, and wiped away her tears. Roxana heard her father's voice on the line.

"Princess, are you there?" he asked.

"Yes, I am," Roxana said, choking back sobs. She couldn't make sense of things. Why would her family have kept this from her?

"Your grandmother died a week after the hostage taking. You were going through a tough time in New York. Then, in January, I was almost killed in a car accident."

The telephone fell to the floor; Roxana had to sit down.

"You should be grateful your father didn't die," Puri said.

Roxana sat there motionless.

"It was a cold January evening, and it was dark," her mother continued. "When your father exited the cab on the highway and tried to cross the road, a driver with impaired vision didn't see him. He didn't even notice he had hit your father and dragged him a long way before he realized his car was hard to steer."

Roxana listened and cried quietly. Her father had gone through two surgeries within a month in order to correct his fractured shoulder.

She wiped her tears and then picked up the receiver from the floor.

"Father, are you okay now?" she asked.

"I'm as healthy as a roaring lion!" he answered.

Roxana ran to her bedroom and pulled an old photo album from one of her bureau drawers. She turned the pages until she found her grandmother's photo. She caressed the photo. Her tears dropped on the photo; she wiped them and kissed the photo. *My friends always named famous people as their heroes. You were mine. How could you die without seeing me?*

Chapter 15

The puzzle was solved now. Her mother had been putting up with the *Noruz* excitement for Roxana's sake. Roxana knew that families who lose a loved one do not celebrate the first *Noruz* after the death. She felt guilty that she had enjoyed an exciting *Noruz* celebration without knowing her family was in mourning.

Despite her mother's advice, Roxana insisted on visiting her grandmother's grave. She couldn't believe her eyes when she saw her mother wearing a black *chador*.

"What's that for?" Roxana asked.

"A middle-aged woman cannot go to the south of Tehran without proper *hejab*," Puri said. "You're young; you don't have to. But you'd better wear a conservative outfit and a scarf."

On another day, Roxana might have chafed at these instructions, but today, in her grief, she simply did as her mother advised.

This was Roxana's first trip to Behesh-e-Zahra—the largest cemetery in the south of Tehran. At first she was confused when she saw many avenues, squares, and rows of graves. She followed her mother blindly. Puri knew how to find her mother's grave. Not too far from the entrance of the cemetery, Roxana's mother pointed to a woman sitting by a grave and whispered in her ear, "Look at this woman and this grave. I have a sad story to tell you."

The woman appeared to be fifty-something, wore a black *maghna-eh*, a long scarf fastened under the chin. She also had a black *chador* hanging loosely on top of her head. She wore a long-sleeved black dress under her two layers of *hejab*. An enlarged photo of a young man was fastened to a black fence on top of the grave. On the ground beside her rested a tray of halva, a sweet pudding specifically made for funerals or visits to the cemetery.

"What about her?" Roxana asked.

"She's only thirty-five years old. That was her only child—nineteen years old when he got killed during the Kurdistan unrest. The woman cursed the government, including Imam Khomeini. At first they arrested her, but then they didn't know what to do with her, so they let her go. Look at her. She barely moves. Her gaze is fixed on the picture. She comes here early in the morning, sets up her flowers and her tray of sweets and fruits, sits there until it gets dark, and then she leaves. She repeats the same ritual day after day."

They continued on, arriving at her grandmother's grave. Roxana restrained herself, pretending to be brave. But the minute she saw the engraved inscription on the modest marble headstone, she burst into tears. Like her mother, she picked up a small stone, tapped on the tombstone three times, and said a prayer.

Puri rose and told Roxana that she was going to distribute the halva she had made. She also wanted to give *Sadagheh,* charity money, to the poor in the other section of the cemetery.

Once her mother was gone, Roxana sobbed in earnest. The grave appeared lonely to her. She kept looking at the words on her grandmother's tomb.

Talat Fatemi

The Beloved Mother of Pourandokht and Parviz

Below that was her grandmother's favorite Omar Khayam verse:

The Ones Not Arrived,

Had They Known

How We Suffer On Earth,

Wouldn't Have Come Anymore.

She remembered her grandmother's life. *Talat* or *Tala*, meaning gold, as her friends called her, was the daughter of the governor of a small beach town near the Caspian Sea. At age thirteen, she was so beautiful that every eligible bachelor in town desired to marry her. One of those suitors was the son of a rich man. Tala's father asked the young suitor's family to wait for another two years for his daughter to reach age fifteen. The family felt insulted, so they arranged for Tala to be kidnapped.

Tala and the rich man's son were taken to Tehran. He raped her during the trip but subsequently married her in Tehran. The family got them a nice house in the *Amirieh* neighborhood. Despite Tala's pleas to visit her family, she was forced to live with her rapist husband.

She didn't respond to the husband's demands or to her mother-in-law's orders. She couldn't be tamed; as a result, she was beaten up every day.

After eight months of abuse, Tala escaped one night. She kept running until she reached a mosque and went inside. It was the month of *Ramadan,* and they were serving food during *Iftar,* the end of fasting.

Tala befriended an old widow and told her how she had been kidnapped, raped, and forced to marry the man she didn't love. She told the woman about eight months of sexual and physical abuse. The old woman lived in *Monirieh* and had come to this mosque because of the special *Iftar.* She felt sorry for Tala and took her to her house.

Life was peaceful for Tala for a few weeks, until the woman's nephew came for a visit. He fell in love with her and asked her to marry him, which she did.

She had a month of happy life before husband number two became abusive.

The pattern of abuse and fleeing continued until husband number seven, a sergeant in the neighborhood's precinct. Tala had gone to the police to complain about her current husband. Amir, the handsome sergeant on duty that night, told Tala that he had no authority to arrest a man for disciplining his wife. However, he took Tala to his mother's house for protection. Amir waited for a few months, and then he married Tala after he made sure that she was legally divorced.

One day, Roxana had asked her grandmother how she could've possibly gotten married so often without being legally divorced. She was surprised to learn that during those years, and before the Family Protection Law of 1967, a man could go to any *Mahzar,* a notary-like office, and unilaterally divorce his wife. The shame of having a runaway wife was so serious that each one of Grandma Tala's husbands went to one of those *Mahzars* and got a quick divorce in order to tell people that he, the husband, was the one who had divorced her.

Life brought happiness for Tala for a while. She was pregnant with Puri, Roxana's mother, so she thought that this was probably her fairy-tale story at last. Unfortunately, Amir cheated on her and moved in with her best friend, making that friend his *sigheh,* concubine.

Another quick divorce and another homeless period ensued. But this time Tala was pregnant. After a few weeks of living with friends, she began looking for a job.

Finding a job in a country where no women worked was like climbing Mount Damavand in high heels. Surprisingly, she found a job, first with a textile factory, and then, when she was laid off, with a glass factory.

It was at the glass company that she met Yousef (Joseph) and fell in love with him. She was now seventeen, and Yousef was thirty-seven. He was a gentle man who understood he could not put Tala in a cage. He gave her freedom and a sense of respect and independence. Yousef raised Puri as if she were his daughter. Three years later, Tala had a boy with the man she loved. She named him Parviz.

When Yousef died, Tala was thirty-seven years old, still a young, attractive woman. She had stayed married to Yousef for twenty years. He was her soul mate.

After Yousef's death, Tala still had marriage proposals despite having two children, but she never remarried.

Roxana remembered bragging to her American friends about her feminist grandmother: "You think that Elizabeth Taylor broke the record? My grandma married eight times in a conservative Moslem society—where divorce was considered a *taboo*."

She couldn't help being proud of her grandmother. She had heard stories from older relatives that when Reza Shah banned the *hejab* in 1936, Grandma Tala was the first woman running to the streets of Tehran without *chador*. Tala was insulted, physically abused, and spat upon in Conte intersection on Reza Shah Avenue.

Unlike Roxana, Puri didn't feel proud of her mother's past. In fact, she was ashamed that her mother had married eight times. She was embarrassed when her mother forced her to wear fashionable French clothes just to irritate people on the street. Every time her mother got into a street fight about the *hejab*, the frightened six-year-old Puri cried.

It took several decades, a revolution, and the imminent threat of the return of the *hejab* to make Puri understand her mother's heroic struggle.

Roxana marveled at the challenges her fearless grandmother faced and the obstacles she overcame. She wondered whether she had it in her to do the same.

"What are you thinking about?" Puri asked her daughter as she put the tray of halva on the grave.

"Just remembering the stories about Grandma."

"She would roll over in her grave if she knew they're bringing back the *hejab*."

"I'm ready to go now."

"Let me finish distributing this halva. More people just entered the cemetery."

Puri took the tray of halva to a group of *chador*-clad women who had gathered around a grave.

Roxana waited for fifteen minutes for her mother's return. She grew impatient and went in search of her. She tapped on the shoulders of several women in black *chador*, calling them *Maman*. With their backs to her, they all looked alike. She felt like a little girl who had just lost her mother in a big amusement park. She moved back to her grandmother's grave thinking about *chador*. What was it about this piece of cloth that could make a woman's identity disappear?

Puri appeared from an opposite corner of the cemetery with an empty tray. Her mission was accomplished.

Roxana looked at the cemetery once more. She promised herself that she would never revisit the depressing place. She didn't know that she had to return again.

Chapter 16

The visit to the cemetery was therapeutic for both Roxana and her mother. Puri no longer pretended that everything was nice and joyful. She could now cry whenever she talked about her mother.

One day Roxana found her sitting on her bed looking at some pictures. The bedroom door was open, but because Puri was crying, Roxana knocked on the door.

"May I come in?"

"Yes." Puri wiped her tears quickly and motioned Roxana to sit on the bed. "I've been meaning to show you these pictures for years." She handed the pictures to her daughter.

There were four old faded pictures. In one picture, Puri was holding hands with a tall foreign-looking man. In the other three pictures, in addition to Puri and the foreign man, the young, attractive Tala was standing next to her husband, Yousef, and holding a boy's hand.

"The boy is your uncle Parviz. Of course, you recognize Yousef—"

"The question is who is the man next to you, and why are you wearing a white satin dress?"

"That's Charles, my fiancé."

Roxana's jaw dropped. For the next hour or so, she sat on her mother's bed speechless and listened to an unreal tale.

When Puri turned fifteen, her mother found her a job at Iran's Tobacco Company, where she worked. Like a perfume connoisseur, Puri could distinguish the aroma of different tobacco leaves. The company had employed several tobacco experts from Greece, Belgium, France, and England. While the French and the Belgian men flirted with both Puri and her young, attractive mother, a Greek employee and a young British employee competed with each other to win Puri's heart. Tala accepted the British suitor's marriage proposal on behalf of her daughter, knowing well that Puri loved Miremad, the young neighbor who lived across the street.

"What happened?"

"You thought your feminist grandmother was perfect. She forced me to accept the man, but, thank God, the engagement lasted only for one week. The clergy in the Marriage Office first asked Charles to convert to Islam, because a Moslem woman could not marry a non-Moslem."

"Did he?"

"Yes. Then the clergy claimed that the law required Charles to become an Iranian citizen. Thank God he couldn't comply with that condition because he would've lost his diplomatic status at the British Embassy. I thought that was God's intervention. If he hadn't, like Lili, you would've been half British."

"How come Lili's father didn't have any problem marrying Lili's mom?"

"Because he was a man. All those restrictions existed for women."

"How did my poor father react?"

"He was heartbroken, of course. But after the engagement fell through, he was so happy that he immediately forgave your grandmother. It took me a long time before I could forgive her. I finally did when she told me her story of being raped and kidnapped, and all those abusive husbands. She was trying to protect me. She thought that a British man wouldn't abuse his wife."

Roxana was energized by the stories about her grandmother and her struggle to find a job in an era when only a handful of Iranian women worked.

She could no longer sit around and wait for someone to knock on her door and offer her a job. She realized she had to put her legal expertise on hold for a while and look for work in other areas.

During the last three years of high school, Roxana had worked for two different women's magazines as a reporter. She had also obtained a certificate in journalism from Tehran University. She had published several poems and short stories in literary magazines.

Many newspapers and magazines were shut down after the revolution, but new publications were surfacing every day.

Kayhan and *Ettelaat*, the two famous daily newspapers in Iran, showed an interest in publishing some of her articles and essays, but they had no job offer.

Kayhan published a series of articles by Roxana on slavery, which ran for three consecutive days. The *Tehran Times,* which was published in English, ran her article on Iran's revolution. This article was praised and brought her personal satisfaction.

After the hostage taking, she had sent several letters to the *New York Times* and the *Washington Post*, pointing out the inaccuracies of some of their editorials. But none of those letters were even acknowledged, much less published. She felt by ignoring her, the two papers sent her a message: "If you're a hostage-taker, no one is interested in your point of view."

Among many issues discussed, Roxana's article on the revolution had referred to conversations she'd had with a New York cab driver and a prominent Washington, DC–based attorney. She enjoyed the driver's Brooklyn accent, but his opinion was shocking to her.

"Those Arab nomads have too much oil, which we need. Why can't we send our marines to get that oil?"

The following week, the well-known attorney in Washington, DC, tried to explain the cab driver's thesis. "You see, the important natural resources in the world are like a trust that belongs to all the peoples of the world—a common heritage of mankind."

When she asked the attorney whether he would consider sharing the US coal resources, known as the world's largest reserves of coal, with other nations, he said, "It's not the same."

Nina invited Lili and Roxana to visit her in Shiraz. "I have invited Steve too. I want to show him our Persepolis," she said. "Kayvan is driving him first to Isfahan, then to Shiraz. Why don't you two come? It'll be fun."

Chapter 17

Steve ran back and forth from the Gates of Xerxes to the Apadana Palace, taking as many pictures as he could. He was so impressed by Darius's Palace and the carved images of Darius and his guests on the walls that he forgot he had come to Persepolis with a group of friends.

Lili had her own camera. She also took many pictures.

Kayvan, Nina, and her husband toured the place together.

After a long period of taking pictures, Steve noticed that Roxana was walking by herself, being aloof. He was surprised to see the cheerful and witty Roxana so preoccupied. When he found her staring at the Throne Hall, an impressive site in Persepolis, he approached Lili. "She seems so sad; what's wrong?" he asked her.

"She just found out that her grandmother died in November when she was in New York. She was Roxana's hero, a feminist who was way ahead of her generation."

"I felt awful when my grandmother died."

"Grandmothers play a great role in their grandchildren's lives," Kayvan said as he joined the conversation. "People in the West think Iran is a patriarchal society, but believe me, if you peel off the layers of authorities and powers in many Iranian households, you will see that somewhere, there is a grandmother who rules."

Steve saw Nina and Bijan talking to Roxana, so he walked toward them.

"Roxana, I'm so sorry about your loss," he said. "I hear that your grandmother was a feminist."

"Thanks. Indeed she was. My grandmother was one of the first women who appeared without *hejab* in public. Feminist groups in

Iran should put a statue of my grandmother in one of Tehran's squares to symbolize Iranian women's struggles against *hejab* in the 1930s."

"Why don't you campaign for that?"

"Are you kidding me? With a Moslem government that is planning to reinstate the *hejab*?"

"Don't you know what they did to the grave of the shah's father?" Nina chimed in. "He was the one who banned the veil. They destroyed his grave and replaced it with a new public toilet."

"Haven't you seen some of the slogans about *hejab* in the streets of Tehran?" Bijan added. "The most popular one reads, 'A woman in a veil is protected like a pearl in an oyster shell.'"

"I can't believe this is the same country that had two women ruling the Persian Empire for several years," Roxana exclaimed.

"Who were those?" Steve asked.

"Purandokht and Azarmidokht, two Persian queens during the Sasanid Dynasty. And, of course, who can forget Queen Vashti, the first feminist woman in the world?"

Steve was eager to hear the story, so Roxana proudly talked about the wife of King Xerxes, who refused to display her beauty by appearing before the king's guests.

"Queen Vashti's story is told in the book of Esther in the Bible," Lili said. "Esther was the Jewish queen who saved her people. After Cyrus the Great conquered Babylon in 539 BC, he released the Jews who had lived in captivity under Babylonian rule. He gave the liberated Jews two options, either to return to Jerusalem or to stay in Persia. He also gave them the money that the Babylonian King Nebuchadnezzar II had taken from Jerusalem. Esther (Hadassah), an orphaned Jew, and her cousin, Mordecai, stayed in Persia. Esther married King Xerxes after he divorced Queen Vashti. That's why I don't feel British. This is my home. My ancestors have lived here since biblical time."

"My ancestors came here after the Armenian massacre," Nina said. "We haven't lived here for thousands of years, but I also feel this is my home, mostly because of Cyrus the Great. I have read he was kind to the Armenians who lived in his empire. He even mediated between Armenians and their enemies in order to establish peace among them. What a great man!"

"I'm listening to all these patriotic stories, but you guys all chose to live outside Iran," Steve said.

"We didn't have any political freedom. That's why we left," Kayvan said. "Steve, you should write about Cyrus the Great and the fact that we are all his children."

"He was the first ruler who inscribed a charter of the rights of nations on a clay cylinder," Roxana added. "In his human rights charter, he declared that everyone was free to choose his religion and the place he wanted to live. Everyone had the right to choose his profession. He abolished slavery, but most significantly, he said that he would not impose his rule on anyone. His subjects were free to accept or reject him as their king."

"I don't believe any of today's modern kings and queens have the guts to make such a suggestion," Steve commented.

Nina encouraged Steve and her friends to visit the Eram Garden, one of the shah's favorite vacation places. After the Eram visit, she took them to the Shah-e-cheragh Mosque, Vakil Bazaar, and the tombs of Hafez and Sa'di.

When visiting Hafazieh, Roxana told Steve, "You may find some Iranian families who don't have a copy of the Koran in their homes, but I bet those families have a copy of Hafez's collection of poetry."

"Why don't you read some of his poems to me?" Steve asked, stepping closer to her. "Maybe Hafez can teach me how to find a way to your heart!"

Roxana smiled.

Chapter 18

On the thirteenth day of *Noruz*, which sometimes coincides with April Fools' Day, most Iranians go on a picnic. Popular places include recreation parks, gardens, woods, and mountains alongside streams and rivers.

To celebrate the *Sizdeh-be-dar*, another Zoroastrian tradition, Lili invited her friends to their family vacation home in Karaj outside Tehran.

Roxana took her younger brother and sister along with her. This was Roxana's first visit in Karaj. She admired the garden that Yahya, Lili's father, had created. He had planted several weeping willows around the creek that went through his property. There were several separate beds of yellow hyacinths and purple and red tulips. She saw many blooming plants on each side of the creek.

Everyone helped Yahya, while he grilled the *kabab*. Narges, Lili's aunt, had already cooked rice and *Ghormeh sabzi*. Nina had baked a cake and lots of cookies.

At the lunch table, Roxana felt relaxed and happy. Pleasant Persian music played on the cassette player, and the soothing sound of the water running in the creek filtered through every now and then.

She had to rid herself of the pain of losing her grandmother. Her father was right, "Death is a part of life."

She saw Narges happy. She couldn't help remembering her difficult life. The shah executed her communist husband when she was only twenty years old. Her brother Yahya helped her raising her one-year-old son, Iraj.

When she compared her life to the lives that Narges and her grandmother had endured, Roxana admitted that she had had a pain-free life. She realized that she was feeling relaxed mostly because of Steve's absence. Though he intrigued her, he was also a constant reminder of America, the Americans, her life in New York City, and, ironically, the hostages—all the things, people, and places she was trying to forget. She wondered how her life would have changed had she met Steve in New York City and before the hostage crisis.

After lunch, Yahya, Bijan, Iraj, Roxana's brother Syrus, and Nina's two sons began playing soccer. As they ran in the sunshine, the five women sat at the table and enjoyed their afternoon tea with cake.

Nina was the only married woman in the group, so she took it upon herself to remind the three young single women to knot the grass. This was a part of *Sizdeh Be-dar* tradition, in which single women were encouraged to tie blades of grass and make a wish to be married in the New Year.

"Are you kidding?" Roxana asked, incredulous.

Her mother had never urged her to follow the old tradition. All she had heard was, "Study hard and choose a profession that makes you independent, so you won't be needing any husband."

Iraj, Lili's cousin, changed the music to a happy song. "Come on now, this is *Sizdeh be-dar*. You've got to dance," he demanded.

He pulled the women up out of their seats and led them to the flat area in the garden. Pretty soon all the *Sizdeh be-dar* celebrants were dancing and having fun.

At the end of the day, each family threw their *Sabzeh* into the stream, confident that they had thrown away all the evil things waiting to haunt them in the New Year. They didn't know about the New Year's surprises changing their lives.

Chapter 19

Roxana had a busy New York lifestyle in Tehran long before she became a Wall Street lawyer. In high school, she was the president of several student clubs and was the editor of her high school's weekly journal. So when one of Iran's famous women's magazines decided to recruit reporters from high schools, she was the obvious choice.

After competing with forty thousand students and passing all levels of college tests, Roxana's average was on the top ten in both medical and law schools. She knew that medical school meant a lot of sleepless nights. Even at age eighteen, she was wise enough to know that she could not make a great doctor. So, over her mother's objections, she chose law, but deep down she was not sure whether she had made the right choice. Every day for a month, she entered Tehran University with that nagging question pounding her head.

Nina got admitted to medical school at Pahlavi University in Shiraz. Lili passed the test for law school but chose economics. Since economics and political science departments were part of the law school, Lili shared classes with Roxana during their freshman year.

Roxana enjoyed the law school tremendously, but, with the exception of her father, every relative or family friend had joined her mother in reminding her that choosing law school over medical school was a big mistake. She had to put up with negative opinions for a month because she herself wasn't convinced that she had made the right decision. However, at the end of the first month, something happened that changed her future.

On that decisive morning, she couldn't find a taxi, so she was late for her sociology class. Luckily, Lili, who had to take this compulsory course with law students, had arrived on time. Roxana sat next to her, borrowed her notes, and started copying. She didn't pay attention to the debate that was going on at the lectern between a female political science student and a clergy law student who had a degree in theology.

The professor who taught this sociology course was one of the judges of Iran's Supreme Court. Roxana heard a few words about "polygamy" and "adultery," so she tuned in and listened to the debate. The clergy law student was actually advocating polygamy and justifying the wife's killing by her husband if he had found his wife and her paramour in an adulterous relationship. Roxana waited for her female classmate who was debating the clergy to say something. She was obviously upset and angry, but she was mumbling.

Roxana raised her hand and asked the professor to allow her to participate in the debate. He agreed.

The classroom resembled a courtroom with an elevated bench. One had to climb several steps in order to reach the podium that was next to the professor's seat. Roxana ran—that made the students laugh.

After twenty minutes of nonstop argument, she bombarded the clergy student with Koranic verses, specifically emphasizing two. "In Surat 4:3, it's stated that 'You can marry up to four women,'" Roxana explained. "But it specifically adds, 'If you fear that you shall not be able to deal with them justly, then limit yourself to one. That is to prevent you from doing injustice.'" Furthermore, Roxana added. "Surat 4:129 states, 'You will never be able to do perfect justice between wives even if it is your ardent desire.'"

On the subject of adultery, Roxana cited Koranic verses and Hadith from Prophet Mohammad, indicating that Islam had made it almost impossible to prove adultery. Besides, the punishment was to humiliate the adulterers, not to kill them.

The clergy stood there not being able to respond. Roxana was so preoccupied with her debate that she had not noticed the roar of applause until she stopped talking. Three hundred students—fifty of whom were women, had stood up and applauded her. Some male students in the back of the classroom had climbed on top of their chairs to make their enthusiasm and support more visible.

The professor, who was full of smiles, thanked Roxana. By the time she went back to her seat, the session was over. Many students gathered around her and congratulated her. When they asked her where they could find her sources, she simply said, "Go and read the Koran. The information is there."

Lili was trying to push back the students who had hovered over their desks. After they left, she turned to Roxana and asked, "What did you have for breakfast this morning?"

"Actually, nothing, because I was late for school."

* * *

Beginning with her internship in the second year of law school, Roxana's day would start at 6:00 a.m. and end around 10:00 p.m. She had five hours of internship at the Senate's Judiciary Committee. She had to attend law school, and teach English to seventh-graders, six days a week.

The tough Iranian educational system and the fast-lane lifestyle in Tehran had prepared her to walk down tough roads and face harsh realities. The two factors played a significant role in her success in New York.

But none of her experiences in the past had prepared her for how to live a revolutionary life. She had passed the tough tests and had done the hard work. This was the time for her to relax and enjoy life. She didn't know that, instead, she was destined to sail on a stormy sea, like a lost boat.

Chapter 20

Lili was offered a job by Iran's Bank Markazi in mid-April, working in their international division. Roxana had suspicions that Kayvan must have had some involvement with the sudden job offer. But Lili told her that it was the director of the division who had reviewed her resume, and he was the only one who had the power to hire her. "You should've seen Kayvan's face! He was shocked to see me at the bank, but very happy," she told Roxana.

Roxana didn't make any comment on Lili and Kayvan working together. Recently she had found herself getting ready to agree with Nina, *maybe these two are meant to be together.*

As happy as she felt for Lili's new job offer, she was getting frustrated with her own unemployment. So one day she applied for a teaching position at the former Iran-America Society, and she got it. The revolutionary government had changed the name but had kept the building. Roxana's job involved teaching an intensive English course to Iranian businessmen who traveled abroad.

On her first day, she was surprised to see thirty students in her class.

During the break, she needed to make copies of the handout she had prepared for them. The copier was inside a small room located in the faculty lounge. There was no one in the lounge, so Roxana felt relaxed, but when she came out of the copy room, she saw a blonde woman sitting at one of the tables looking out the window. The woman looked American. *Is it possible?*

"Excuse me," Roxana said as she approached her. "Are you an American, by any chance?"

"Yes. My name is Susan."

"Nice to meet you. My name is Roxana. I just started working here today." She shook Susan's hand.

Susan invited Roxana to join her and have a cup of coffee. "You probably want to know why I'm still here," Susan said.

"If you don't mind."

"Well, I'm married to a wonderful doctor. We have a two-year-old boy and another baby on the way. I don't want to go back. I'm happy here."

"Are you treated well?"

"We live in the Zafar area, as we did before the hostage taking. No one bothers me."

"We live in the same area. You should come and have dinner with us sometime."

"I'm so glad you're here. All teachers here are men. I can use a female companion."

Roxana and her new American friend learned more about each other over coffee. Susan was from Rhode Island and had lived in Tehran for five years. She felt safe, but her parents were worried about her.

"Please tell them we aren't hostage-takers. Actually, we're really nice people."

"I know. Do you know that one of the hostages is Kathryn Koob—the last director of the Iran America Society?"

"No, I didn't. I hope they all go home soon."

"I hope so too."

When Roxana went home that night, she was excited to share the news about Susan with her family. But as she entered the hallway, she saw her family gathered around the TV in the living room watching an exciting program. Her uncle was there too. She thought maybe her uncle had brought a new video. After the revolution, many families in Iran used to watch videos of the American TV programs, music, and movies. Uncle Parviz was the one who always brought videos to Roxana's family.

The first time Roxana asked her mother why nobody was watching TV anymore, her father volunteered to answer, "Because the TV programs make your mother angry."

"What programs?" Puri snapped. "We have two TV channels. One belongs to the white-turbaned clergies, and the other belongs to the black-turbaned clergies. It's all political lectures and teachings. I'm past school age."

Roxana went to her room, changed her clothes, and came back downstairs to the living room. No one noticed her. Finally she asked, "What's the big excitement about the TV program tonight?"

Roxana's mother looked at her, motioned to the TV screen, and said, *Amrika be ma hamleh kardeh,* the United States has attacked us.

Roxana's heart stopped for a moment. She felt the same twinge of pain she had felt when she first heard the news about the hostages.

Uncle Parviz pulled a chair for Roxana. Puri brought her dinner on a tray and put it on the table for her.

"What do you expect?" Parviz said, "When a bunch of *akhunds,* clergies, humiliate a superpower for months, that's what you get. You can't pull the tail of a lion for so long!"

"The action of some students shouldn't justify the attack on the country," Syrus commented.

Roxana's father was quiet as usual, and her sister had a frightened look on her face.

She watched the footage of the smoking remains of the American helicopters in Tabas. She heard the gleeful broadcaster talking about America's impotence and the divine intervention in Tabas where the rescue operation failed. She looked at her dinner. For a moment the image of her unfinished TV dinner and melting ice cream in New York City flashed through her mind. She felt she was back in her apartment and watching the TV coverage of the hostages all over again.

The next day, Susan greeted Roxana at the faculty lounge of Iran America Society. Susan had a sad expression on her face. "I'm so sorry. I don't know what to say," she said as she hugged Roxana.

"You're responsible for your government's attack as much as I am for the hostage taking."

Chapter 21

Despite the joy displayed by the government authorities over the failed American rescue mission, and despite their popular slogan, "America cannot do a damn thing," the majority of people in Iran, especially in Tehran, were fearful about another military attack by the United States.

The editor of the *Tehran Times* called Roxana and said, "This was like the Entebbe attack on Uganda. You published an article on Entebbe. Why don't you write an article on the Tabas attack focusing on violations of international law?"

Roxana's response was that she needed to do some research on the subject. In reality, she didn't need any research. She had exhausted all the sources in international law for the Entebbe article.

The United States could have used Israel's self-defense argument in Entebbe that the attack was justified to rescue the American diplomats held hostage in Iran.

The self-defense doctrine, however, required an armed attack on US territory first. Roxana wondered whether the act of the Iranian students and the government's subsequent blessing could be interpreted as an "armed attack" on American soil to justify the Americans' self-defense theory.

She decided not to write about the Tabas incident. International law didn't have any answer to resolve a unique conflict like the American hostages. However, she felt compelled to write to Judith. She also decided to send her a nice piece of Persian souvenir. She searched in Manouchehry—Tehran's Madison Avenue—where many antique shops were located. She began browsing inside a large shop.

All items were unique and beautiful. She felt like a kid in a candy store; she didn't know which one to choose. Finally she picked out a large, shiny, navy-blue goblet that could be used for wine or simply as a chocolate holder. The exterior of the goblet was embossed in gold color with images of classic Persian miniatures.

The price was more than Roxana had anticipated. She asked the shop owner to hold the goblet for her until the next day so that she could bring more money. "I'm sorry; I'm still not used to these new notes," she explained.

"Pish kesh. Ghabeli nadereh, it's yours. It's not worthy."

Roxana loved her countrymen's *Ta'arof*—the first thing she had taught Steve about the Persians. The item was worth more than two thousand tomans (close to $300), and he was saying, "It's not worthy."

She insisted on putting some down payment on the item and coming back the next day.

"How much money do you have?" the shop owner asked.

Roxana kept some money for her cab fare and put all her money on the counter. The shop owner counted it and smiled. "You're two hundred tomans short. Take it."

"I can bring the two hundred tomans tomorrow."

"It's yours. You see, your name is etched on the bottom of the goblet." The shop owner turned the goblet upside down and pointed to the bottom. Despite feeling proud of her countryman's generosity, Roxana still felt like teasing him a little. "I don't see my name there!"

"It's invisible to you. Only I, as the owner, can see it."

Roxana smiled, thanked the owner, and left the shop feeling proud.

* * *

A week later, when Judith came back home from one of her most hectic days in Manhattan, she found a package from Iran in her mailbox. She opened it and pulled out the beautiful goblet. She put the goblet in her glass display case and sat gazing at it for a long time. She couldn't help admiring the work of the artist.

She then opened the letter and read:

Dear Judith,

I hope you are doing well. It's been three months since I left America, or as we call it here, *Amrika.* After some forty-five days of soul-searching in Paris and Rome, I arrived in Tehran. My first experience was seeing fatigue-clad, bearded young men carrying machine guns searching the passengers inside the plane, and outside in the terminal. For a moment I felt I had landed in a wrong country.

The first few weeks were very exciting, observing political freedom I had never experienced. We have rows of newsstands in some parts of Tehran, just like Paris's Quartier Latin. You can buy all kinds of newspapers, magazines, and books. I have access to American newspapers and magazines here. I still read them despite the fact that after the hostage taking they published a lot of biased, unsubstantiated articles about Iran and Iranians.

People criticize government authorities here on the streets without any fear of SAVAK. But then I witnessed a questionable arrest in front of Tehran University. I heard about the past assassinations of the shah's cabinet members and those who had high government positions.

I'm teaching English to some businessmen at the former Iran America Society. Can you believe it? I studied here when I was a teenager. There is no sign of legal work yet.

When I first came back, I felt that someone had kidnapped the Tehranians, especially the women. I could hardly find them in downtown Tehran. But then I found them inside their homes enjoying their private parties.

The streets of Tehran are full of people from other cities, provinces, and villages, and Afghan refugees. Can you visualize in your head that one day you come back to Manhattan after ten years of absence, and all the people you see are non-New Yorkers?

You must know about President Carter's failed attempt to rescue the hostages. He's a nice man, but I don't know why he attacked Iran. Maybe, as everyone believes here, it's because of the election season.

My brother Bahram tells me that based on the Beach Boys song "Barbara Ann," a music group has composed a new song with new lyrics that goes something like, "Bomb, bomb, bomb, bomb, bomb Iran." The following two lines of the lyrics are very interesting to me, "Ol' Uncle Sam's getting pretty hot. Time to turn Iran into a parking lot. Bomb Iran…"

I wish someone would tell the artists that even Alexander the Great, who burned Persepolis, could not turn Iran into a parking lot.

In fact, I wish more Americans would read history books, or at least some paragraphs about Cyrus the Great. This is the man who liberated the Jews of Babylon and created peace between the Armenians and their enemies. I wish I could reach all Americans, telling them that we are not hostage-takers.

I miss you a lot.

Love,
Roxana

Judith stared at the goblet for a while, and then looked at the letter again. "I miss you too, my dear."

Chapter 22

Dr. Hatefi, the president of Tehran's Bar Association, called Roxana in mid-June and informed her that he had found a job for her in a big company. The company had fourteen subsidiaries, and in the past had transacted with multinational companies from France, Italy, Poland, and Israel.

Dr. Hatefi alerted Roxana that the company was taken over by *Bonyad-e-Mostazafin* (the Foundation of Poor)—a very revolutionary group.

"How can I thank you?"

"You may not like to work with them."

"I can work with any group. I'll do my research on *Bonyad*. Thanks again for helping me."

She went to her father for more information about *Bonyad*.

"I've kept all important newspaper articles for you since 1978. I thought you might need them someday," Miremad told his daughter.

Roxana hugged her father and went straight to the attics, where stacks of newspapers were waiting for her, all in chronological order.

The newspapers were full of stories about strikes and antishah demonstrations in 1978. When the government introduced martial law, banned demonstrations, and set a curfew at night, Ayatollah Khomeini encouraged the people to go to their rooftops and continue their protest. The chant of "Death to shah," and *Allahu Akbar* (God is great) could be heard from rooftops throughout Tehran and other major cities.

Roxana was amazed to read that the number of demonstrators had reached more than six million in December 1978. The figure represented the largest protest in history, surpassing the French Revolution of 1789 and the Russian Revolution of 1917.

Roxana found her answer why the revolutionary government had created so many new entities to carry on the day-to-day operation of the government. They didn't trust the shah's organizations. The new entities included *Pasdaran-e-Engelab* (the Revolutionary Guards), *Baseej-e-Mostazafin* (the Oppressed Mobilization), and *Bonyad-e-Mostazafin* (the Foundation of Poor), and thousands of *Komitehs* (revolutionary committees). The *Komitehs* were created to act as "the eyes and ears" of the revolution. They were empowered to arrest, confiscate property, or simply act as a police precinct.

After reading all the important news articles, Roxana felt confident. However, she still needed someone to tell her about the power exercised by each one of these government entities. She needed someone to analyze this revolution and connect the pieces of the puzzle for her. She called Yahya, Lili's father, and made an appointment with him.

Yahya, a prominent attorney during the shah's regime, had stopped practicing law even before the revolution. He greeted Roxana with a fatherly hug in his library. Roxana was amazed by the number of books on Yahya's bookshelves. When she was seven years old a relative once asked her, "Do you know what heaven looks like?" She'd immediately responded, "Like a library." She envied Yahya because he possessed more books than she had. When he saw the expression on Roxana's face, Yahya smiled. "Don't worry; by the time you reach my age you'll have more books in your library." Yahya was excited when he heard about Roxana's new job. "Someone with your educational background should be advising this government what to do."

"I'm so grateful to Dr. Hatefi to find me this job."

"I know him. He's a decent man who is trying hard to keep the integrity of the bar, but what can he do when the government prefers the advice of their clergies rather than the lawyers? Do you know that the judges in the family courts are all clergies now?"

"That's a sore subject for me. I published an article on our old family law. I thought that law needed a lot of improvements, but now, I hear that they don't even bother with it."

"I know that you always advocated for women's rights. But these days, everyone's rights are jeopardized. You have to start thinking outside the box. Do you know how many publishers and journalists are in jail?"

"I know. That's sad, but I have to worry about women more. I see too many women with *chador,* or scarves. I'm so scared that they are going to make it mandatory soon."

"I need to know your view on our constitution. Lili told me that you wrote a thesis sometime in *Amrika* comparing the Russian, the French, and the American constitutions. Is that right?"

"Yes, I did."

"So what do you think about the new constitution?"

"It's a beautiful document. It treats men and women equally. It protects all citizens, including minorities. But at the end of every right they have created, they repeat the familiar phrase, 'as long as it is in conformity with Islamic criteria.'"

"*Marhaba*, Bravo, that's exactly the way I see it."

"Are minorities treated well?"

"Well, they don't have problems with the Jews and Christians because we are repeatedly referred to as *the people of scripture* in the Koran, but the Bahaiis have a problem here."

"So you and Narges haven't had any problems?"

"Look, the Iranians have a different view about the Jews. We have lived here for thousands of years. When Hitler was rounding up the Jews and sending them to concentration camps, the Moslem Iranian diplomats in Paris and other European cities were issuing hundreds of Iranian passports to European Jews. That's why we have a number of European Jews in Iran. So, it's not surprising that after Israel, we have the largest Jewish population in the Middle East. I've got to tell you a story. During the early part of the revolution, we had a clergyman who was given a great deal of power. He was intimidating the Jews. So one day, our chief rabbi got an appointment with Ayatollah Khomeini and told him about the clergy. He was fired immediately. I was very impressed."

Roxana gathered the information she needed about *Bonyad,* thanked Yahya, and called her new employer.

Chapter 23

Tehran Industries Company was located on Kakh Avenue, one of the most elegant areas in Tehran. It was a few blocks away from Iran's old Senate building, where Roxana had done her internship. With its strictly aligned majestic sycamore trees, fancy restaurants and shops, Kakh Avenue still looked as charming as Roxana had remembered it. The sound of the water in its *jube,* a narrow canal running through many streets in Tehran, was soothing.

Mr. Kasravi, the company's general director, greeted Roxana warmly. Contrary to her expectation, the forty-five-year-old director did not look Islamic at all. In fact, he looked more like a Hollywood actor or a movie producer. He had beige-colored pants with a matching short-sleeve shirt.

Roxana was led to a large conference room with some twenty men sitting around the conference table waiting for her.

Mr. Kasravi introduced her to the men, each of whom shook her hand except the two bearded *Bonyad* men, who stepped back. Disregarding her father's advice, Roxana took a few more steps forward and extended her hand. The two bearded men, although hesitant, could not resist her friendly gesture and shook her hand.

The company belonged to a famous rich family that had fled Iran before *Bonyad's* expropriation. It constructed roads, buildings, and dams, and provided heavy equipment to other companies, such as National Iranian Oil Company (NIOC).

"We have settled with the Israelis but not with other foreign companies," Mr. Kasravi said. "We have bought the shares of many foreign shareholders, but there are some who refuse to be bought. We really need your help."

"When can I meet with them?"

"Tomorrow, at noon. Do you think you have enough time to read several thick files tonight?"

"Yes."

Mr. Kasravi introduced her to Afshin Imani, the director of the heavy machinery department. He served as Roxana's tour guide and took her to different offices of the company.

Roxana didn't feel comfortable with Mr. Imani. He was a tall man with broad shoulders and muscular chest. His swept-back hair made his high forehead more noticeable. He had stared at her and listened to her every word the entire morning with an unabashed admiration written all over his face.

He was one of the few nonengineer employees working at the company and the only one who had studied in the United States. The rest of the employees were educated in European universities.

Mr. Imani was more interested in getting personal information about Roxana than in providing details about the company. She had to interrupt his questioning numerous times by asking him about the company's projects—a polite way of directing him to do his task.

"I have an MBA from MIT. Where did you get your JSD?" Mr. Imani asked when the company tour was over.

"From NYU."

"I took some PhD courses, but when the revolution started here, I was so excited, I couldn't concentrate on school anymore. I had to come back home."

Roxana learned that Mr. Imani's mother was Russian. When she lost both her parents in Baku, a relative adopted her and brought her to Tehran. She married Mr. Imani's father—a builder—and gave birth to two boys.

"I don't see any ring on your finger. Do you have a boyfriend?"

"That's a very personal question."

"I thought we could have lunch sometime."

"I was engaged once. No, I don't have a boyfriend, but I'm not ready to date either."

Roxana looked at her watch; she had to leave to participate in an anti-*hejab* demonstration. She said good-bye to Mr. Imani, ran to the street, and hailed a taxicab.

She had asked her mother and sister to meet her at the big newsstand across the street from the Ministry of Justice. She found them easily. She felt proud to see hundreds of women accompanied by their husbands, brothers, fathers, and male friends. Women were carrying banners and chanting against *hejab*, or veil. The protest organizers had advised women who couldn't come downtown to simply come out of their houses, go to their nearest street, and chant against veil.

On that hot July day, many Iranian women complied, but the state-controlled TV did not show any footage of the huge demonstrations in Tehran or any other major Iranian city.

Chapter 24

She went to work an hour early to get settled in her new office and prepare for the meeting with the French shareholders. Her office was on the sixth floor of the building, with two large windows opening to the street. The view from one window was totally obscured by branches of an old sycamore tree. Through the other window she had a picturesque view of Kakh Avenue.

As soon as she sat behind her desk, she heard a mourning dove cooing. She tried to locate the bird, but the tree branches were too thick for her to see anything but the leaves.

She took the bird's presence as a good omen. She remembered the places she had encountered the bird in the United States. The first time was when she had rented an apartment on Connecticut Avenue in Washington, DC. Her windows opened onto a large park full of tall trees, and often there was a mourning dove cooing among the branches.

Like Damavand Mountain, the mourning dove also gave her the same message: nothing has changed drastically in your world.

Roxana found the French shareholders' representative very arrogant. The man's name was Jean Voltaire. As a Tehranian with a sense of humor, Roxana started the session with some jokes about Voltaire. Mr. Voltaire was not amused. She didn't bother to tell him how she admired Voltaire. She got serious and attended to the business at hand. She even stopped speaking in French.

"I've reviewed all the documents, and you've been treated like other foreign shareholders," Roxana said. "I don't know why you're giving Mr. Kasravi such a hard time."

"The company is losing thousands of dollars because of poor management of *Bonyad*," Mr. Voltaire responded in anger. "This cannot go on."

"Mr. Voltaire, in case you haven't noticed, a historic revolution has happened in this country. There are hundreds of companies in the same position. You can sell your shares and go back to Paris."

"No, we don't want to go back. We love it here. We want to see the company start functioning again."

A few months later, when Mr. Voltaire's wife, a shareholder herself, attended a brief meeting to sign some papers, Roxana realized why they loved it in Iran. On a mild autumn day, Mrs. Voltaire was wearing an expensive mink coat. Her chauffer was waiting in a Mercedes to whisk her away to another event. *Even Catherine Deneuve wouldn't wear a mink coat in a revolutionary country.*

* * *

After Mr. Voltaire left, Roxana started reviewing the company's other urgent matters, but she was distracted by the commotion in the reception area just outside her office. She left her office to check on the disturbing noise. She found all the female secretaries gathered around Mara, the company's Armenian receptionist. The reception area was large but not fancy. It had a large desk for Mara and a few file cabinets against the wall at her reach. In addition to being the company's receptionist, Mara also acted as Mr. Kasravi's secretary. Her main job was to answer the phone and to do whatever her boss needed. Roxana noticed that the secretaries all were making hostile gestures targeting Kazem—a *Bonyad* employee.

Kazem was one of the bearded men who sat through Roxana's all-day interview and shook her hand reluctantly. He was in his early twenties, but his beard and mustache made him look older.

"What's going on here?" Roxana asked.

"Dr. Ramsy, could you please help us," Mara said. "Mr. Kasravi's out of town, and Kazem is acting like he's the boss."

Roxana turned to Kazem and asked, "May I call you by your first name?"

"Yes, my last name is long and difficult. Everyone calls me Kazem."

"Okay, Kazem, what's the problem with the ladies here?"

"They laugh every time they gather here. Moslem women are not supposed to speak or laugh loudly."

"He always calls us *taghouti,"* one of the women complained. "We don't call him *hezbollahi,* which he is."

Roxana had heard the two terms many times since her return to Tehran. She had found the Arabic definition of the two terms in the Koran. So she retrieved a copy of the Koran from her office, came back to the reception area, and said, "Kazem, look, this is the meaning of the word *taghouti.* This is Surat 2:256, and its footnote, which says *taghouti* means, "Anything worshipped other than the real God." For example, worshipping false idols, stones, sun, stars, etc. These ladies don't worship any of those things." Roxana turned to Mara and other secretaries and asked, "Do you?"

"No, we don't," they all said simultaneously.

"You see, Kazem, next time you call someone *taghouti*, you have to know for sure that he or she worships anything or any person other than God."

Kazem looked at the pages of the Koran and said, "This is in English. I don't know what it says."

"Look at the Arabic version next to it."

"I don't know Arabic either."

"I'll get you a Farsi translation of the Koran."

She called her father and asked him to buy a Farsi translation of the Koran from a religion bookstore she knew in Bazaar.

That night, Roxana's father handed her the copy of the Koran in Farsi as soon as he entered the house. "According to the bookstore owner, this is the best translation," he said. "You're gonna love to hear this. The translator is a Jew. I thought you'd like that. After all, your best friends are non-Moslem."

"I have many Moslem friends. It's just a coincidence that my two best friends are not Moslems."

"I was just joking!" Miremad said, smiling. "I love Lili and Nina as if they were my own daughters."

After Roxana told her parents about the confrontation between Kazem and the female employees of the company, Roxana's mother looked at her admiringly. "You know, my dear, you should be working for the United Nations. I always tell my friends that if the

UN chooses my daughter as a peace ambassador and sends her to the troubled areas of the world, there will be no war."

"Maman, you're so biased. There are people who have dedicated most of their lives to negotiating peace, and they haven't succeeded."

"Because they're not women. Look how you stopped a conflict between a fundamentalist Moslem and the modern women in your office. If we had more female leaders in the world, we wouldn't have any war."

"I caution you," Roxana's father said, "some of those *Bonyad* employees may resent your interference."

"I had a legitimate reason to get involved. The man was basically saying to the women that their voices should not be heard. Mara is a receptionist. She answers the phone at least fifty times a day. Is she supposed to answer it in sign language?"

Chapter 25

Nina planned a big party celebrating Roxana's new job. She allowed her to invite more friends. Roxana invited Susan from the Iran America Society, and Gelareh, her lawyer friend. She planned to introduce Susan to Steve Radcliff, who was still in Tehran. She also needed to talk to Gelareh who practiced family law.

On the day of the party, she worked until 7:00 p.m. She had to write a report on the company's contracts for the general director, Mr. Kasravi. She also had to mediate another problem between Kazem and the female employees. This time, she took the Farsi copy of the Koran to Kazem. "You said you don't read Arabic. This Koran is in Farsi," Roxana said, handing the Koran to Kazem. Please go and read it."

"This is a thick Koran. I can't read it fast."

"Take your time. I want you to show me where it says that women cannot laugh. I also want you to ask your imam at the mosque, next Friday, where in the Koran it says that men and woman cannot talk to each other. Please ask him how Mara is supposed to answer the phone."

"I know what my imam would say. A man should answer the phone."

"You know, Prophet Mohammad was the employee of his wife, Khadijeh, before he married her. So please ask your imam how the prophet got his job if he could not talk to Khadijeh—a woman. Please also ask him whether he knows about Hazrat-e-Zeinab. When she went to Caliph Yazid's court and chastised him for killing her brother Imam Hussein, she didn't even have any head cover. She was also talking to a group of men. Your imam should know about her historic speech."

Kazem started walking away, but he took the Farsi Koran with him.

* * *

At the party, Roxana apologized to everyone for being late and went directly to Susan. She had already met Steve.

"Thanks for inviting me," she said. "Your friends are so wonderful. I'm so excited about your new job."

"I hear that someone finally discovered your brilliant legal mind."

Roxana recognized the voice behind her. "Hi, Steve," she said. "I see that you're still in Tehran."

"I like it here. People are nice to me, except one individual."

"How can your editor allow you to stay here for such a long time?"

"I'm gathering information for my book."

"A book about the revolution?"

"Revolution, people, places and—you."

Roxana was rescued when Nina's husband came over and took Steve away. He was gathering the men and taking them to the basement to have drinks.

He had to hide his drinks in a safe place so that the *Komiteh* couldn't find them. It was not unusual for a *Komiteh* member to knock on someone's door and search the house for alcohol and modern music.

While Nina, an Armenian, was allowed to consume alcohol or to serve it to other non-Moslems, Bijan, her Moslem husband, could not.

Susan told Roxana that her husband had already made friends with Bijan and Steve. "I have a question. Steve tells me he's crazy about you, but you're so cold. What's going on?"

"Susan, I'm living in a revolutionary country; I can't get involved with Steve. I should've met him in the States, not in Paris, Rome, or Tehran."

Gelareh showed up exactly when the dinner was being served. "I'm sorry for being late," she said as soon as she entered the house.

Roxana took her to the dining room and introduced her to the rest of the guests. At dinnertime, she sat next to her so they could talk. "I'm dying to know what has happened to the Family Protection Law. Did they abolish it?"

"They tried, but they had so many divorce and child custody cases that they didn't know what to do. They are still using the law."

"I remember I was reading about Ayatollah Khomeini's speeches when I was in New York, and there was no trace of antiwomen sentiments in them. I also read that he believed in human rights and didn't believe that religious dignitaries should rule."

"Yes. That was at the beginning, but now that he has the power of *Velayat-e-faghih,* guardianship of the jurist, as a supreme leader, he is the law."

"So how do you practice these days?"

"I don't because I don't want to wear a scarf and that crazy uniform. The regime had its administrative revolution by forcing women to wear *hejab* in government offices. Now they are going through a cultural revolution by closing the universities and putting women who work in the private sector under *hejab*. I'm surprised that you're still going to work without a scarf. I think *Bonyad* is too busy with other matters. I'm sure they will hit your company soon, and then the public places such as parks, streets, and shopping malls."

"I hope not."

The party was winding down, but there was still no sign of Lili. When Steve was leaving, he kissed Roxana's hand and said, "You still owe me a dinner date."

"That line is getting too old."

"I'll repeat it until you say yes."

As the last few guests were saying good-bye and leaving Nina's house, the doorbell rang. Roxana opened the door and found Lili standing there frightened and shaken. "What happened to you? Why are you so late?"

Lili came in, went directly to the kitchen, and poured herself a glass of water. "My cousin Iraj is in trouble," she said. "They're going to put him in jail."

"What has he done?"

"It's complicated, Roxana. Are you free to have lunch with Iraj and me tomorrow?"

"Yes. Come to my office."

Roxana and Nina tried to calm Lili down. "Iraj is not a political person. They can't put him in jail," Nina said. "For God's sakes, his father was executed by the shah. That should give him political immunity for life."

"It's not political; it's about money, millions of dollars," Lili said.

"Lili, you're driving me crazy. Could you please spit it out? Millions of dollars where?" Roxana asked.

"His cousin, who is a US citizen, made him sign a multimillion-dollar contract deal with the government promising them that his company would get the government spare parts that were frozen by the United States. He took millions of dollars of the Islamic government's money and left. The government is asking Iraj to give the money back. He doesn't have that kind of money. He's gonna go to jail."

Chapter 26

Roxana was speechless when she arrived at the restaurant Lili had selected for their lunch meeting. It was located in a garden full of flowers; a small Italian-style fountain added to its ambience. Roxana couldn't believe that there were so many luxurious restaurants still left in Tehran. She soon learned, though, that despite the revolutionary mood of the government and their adherence to a modest Islamic lifestyle, they didn't close Tehran's fancy restaurants as long as their owners didn't serve alcohol and didn't play Western music.

Iraj had brought his fiancée, Fereshteh, who at first seemed a little anxious to Roxana. As soon as the waiter took their orders, Roxana asked for Iraj's documents. "Please let me look at the contract," she said.

"I want you to have your lunch first," Iraj insisted.

"All my life I've been eating lunch while reading something. Let me see it."

Iraj handed a voluminous file to Roxana, pointing to the contract. He stared at her to observe her reaction. After a few minutes, Roxana, who was aware of the stare, finally closed the file and said, "Hey, you're safe. This is not a death sentence."

Lili and Fereshteh sighed, but Iraj still had a worried expression on his face. "They keep threatening me that I'll go to jail unless my cousin delivers the equipment or I pay the millions he took."

"The government signed a contract with him, not with you. All you signed was a direct contract with your cousin and his company, not with the government. Your company is supposed to provide transportation of the equipment when it arrives at the Persian Gulf. Your cousin also has breached his contract with you. So, like the government, you can have a cause of action to bring a lawsuit against him."

"Oh God. Thanks, Roxana," Iraj said with a sigh. "You saved me once before from going to jail during the shah; I hope you'll save me again this time."

"No thanks necessary. You're family."

When the lunch was over, Roxana asked if there was wedding bells ringing sometime in the future. Fereshteh blushed, but Iraj answered quickly. "Yes, as soon as I solve the mess my cousin has created."

"Congratulations. I'm dying to see a wedding. Since I've returned home, all I hear is the number of people who have been killed because of the revolution. I need a happy event."

Fereshteh blushed again and smiled.

Roxana said good-bye to everyone and started walking toward her office building.

As she got closer, she heard the chant of *Marg bar shah* (Death to shah), and *Marg bar Amrika* (Death to America). The chant was coming from a main road near Kakh Avenue. She was curious, so she walked in the direction of the chant. Hundreds of men were followed by dozens of black *chador*-clad women who were chanting. The mood of the demonstrators was jubilant. Roxana asked one of the onlookers about the commotion.

"Didn't you hear? The shah died in Egypt today, and they are celebrating it," the man said.

Back in her office, Roxana was numb for a few minutes. She thought about the shah and the historic picture she had seen during one of her researches at the United Nations. The picture showed the twenty-four-year-old shah in Tehran's meeting of 1943 posing with Churchill, Stalin, and President Roosevelt—the world leaders who had just sent his father to exile.

She remembered the face of the shah's youngest child, an eight-year-old daughter named Leila. She had either read or heard from someone that she was very close to her father. *What does an eight-year-old do when she loses her father?* Roxana didn't know that many years later, Leila, who had never gotten over her father's death, would commit suicide.

She wondered about the sins of the wife or the children of a dictator. Did the shah's wife have power to order SAVAK not to torture someone? Could she make the shah change his decision about anything?

As part of his White Revolution, the shah bestowed equal rights upon women. Iranian women whose grandmothers had carried guns in the 1906 Constitutional Revolution, who had campaigned against illiteracy, who had organized the textile industry, who welcomed Reza Shah's banning of the veil in 1936—thirsty for equality—had welcomed those rights, and had exercised and expanded them.

While she appreciated the shah's grand gesture, Roxana was disappointed when she read about the shah's famous 1977 interview with Italian journalist Oriana Fallaci. He had made several shocking sexist remarks. He had said that even though women were equal in "the eyes of the law," in reality they were not because women never produced a Michelangelo, a Bach, or even a great chef. He repeated the same remarks during a TV interview with Barbara Walters. This time, Barbara Walters asked Queen Farah if she agreed with her husband. Roxana felt bad when the queen struggled to explain the shah's comment.

The next day at the supermarket, Roxana saw several female customers talking about the shah's death. The antiregime customer who had spoken to Roxana before wore a black dress showing that she was mourning. "They killed him," she said to another customer.

"But he died of cancer," the other customer commented.

"I never thought for a moment that a king could become homeless," another customer added. "Poor man had to go to Egypt, Morocco, Panama, the Bahamas, Mexico, *Amrika*, and back to Egypt again."

Roxana heard a third customer, who wore a scarf, muttering, "That's the price you pay when you kill so many people."

As Roxana was paying for her groceries, the woman in the scarf muttered again, "I'm glad he died. He was a dictator. He spent all our oil money."

Roxana picked up her groceries and didn't hear the customer's final remark. *He was a dictator, but he was also a little girl's father, Leila's father.*

Chapter 27

Roxana was surprised to see Mr. Imani in her office, sitting at a desk across from hers. After greeting him and setting her briefcase down, she immediately asked, “Do you need my help with anything?”

“No. They took my office from me. They needed it for two new *Bonyad* employees. We are supposed to share the same office.”

“This cannot happen. Please don’t take it personally. I can’t work with someone else. I’m drafting documents. I need an absolutely quiet environment.”

“Talk to the administrative director.”

Roxana stormed out of her office. She tried to swallow her anger before talking to the administrative director. His office door was open.

“I need my office back,” Roxana said as she entered the room. “I’ve nothing against Mr. Imani, but he has visitors and phone calls to make. I need a quiet office.”

“I understand, but I’m sorry,” the administrative director said. “They have sent two new individuals from *Bonyad* to supervise the company’s day-to-day operation. You and Mr. Imani are the only two employees who have single offices. I had to put one of them in your office and one in Mr. Imani’s office. I figured out you two prefer to share an office rather than working with a *Bonyad* supervisor.”

“Can I use the conference room?”

“*Bonyad* people are using that for the noon prayer.”

She went back to her office. Mr. Imani had left. She sat in her chair, put her elbows on her desk, took both sides of her face in her hands, and tried to think of a solution. She couldn’t. She closed her eyes, trying to enjoy the last few minutes of her privacy at her office when she heard her mourning dove cooing. She went to the window. The bird was still hidden in the thick branches of the sycamore tree.

Mr. Imani came back. When he heard about Roxana's unsuccessful attempt to have a separate office, he promised her that he would leave the office as often as he could to give her peace and quiet.

Although she appreciated his kind gesture, she felt that deep down, he was very happy.

She started reading from a pile, but a knock on the door interrupted her concentration. Mr. Imani opened the door. Kazem was outside with a lunch-like bag in his hand. *"Khanoom doctor,* lady doctor, can I talk to you?"

"What's on your mind?"

"I showed your Farsi Koran to the imam in our mosque. He said this is no good because it's been translated by a Jew."

"Oh, poor Kazem! Do you believe for a second that a Jew living in a Moslem country would dare to falsify the Koran? He would be hanged not only once but many times in every intersection of the city."

"I believe you, but—"

"Listen, Kazem, every time your imam debates something in that Farsi Koran, please bring it to me. I'll compare it with the Arabic Koran and the English one and let you know if your imam is correct."

"*Rooy-e-Chashmam*, upon my eye."

"By the way, if your imam had read the Koran completely, he would not object to a Jewish translator. Did you know that Moses has been mentioned in the Koran more than one hundred times? That makes you wonder whether Moses was God's favorite prophet!"

"I have something for you." Kazem approached Roxana's desk and pulled four cassette tapes from the bag he carried. "These are for you," he said. "You bought me a Koran; I brought you some revolutionary songs."

"Thanks, Kazem. I will listen to them tonight."

Kazem left the room. Mr. Imani, who had kept quiet, put away the pamphlet he was reading. He raised his gaze and stared at Roxana for a long time. Roxana felt the stare like a stubborn summer sun that could not be avoided. "What?" she asked. "You have a comment?"

"You have read the Koran in three different languages?"

"Yes."

"Is your family religious?"

"No. Is yours?"

"No. I told you that my mother grew up in Russia. Even after she was adopted and raised by her Moslem relatives here in Iran, she wasn't interested in any religion."

"Is she communist?"

"No. She isn't interested in religion."

"What about your father?"

"He and my brother are moderate Moslems."

"And you?"

"I studied Maoism during my college years. He was way ahead of Lenin and Marx."

"I hope what I'm about to say won't offend you. Anytime someone talks about Mao or Maoism, all I can help thinking about are labor camps or reeducation camps."

"I'm not a Maoist; that was a college fascination. But Mao's revolution was misinterpreted. There's misconception about every revolution. Look at ours. *This* revolution was not supposed to be an Islamic revolution. Everyone was involved, but at the end it became the ayatollahs' revolution."

"So, you disapprove what they're doing?"

"No, I still hope we'll have a democratic system someday. My twenty-year-old cousin died for this regime. I owe it to him to believe in this revolution."

"I'm sorry to hear about your cousin."

"Thanks. A lot of people died during the revolution. But, hey, I still haven't heard your explanation for why you're so interested in the Koran."

"My profession."

"But you're an international lawyer."

"Yes, but I'm also a woman and an advocate for women's rights. In an Islamic country, I should know what the Koran has to say about women."

"Now I can understand. I'm a feminist myself."

"Are you?"

"Now look who's surprised. I marched with many of my male friends in women's demonstrations against *hejab* when you were still in the States."

"Did you?"

"Yes."

Roxana killed a "wow" inside and said, "Someday when you have time, I'll show you the Koranic verses that have been repeatedly misinterpreted by the Moslem clergies for hundreds of years. Those are the ones that affect women's rights."

* * *

When Roxana left the building it was still daylight. She started walking to the taxicab stand. She saw two teenage boys coming toward her. They looked lost. She asked them if they needed any direction. The boys did not respond. Instead, they laughed and ran. All of a sudden, she felt a sharp pain in front of her right ankle. She couldn't figure out what caused the pain. She continued walking. She had one more block to reach the taxi stand, but the pain had crippled her. She turned around and returned to her office building. Everyone was gone except Kazem. She was happy to see him. "Kazem, do we have a first aid kit here? Someone threw something at my ankle. Please hurry up."

Kazem came back and gave her a bottle of alcohol, some cotton balls and bandages. She looked at her ankle. The shiny metallic thing that had penetrated into her skin looked like a large, wide staple. After several unsuccessful attempts, she finally removed the flat metallic object with a staple remover. She washed her wound with alcohol and put some antibacterial ointment on it. She wrapped her ankle with a wide tape, thanked Kazem, and started walking.

"I feel guilty. I couldn't help you," he said.

"I know I am *Na mahram,* not related to you, and you're not allowed to touch me, but next time, if you find a woman in need of medical assistance, you should think of yourself as a paramedic."

Roxana started walking toward the taxi stand but noticed that Kazem was walking behind her, keeping a few feet distance. "Why are you following me?"

"I won't allow anyone to attack you again."

"Thanks," Roxana said and smiled.

That evening, Roxana learned from her brother Syrus that a special gun was used to harm women without *hejab*.

"I wear my mandatory office *hejab* everywhere because they are throwing acid on the faces of women who don't wear the veil," Elli said.

"Can you wear a scarf until you go into your office building?" Roxana's father asked.

"Absolutely not."

After dinner, Roxana went to her room and listened to the tapes of the revolutionary songs Kazem had bought for her. The songs were so powerful that they raised the hair on her skin. The last one brought tears to her eyes. The song was based on the lesson printed on the first page of the textbook for first-graders. The basic chosen words were meant to teach the first-graders how to write the Farsi alphabet. The text read:

"Dad gave bread,
Dad gave water."

The lyrics were changed to,

*"Baba noon dad digeh shoar ma nist
Baba khoon dad. Baba khoon dad."*

"Dad gave bread is not our slogan anymore.
Dad gave blood; Dad gave blood."

A poetic revolution in the lands of poets, Roxana thought.

Chapter 28

Despite the pain in her ankle, Roxana went to work the next morning. She was surprised to see the French shareholder, Mr. Voltaire, and another elderly Frenchman sitting in her office. Roxana heard Mr. Voltaire whispering to the other guy, "Don't speak in French; she knows French." The old man didn't hear him, so he asked, "Qu' est-ceque vous dite?"

Roxana said, "Bonjour," to both men, shook their hands, and said, "Mr. Voltaire told you that I know French, but that's okay; we're all going to speak in English. What can I do for you?"

"This is our parent company's president, Monsieur Pitofsky. He has come from Paris to finish the deal."

"Nice to meet you, Monsieur Pitofsky. Which deal are we talking about, Mr. Voltaire?"

"The last proposal you drafted. It has been approved by the board of directors of our parent company."

"Fantastic. Then let's go to Mr. Kasravi's office and sign the documents."

After the two French shareholders left, Mr. Kasravi couldn't hide his excitement anymore. "I cannot believe it. This is more like a miracle. The man has been chewing my brain for months. How did you do it?"

"One simple provision of your contract did it. The dispute settlement clause refers to the Iranian laws and the Iranian courts. I asked Mr. Voltaire if he believed they had a better chance litigating their dispute in a clergy-run court."

"Now I have to get *Bonyad*'s approval. They feel that since the foreigners have ripped us off for so many decades, now that we have had a revolution, we don't owe them anything."

"Tell them even the Koran forbids *unjust taking* of one's property."

Back in the office, Mr. Imani, who had learned about the deal, congratulated Roxana. "Maybe we should have lunch to celebrate this," he said.

"Okay," Roxana said. "I really feel someone has lifted a heavy burden off my shoulders. This was our last and the most difficult settlement."

Mr. Imani insisted on paying for the lunch, but Roxana refused. He had heard about the wound to her ankle and volunteered to escort her to the taxi stand every evening. At first Roxana was hesitant, but the pain in her ankle was a reminder that a similar incident could reoccur. She felt sad that in the revolutionary Iran, women needed male protection.

Since he was sharing an office with Roxana, Mr. Imani knew when she was breaking for lunch. He had gotten into the habit of going to lunch with her every day. Roxana was resentful at first. Sometimes she pretended she was busy and had to take lunch later, but every time she walked alone to a restaurant, a man followed her. At the restaurant, men stared at her while she was eating alone. Tehran was not the old Tehran anymore. It had turned into a "Moslem Rome," where men still followed unescorted women.

One day, she discussed the situation with Mr. Imani and told him how surprised she was. "This is an Islamic republic, and men are still chasing women?"

"Men chase even unattractive women when they walk alone on the streets. You're attractive, look European, and smile a lot."

"I don't smile a lot. In fact, when I returned home, one of the first things I learned was to have a serious face."

"You don't notice it yourself, but I've seen you smiling at people even when waiting for the elevator and at company meetings. You smile a lot. I know that this is an American trait, but not everyone knows that your smile is a sign of politeness and not an invitation to be chased."

That night, Roxana remembered her first few months in Georgetown Law School. After she forbade everyone from messing up her name by calling her Rocky, or Roxy, her friends gave her another nickname, Smiley. "You have such a beautiful smile," they said. Her smile was not acquired from Americans; it was the smile of a typical Tehranian.

The following week, Mr. Imani found a taxi stand at the intersection of Kakh Avenue and Queen Elizabeth's Boulevard. The cab would take her directly to Zafar Avenue. The walk was longer, but she could not resist. She never got tired of walking on Kakh Avenue, the same way she could never get enough of walking in Paris's Quartier Latin. Besides, this new taxicab line eliminated having to connect with another taxi and would drop her one hundred feet away from her house.

A price tag was attached to Mr. Imani's kind gesture. In addition to having lunch with her and sharing too many office hours together every day, now he was walking with her for twenty minutes on Kakh Avenue to reach the taxi stand.

Despite Mr. Imani's efforts to provide a quiet office environment for Roxana, she checked with the company's administrative director every few days to see whether there was a new office available. She felt uncomfortable to work with Mr. Imani in the same office. It was obvious that the man had a great deal of affection for her, maybe even love. He had invaded her world. She wanted to be left alone to concentrate on her job and the revolution that was moving in the wrong direction. She still couldn't get rid of the image of the arrest she had witnessed in front of Tehran University. She was still expecting to receive a phone call from the young man. Mr. Imani had become a distraction.

One day, she had a lot of visitors from the company's subsidiaries; she also had deadlines to meet and reports to submit to several boards of directors. She came in and out of her office dozens of times. The last time she came in, before she could sit down, Mr. Imani complained. "Could you stop working this hard? You're killing yourself."

"I've been running all day because I have deadlines."

"This is not a Wall Street law firm. Your boss is *Bonyad*, which needs three weeks to finish a three-line letter."

"If they are slow, that doesn't mean I should follow them."

"Have you ever thought how your work impacts us, the rest of the company employees? They expect us to kill ourselves like you."

"I'm sorry. I never thought of it that way."

"You've turned into a one-woman law firm, handling legal problems of fifteen different companies. Slow down. Pretty soon you're gonna eliminate your job by finishing all their legal work."

Roxana moved her work to Mr. Kasravi's office two doors away for the next few days, since he was out of town. She also changed her lunchtime and departure from the office to avoid Mr. Imani. *How dare he talk to me like that!*

Mr. Kasravi's trip took more than a week. That was a great opportunity for Roxana not only to avoid Mr. Imani, but also to have a quiet place to work. But one day, there was a commotion coming from the reception desk. Roxana and Mr. Imani came out to the reception area at the same time. They greeted each other politely.

She went to Kazem, who was in the middle of a heated argument with the female employees of the company. "What's going on?" she asked, tapping on Kazem's shoulder.

"They call me *dahati,* peasant," he said. "I know that I come from a village, but I'm going to night school to get my high school diploma."

Roxana looked at the women and said, "Ladies, may I see all of you in Mr. Kasravi's office?"

Back in Mr. Kasravi's office, there was an outburst of anger shown by the five female employees and Mara, the receptionist. Most of the complaints related to Kazem's criticism of their dresses. "We're trying to wear long sleeves and long, thick stockings, but that is not good enough," one woman said. "The only thing that makes Kazem happy is for us to wear those ugly uniforms, large pants, and scarves."

"This is not a government job; it's a private company," another woman said.

"Listen, ladies, I'm with you. No one should tell you how to dress up," Roxana said, "but don't forget, except in private companies, all female government employees have been forced to wear mandatory *hejab.* I hate to inform you that *Bonyad,* which is controlling our company, is actually a government entity. The fact that they haven't imposed the *hejab* on us yet is because they have so many urgent matters that they haven't had time to get around to our dress code."

"Kazem and the other two new bearded guys are their spies," one of the female employees said.

"Kazem is doing his job; don't kill the messenger," Roxana said. "But I think he is actually trying to protect us by nagging about the dress code. Otherwise, he could have just simply reported all of us to *Bonyad*."

"He calls us *taghouti*, yet he's the one who lives on Kakh Avenue," complained another female employee. "He and his entire family live in this huge mansion that belonged to a rich family; they fled Iran last year."

"I'm sorry for the family. If they had retained me to file a case against the authorities in court, probably I would have. But they're gone, and what's so wrong for a poor family living in a mansion for a short period of time? To me it's poetic justice, don't you think so?"

"What bothers me is that he thinks since his brother is a revolutionary martyr, we owe him something for the rest of our lives," Mara said.

"I agree with Mara. He lost a nineteen-year-old brother during Kurdistan's unrest," another employee said, "but now he has a job. He lives in a mansion, and they have even named a street after his brother. So he should be happy and leave us alone."

Roxana thanked the women for listening to her. "Please don't call him *dahati*. It's a derogatory term."

That afternoon Roxana received a phone call from Lili. She had planned a party to cheer up Iraj. Apparently the government's pressure and ultimatums had put him in a depressed mood.

The next day when Mr. Kasravi returned from his trip, Roxana knocked on his door and asked him if he could talk to some influential *Bonyad* people about Iraj's problem. He promised her that by the end of the day he would have some answers for her.

Roxana thanked him and went back to her office. Mr. Imani greeted her warmly, as if the two had never quarreled about anything. "Please let me know when you need the office all to yourself. I can get all my stuff and find somewhere else to do my work," he said.

"You'd really do that for me?"

"Yes. I'll do anything to make your life easier here."

Roxana found herself speechless. She never expected such a generous offer. She felt an urge to express her gratitude instantaneously. "My friends are having a party this weekend. Would you like to come?"

"I'd love to."

"You'll meet not only my friends but also an interesting American journalist."

"I'm looking forward to meeting all of them."

Roxana was eager to introduce Mr. Imani, a former Maoist, to Steve Radcliff, an American capitalist. She anticipated an exciting and thought-provoking conversation between the two, not knowing that each man would play a significant role in her life.

Mr. Kasravi stopped by Roxana's office before he left. The sad expression on his face indicated that he didn't have any good news. "I'm sorry, Dr. Ramsy," he said. "Your friend has been playing with the big guys. These are defense contracts, and none of the powerful people I know are willing to touch them. I really did my best."

Chapter 29

At Lili's party, Roxana was anxious to find Steve. She was encouraged by the news earlier in the month when the government released one of the hostages, Richard Queen, due to his illness. So as soon as she saw Steve, she asked, "Do you have any more information about the hostages' release?"

"There have been ongoing efforts to release them since November."

"I mean, behind-closed-doors negotiations."

"Hamilton Jordan and Secretary Vance have used many hours through diplomatic and sometimes even secret channels to release them."

"I didn't know that. All I know is that the CIA is not sitting quietly. I'm sure they had something to do with the rescue of the six American diplomats hiding at the Canadian Embassy."

Roxana remembered seeing the signs of "Thank You, Canada" in the newspapers when she was leaving New York. She didn't have time to follow the story.

She was so preoccupied with the thoughts of the hostages that she didn't notice Mr. Imani had arrived. He had already introduced himself to Lili and her father.

She introduced Mr. Imani to Steve, but contrary to her expectation, there was no exciting conversation between the two men. Actually, Mr. Imani preferred to talk with other guests than Steve. But from time to time he was standing in a corner by himself looking at Roxana as if she was the only guest at the party.

Steve was talking mostly to Kayvan and his fellow American, Susan, but once, when Roxana passed by him, he pulled her arm gently and said, "I thought your revolutionary mood didn't allow you to date. Who's that character?"

"He is the director of the heavy machinery department in our company. We share an office."

"Are you telling me that he sits in your office every day, looking at you with all the lust in his eyes, and you don't mind that? I can't believe it! You break my heart every time I invite you to dinner, and yet that man can see you every day for eight hours?"

"I'm working with him, not dating him."

She ignored Steve and turned to Susan to talk to her. "When is the baby due?" she asked.

"Sometime in August," Susan responded.

"So your baby is gonna be a Leo, like me!"

"We have decided to name the baby Roxana if it's a girl. Is that okay with you?"

"I'd be honored."

* * *

It was 9:00 p.m., but there was no sign of Iraj. Lili and her family were all worried, but as good Persian hosts, they hid their concern well. Only Roxana knew how anxious they were.

"Where is he?" she finally asked Lili.

"I don't know. He said he had to go to Ray at 5:00 a.m. to check on some of his company's equipment. He hasn't called anyone."

"Maybe we should have told him that we were going to have a party, rather than surprising him," Narges said, hiding her anxiety.

"He's caught in the traffic," Roxana suggested. "It's impossible these days to drive from southern Tehran to the northern suburb."

"Roxana is right," Yahya said. "Let's have dinner. Our guests are hungry. He'll probably show up at 10:00 p.m. as usual."

Everyone's mood was happy at the dinner table except Iraj's relatives and Roxana. She was put in an awkward position, sitting between Mr. Imani and Steve. Each man was trying to have a conversation with her, ignoring the other. She tried to initiate a discussion between the two by bringing up some topics that interested both, such as the Soviet invasion of Afghanistan, but the conversation died after a few reluctant remarks.

Roxana gave up and asked Kayvan if he would switch his seat with her so that she could talk to Lili and Susan. He agreed, and Roxana was saved, but before she took her plate to move to the opposite side of the table, Mr. Imani asked her in Farsi, "Where did you meet this *Sia,* CIA agent?"

"Please don't call him that. He has passed all our tests. He's a journalist."

Roxana sat between Lili and Susan, feeling satisfied that Kayvan would carry on a conversation with both Steve and Mr. Imani. She turned to Lili and asked her why Nina had not come to the party.

"They're visiting Bijan's parents in Shiraz again."

"Has anyone called Fereshteh? Maybe Iraj decided to have dinner with her tonight."

"Aunt Narges has been calling her since 8:00 p.m."

It was 11:00 p.m. when the guests started leaving the party. Mr. Imani thanked Roxana and his hosts, telling them he had a wonderful time. Steve repeated his routine line when he said good-bye to Roxana, "You still owe me a dinner date."

After everyone was gone, Roxana and Lili started cleaning up. Yahya gathered the dirty dishes in the sink and asked Narges to sit down and relax. "You cooked all day. Now it's my turn to wash the dishes."

"There are two bottles of wine unopened. I'm gonna hide them in the basement. Then I'll come back and relax."

"We're Jewish; we can drink wine."

"I know, but I don't want our Moslem friends to get into trouble if they are here."

"Komiteh has never bothered us."

"You never know," Narges said as she walked to the basement.

Roxana was the first one who heard a loud scream. "What was that?" she asked panicking.

"What was what?" Lili asked.

The second scream was louder, followed by Narges's moaning.

"Khoday-e-man, be man nagoo. Eltemas mikonam nazar bemireh. My God, don't tell me. I beg you, don't let him die."

Yahya, Lili, and Roxana ran to the basement. They saw Narges hugging Iraj's body lying on the floor. As Roxana ran upstairs to call for an ambulance, she heard Yahya say,

"They finally forced him to kill himself."

Roxana's heart was beating fast in her chest. She was trembling when she called the Zafar hospital. She then called her home. Syrus answered the phone.

"What's wrong? Why are you crying?" he asked.

"Please come to Lili's house. Iraj is dead."

Roxana left the house's front door unlocked and rushed back to the basement. Yahya was holding her sister and crying quietly. Narges was moaning and saying incoherent words. Roxana walked toward Lili, who was sitting on the floor weeping. She hugged her and sat by her side. "I'm so sorry. He was like a brother to me too."

She heard some footsteps. Before she could turn around, the basement door opened. She saw her father, mother, and brother. She threw herself into her mother's arms. "Maman, he's gone."

Puri rushed to Narges while Miremad helped Yahya get up from the floor. Puri offered Narges some sherbet she had prepared in a hurry. "Narges Joon, please have a sip."

She took a few sips of sherbet. "Did you see what they did to my child?" Narges muttered.

"I'm so sorry." Puri's voice cracked and tears rolled down her face.

Syrus found an empty bottle of vodka, two bottles of sleeping pills, and two boxes of rat poison. He threw the vodka bottle in the trash can for fear of some investigation by the neighborhood *Komiteh*. He kept the poison boxes and the sleeping pill bottles for the doctors to look at.

The paramedics took Iraj's body to the hospital. Everyone followed the ambulance in Syrus's car. Roxana stayed behind to be with Lili. The two friends sat on the basement floor and cried quietly. For the first time in their lives they couldn't talk. Their silence expressed their unspoken words.

Chapter 30

The doctors at the hospital determined the time of Iraj's death at between 5:00 and 7:00 a.m. He had taken the poison, the sleeping pills, and a full bottle of vodka the night before when everyone was asleep. He died when his family was planning the party to cheer him up. He had left two envelopes on his desk in his home-based office, one labeled "To My Mother," the other "My Will."

Roxana avoided looking at Iraj's face throughout the whole ordeal. She wanted to keep that image of a young Robert Redford look-alike in her mind. When Iraj traveled to the south of Tehran to work on a project or inspect equipments in his company's warehouse, at first the workers thought he was a movie star shooting a film, but they soon found out that he was an engineer. When he sat with them and dipped his bread into their *abgusht,* traditional Persian stew, and when he tucked his sleeves and got his hands soiled with oil and dirt, he was one of them. Iraj's down-to-earth personality, his sense of humor, and his enthusiasm for work had brought him not only success, but also a good relationship with his employees.

Roxana got the difficult task of reading the will and the letter Iraj had written to her mother. Narges started crying as soon as she saw the label, "To My Mother." Iraj had always called his mother by her first name. Narges, who was followed by SAVAK for twenty years, had asked him not to call her *maman*, the term used by many Iranian kids addressing their mothers. Narges never took him anywhere out of fear that the SAVAK men who followed her would recognize him as her son.

Iraj's family gathered in the living room for the reading of the letter and the will. Roxana tried to mask her pain and began reading the letter out loud:

> My dearest *Maman*,
>
> Everyone thought that I was proud of my father, who was executed because of his beliefs, but they were wrong. He was not my hero. You were.
>
> As a child, I couldn't understand why you didn't let me call you *Maman*, why you carried three different-colored *chadors* in your bag, and why you didn't take me with you anytime you left the house. But when I grew up, I realized that for twenty years, everything you did was for my protection. I still remember the days you entered the house, panting because you had to run fast to lose the SAVAKI men. I still remember your rapid heartbeats when you took me in your arms and kept kissing my face.
>
> You were a great mother, but I also have to acknowledge other people who had significant roles in my life. My uncle Yahya was the only dad I knew. I'm grateful to Roxana's father, who was my second dad when Uncle Yahya was away. Roxana's mother was always around to respond to the needs of a little lost boy whenever you were hiding from the SAVAK. I have to acknowledge my gratitude to my paternal grandparents. Despite their mourning for their son's execution, they were always cheerful around me.
>
> What can I say about my beautiful cousin Lili, who always acted like a wise older sister? She lost her mother at a young age, but I learned from her how to be cheerful, not to fuss over stupid things, and, most of all, how to be happy.
>
> Having Lili in my life had other advantages too, like receiving love from her friends Roxana and Nina, who treated me like a brother.
>
> So, *Maman*, as you see, I had a happy life being surrounded by people who loved me, but the problem with the government was too big for me to handle. When I served in the shah's army for two years, I thought I liberated both of

us. They realized that I was not political, and we were not plotting a coup d'etat, so the SAVAK stopped bothering you. After establishing my business, I thought that was the end of our problems. I never imagined life would plan another impossible situation for us. They have expropriated my company, confiscated my assets, and fired my employees. When I decided to commit suicide, they were drafting a warrant for my arrest. I was not going to rot in their jail.

I have a request which I hope doesn't disappoint you. As you know, my father was a communist and didn't believe in any religion, but his parents were Moslems. I know that according to Jewish laws, I'm the real Jew because my mother is a Jew, but neither you nor Uncle Yahya ever took Lili or me to a synagogue. I saw my grandparents observing their religion. All of my friends and my employees are Moslems, so I think I'm a Moslem too. I wish to be buried next to my grandparents' graves.

I've left a letter for Fereshteh that should be delivered to her immediately. Please give her your love and support until she finds a man who can make her happy. Her life would've been miserable with me in jail.

Sorry that I have caused you pain. I love you all.

Iraj

Roxana could not read the will immediately. She had to get her composure back. Her voice had cracked many times during the reading of Iraj's letter, and she had to constantly wipe her tears, as did the others.

Roxana called Kayvan and informed him of Iraj's death. "I can't believe I'm asking you to come and be with Lili. She needs you."

Puri prepared a big lunch for Lili's family. Miremad and Syrus were also busy making arrangements for the funeral.

Iraj had written his will a week before his suicide, so at the time he didn't know that his company and its assets would be expropriated.

He had bequeathed three million Tomans, about $215,000, to Tehran's Orphanage House. He had established a one million toman education fund for the two young children of an employee who had recently died. The rest of his wealth was bequeathed to his mother, Narges.

Chapter 31

Roxana felt a great deal of respect for Narges when she honored Iraj's wish and buried her son in Behesht-e-Zahra Cemetery near the graves of his paternal grandparents. Earlier in the day, Roxana was informed that Iraj's family would have a small ceremony with close friends and relatives, but she became overwhelmed when she saw dozens of Iraj's friends, colleagues, and employees showing up with many wreaths and bouquets of flowers.

Roxana saw that everyone's attention was drawn to Fereshteh, Iraj's fiancée. Her loud wailing could be heard a few feet away. At some point, Narges had to stop weeping to console her. "Just pray to God to help us to get through this," she said.

Roxana was the first one who noticed that Fereshteh had stopped crying. She followed Fereshteh's gaze and noticed that she was focusing on three chic women, all dressed in black. Suddenly Fereshteh pointed to the three women and commanded in a loud and angry voice, "Get those whores out of here!"

It was not clear who was supposed to get rid of the women. Lili turned to Roxana, who was standing near her, and said, in a hushed tone, "Could you please handle this. Those are Iraj's former girlfriends."

Roxana ran to Fereshteh, put her arms around her, and whispered in her ear, "Look, he chose to marry you. It shouldn't matter that they're here."

"I want them out of here," Fereshteh ordered again loudly.

Roxana rushed to the three women, who were standing a few feet away, and pleaded with them, "Ladies, out of respect for his fiancée, please leave. You can always come back here later."

Syrus volunteered to take most of the flowers in his car to distribute among several hospitals in the poor neighborhoods of Tehran.

Roxana's family stopped by her grandmother's grave and said their prayers. As they were leaving the cemetery, Roxana noticed the woman who had lost her only son in the revolution. She was still sitting by the grave staring at her son's picture and murmuring something. She wondered what would happen to the woman on snowy days.

Once more, she promised herself that she would never come back to a depressing place like Behesht-e-Zahra Cemetery.

* * *

The next day, back in her office, Mr. Kasravi and Mr. Imani met with Roxana and extended their condolences. "Your brother called the other day to explain why you couldn't come to work," Mr. Kasravi said.

"He told us about the tragic death," Mr. Imani added. "I'm so sorry."

After thanking both of them, Roxana provided Mr. Kasravi with all the details in Iraj's letter regarding the government's ultimatum, expropriation of Iraj's company, and firing his employees. "You've got to help me meet with a top authority in *Bonyad*," she pleaded.

"I'll make some phone calls immediately."

"Thanks."

After Mr. Kasravi left Roxana's office, Mr. Imani tried to comfort Roxana. She needed to talk to someone about Iraj. Since his death, she had tried to console everyone, but no one had noticed her pain. She talked about Iraj's childhood, his father's execution, and his shocking suicide.

"I know his father through some literature I received from the Iranian Students' Movement," Mr. Imani said. "He's a well-known name and a hero among the Iranian communists."

"I didn't know he was that famous. I was two years old when he was executed."

At the end of the day, Mr. Kasravi informed Roxana that he had made an appointment for her with a powerful authority from *Bonyad* who had agreed to meet with her.

When Roxana left the company, it was dark. She was apprehensive about the possibility of facing another staple gun attack, and was on the lookout for potential attackers. At one point, she heard some footsteps, turned back, and saw Kazem a few feet behind her. "You scared me."

"Khanoom Doctor, it's dark. I'll come to the taxi stand."

"Thanks, Kazem."

Roxana found an empty taxi, and as she entered the cab, Kazem turned to her and said, "*Tasliat migam.* My condolences."

The taxi drove off before Roxana could say anything.

Chapter 32

Roxana knew the significance of the meeting she was about to have with *Bonyad*'s representative, so she was careful not to offend him. She brought a scarf to the office and, for the first time, wore it to the meeting. She was not worried about Lili, because she had been wearing the Islamic *hejab* since she got the job with Iran's Bank Markazi.

Roxana and Lili met with Mr. Kasravi in his office. He took them to the conference room where the *Bonyad* representative was waiting for them.

Again, for the first time, Roxana broke her rule and didn't shake hands when she was introduced. After everyone was seated, the *Bonyad* representative turned to Roxana and said, "Before we talk about Mr. Razavi's unfortunate departure, I'd like to thank you for what you've done for this company. Mr. Kasravi has been reporting to us on a daily basis about your hard work—"

"No thanks needed," Roxana interrupted him. "I was doing my job."

The man then turned to Lili and said, "I'd like to extend my condolences to you and your family for your loss. No one ever knew he was under so much pressure."

"Iraj's cousin, who took the money, his brothers and other family members living in Abadan weren't pressured at all," Lili said. "They were more in contact with him than Iraj." Lili's voice cracked, tears pushed through her eyes, and she couldn't continue.

Roxana started piling up documents on the conference table as the *Bonyad* representative defended his agency's position.

"It's true that he didn't sign any document with us, but he brought his cousin to us. He vouched for him, so when the man disappeared with millions of dollars, we had no choice but to assume that there was a conspiracy here—"

"Forgive me, sir," Roxana interrupted the man. "There was no conspiracy whatsoever." Pointing to the pile of documents on the table, she continued, "I've brought a dozen documents for your review. But first, I'd like to tell you what kind of a man Iraj was. He loved his country. He was a dedicated engineer who treated his employees like his family. He gave the government the lowest bid and built a new technology college for you. He worked ten to fourteen hours a day. If he had conspired to steal the government's money, he could have left with his cousin months ago. His passport will expire two years from now. He could have fled the country as soon as he was being questioned. But he stayed here and faced the problem. We have copies of dozens of letters he wrote to his cousin begging him to return the money, but the letters always came back, stamped Address Unknown. We have his telephone statements showing how many times he had called other relatives in California to find a clue about his cousin's whereabouts."

The *Bonyad* man started looking at some of the documents. Meanwhile, Lili passed a note to Roxana that read, "Tone it down. You're gonna lose your job." Roxana wrote on the bottom of the note, "I don't care. I'm just warming up," and passed it back to Lili.

As the *Bonyad* man was carefully reviewing some of the documents, Roxana said, "I have a question."

"Go ahead," the man said.

"With all due respect, sir, how can you possibly give millions of dollars to someone you don't know without checking his background first?"

"We were desperate to get the spare parts we had purchased from *Amrika*. As you know, they were frozen. We thought Iraj was an honest man, so we assumed his cousin was honest too."

"You see, you said the magic word. Yes, Iraj was *honest*. Your agency's unintentional pressure killed him. But please don't kill his legacy. Let his company continue to run. There are more than fifteen construction workers who have lost their jobs since you closed the company. These men support wives, children, and elderly parents, and who knows how much financially and emotionally they have suffered because of the company's shutdown."

"I'm gonna look into this."

"I really appreciate your time, sir, and your kind consideration. I also have a message for your colleagues, the final decision-makers. This is my legal advice. There is no conspiracy theory in our legal system that can justify the closing of Iraj's company. Should the family decide to bring litigation in court, they will win. Taking property without just compensation is not a Western legal concept. It's also recognized in the Islamic law. I'm sure you know the specific Koranic verses I'm talking about."

The *Bonyad* man raised his gaze, took his beard in his left palm and stared at Roxana for a while. Then, as he gathered the documents on the table, he said to her, "Thanks for the documents and the information. I'll see what I can do."

After he left the conference room, Mr. Kasravi took a deep breath and said to Roxana, "Do you know how many times you came within an inch of losing your job?"

"I know, and I didn't care."

* * *

Roxana wore black for one week, which is traditional for the death of a friend, then went back to her regular clothes. A month had passed since the meeting with the *Bonyad* man, but there wasn't any news regarding Iraj's company.

One afternoon instead of going home, Roxana decided to work even longer. Iraj's tragic death, her failure in saving his company, and the ongoing hostage crisis had created a somber mood for her.

She looked out her window. Kakh Avenue was getting emptier as office workers, shopkeepers, and pedestrians hurried home. She was thankful that there was no anti-*behejab* demonstration on that day. In recent weeks, the revolutionary marchers had intensified their protest against women who didn't wear the Islamic *hejab*.

She sat behind her desk, still looking out the window thinking that the threat was imminent. After almost half a century of wearing European clothes, Iranian women were being forced to wear an ugly uniform that was not recommended in the Koran; nor did it have any connection with their old Persian costume. This was not the sari of the Indian women or the kimono worn by the Japanese women.

Roxana's thoughts were interrupted when her favorite mourning dove began cooing. She picked up her briefcase and left. *Does the bird know about Iraj's suicide?*

She arrived home at 7:00 p.m. From behind the large-laced windows of their living room, she saw the images of three people in addition to her parents and her siblings. She wasn't in a mood to socialize with any unexpected guests that evening. As she tried to sneak through the hallway and climb to the second floor, the large door of the living room opened. Her father was the first one who appeared at the door, and he said, "Happy birthday, princess."

Roxana entered the room; she was surprised to see Lili, Narges, and Yahya. "What are you doing here?" she asked.

"Celebrating your birthday," Narges said while hugging Roxana. "Boy, have we got a birthday gift for you!"

"I honestly had forgotten that today was my birthday!"

"After what you went through over the past two weeks, I don't blame you," Yahya said.

"I have to confess, I had forgotten your birthday too. Guess who is the one who never forgets birthdays," Puri said, pointing to Roxana's father.

She looked at her father. He was the one who had bought the birthday cake from her favorite bakery. Miremad never forgot his children's birthdays, even during the year he almost went bankrupt.

The dining table was full of food. Roxana's mother and sister had made some of her favorite meals. There was a large rectangular birthday cake in the middle of the table wishing Roxana "Happy Birthday."

After dinner, Roxana blew out the candles and opened four boxes of gifts from her family, but she was anxious to know what was inside the small cylinder Narges was holding.

Roxana's mother and sister had bought her a conservative-looking skirt and blouse. Her brother had bought a tape of famous revolutionary songs. But her father had continued his tradition by giving her a Swiss wristwatch. Roxana couldn't help laughing. Everyone knew why. Ever since her sixteenth birthday, Miremad had given her an expensive Swiss watch as her birthday gift, every year. The problem, as she explained it once to her friends, was that "Swiss watches never go bad; they never die." So every year, she gave the old watch to a poor person.

After everyone heard and laughed about the Swiss watch stories, Narges put the nicely gift-wrapped cylinder on the table in front of Roxana. "We couldn't think of a better gift," Narges said. "It came from a higher authority to us."

She opened the gift. Inside was a small notarized letter with the stamp and seal of the *Bonyad.* The letter read:

> Temporary Board of Directors of
> Razavi Construction Company,
>
> This is to inform you that as of today, the twenty-sixth day of the month of Mordad, August the seventeenth, the ownership and management of the Company shall be transferred to the Executor or Principal heir of Iraj Razavi according to the terms of his last will and testament.

Roxana sighed and said, "Oh my God. Oh my God!"

Iraj's family gave her a group hug while her proud parents watched tearfully.

Yahya took the letter back and said to Roxana, "Thank you, counselor. I'll take it from here and make sure that the company opens immediately."

"This was the best birthday gift that . . ." Roxana couldn't finish her sentence. She burst into tears and covered her face with both hands. Lili came to her and hugged her. "He didn't die in vain. Now he has left a legacy behind," she said.

Before leaving Roxana's house, Yahya had a chance to talk to her alone." Narges, Lili, and I appreciate so much what you and every member of your family have done for us during these difficult days," he said, "but you've got to ask your father to give us a list of the funeral expenses he has paid for."

"Save your energy, Mr. Cohan. He's not going to do that."

"Look, I know how expensive a funeral can be."

"My father grew up as an orphan, so Iraj had a special place in his heart. He treated him like a son. He's not going to accept a penny."

"Your father is a noble man."

"I've heard that many times before."

Chapter 33

September 22, 1980

Roxana was writing a legal brief when the power went out. Before she could find a flashlight in her room, she heard nonstop gunshots, or she thought they were gunshots. She ran downstairs to the first floor and saw her mother holding a candle. Soon her father, brother, and sister joined them.

"Either there is a coup d'etat, or we are being attacked," Syrus said.

"Let's take shelter under the big dining room table," Puri suggested.

"This is not like cowboy movies. That was the sound of antiaircraft artillery," Miremad said.

Roxana's heart was beating fast now, and her body was trembling. She looked at the panicky expression on Elli's pale face. She was the older sister. She was supposed to say something to reduce Elli's fear. But she stood there feeling helpless. She couldn't do anything to alleviate the fear in that room. Her family stood in the middle of their living room and listened to the deafening sound of antiaircraft artillery. Finally, Syrus went to his room and brought his battery-operated radio to the living room. He couldn't find any station to give them information. After several efforts, he found a station that announced Iraq had attacked Iran. They listened to the broadcaster, who advised the public not to worry about imam's health (referring to

Ayatollah Khomeini) because he was safe. The station started playing revolutionary songs without any further detail.

Syrus tried another station, which informed them that Iraq had invaded Khuzestan, and the antiaircraft artillery was an exercise to prepare the Tehranians for future attacks.

That mock exercise caused dozens of Tehranians with heart conditions to have heart attacks, some fatal.

The next day, Roxana, who had not slept at all, went to work feeling distraught.

Mr. Imani greeted her with his usual welcoming smile. "You look pale. Are you sick?" he asked.

"After last night, how do you think I should look?"

"Oh, you didn't know that was a mock exercise?"

"No. Did you?"

"Yes. My older brother is very active in our local *Komiteh*. He told us about the exercise last night."

"Good for you. We didn't know."

"Saddam is digging his own grave, even though he has the Americans' blessing. He knows Iran is four times the size of Iraq."

Roxana didn't make any comment, but deep down she agreed that Iraq, with a population one third of Iran's, could not have risked starting a war without the United States' support.

The entire day at the office Roxana heard different opinions about the attack. Some believed that because the government had dismantled the shah's military, Saddam felt confident that he would win the war. Others believed that by attacking Iran, he had planned to obtain exclusive jurisdiction over Arvand-Rood (Shatt-al-Arab) River, and gain more access to the Persian Gulf.

Mr. Kasravi, who traveled routinely to the Iranian port cities on the Persian Gulf, had a different view: "He plans to capture and annex rich oil wells of Khuzestan."

"Saddam is acting like an Arab leader, as if he's another Jamal Abdul Nasser," Mr. Imani said. "He's also trying to replace Iran and become a dominant power in the region."

A few days after Saddam's initial attacks, Iranian pilots flew the American-made F-14 Phantoms and bombed many major Iraqi cities and oil installations.

Chapter 34

Saddam's nightly bombing of Tehran had ruined the lifestyle of its inhabitants. The brave revolutionary Tehranians who poured into the streets by the millions, who marched fearlessly to the army's tanks during the revolution, were now rushing home before dark, wondering whether their neighborhood or their homes would be Saddam's next target.

Every night, Tehran, the Paris of the Middle East, the city that never slept, was buried under darkness like an abandoned ghost town. There were no more exciting nights at *pole-e-Tajrish,* the large square in the suburb of *Shemiran* where people shopped and ate skewered kabob, roasted corn on the cob, and saffron ice cream. There was no more strolling on Pahlavi Road—Tehran's Champs-Élysées.

A great sense of sadness had fallen over Tehran like an invisible smoke that escaped the naked eye but could be smelled all around. People had stopped the early-morning jokes around the teapots in offices throughout the city. Now the conversation was all about the war. "Did you sleep last night?" "How could I, with the antiaircraft artillery deafening me all night." "I heard Saddam bombed . . ."

The thick X-shaped tapes that were intended to protect the window glasses from being shattered had changed the beauty of the houses and buildings in Tehran.

Roxana felt that even the sound of her mourning dove's cooing had changed. She remembered one of her favorite poems by Forough Farrokhzad, titled, "The Bird Was Only a Bird." The portion of the poem she liked the most read:

"The bird was small,
The bird didn't think,
The bird didn't read the newspaper."

Roxana tried unsuccessfully once more to locate her mourning dove, but it was hidden as usual. *The bird doesn't know about the war.*

The war had changed people's mood and behavior. Despite the government's organized marches on the streets of Tehran and the playing of the revolutionary songs on the state-controlled radio stations and TV channels, the revolutionary excitement had died away for the majority of the Tehranians.

The only person whose mood had not changed was Mr. Imani. The war had given him more courage to express his affection for Roxana.

One day as Roxana was walking with him on Kakh Avenue to her taxicab stand, she expressed her concern about the tone of the government demonstrators. "Now, in addition to 'Death to Saddam,' and 'Death to *Amrika*,' they have added, 'Death to *behejab*, women without Islamic *hejab*,'" she said. "I'm afraid one of these days, they're gonna stop us. Maybe I should walk by myself."

"We can tell them we're engaged."

"Excuse me?"

"All we have to do is to buy two wedding bands."

Roxana stopped walking. "Are you joking?"

"No, I'm not joking. You know how I feel about you. I want to marry you."

"Even if my mind was not preoccupied with the revolution and this horrible war, I couldn't marry you. You're four years younger than me. Besides, we're friends."

"I look much older than my age, and you look like a college freshman; no one will ever know."

"But I know. Forget about me. I'm not going to make a good wife for anyone. I'm always buried in my work or concerned about what's happening in the world."

"Maybe that's why I love you. I've never met anyone like you. Women I have met so far have been shallow or self-centered. You're so different."

"You'll meet someone who'll impress you."

"But she won't be you."

Roxana's cab arrived. While opening the cab door for her, Mr. Imani whispered, "Remember, no one is gonna understand you or love you more than I do."

Roxana waved good-bye.

She tried to dismiss Mr. Imani's daring marriage proposal, but she couldn't. During the entire taxi ride she wondered why he was so relaxed that he could think about marriage, while she was so preoccupied with the war, the hostages, and the revolution.

Back in her room, she stopped thinking about Mr. Imani. She had to worry about the night—the sound of the sirens, the length of time she had to hear the antiaircraft weapons, and whether her family's house or their neighbor's house would be the target of Saddam's bombing that night.

She was not afraid of dying, but she couldn't bear seeing her parents or siblings die before her eyes. Since the start of the war, her daily prayer had become lengthier because her list of requests from God had become longer. All her adult life, Roxana's prayer included asking God for peace in the world, whether it was the Vietnam or Arab-Israeli wars, or the 1979 Soviet invasion of Afghanistan. But since Saddam's nightly attacks on Tehran, she had added an additional request, "God, please let me die first."

The government advised people to go to a shelter when the siren rang, but, in reality, there were no shelters. The government never built any shelters, even years after the war started. Shelter basically meant the basement of the house, or, for those who didn't have a basement, it meant a room or a space in the middle of the house far from the windows.

Roxana's mother designated their large windowless kitchen as their shelter. They had several kerosene lamps that provided light in the room, creating an illusion that the electric power was not out.

During the first few nights, it was very difficult for Roxana to adjust to the family gathering in one room. She could not concentrate on her books. Even though she was pretending to read, she was reviewing the life of her family members as if that night was their last night together.

She thought about her father, a loving family man. Miremad was from a prominent family. An old cousin had kept the family tree written on the skin of a gazelle. The family tree placed him as a descendent of Yazdegerd III, the last king of the Sasanid Dynasty. Miremad, a humble man, never bragged about his ancestors, but the story was intriguing to Roxana. Yazdegerd's daughter, Shahrbanoo, had married Imam Hussein, Prophet Mohammad's grandson. When the Arab caliph killed him, some fifteen hundred years ago, Shahrbanoo got back on her horse and escaped from the city of Karbala in Iraq and headed toward Iran. According to a myth, there was a mountain on her way that stopped her horse. She told the mountain to open up, and the mountain did. People who believed she was a saint built Bibi Shahrbanoo's mausoleum near Tehran.

Roxana looked at her brother. Syrus, a twenty-six-year-old computer engineer, unable to find a job, was helping his father in his business. *He's a handsome man who should be partying every night instead of hiding from Saddam's bombs.*

Elli had planned to major in music, but the universities were closed. Even if they had opened, in an Islamic country where there was a ban on modern music, she could not have pursued a career in music. She was twenty and not in college. Roxana looked at her sister's flawless face and long, chestnut-color hair that matched her light brown eyes. She wondered about Elli's future. She felt thankful that at least her youngest sister, Neghar, lived in the States and attended college.

The deafening sound of antiaircraft artillery interrupted Roxana's train of thought. Saddam was busy destroying some part of Tehran. If she were lucky to live that night, she would read about it in the papers the next day. She felt all the blood in her body was rushing under her skin. Her body was burning with fever now.

When she visited Paris and Rome, she had never anticipated Saddam's attack on Iran. But a nagging voice in the back of her head kept telling her that, once in Iran, she would never leave the country again. Her nightmare had now become a reality. Even if the borders were not sealed, how could she leave her family behind?

Chapter 35

Proud of his army of 190,000 men, Saddam sent his army across the Arvand Rood in October. The Iraqi troops advanced eighty kilometers inside Iran. On November 10, 1980, after a bloody house-to-house fight, they captured Khorram Shahr. Roxana was shocked to hear the news of inhuman killing of the innocent civilians and the raping of women in Khorram Shahr. *How can a Moslem commit such crimes?*

Roxana learned through the media that the revolutionary government had aggressively recruited one hundred thousand volunteers to fight the imposed war. In addition to Iran's regular army, navy, and air force, the government had also mobilized members of the Revolutionary Guard and the *Basij*—what Ayatollah Khomeini referred to as the "army of twenty million," or "the people's militia."

By the end of November 1980, Iran had sent two hundred thousand ideologically committed troops to the battlefield. Some members even carried their own shrouds, expecting martyrdom.

Retaliating against the Iraqi troops' atrocity in Khorram Shahr, Iran attacked major Iraqi oil export terminals at Mina al Bakr and Al Faw on November 29, 1980.

When Saddam's nightly bombing intensified, Nina decided to leave Tehran. She had a job waiting for her in Shiraz. Before her departure, she invited her friends to her house for a casual lunch. She had assumed that no one would enjoy a dinner party with the sound of antiaircraft artillery. "My four-year-old is so scared here," she told her friends. "Every time he sees a passenger plane in the sky, even during daytime, he starts crying. He thinks they are enemy planes here to bomb us."

Unlike previous gatherings, everyone's mood was somber at the luncheon. Roxana noticed the sadness in Nina's voice when she explained why she needed a safer place for her children. In addition to Yerem, her twelve-year-old son, Ramin, couldn't sleep well at night. "I know I sound like a selfish bitch because there are many twelve-year-olds who are fighting in the battlefield, and here I am worried about my son's sleeping pattern. But I have to protect my kids," Nina said apologetically.

"You're a mother, so you don't need to explain anything," Roxana said. "I'd be worried too, if I had kids."

"That's why I never want to have any children," Lili said.

Kayvan and Steve arrived soon and joined their friends. Unlike the rest of the group, Steve was in his usual jovial mood. "You guys worry too much. This war will be over soon."

Nina's husband, who was fixing drinks for his guests, heard Steve's remark. He stopped pouring drinks, turned to Steve, and said, "I don't know where you get your information, but Saddam has just started."

"All I'm saying is that this will be a short-term war."

"Even if Saddam stops the war tomorrow, it'll take a decade to reconstruct the cities he has destroyed," Lili chimed in.

"Do you know the number of refugees in Shiraz?" Bijan asked.

"What refugees?" Steve asked.

"In addition to the camps for the many Khuzestanis that have fled their destroyed cities, Shiraz has refugee camps even for Iraqi-Iranians that were expelled by Saddam. Please write about Saddam's violation of his own treaties and even human rights."

"I can write about the destruction of the cities and the killings, but violation of which treaties?" Steve asked.

"Why don't you get Roxana to help you? She's an expert in international law," said Kayvan.

"I'm writing an article on the war for *Kayhan*, one of our daily newspapers, but that's gonna be in Farsi. Your article in the *Washington Post* can reach millions in the world," Roxana said.

"Okay, then I'll need your help in identifying which international treaties he has violated."

"I'll be happy to help."

Before leaving Nina's house, Steve found Roxana alone in the kitchen, drowned in her thoughts. "You're thousands of miles away. I'm concerned about you."

"Can you blame me?"

"Well, this is the ugly face of war. What do you expect?"

"This is the twentieth century. Why do we still have wars? Why do innocent, helpless people still get killed? Why—"

Roxana choked. She couldn't finish her sentence. She couldn't fight her tears anymore.

Steve got closer, gave her a hug, and kissed the top of her head. She needed that hug. She stayed in his arms for a few minutes, and then she pulled away. "I'm sorry. I hate to see myself this emotional."

"That's what I love about you. You're such a caring person."

"I'm a useless coward who cannot do a damn thing about this war, the hostages—"

"Stop it. What do you expect? To fight on the battlefield against Saddam? Or to rally against the hostage taking?"

Roxana didn't comment. She went back to the living room and said good-bye to Nina and Bijan. She promised that she would visit them in Shiraz.

Back in her room before nightfall, she thought about Steve. *He's such a good friend.* To distract herself, she decided to hear some music. A friend had told her that listening to Tchaikovsky would reduce the pounding sound of the artillery. She had enjoyed Tchaikovsky at the Lincoln Center, the Kennedy Center, and even in Central Park, but she quickly found out that Tchaikovsky's music wasn't so soothing during antiaircraft artillery—it didn't mix with Saddam's bombs.

She put on one of Adamo's records. The French singer had always played a significant role in her life, in sadness or in happy times. She liked to believe that she was the first Tehranian who had discovered Adamo's music.

One day after finishing her classes, as she was waiting to get a cab on the opposite side of Tehran University's main entrance, she heard nice music coming from one of the record stores behind her. She listened to the French song, went inside the store and asked the salesman about the singer. He informed her that his name was Salvatore Adamo.

That was the beginning of an eternal love affair between Roxana and Adamo's music. The music helped her through tough times.

That night, she needed to hear Adamo's songs before the start of Saddam's symphony. She hummed or sang along to "*Quand Les Roses*," "*A Demain Sur La lune*," and "*Printemp Sous La Neige.*"

Listening to Adamo made her forget for a moment that she lived in a war-stricken land. She felt like she was back in New York. She decided to write a letter to Myrna, her friend from her Georgetown years. She assumed that her American friends were worried about her.

She wrote:

> Dear Myrna,
>
> I'm sorry that I couldn't come to Washington and say good-bye to you in person. These days, I think a lot about the decade that I lived in the United States. When I came back to Tehran, I found it tough to live in revolutionary Iran, but I hadn't tasted the war yet. Night after night, Saddam's Russian-made MiGs bomb Tehran and other large cities. We gather in one room for several hours until the bombing is finished. If we are lucky to escape this nightly Russian roulette alive, then we can get some sleep.
>
> My generation, which opposed the shah's oppression, was elated with this dream-come-true revolution, but soon the religious group that took power and formed the government acted like the Bolsheviks, and treated us like the bourgeois. We are the Dr. Zhivagos of the Iranian revolution. Thank God we don't have a Siberia or the Gulag Archipelago.
>
> Please pray for the end of this war and the hostage crisis.
>
> Love,
>
> Roxana

Chapter 36

Roxana was surprised to see Steve waiting at her office. "What are you doing here?" she asked, feeling awkward.

"You promised to help me write about the war. I need the materials on Saddam's violation for my article. Can we talk somewhere?"

"Yes, we have a conference room."

She took Steve away as fast as she could. Mr. Imani's grim expression warned her that Steve was not welcomed in their joint office.

At the conference room, Roxana sat far away from Steve and left the door open so that the *Bonyad* overseers wouldn't suspect anything.

"How did you pass the reception desk?"

"Relax. I have my journalist ID card issued by the Islamic Republic."

She pulled a legal pad from her briefcase, and as she talked, she wrote about Saddam's violations of international law. "Do you know that in 1961, Iraq attempted to exercise its dominion over Kuwait?" she asked.

"No, I didn't."

"The neighboring Arab states interfered and stopped Iraq. In 1975, Iraq entered into an agreement with Iran that declared Arvand Rood or Shatt al-Arab, as it's called in Arabic, as a navigable international waterway. They followed the universally accepted median line for demarcation of the river boundaries for the two countries. Saddam has unilaterally abrogated that treaty. He has also violated the 1949 Geneva Conventions of war addressing the treatment of POWs, wounded soldiers, and civilians. The list can go on. You can add violations of Articles 24, 39, and 99 of the United Nations Charter, as well as the 1980 Law of the Sea Treaty."

Roxana picked up her pad and briefcase, but as she was ready to say good-bye, Steve ran to the door, closed it, and said, "I'm not finished here. I still need to talk to you."

"What about?"

"You and me."

"There is no you and me."

"I was away for more than a month. I wanted to talk to you as soon as I got back. I wanted to tell you that I'm officially divorced now, and my boss wants me back in Washington. Why don't you marry me and come to Washington? You don't belong here."

"What's this, Propose to Roxana Week? I just had one the other day."

"Don't tell me that it came from that character who shares the office with you."

"He's not a character. For your information, he's a very intelligent person."

"Please don't marry him. I don't have a good feeling about you and him."

"I'm not marrying anybody. I'm telling you what I told him."

"Have you read Somerset Maugham's *The Moon and Sixpence*?"

"Yes, I have."

"He said, 'A man might fall in love without making a fool of himself.' Boy have I proven him wrong."

"He also believed that during the time men are in love, they can 'do other things which distract their minds.' That means men can love sometimes, but when a woman loves, she loves 'all day long.'"

"So if you love, it has to be uninterrupted?"

"Yes, and it has to be at the right time and the right place. For God's sake, I was struggling to understand this revolution when I was hit by the war. What you're offering me is like a delicious ice cream dish to a patient who has just gotten out of surgery. I have to heal before I can enjoy any delicious food."

"I have to leave Iran, but I'll be devastated if something happens to you. Do you know that?"

"My blood is not redder than those who get killed every day."

"I'm sorry, I don't know them. But I know you, and I don't want anything to happen to you. If you're staying here, then I have to convince my boss that I need to return to Tehran."

She was silent. He gazed into her eyes lovingly and kissed her hands. "You owe me a dinner date. I'm gonna repeat it until you say yes."

She pulled her hands away, went to the door, and said, "See you when you come back."

She stood there for a few minutes. She was already missing him.

Back in her office, she saw Mr. Imani pacing in the room. "That was a lengthy meeting. What did he want?" he asked as soon as Roxana entered the room.

"Not that I owe you any explanation, but he needed to know about Saddam's violations of international law. He is writing an article for the *Washington Post*."

"Was that all you talked about?"

"No. He also proposed. Don't worry, I told him the same thing I told you."

"He doesn't know you the way I do. I know exactly what you want in life."

"And exactly what do I want in life?"

"Aside from wishing an end to the hostage crisis and this war, you want to continue your independent professional life. You want to be left alone to do your research, to write, and to solve all the problems in the world. I know you have helped battered women. You have represented women in their divorce and child custody cases pro bono. You've even written about *bride burning* in India."

"How do you know so much about me?"

"First of all, I was a member of the hiring committee here, so I reviewed your resume. Second, I know some lawyers who have known you since law school. If you marry me, you'll never have to worry about your career."

"You're offering me a walk in paradise, but I feel I've an injured knee. I can't take that walk."

That afternoon, she didn't take her usual route to the taxi stand to avoid Mr. Imani. She walked alone and listened to the crunching sound of the dry, fallen leaves under her feet. She was angry at Mr. Imani for daring to talk about her life and her future. She was angry with herself for talking about the injured knee. She thought about Steve. He had not left the country, yet she already felt a void in her heart. She wondered why she didn't feel pressured every time Steve expressed his love for her, and why she felt trapped every time Mr. Imani talked about their future. *Why didn't I meet him back in the United States?*

Chapter 37

Roxana read Resolution 479 issued by the United Nations Security Council calling upon Iran and Iraq to immediately cease any further uses of force and to settle their disputes through negotiations.

This was the first reaction from the world community. She understood why the resolution had angered the Iranians. Not only had it not identified Iraq as the aggressor, but also it had failed to recognize Iran's right of self-defense.

Kayhan, the famous Tehran-based daily, published Roxana's article on the war in two consecutive issues, but when they asked for more, she declined. It was frustrating for her to see how callously the world was ignoring the war. Her articles would not help anything because they were not published outside Iran.

Tehranians soon learned that time would pass faster if they shared their horrible nights during the bombing hours with friends and relatives.

Roxana's father refused to leave the house. His motto was that if he was destined to die, he preferred to die at his own home. One night, Parviz invited his sister's family to spend the night at their building, which had a deep but large modern basement. The building had ten apartments. Each family had brought their favorite entertainment. Some neighbors played chess or cards. Some listened to Farsi-speaking *Radio Israel.* There was always plenty of tea, pastry, fruits, pistachios, and *tokhmeh*, roasted watermelon seeds. Parviz was serving a few of her male neighbors with his homemade wine.

Roxana admitted to her mother that the sound of the antiaircraft artillery was more tolerable in that basement than in their home, but she couldn't go through "the hell with Saddam's bombs picnic" night after night. She needed her books to take her away from the war. She had planned to reread *Doctor Zhivago* that night, but the place was too noisy.

She was actually enjoying herself until her uncle and one of his neighbors started a political debate. The neighbor insisted that people were correct to stand with the government against Saddam. Uncle Parviz, on the other hand, believed that the Islamic government was using the war to strengthen its power. "You never appreciated what the shah did for you," he said. "This is what you get when you have a bunch of *Akhunds,* clergies running the country."

"The shah didn't do anything for us. He took all the oil money for himself and his *Hezar famil,* one thousand families. This government is at least spending some of the oil revenues building roads in villages and giving them electricity, schools, and farming equipment."

As the debate was getting more heated, Parviz's wife approached Roxana and said, "You see what your uncle is doing to me. I'm so sick and tired of his political fights with people. Can you please help me get a divorce?"

"Are you nuts?" Roxana looked shocked. "I don't agree with him politically either, but how can you possibly expect me to hurt my uncle."

"You're a feminist. You've helped many women with their divorces."

"Yes, battered women, abused women. My uncle is a good husband and a good father. You have your BMW, your parties, and your European trips. You never had to work a day in your life. But he has worked his tail off to give you and your kids the best life. He cooks more than you do and does housework more than you do. You've got yourself a male Japanese geisha."

"I agree with everything you said, but his political discussions are killing me."

"I'll talk to him."

Puri, who had been listening to her sister-in-law's compliant against her brother, whispered to Roxana, "I'm proud of the way you told her off. How dare she expect you to ruin your uncle's marriage? I admit my brother is driving me crazy too, but he's a good family man."

Syrus, who was playing chess with one of the building's occupants and listening to the radio, stopped playing and said, "There is a white siren. We can go home now."

Roxana thanked her uncle and his wife for the invitation. As she was leaving, she whispered to her aunt, "I love you as much as I love my uncle, but political beliefs can't establish a ground for divorce in any legal system."

Her aunt smiled. "Sometimes I get desperate and say things that I really don't mean. I love him too."

They began walking toward their home. They seemed happy and relaxed for having survived another night of bombing. Their home was three short blocks away. The pale moonlight was guiding them. When they turned to the narrow alley that led them to their house, they heard the antiaircraft artillery again. Syrus turned his radio on quickly and heard the red siren—the Iraqi MiGs were back again. The war broadcaster on the radio advised people who were in the street to lie down on the ground on their faces. "Get down and close your eyes," Puri commanded. Before closing her eyes, Roxana saw her helpless mother and brother lying next to her. She felt a rush of adrenaline in her heart.

"God, please don't let me witness my family die," she begged. She opened her *Doctor Zhivago* book, placed her face on it, and put the palms of her hands on her ears. She heard the blast of an explosion somewhere to her left and guessed that it must have come from Zafar Avenue.

After a short period of time, which seemed endless, the antiaircraft artillery sound stopped. Roxana got off the ground, dusted off her book and her clothes, and watched her mother and brother do the same. "Are you okay?" she asked her mother. There was no response. She was able to see the footprint of fear on her mother's face even under the pale moonlight.

The next day, everyone knew that Zafar Avenue had been bombed. Fortunately the bomb had hit the pedestrian sidewalk, not a house. Although there were many shattered windows, no deaths or injuries were reported. The government authorities had removed the evidence of the damage quickly at night before anyone could see it, but they couldn't hide the deep crater the bomb had created.

"It's as deep as a well!" an onlooker commented. "Is Saddam trying to find oil here?"

Although frightened by the extent of the damage, other onlookers laughed.

* * *

After the terrifying Zafar Avenue bombing experience, Roxana didn't go back to her uncle's home for another nightly "picnic." She kept busy with her books.

Every night, in their large kitchen that had been converted into a family shelter, Miremad read his newspapers. He seldom talked about politics. Syrus listened to his radio, usually getting the BBC news. Puri and Elli were the ones who talked about their daily routines. Roxana participated in the conversation sometimes, but mostly she kept reading her book.

She had heard many people comparing the Iranian Revolution to the French Revolution of 1789, but the more she read her old history books on the French Revolution, the more she was convinced the two revolutions were different. She found more similarities between the Iranian Revolution and the Russian Revolution of October 1917. One night she shared her views with her father. He agreed. "There have been revolutions within revolutions in both countries," he said. "For example, the cultural revolution in Russia to exterminate the bourgeoisie as a class is similar to *pak sazi,* cleansing, here in Iran. The cultural and administrative revolutions in Iran were designed to get rid of the Iranian bourgeois, called *taghouti*, by eliminating them from government agencies, university posts, and even the military."

"At least the Russian Revolution didn't eliminate art, music, or sports."

"This revolution would have gotten better if we didn't have to fight a war."

"I admire your optimism."

Roxana went back to reading her book—*Doctor Zhivago*—a story that had fascinated her long before the Iranian Revolution. She revered the way Boris Pasternak had described the revolution:

"The whole Russia has had its tail torn off, and freedom! Real freedom dropped out of the sky . . . Mother Russia is on the move.

She can't stand still. She is restless. She is talking and she can't stop. And it isn't as if only people were talking. Stars and trees meet and converse, flowers talk philosophy at night, stone houses hold meetings . . ."

She saw a parallel between the revolution Pasternak had described and the excitement she had witnessed during the first few months after her arrival in Tehran. One could breathe freedom at the bookstands and in every corner of the city.

It seemed as if Pasternak was describing the Iranian Revolution when he wrote, "It broke out . . . like a sigh suppressed for too long . . . everyone was revived, reborn, changed, transformed. Everyone . . . had gone through two revolutions, his own personal revolution as well as the general one."

Roxana had observed that *personal revolution* in people she knew. Everyone had turned into a revolutionary person in their own way, even apolitical individuals like her mother, her siblings, the neighborhood baker, and the cab drivers. Political discussions were no longer the realm of a professor and his political science students within the walls of a college classroom. The Iranians' internal revolution had been erupted like a volcano that had stayed dormant for too long.

Chapter 38

When Roxana got out of the elevator, she saw Mara and other female employees chatting, but everyone had a sad face. "What's going on here?"

"Kazem has joined the troops in Khuzestan," Mara volunteered.

Back in her office, she prayed for Kazem's safe return.

She had a surprise visitor in the afternoon. It was Gelareh, her lawyer friend. "I'm here to take you to lunch—in my house. I want to show you some tapes. You're gonna die laughing," she said.

"What's happening with you and your practice?"

"Well, I had to wear the stupid scarf, open my firm again, and continue my practice. You know, sooner or later, they're going to make *hejab* mandatory. In the next few months probably I have to wear it in order to put my garbage out. I'm too tired to fight, but I'm proud of the way you have been fighting it for so long."

"It's not easy. I expect any day now that someone from *Bonyad* will barge into my office and order me to wear *hejab*."

"You have no idea how many times women poured into the streets of Tehran and demonstrated against *hejab*. The last time, many were beaten up, and that ended the demonstrations. Now, with this war going on, no one dares to talk against *hejab*."

Back in Gelareh's home, after a delicious lunch, Gelareh talked about a funny clergy whose TV shows entertained many people.

"This is one of his TV speeches talking about the Indian women's sari."

Gelareh put the tape in the video cassette player and forwarded it to the segment she had chosen to show Roxana. A clergyman appeared on TV. "I don't know why our sisters are making such a big deal about *hejab*. The Indian women have their *hejab*. It's called sari. It's their national dress."

Gelareh stopped the tape. "Can you believe this man? He doesn't even know what a *sari* looks like," she said. "First of all, Indian women don't wear a head scarf. A *sari* has short sleeves, and one can see the woman's neck, arms, and a portion of her body between her breasts and her waistline."

"The model *hejab* the government is suggesting is not our national clothes. If they want to go back to the Persian Empire era, or even to the *Ghajar* Dynasty period, the clothes those women wore were very seductive."

Gelareh inserted the second tape in the video cassette player and said, "He's gonna talk about *ghosl*, now. As you may remember from your Islamic courses, married couples who have had intercourse should perform *ghosl*—shower and cleanse their bodies before their Moslem prayer. Listen to him."

The clergy's face came on the screen again. "Sisters are complaining about *manteau,* pants and the scarf, but this is not really a true *hejab*. The other day when I was on my way to the mosque, a sister was walking in front of me. She was fully covered, but still, the way she walked made me go home instead of to the mosque, take a shower, and perform *ghosl*."

Roxana screamed. "They showed this on TV?"

"Yes, they did, but unfortunately they canceled his show after that. Alas, that was our only comedy hour."

Roxana couldn't stop laughing for several more minutes. The image of a clergyman having an orgasm in the middle of the street and ejaculating in his pants on his way to the mosque was hilarious.

* * *

Roxana accepted a dinner invitation from Lili's family and went over to their house one night. She also agreed to spend the night there to avoid walking in the dark. She was tired of sitting in one place night after night listening to Saddam's bombing. The family's kitchen-shelter had become more like a prison. She felt she was under house arrest at nighttime.

After dinner and before the siren wailed, they went to the basement. Lili had told Roxana how painful it was for Narges to go back to the place that she had found Iraj's dead body. But she had no choice. The basement was the only safe place in the house, since it didn't have any windows.

Roxana saw Narges holding a heavy book. When she got closer, she saw that it was the Torah. "I've read that once. Some parts of it were a little complicated for me," Roxana said.

"I hear they call you Ayatollah Ramsy in your company after they heard that you had read the Koran several times. Is that true?" Narges asked.

"My boss was joking one day. He meant it as a compliment."

"What makes you interested in researching different religions?"

"I had a course comparing the world's three popular religions, so I had to read each religion's holy book. The fascinating discovery for me was that the three religions were all saying the same things, so I don't understand why there have been so many religious wars in the world!"

"If you become an expert in interpreting our Torah, then we have to start calling you Rabbi Ramsy," Narges laughed.

"Don't worry. Some of our friends have already called her rabbi," Lili chimed in. "One day three of our friends were arguing. I don't remember about what. As usual, they asked Roxana to arbitrate their dispute. When she concluded that everybody was right, they told her that she sounded like the old rabbi in *Fiddler on the Roof.* You remember the dispute at the wedding?"

"No, I don't," Narges, said.

"When the rabbi told the two opposing sides of the dispute that they were both right, someone yelled out, 'Rabbi, they cannot be both right,' and he said. 'You're right too.'"

Roxana had come to Lili's home specifically to talk to Yahya. She needed to hear his views on the war. "What do you think about this war?" she asked him while moving to a chair next to him.

"You mean aside from being scared for my life and my family's," Yahya said, and smiled. "You know what our problem is? Our geographic location! The ideal location for Iran would have been someplace among the old civilizations. We should have had Greeks, Egyptians, and Italians as our neighbors, not the Arabs, who hate us. They fear that we're gonna build up a modern Persian Empire sometime soon."

"All these Arab countries were ruled by the British after the fall of the Ottoman Empire. We have a good relationship with Turkey, which is the legitimate heir to the Ottoman Empire, but I don't know why we can't have the same relations with our Arab neighbors."

"The Arabs have oil. They are spoiled by the Western powers, which need their oil. The American presidents are bowing to the Saudi kings more than their ancestors ever bowed to the kings and queens of England. Do the Americans even know that Iraq became independent in 1932, Saudi Arabia in 1953, and Kuwait as late as 1961?"

"I don't think an average American knows about the history of the Arab countries, but I'm sure their politicians know. I think oil is just one element for the American interest in the area. They need these countries for their military bases and for their presence in the Persian Gulf."

"The Arab states of the Persian Gulf collectively have more power than Iran. Even the shah didn't have power to stand up to them. He lost Bahrain, which belonged to us when the British left in 1971, remember?"

"You still haven't answered my question," Roxana insisted. "What do you think about this war?"

"I'd be surprised if this war ends soon. *Amrika* loves it. It's a sweet revenge for hostage taking. Israel loves it. Thanks to the ayatollah's rhetoric, Israel thinks Iran is an enemy like Iraq. They love to watch their two enemies destroy each other. The Arab states who hate the *Shiite* Iran cannot attack a Moslem country; therefore, they support Saddam, who's doing it for them."

"I heard there are a million Egyptian laborers imported by Iraq so that the Iraqis can concentrate only on the war," Lili said.

"If the war lingers, what impact is it gonna have on our revolution?" Roxana asked.

"Our revolution was stolen a year ago. This is the clergy's revolution now. This war is a blessing in disguise for them. Now they can silence all the opposition voices."

"Do you agree with those who believe that the Iranian revolution was similar to the French one?"

"The only similarity was the killing, the bloodshed. The French Revolution was the uprising of the middle class against the privileged nobility and clergy. The Iranian Revolution occurred because the intellectuals, the middle class, the poor, and the clergy were all fed up with the monarchy, but as I said before, the clergy stole our revolution."

"Dad, you said bloodshed. Doesn't every revolution have bloodshed?" Lili asked.

"You're right. I love what Mao said, 'Revolution is not a dinner party. It cannot be advanced safely, gradually, carefully, considerately, respectfully, politely, plainly and modestly.'"

"I love the notion of a *polite revolution*," Lili said with a laugh.

"In an ideal world, revolutionary leaders would've learned from each other," Roxana said. "For example, Lenin would not repeat the mistakes of the French revolutionary leaders. Mao, Castro, or our own revolutionary leaders would have remembered the errors of previous leaders."

"Revolution is not like a coup d'etat, where you already have a leader imposed on you. It's a long process through which you find your leader," Yahya said.

Back in her room, Lili helped Roxana to unfold the sofa bed. When it was done, Lili said, "Your idea of learning from mistakes of previous revolutions has started me thinking. Even the kings didn't learn from previous kings' mistakes. I'm sure you have read a lot about Louis XIV."

"You mean, Monsieur, *L'etat c'est moi*, 'I am the state'?"

"Yes. Napoleon didn't learn from him. Instead, he went so far as to call himself an *emperor*."

"I saw a painting that showed similarity between his coronation and our own shah's coronation during the twenty-five hundredth anniversary of the Persian Empire."

"Yes, I saw that too. Napoleon's queen knelt before him to be crowned just like Empress Farah knelt before the shah."

"Forget about the revolutions. How's everything between you and Kayvan?"

"We're just friends."

"And you still remember he's married, right?"

"Look, we have a war going on. I don't know whether I'll get killed under Saddam's bombs or not. Kayvan makes me forget about the war."

Chapter 39

Roxana was about to enter Mr. Kasravi's office to talk about a case when she heard a heated debate going on inside. She couldn't recognize the voice of the man who shouted, "This is an Islamic country."

Roxana noticed Mara was holding a file and waiting close to Mr. Kasravi's office door. She also noticed Mara wore a scarf. "What's going on, and what's with the scarf?" she asked.

"One of *Bonyad's* powerful men is in there," Mara whispered. "Every time he comes here, Mr. Kasravi warns us ahead of time to wear our scarves."

"Why are you standing behind his office door?"

"Mr. Kasravi asked me to bring a file. I'm afraid to go inside."

"I need to talk to him about a case. Give me the file. I'll give it to him."

"Oh no, please don't, Dr. Ramsy! The man is shouting about you. This is your file."

Mara took Roxana's hand and led her to the conference room. She closed the door and whispered, "The man is yelling because you're not wearing *hejab*."

"There are several female employees here. No one wears *hejab* in this company."

"But we all have scarves in our drawers. As soon as we hear an important *Bonyad* man is coming, we wear them."

Roxana pressed the documents she carried to her chest and took a deep breath. As she was about to leave the conference room, Mara said, "I wish you could hear how Mr. Kasravi defended you. He said that you were a brilliant lawyer, and he couldn't run this company without you."

Roxana went back to her office, sat down, pushed her fingers through her hair, and pressed her skull hard with both hands. She felt like her brain was about to explode. She wasn't ready to wear a scarf, much less a full *hejab*. What would her grandmother think? History was repeating itself with a little sense of humor. Her grandmother fought against *hejab* with religious people in the street who intimidated her, but the law and her government protected her. For Roxana, the fight was against her government, which was imposing the Islamic *hejab* on her, not the people.

"What's the matter, did someone die?" Mr. Imani asked as he entered the room.

"Yes, my freedom."

After hearing the detail of what had happened at Mr. Kasravi's office, Mr. Imani became angry. "Damn it, the country is falling apart," he said as he banged his fist on his desk. "There is a horrible war going on, and all they are concerned about is women's *hejab*."

"That's their real war, an invisible war no one can see except women."

"That's their opium. Remember what Karl Marx said, 'Religions . . . are the opium of the people.' I believe he meant religious people."

"What saddens me is that even our intellectual president is advocating *hejab*. This is a man who lived in Paris for fifteen years and who told Jean Paul Sartre that he'd be Iran's first president, and he made it. But now, in order to strengthen his position, he sides with the clergy and declares that 'women's hair emits rays that arouse men.' How shocking is that?"

"I don't think he personally believes in *hejab*, but he has to work with these people."

"By sacrificing women's rights?"

Before Mr. Imani could comment, there was a knock on the door. He opened it and let Mr. Kasravi in.

"There will be a significant meeting at one of *Bonyad's* companies tomorrow. They want you there to explain about our company's litigations. They expect us there at 6:00 p.m. It will be late, maybe

10:00 p.m. after we finish, but the company driver will take you home. I have to ask you a favor. I don't know how to—"

"Don't worry, I'll wear a scarf."

"Oh, thank you. One more favor—"

"I won't be shaking hands with them, either."

"Thanks so much; you're a lifesaver."

I'm a coward and a compromiser, Roxana thought.

Chapter 40

She examined a dozen scarves that her mother had gathered for her. She picked up a small beige scarf adorned with golden lines. She put her chocolate-brown business suit on and tried the scarf. It was too small to cover her long hair. She made her hair into a French twist and used some pins to hold it back, and then tried the scarf again. The see-through scarf still revealed her reddish hair.

"You still look very chic," her mother said, "but this is a flimsy, see-through scarf."

"That's the best *hejab* I can put on."

She thanked her mother, went to her room, and listened to some of her Adamo records. She then took her book and went to their shelter—the kitchen. It was dark, and Saddam had started his bombing. Soon, the horrible, loud, and monotonous sound of antiaircraft artillery ensued.

That night, she decided to reread Solzhenitsyn's book, *The Gulag Archipelago.* She had read the book in 1975. The terrible stories about the Soviet penal system of labor camps had created an image in her mind similar to the Nazi concentration camps. She couldn't believe the extent of the atrocities.

She read Solzhenitsyn's criticism of the Soviet system of arresting people without giving them a trial. He had wondered why people so easily submitted to arrest. He had admitted that he himself should have shouted, "Why are you arresting me?"

Roxana remembered the young man who was arrested in front of Tehran University. He objected, but no one cared.

Solzhenitsyn then tells his readers that if he had cried, only two hundred people would have heard his cry. "I had a vision that someday my cry would be heard by two hundred million."

When Roxana put the scarf over her hair, she felt she was under arrest. She had lost her freedom, her identity. The threat of wearing *hejab* and the endless hours she had spent in their so-called shelter had created a new form of revolutionary confinement. She closed her eyes and dreamed that one day her pain would fill the pages of a book read by two hundred million people.

* * *

When Roxana and Mr. Kasravi entered the conference room of *Bonyad's* largest company, eighteen men already were seated around the conference table waiting for them. It was not difficult to detect the *Bonyad* men. They were all bearded.

Roxana said, "Hello," flashing a half smile, and sat down in the chair they had designated for her. Two huge piles of files were in front of her.

One of the *Bonyad* men, who was seated at the head of the table, welcomed Roxana and Mr. Kasravi. "We are thankful to Brother Kasravi and Sister Dr. Ramsy for accepting our invitation and coming here today," he said. "Brother Kasravi had advised us to separate the files of our European companies from our American companies. The pile on Sister Dr. Ramsy's left is the American ones."

Roxana pulled out her legal pad and went though the piles on her right side first. Although she was concentrating on the essential provisions of each contract, she was aware that all the conference attendees were staring at her except the *Bonyad* men.

She finally finished reviewing all the relevant portions of the files belonging to the European companies. She created two separate piles and leaned back in her chair. She took a hidden long breath and said, "Okay, gentlemen, I am ready for your questions."

One of the engineers, who were staring at Roxana's action the entire time, raised his hand. "How on earth could you go over those contracts so quickly?"

"All I had to do was to look at only one significant provision of the contract, the dispute settlement clause."

"How can we get rid of these foreign companies?" one of the *Bonyad* men asked without looking at Roxana.

"Wait a minute. We need these companies," one of the engineers said. Several others agreed.

"Gentlemen," Roxana said, "if you don't have the technology or the needed equipment, I recommend that you continue your transactions with these European companies, since their governments still have diplomatic relations with Iran."

"What if they don't want to work here?" asked a *Bonyad* employee, again avoiding eye contact with Roxana.

"You are lucky," Roxana said as she showed the tall pile she had created. "These are the companies whose contracts refer to the Iranian laws and the Iranian courts when there is a dispute. The three companies on my left refer to arbitration, but they don't say arbitration according to whose laws."

"How can you help us with the mess we have?" asked the *Bonyad* man at the head of the table, staring at his notes.

"I believe you should first negotiate with the European companies to see whether there is a possibility to continue working with them. If anyone of them says no, then I will get involved and negotiate a settlement with them," Roxana said.

Before Roxana had a chance to talk about the American companies, the power went out, the siren wailed, and everyone began running out of the conference room. Someone struck a match to find the staircase.

She was walking next to Mr. Kasravi surrounded by all the meeting attendees as well as other employees in the building. She was not pushed, but she felt the panic around her. Everyone was rushing to get out. They were on the fourth floor. The stairway was large but it had no handrail. Roxana took her first step down, but before she could reach the second step, she lost her balance and her body plunged down the staircase. She heard a man's cry, "Someone fell down." Her head hit every step, sounding like a bouncing basketball. The pain was so excruciating that she thought her brain had ruptured. Her body finally landed on the first floor. The building janitor, who had a large flashlight, discovered her. He momentarily forgot the Islamic code prohibiting him from touching a *na mahram*, a woman not related to him. He picked up Roxana's bruised body and helped her to a chair.

The flashlight had made it easier for the other people to find their way to the door. Mr. Kasravi rushed toward Roxana. "I kept calling you. Oh my God. You were the one who fell down? How can you forgive me for bringing you here?" he said with a painful expression on his face.

"Please have the driver take me home," Roxana asked.

"We're going to a hospital. There are at least forty steps here. This was a bad fall."

The pain in Roxana's head indicated she needed medical attention.

* * *

After reviewing the X-rays and examining Roxana for the last time, the doctor let Mr. Kasravi into the examination room. He said, "There is no fracture in the skull or any bone. However, for the next twenty-four hours, there is a possibility of a brain hemorrhage or internal bleeding."

Roxana didn't pay attention to the rest of the doctor's explanation. She was testing her brain to see whether it was damaged. She started writing an imaginary brief in her head in response to a lawsuit brought by an imaginary corporation. She was halfway through her legal argument when she heard the doctor addressing her. "We can observe you here for the next twenty-four hours, or you can go home and come back if there is any trouble."

"Thanks, Doctor. I prefer to go home."

Roxana had tested her brain. She hadn't detected any problems, but the bump on the left side of her skull was the size of an egg. "Mr. Kasravi, could you please ask the driver to take me home?"

"Could you ever forgive me?"

"It was my fault. I wanted to get out of there fast, so I decided to fly down the staircase," Roxana said with a smile.

Back in her bedroom, she checked the bruises and the scratches on her body. They were all on the left side where her body and head had hit the steps repeatedly.

She lay down in her bed trying to forget the unexpected event, but she couldn't. She had almost died that night. Before the war, she thought she would live a long life. She also desired to have at least one child. She was planning to teach that child about the horrors of the war, the Holocaust, and good leaders like Gandhi, Mandela, Dr. King, and Cyrus the Great. She believed that if parents taught their children about the mistakes of older generations and about their sins and crimes, future generations would avoid racism, hatred, and wars.

Unlike typical Persian mothers, Roxana's mother had never rushed her to get married, but she had recently hinted that she would like to see a grandchild before she died. Puri was always telling people stories about Roxana's childhood. One story she repeated often related to the time Roxana was only four years old. An older boy in their neighborhood used to hit her with his soccer ball. One day, Roxana got mad and threw the ball back at him. He lost his balance, fell down to the ground, and got scratches on his elbow. The kid's mother told Puri that Roxana had pushed her son. Puri, believing the neighbor's story, rushed to Roxana to punish her. Roxana, who was tall enough only to reach her mother's knee, managed to hold her mother's hand in the air and said, "Maman, let me explain. He hit me first with his ball many times. I was defending myself. It was not my fault that he fell."

Puri proudly explained to her listeners that, "She was using a self-defense theory at age four, yet I kept pushing her to go to medical school."

Had she died that night, she would not have experienced what her mother had. She would've left no legacy behind.

She wondered why she was having all those thoughts. After all, she had prepared herself for the possibility of dying under Saddam's bombs. What was the difference? Why was the '*near death*' experience more frightening than *death* itself?

She remembered Albert Camus's character in *The Stranger.* Meursault, while waiting for his execution, thought a lot about death. He had concluded, "Whether it was now or twenty years from now, since everybody was going to die, it didn't matter when and how."

She struggled in her head with the issue of death. Was death under Saddam's bombing nobler, more heroic than falling down the staircase? Did it matter if she died twenty years later? Yes, it did, she concluded. She wanted to live to see the hostages released and the end of the wars in Iran and Afghanistan. She wanted to see the Iranian Revolution blossom into a democratic system. And she wanted to have a child, a child who could do what she couldn't—preach peace and touch the souls of millions.

Chapter 41

"Oh my God; oh my God!" Puri cried out the next morning, as soon as she heard about her daughter's accident the night before.

"I'm fine. No hemorrhage last night, so I'm not gonna die."

Puri, who was holding her face with both hands, burst into tears. She was a strong woman, who only cried when someone died. But the pain of going through an uncertain revolution and Saddam's war had turned her into an emotional person. "After my mother's death, and losing Iraj, I can't bear losing anyone else, especially you, my precious child. I never tell you this, but I dream of seeing you get married someday, of having a grandchild and all the dreams that mothers have for their daughters."

"Look at me. I walk; I talk. All my limbs work."

"First the attack with the staple gun, now this. You're not wearing their stupid *hejab*. I'm so afraid that next time someone will throw acid on your face."

"Maman, nobody pushed me—this was an accident. I'll be very careful from now on."

"I forgot to tell you, someone named Mr. Imani has called here several times while you were asleep."

"If they called me from the office, tell them I'm resting."

She went back to her room and lay in her bed. Despite the headache from the fall, she managed to get into a comfortable position and read her book—*The Gulag Archipelago*. To Roxana, reading about the horrific stories in the Soviet labor camps was as painful as reading about the Holocaust. Solzhenitsyn's words, however, were soothing, as if he was telling her in a fatherly way, "Yes, your country is torn up by revolution and the war, but, believe me, you still don't have it as bad as we did."

Solzhenitsyn had criticized New York Supreme Court Judge Leibovitz, who had praised the condition of labor camps in an article in *Life* magazine.

Disappointed by the West's indifference, he especially criticized the French intellectuals' flirtation with Soviet communism. "All you freedom-loving left-wing thinkers in the West! You *Laborites!* You progressive American, German, and French . . . As far as you are concerned, none of this amounts to much . . . You may suddenly understand it all someday, but only when you yourself hear, 'Hands behind your backs there!' and step on our Archipelago."

Roxana knew exactly what Solzhenitsyn meant when he talked about the "West's indifference." They had remained indifferent toward Saddam's war too, the war that had killed thousands of people.

She stayed at home and rested for one week. She ignored Mr. Imani's telephone messages—she didn't want to talk to anyone from the office.

Saddam's bombing of Tehran had temporarily stopped, although a brutal war continued in Khuzestan. The power outages still forced families to spend their evenings together in their so-called shelters.

One evening when Roxana was reading, Uncle Parviz knocked on her door. She opened it and let him in.

"How's my favorite niece doing?" He was very jovial.

"I'm fine. You seem very happy. What's going on?"

"I have some good news that'll make you forget about your head injury."

"What?"

"I heard it both on BBC and Radio Israel that the hostages are gonna be released. They will be flown to Germany as Reagan is having his inauguration tomorrow."

Roxana jumped to her feet. She hugged her uncle, took a long sigh of relief, and said, "Thank you, Uncle Parviz. This is the best news I've had in 444 days."

Parviz went downstairs to share the news with the rest of the family. Roxana felt she had carried an expensive, heavy crystal ball for many days while climbing a mountain. She had reached the peak, and the crystal was not damaged. What a relief. She felt her eyes filling with tears—happy tears.

She called Susan and found out that she and her family were exhilarated. "Now my parents can sleep better," Susan said.

"You have no idea how happy I am."

"I know how you suffered, but now let's hope for this war to end."

"We're all praying."

Lili's reaction was more casual. "What a Hollywood moment for a Hollywood actor," she commented.

"I don't care about the inauguration show or the hero's parade that they will probably have on Fifth Avenue, though justifiably. I'm happy that they're out of here and heading home."

"Our government says that they were our guests for 444 days and not even a nose bleed. I bet that once they're back in the States, they will flood the American courts with lawsuits against Iran. Oh! Wait a minute, that'll be your problem, not mine," Lili said with a laugh.

* * *

Two days later, Roxana still felt ecstatic, so when Mr. Imani called and asked her to meet with him in a park, she agreed. They met in Saei Park, located at Vali Asr (formerly Pahlavi) Avenue. Saei, one of Tehran's most attractive parks, was situated on a hilly area, so Roxana and Afshin had to descend some steps. During spring and summer, the park's flower gardens were adorned with various roses, geraniums, violets, marigolds, and many other flowering plants, but even on a cold January day, the sycamore, pine, and cypress trees still preserved the park's charm.

Since her accident, Roxana had realized that the cold weather would increase the pain associated with the bump on her head. She didn't walk very far inside the park. She found a bench near a small, strange-looking structure, sat down and invited Mr. Imani to sit down as well. "So what was this urgent matter that you had to call my house a dozen times?" she asked.

"This past week has been the longest and the most painful week of my life," he said. "I was so worried about you. I knew that something bad would happen to you the minute I heard you had to wear a scarf in that meeting, but I anticipated that you would end up having an argument with one of those *Bonyad* guys if they lectured you on your *hejab*. I never expected a near death accident. Mr. Kasravi gave me the details when you didn't show up at work."

"Since the news about the hostages, I've forgotten about my accident. I'm in a state of euphoria. I feel like going out and dancing all night. Too bad we don't have any nightclubs anymore."

"I'm also happy that the hostages are gone. Now out of the three anxieties you had, one is gone. You should leave the war and the future of the revolution to the government."

"Believe me, after my accident and the good news about the hostages, I'm taking a little time off. I need to feel happy again. I disagree with the Americans who believe one person can make a big difference—maybe in a democratic society, but not here. I have fought long enough against the *hejab*, but I cannot change the system. I don't need seventy-five lashes and the humiliation that goes with it."

"You deserve to be happy. Why don't you let us build that happiness together? Roxana, please marry me. I can't live without you anymore."

"Wow!" Roxana's eyes got wider. She was speechless, but finally she gathered her thoughts. "You've known me only for eight months, and as a coworker. We haven't even had a date."

"Every lunch we had and every day I escorted you to the taxi stand was a date to me."

"I'm not housewife material, spending all day in the kitchen cooking and doing housework. If you want to marry, you'd better look for someone else."

"Just give me a chance. I'll do everything. Your professional life will never change."

Roxana became speechless again. Her image of plunging into the staircase was a constant reminder that life was too short. She remembered her mother's tearful description of her wishes, her daughter's marriage, and a grandchild. Had Puri made that emotional statement before the accident, Roxana would've simply shrugged and left the room. She was amazed how she had changed since the accident. She was sitting on a park bench talking marriage. *What's happening to me?*

Mr. Imani took advantage of Roxana's long silence. He moved closer, held Roxana's hands, and kissed them repeatedly. He now had tears in his eyes. "Please say yes. I can't live without you. Please say yes."

"Okay, yes." she couldn't believe those words came out of her mouth.

Mr. Imani saw the doubt, the hesitation written all over Roxana's face. "You said yes. Remember, you can't take it back. You said yes," he repeated.

"I said yes, didn't I?"

Mr. Imani hugged and kissed Roxana. He stopped when he heard a man coughing. The bearded man, who came out of the strange-looking structure, looked the other way in a shy manner when he passed them. Roxana got up from the bench and looked at the structure closely. There was a sign that read, "The Park's Mosque."

She showed the sign to Afshin. They both laughed and started running. As they got farther away from the mosque, they held hands and started walking normally. He was staring at his future bride passionately. She was watching the tall trees when she first felt the snowflakes falling on her face. It was an amazing scene. The sun was still shining, but the soft snowflakes were dancing in the air. *Maybe that's a good omen.*

Chapter 42

Back in her room, she felt sick. She went to the bathroom several times and threw up. Her fear had finally settled in like a stubborn black crow sitting on an old tree crying, "Oh my God. I said yes. Oh my God." Finally, she pulled herself together and built up enough nerve to walk into the kitchen. "You're not gonna believe this, but I'm getting married," she announced the news to her family.

Roxana's mother jumped to her feet, raised both arms, looked up to a presumptive sky, and said, "Thank you, God."

She and Elli both hugged Roxana and congratulated her. Then it was her father's turn to do the same. "Who's the lucky man?" her father asked.

"You don't know him. He works in my company. His name is Afshin. He's an economist—left his PhD program in the United States when the revolution started. He's been in love with me since the day I was hired by the company. He had proposed before, but I ignored it until today."

"What made you change your mind this time?" Syrus asked.

"Maybe because my head hit the ground many times and shook my brain," Roxana said with a laugh.

Roxana's family was surprised when they first met her fiancée. Afshin was not good-looking like Roxana's previous suitors, but he was tall, square-jawed, and looked athletic. At the end of the evening, the family agreed, however, that he was very intelligent and likable.

Afshin had suggested to Roxana that he wanted a small wedding with family and close friends. When Roxana mentioned that to her mother, Puri blasted, "You're not a widow. This is your first marriage. You're my firstborn, first daughter getting married."

"We have a war going on. Our young soldiers are getting killed every day. I don't feel like having a fiesta."

"My heart goes out to our soldiers' mothers, but this is my moment of happiness as a mother, and I'll be damned if I let anyone ruin it."

"All nightclubs are closed. You can't even use music. And what about the *Komiteh*?"

"You leave that to your uncle Parviz and me."

"Even if he finds a place, it would be expensive."

"Look, your father and I will give you an extravagant *Jahaz* (dowry), so wedding expenses are the groom's responsibility."

"He shouldn't spend a lot of money because you want a big wedding."

"Listen, you're not in *Amrika* anymore. You have to follow our tradition. Here the groom pays all the wedding expenses. The bride's family gives *Jahaz*."

Roxana declined her father's offer of buying her a house as part of her *Jahaz*, but allowed her mother to buy household furniture.

She was excited and eager to meet her future in-laws, but contrary to what she had envisioned, the meeting didn't go smoothly. She had expected her future in-laws to greet her at the door with open arms, the way her family had treated Afshin, but the house was empty.

Afshin led Roxana to the family room. "My mother's in the kitchen cooking for us," he said.

"We didn't have to have dinner here. I just wanted to meet your family."

"She insisted."

Roxana waited for her future mother-in-law for a long time. Finally, after a forty-minute wait, Afshin's mother showed up with a loose light-colored *chador* hanging on her head. Roxana rushed to her to give her a hug. "I've been so excited to meet with you," she said.

Afshin's mother gently pushed Roxana's arms away. "I'm sweaty. Please, no hug. I've been in front of the stove too long."

"You shouldn't have cooked at all. I just came to say hello."

"Thanks, but I had to cook something. My son tells me you're gonna get married next month. What's the rush?"

"It's my decision," Afshin volunteered. "I want to start a new life beginning with Persian New Year, which happens to be next month."

Afshin's mother excused herself to check on her food again. As she was leaving, Afshin's father and brother came in.

"So this is my beautiful daughter-in-law," his father said as he gave Roxana a big hug. His brother shook Roxana's hand. "I'm Armin; I'm four years older than Afshin."

"Nice to meet you, Armin. I hear that you're a savvy businessman."

"My father's eyes are getting bad. He needs my help."

"My brother has sacrificed a lot for the family," Afshin said. "He's been in and out of college so many times. This time he was determined to get his degree, but the universities are closed now."

"Afshin is being kind. I don't have his brain. I should have finished college a long time ago. I like business more than studying," Armin commented.

When the evening was over, Roxana didn't have a very good feeling about her future in-laws. With the exception of her father-in-law to be, she sensed that she was not received well. Afshin's mother seemed overbearing, and sometimes simply cold and distant. His brother's remark that he was four years older troubled Roxana. He could have simply said that he was the older brother. Was he giving her a hint that he was aware of the four-year age difference between her and his brother?

One day, Roxana shared her concerns with Afshin. He smiled and assured Roxana that no one in his family cared about their age difference. Roxana also asked about her mother-in-law's *chador*. "I thought you said she grew up in Russia. What's with the c*hador*?"

"Her adoptive mother was very religious, but my mother is not. It's her laziness. She doesn't want to dress up."

Roxana picked out a simple engagement ring. When Puri saw it for the first time, she tried to mask her disappointment. "It's beautiful," she said, "but not an eye-catcher."

"I live in the Islamic Republic. When I'm in a meeting, I cannot wear a ring that attracts everyone's attention."

"Living in the Islamic Republic doesn't mean we should all put our heads down and die."

Roxana and Afshin rented a nice two-bedroom rambler on one of the side streets of Vali Asr Avenue. The house was near Tehran's

Sheraton Hotel, surrounded by several supermarkets and good restaurants.

Afshin objected to the expensive rent at first, but he eventually agreed when he realized that Roxana had grown up in the area.

After viewing the house, Puri started buying furniture and almost every item that newlyweds needed. Her brother, Parviz, found an abandoned nightclub for the wedding reception. "The rich owner has fled the country, and the new owner shares his profit with the *Komiteh*, so they won't be bothering us," Parviz said.

"Uncle Parviz, are you sure that the *Komiteh* is not gonna raid the place?"

"I'm sure."

Roxana angered her mother once more when she chose a simple wedding gown. She picked out the gown in one of the few boutiques still left in Kucheh Mehran—a popular shopping area in Tehran. Her mother desired a fancy wedding gown with a long, sweeping train to be held by a bridesmaid, but Roxana chose a strapless satin gown with a long-sleeved embroidered lace jacket.

After she came out of the fitting room, Puri got tearful eyes. "You're so beautiful that you even make this simple gown look fancy."

"With your veil on top of this long-sleeved jacket, you look very Islamic," Elli commented, laughing.

"Is he gonna pay at least for your gown?" Puri asked with a bit of sarcasm.

"Big wedding was your idea. He wanted a small wedding."

"You're breaking all our traditions. The groom pays for everything. Your father, as generous as ever, is paying for everything, but the groom should at least buy the mirror and the two traditional candleholders."

"Gelareh will lend me hers for the ceremony."

"Is he spending any money on this wedding?"

"He's going to take care of the honeymoon."

That evening, Roxana was reading her book when her father knocked on her door and asked her if they could talk.

"Please, Father, come on in."

Miremad pulled up a chair and sat near her. "I've come to talk to you about something that has been bothering me for some time."

"The wedding expenses?"

"No, princess. I don't care about the expenses. My concern is that we don't know Afshin. I trust him because you trust him. Your mother tells me that you're waiving your *Mehrieh.* As a lawyer, you should know that *Mehrieh* is a deterrent for divorce. You also know that based on present Islamic laws, a man can divorce his wife anytime."

"If Afshin ever wants to divorce me, I don't want to have anything to do with him."

"Suppose you have a kid. You know the Islamic court gives the custody to the father or, if he's dead, to the closest male member of his family."

"What's *Mehrieh* these days for someone like me?"

"At least three thousand gold coins, several million tomans, about half a million dollars."

"That's a price tag. I believe I'm worth more than $500,000."

"Of course you are. Some families ask for their daughter's *Mehrieh* up front, but we are not asking for that. It's just a commitment. *Mehrieh* is even printed in the government's official marriage booklet that you have to sign."

"My *Mehrieh* is going to be a copy of the Koran and a stem of a red rose."

"Please think about this a little longer before waiving your right. You're a lawyer. You should protect your rights."

The conversation with her father didn't change her mind. Roxana was not going to have a price tag. Her father's concern reminded her of another father, Nina's. Vartan stopped Nina's wedding ceremony for hours.

During the shah's regime, despite women's rights movements, married women still needed their husband's permission to travel abroad. Vartan was asking Bijan to waive that right in the marriage contract. Bijan refused. His argument was that he would be traveling with Nina if she desired to go abroad. Roxana remembered how she was running in Nina's home between the first floor, where Vartan had established his bastion, and the second floor, which represented Bijan and his family's battlefield. The eighteen-year-old Roxana finally convinced Bijan to give the traveling rights to Nina, but once the families were ready to resume the ceremony, they found out that the bride was missing.

Roxana thought that Nina might have taken a walk on Queen Elizabeth Boulevard, which was near their home. She started searching for Nina on the east side of the boulevard. She was correct. She found the distraught bride walking in her wedding gown alongside the stream in the middle of the boulevard. She told her the good news. They both started running toward Nina's home, ignoring the honks of the oncoming cars and the cheers of their occupants.

For a moment, Roxana thought all Iranian fathers were overprotective when it came to their daughters, but then she remembered Spencer Tracy in *Father of the Bride.* She had seen the movie on TV many years ago. A father's concern was a universal rule and had nothing to do with his nationality.

She was happy that her father didn't insist on *Mehrieh.* However, she wondered why Afshin was not contributing anything to the cost of their wedding. Covering the honeymoon expenses was just a small part of the wedding expenses. *If he loves me as much as he claims, money should not matter to him.*

Chapter 43

Two days before the wedding, Nina, who had traveled from Shiraz, took Roxana and Lili out for lunch. The three childhood friends shared two hours of worry-free laughter enjoying a delicious meal in one of their favorite restaurants on Vali-Asr Avenue.

During the shah's rein, Vali-Asr was called the Pahlavi Road. According to some report it was considered to be the longest street in the Middle East—some even believed that it was the longest street in the world. With its tall sycamore trees, luxurious hotels, shops, and restaurants, Vali-Asr was one of the most elegant avenues in Tehran.

"I'm so glad that the Iraqi MiGs have spared our Champs-Élysées," Nina said.

"Remember the story about the German pilot who couldn't bomb Paris because he adored the city, and he had fond memories of so many delicious meals there. Maybe Saddam's generals have also been in our restaurants here and have tasted our delicious food!" Roxana said, laughing.

"Well, he's not bothering us in Shiraz, thank God," Nina said.

Nina told her friends how her family was enjoying life in Shiraz. Her four-year-old was not scared of airplanes anymore. "Enough about the war; let's talk about the wedding," Nina changed the subject.

"I remember how Nina's father almost stopped her wedding. Is your father going to ask for traveling rights?" Lili asked Roxana.

"No. But my waiving of *Mehrieh* troubled him. I told him that I was asking for a copy of the Koran and one stem of red rose."

"How intellectual of you. I've never seen a *Mehrieh* like that," Lili said, laughing.

"That's so poetic," Nina said. "He's a nice man. And he loves you."

"I agree with you. Please tell that to Lili."

"I never said anything bad about him," Lili said defensively.

"You didn't, but you're not excited about this wedding either."

"I'm sorry, Roxana. I believe you belong with Steve. There, I said it."

"Lili, why can't you understand that Steve and I are living in two different worlds? Our countries are at war with each other."

"He told me that he proposed to you."

"Why are we talking about Steve?" Roxana asked.

"He sent me a letter telling me that none of the Iranian embassies in Europe are issuing him a visa," Nina said. "I don't have the heart to tell him about your marriage, but do you want me to?"

"Yes, the sooner he knows, the better. Maybe he'll forget all about me, Iran, and the revolution."

"I still believe you should've married Steve."

"Don't be so mean," Nina admonished Lili.

That night Roxana couldn't sleep well. She wondered why Lili believed that she belonged with Steve, and not Afshin.

* * *

Puri bought a fancy s*ofreh-ye-aghd*, a traditional cloth spread on the floor, basically functioning as a table. The s*ofreh* was decorated with a large mirror and two silver candleholders. Other items placed on the *sofreh* included various types of sweets, such as baklava, sugarcoated almonds, cookies, gold coins, a basket of decorated eggs, a container of rose water, and lots of flowers. The selected items symbolized fate, fertility, love, wealth, happiness, and prosperity.

On the eve of the wedding, Puri asked Roxana to take a look at the finished s*ofreh*. "What do you think?" she asked.

Roxana's jaw dropped. "A satin embroidered s*ofreh!*" She was astonished at the luxurious *sofreh* that had covered two-thirds of a large Persian carpet. "This is fancier than Queen Farah's s*ofreh-ye-aghd!* Don't you think you've gone overboard a little?"

"This is the thanks I get. I'll keep it for my other two daughters. Go, go and have a lovely dinner with your fiancé."

"I'm so grateful for all you've done for me, but—"

"Don't you start with that 'we're at war' speech again," Puri said as she gently pushed her daughter out of the room and closed the door behind her.

After dining in a fancy restaurant, Roxana and Afshin walked on the beautiful sidewalks of Vali-Asr Avenue. Two *Komiteh* members stopped them at different places because they were holding hands. Each time, Afshin took Roxana's left hand, raised it, and said, "*Sarkar*, she's my wife."

Despite the fact that Saddam had stopped bombing Tehran for some time, the electric power was still out at night. It was the moonlight that allowed people to see their walking paths.

When Roxana almost fell because tree branches had obstructed the moon's guiding light, she decided to go home. Afshin hailed a taxi for her and kissed her good night. "I can hardly wait to see us married tomorrow."

Back in her room, Roxana felt emotionally exhausted. Although her family took care of every detail of her wedding plan, she felt she was carrying a heavy burden. Did she feel guilty because she was having a wedding celebration while an ugly war was going on? Or was she deep down concerned about Afshin's inaction. He had not lifted a finger to help with any part of the wedding ceremony or reception. And what about Steve? *I owe him an explanation.*

Before going to bed she decided to announce her marriage to her American friends. She wrote:

> Dear Cathy,
>
> I was having lunch today with two of my best Persian friends when I realized how much I missed seeing my American friends. I wish Judith, Myrna, Ellen, and you could all be here. I'm getting married. Yes, you read it correctly. I blame the sudden decision on my near death experience. I fell down in a building, and my head hit forty steps. I believe the antimarriage portion of my brain shifted its position! His name is Afshin. He's an intelligent man. He's very much in love with me. I'm sure I'll gradually fall

in love with him too. But at this point, if we were Russians, you could call this a marriage between two revolutionary comrades.

Next week on the twenty-first day of March, we will be celebrating *Noruz*, the Persian New Year. The state-controlled radio stations and TV channels are criticizing people who are preparing for *Noruz*, saying that celebration should be canceled this year because of the war. However, people are ignoring the government. They are sending them a message that this is still a Zoroastrian nation despite its Moslem religion.

Recently I've been rereading Solzhenitsyn's book, *The Gulag Archipelago.* The book has a different meaning now that I am living in a war-stricken revolutionary country. I feel like printing some of his words in gold, framing, and hanging them in the offices of the Iranian politicians—phrases such as, "Rulers change, the Archipelago remains." He wrote, "Peasants are a silent people without a literary voice. Silent generations grow old and die without ever having talked about themselves…"

The revolutionary Iranians have been silent because this war has forced them to concentrate on their immediate enemy—Saddam. There is a thunderous outcry here about the war, but the West doesn't hear it.

I recently read Albert Camus's speech when he won the Nobel Prize. He said, "The silence of an unknown prisoner, abandoned to humiliations at the other end of the world, should be enough to draw the writer out of his exile…"

We have silent prisoners in Iran. Our intellectuals have remained silent too out of the fear that they would be joining the silent prisoners if they wrote about them. Those who have the power and the freedom to write about the Iranians' suffering are the peace-loving intellectuals in the Western world, but they have chosen to remain silent. No one writes about the political prisoners here or about Saddam's barbaric slaughter of the Khuzestanis. Even though the American hostages are free now, in the eyes of the world Iran still remains a hostage-taker, and, of course, a hostage-taking nation doesn't deserve to exist, much less to complain.

I better end this letter before getting more depressed. For crying out loud, I have a wedding to attend tomorrow—my wedding.

Please share this letter with our mutual friends.

Love,
Roxana

Chapter 44

Roxana had promised herself that she would respect her mother's wish and follow the traditional *Aghd,* marriage ceremony. She sat next to Afshin in a love seat facing a large mirror and the *sofreh.* She let the happily married female relatives hold a piece of white cloth over their heads, and she heard them giggling when they rubbed two hardened sugar cones over her head. The crushing of the sugar cones together was meant to bring happiness for the couple.

She listened to the clergy's lengthy recitation of the Koran in Arabic and his speech in Farsi about the significance of the marriage institution. The clergy then asked the parents of the bride and groom whether the marriage had their blessings. After receiving their approval, he asked Afshin whether he wanted to marry Roxana. Afshin said yes before the clergy had finished his sentence. Traditionally, the bride is asked the question three times, and she is supposed to say yes after the third time. The clergy asked Roxana whether she wanted to marry Afshin. Nina responded immediately, "She's out in the garden to pick up some flowers." When the clergy asked Roxana for the second time, before anyone had a chance to make another excuse, she said yes. The guests laughed. She saw Afshin's wide grin in the mirror.

After they placed the wedding bands on each other's fingers, a female relative offered them honey. Each fed the other with a small teaspoon of honey that symbolized a sweet marriage.

The last part of the ceremony involved the signing of the marriage booklet by the bride, the groom, and their witnesses.

When the clergy announced the couple married, the female guests started singing the traditional "*Mobarak-Baad*" song. The couple kissed among cheers and applause of their guests.

* * *

She was astonished when she entered the abandoned nightclub. Her uncle had turned the place into a fancy wedding reception area. A live band played on the east side of the room. Two royal-like chairs at the top of the room were saved for the bride and groom. The round tables for the guests were decorated with pink roses and were illuminated with romantic candlelight.

On the left side of the reception room, far away from the guest tables were two large tables holding towers of gifts. On a round table in the far corner of the room sat a four-tiered vanilla wedding cake decorated with sugar flowers of roses, calla lilies, lilies, and orchids.

When the bandleader announced the arrival of the bride and groom, all guests stood up, clapping and singing the "*Mobarak Baad*" song with the lead singer. Roxana and Afshin stopped at each guest table and shook hands or hugged their guests.

Susan, Roxana's American friend, was seated at the table with Lili's family. Her husband was holding their baby.

"Let me look at my namesake," Roxana said, admiring the baby. "She is beautiful."

Susan took the baby back and said, "Hopefully you'll have one like her pretty soon."

"Maybe after the war."

Lili gave a lengthy hug to Roxana, then shook Afshin's hand and said, "Congratulations! You'll never know whom you've married."

Afshin seemed puzzled. Narges and Yahya gave Lili a parental look. They congratulated the couple, and as Roxana pulled Afshin's hand to greet other guests, she heard Yahya admonishing Lili. "You couldn't hold your tongue?"

Roxana had never seen so many happy faces in one place before. She felt elated herself, but she couldn't ignore Lili's comment. What terrible thing was Lili seeing in Afshin that she couldn't see?

People were singing, dancing, and having a good time. At one point, she asked her uncle whether she should expect a visit by the

Komiteh members. Uncle Parviz pointed to an unshaven man who was enjoying his meal and said, "You see him. He's from the *Komiteh.* Don't worry. No one is gonna mess up my favorite niece's wedding."

"But people are drinking alcohol."

"I said, don't worry. He and I have come to some kind of agreement."

Afshin was not much of a dancer, but Roxana danced to every song and with everyone who asked her. The wedding photographer followed her like he was following a movie star.

The dance with her father was very emotional for Roxana because he was tearful and quiet the entire time. *Is he also seeing in Afshin what Lili is seeing?*

Toward the end of the party, Nina gathered some guests around the bride and groom and taught them how to do a group Armenian dance.

* * *

When the bride and groom left in their white limousine decorated with red roses, the guests followed them in their cars playing some chords of a Persian wedding song on the horns of their cars. They drove more than a mile on Vali-Asr Avenue, passing a few *Komiteh* headquarters before they reached Tehran's Sheraton Hotel. Roxana had decided to stay at the Sheraton for one night before leaving for their honeymoon.

"You see, I told you not to worry about anything," Afshin said as soon as they arrived at the hotel's reception desk. "Saddam didn't bomb Tehran and the *Komiteh* didn't raid our wedding party. They even ignored the loud sounds of the car horns."

Roxana smiled.

Chapter 45

During one of the dark nights of Saddam's bombing while reading *The Stranger,* Roxana felt like Albert Camus's character Meursault. He was in prison, yet he still felt like "a free man." He had a sudden urge of being "on a beach and to walk down to the water."

She had not been to the Caspian Sea for more than a decade. She craved to walk on the shores. She asked Afshin to take her to Ramsar, her favorite beach, for their honeymoon.

"The water is cold in March. I've heard they have a curtain separating men and women," he said.

"I don't want to swim. I only want to sit by the water and watch the waves."

The government had relaxed its rules on checking the marital status or the family connection of men and women in two areas of activities, climbing mountains and skiing. They could not find enough climbers or ski experts to form a squad, but they could manage the beaches. Had the technology allowed them, they would've probably erected walls on the mountains, the ski slopes, and the sea, Roxana thought.

Ramsar, the most famous resort of the Caspian Sea, sat on the foothills of the Alborz Mountains. The green hills and the palm and orange trees sitting on beds of flowers made it the most charming beach town in Iran.

One of Afshin's rich uncles offered his villa in Ramsar to the newlyweds for their honeymoon. "It is my wedding gift to you," he said. Afshin was so thrilled that he accepted the offer instantly without waiting for Roxana's approval.

Roxana had not anticipated spending her honeymoon in a small room with a small, squeaky bed and an uncomfortable mattress, but she didn't complain. She had come to see the Caspian Sea.

When she walked to the beach and saw the turquoise water of the sea, she felt she was visiting a friend she hadn't seen for a long time. She breathed the air and inhaled the smell of the Caspian Sea, a smell that was different from the beaches of Ocean City or Malibu. This was like a familiar perfume of an old friend.

Despite the golden rays of the sun shining on the water, it was drizzling. She enjoyed the gentle drop of the rain on her face. She felt like a prisoner who had just gotten released. She was free to watch the waves of the infinite Caspian Sea, the beautiful sea birds, and the shadow of the Alborz Mountains all at once.

She felt so serene that she forgot all about Afshin. When she turned to her right, she saw him talking to a local—an old peasant. She walked toward them. Afshin was facing the man; he could not see her approaching. She heard him say to the man, "No one should force my wife to do anything against her will."

"But this is a Moslem country. We are at war," the man said. "At least put a scarf over her head."

Roxana killed an *Ah.* She thought she had left the war and the *hejab* controversy behind. She couldn't pretend she hadn't heard the man. Someone had reopened the old wound in her heart. She sighed and looked at the waves, the mountains, and the sea birds.

As she walked away from the beach, she recalled the good memories of several trips that she had had in Ramsar.

Tehran University used to arrange summer camps for its female students every year. The first camp Roxana and Lili attended was in Ramsar. She edited the camp's daily paper, wrote several plays, and arranged entertainment for three hundred rambunctious female college students. She was responsible for inviting Googoosh and Zia, two of Iran's famous entertainers, to come and perform for the students. Everyone enjoyed her interview with Googoosh published in the camp's newspaper. It was the first time the famous teenage entertainer had talked about her childhood and her difficult relationship with her disciplinarian stage father. No professional journalist had ever been able to get those heartfelt stories from Googoosh.

"How did you get her to open up to you like that?" Lili once asked Roxana.

"I told her that I had sensed sadness behind every smile she flashed on the stage."

For her activities, Roxana was voted Miss Camp, *Dokhtar-e-urdu*, that year. Dr. Parham, the president of Tehran University, handed her a medal, a bouquet of flowers, and a six-month award to study at Tel Aviv University.

"Those were the happy days!"

On the second day of her honeymoon, Roxana was awakened by a loud conversation of several people. The noise came from the first floor. Afshin had left the bed already. She took a quick shower. When she came out, Afshin was waiting for her. "Did you just put makeup on?" he asked.

"No, I just took a shower."

"You look so beautiful."

"Thanks, but who are the noisy people downstairs?"

"The weather has been so warm and nice that my uncle and his family decided to join us here."

"I thought he said we could have their villa for one week."

"I know, but they're here. It's their villa. I haven't seen them for a long time. My two cousins both got married when I was in *Amrika*. This is a good opportunity for me to get to know their husbands."

"On our honeymoon?"

"I didn't know about their plan. Anyway, they have prepared a lavish breakfast and are waiting for us."

Despite the disturbing surprise, she decided to join Afshin's relatives.

Six adults and four children ages two to ten were waiting for her in the dining room. Afshin's maternal aunt gave Roxana a quick hug and went to the kitchen to serve the breakfast. After breakfast Afshin walked to the garden to chat with his male relatives.

Roxana was left alone with Afshin's two female cousins. She had heard from Afshin's mother that at some point the younger cousin, who was Roxana's age, was a candidate to be Afshin's wife, but both families decided against the marriage later because the cousin was older than Afshin.

She greeted Afshin's cousins warmly. The cousins first talked about the wedding—how they had enjoyed it and how much they needed to have a fun night to forget the war.

She had heard similar comments on her wedding night, so she repeated her usual phrase, "The credit should go to my mother and my uncle."

Afshin's cousins then talked about their shopping in Europe for two hours. Roxana learned that the two sisters had never gone to college, and they were both married to two wealthy men.

She played with children for so long that she got Afshin's attention. "You're like me; you love children too," he said.

"I'm crazy about kids. I have one godchild, Nina's younger son. After the fall of Saigon, I was about to adopt one of those South Vietnamese orphans, but my friends reminded me that I couldn't study while raising a baby."

Despite her true affection for children, Roxana didn't appreciate their boisterous behavior at night. She had not planned to spend time with Afshin's relatives either. This was supposed to be her honeymoon!

The next morning she asked Afshin to take her back home. He tried to convince her that she would get used to the noise and could sleep better at night.

"It's too crowded here. I can't make love with so many people next door."

"I love these people. What am I gonna tell them if we leave after two days?"

"I love my family too, but I didn't bring them on our honeymoon."

She took one last stroll by the seashore before her departure. Afshin decided to spend the last few hours chatting with his relatives. She looked at the scenic picture in front of her once more. She promised herself to return to Ramsar in the near future. She didn't know that she would never see the Caspian Sea again.

Chapter 46

Puri was surprised to see the newlyweds back from their honeymoon so soon. "Was the weather bad?" she asked.

"No, Afshin's uncle and his family decided to join us yesterday," Roxana responded casually out of the presence of Afshin.

"On the second day of your honeymoon? This was the honeymoon he had promised?"

"He couldn't do anything. His uncle decided to use their villa."

"I cannot believe it. There are so many empty hotels in Ramsar thanks to the revolution and the war. Couldn't he find a hotel?"

"I wanted to come back."

Roxana appreciated the fact that her mother didn't make any further comment.

That afternoon she received a call from the wedding photographer that the pictures were ready. Puri asked Syrus to accompany his sister to the photo shop. She wanted him to order some wedding pictures for their family album.

The photographer had placed the photos in a wedding album in the order they had been taken, beginning with the *Aghd* ceremony. He had also enlarged four of the photos and framed them.

The photos were incredible. The photographer had captured the best moments of *Aghd*—the dances, cutting the cake, and the happy faces that one could only find at a wedding.

Afshin had told Roxana that he would pay for the photos. He picked up the albums and the framed pictures. "How much do we owe you?" he asked the photographer.

"With my discount for the Ramsy family, who have been our customers for many years, the total will be thirty-five hundred tomans."

"That's too much," Afshin said as he put the albums and the framed pictures on the counter.

"That's only $500. What are you doing?" Roxana whispered in his ear.

"We'll take only a few. He either has to throw the rest of them out, or he's gonna have to reduce his price."

"I want all of those pictures. Suppose he doesn't agree. How are we going to create those moments again?"

Syrus, who was watching Roxana's pleading with Afshin, blurted out, "I'll pay—my wedding gift to you."

"No," Roxana said sharply. "You've already given us a stereo system."

When his young brother-in-law stepped in to pay for the photos, Afshin reluctantly paid the thirty-five hundred tomans.

Despite the fact that she had stocked up Roxana's kitchen cabinets and refrigerator with a month's supply of food, Puri still insisted the newlyweds have dinner with them every night until they got settled.

Afshin's behavior at the photo shop preoccupied Roxana for some time. She couldn't understand his stinginess. Her parents had already spent millions of tomans on the wedding, furniture, and electric appliances for their rented house and other wedding gifts. The two-day honeymoon did not cost Afshin a penny. Why was he debating to pay for the wedding pictures?

Afshin came to his new home with only one suitcase carrying his clothes. His parents' gift to the newlyweds was one small engraved plate to be hung on the wall. His mother also gave Roxana a choker that she couldn't use. She didn't like it because it was tight.

As Roxana was trying to forget the photo shop incident, other daily occurrences all began to point to one thing. Afshin had problems spending money, period. A few days after their return to Tehran, like other Tehranians, Roxana was busy rushing to shops to buy gifts for everyone for *Noruz,* the Persian New Year.

"You're spending a lot of your money on gifts," Afshin complained. "In my family, we don't exchange gifts for *Noruz.*"

"How's that possible? In my family we give gifts to anyone we know."

Noruz parties created another problem for Roxana. Afshin wanted to visit all of his relatives. He took her with him to show her off like a trophy he had won, but he would soon leave her with his female relatives and join the male guests and chat with them for hours. She had nothing in common with those female relatives, yet she was going along with what they were doing. For example, if they were fixing food in the kitchen, she would help out. If they set the table or washed the dishes, she would volunteer. She had become very popular among Afshin's relatives. He kept hearing their compliments. "Not only is she beautiful, she has a great personality," one relative once said. "You're a lucky man. Your wife speaks softly, has a cool temperament, and has a smiley face."

Afshin took these compliments proudly, as if he had something to do with Roxana's personality.

After several days of visiting Afshin relatives, she got tired. "I have seen and talked to every one of your relatives at least four times now," she said. "If you have more parties, please go without me."

"What am I gonna tell them about my missing wife?"

"I don't know. I don't have that much time. Do you know that I haven't even had a chance to see my uncle Parviz and thank him for all he did for our wedding, or for his generous gift of an expensive Persian carpet?"

"Uncles always do things like that. Besides, your parents have given us three carpets already. We didn't need a fourth one."

"One of your uncles is a famous carpet dealer in Tehran. Did he give you any carpet?"

"My uncle Vahid gave us the use of his villa for our honeymoon."

"Do you honestly consider that as a gift after he interrupted our honeymoon?"

"You're not gonna let me forget that, are you?"

"I'm sorry. We were comparing uncles. I will never mention our honeymoon again."

Roxana was in denial that she had marital problems. In her mind, she had concluded that Afshin's behavior was due to his upbringing, which was different from hers. His family had different traditions. So she decided to forget about all the unpleasant surprises she had endured during her short married life. However, whenever she resolved one problem, another one surfaced. She was shocked when Afshin suggested that they should start using the bus for transportation. "Taxi fares are very expensive for the two of us," he said.

"The last time I took a bus in Tehran was in 1963. I've been either driving or taking a cab since."

Roxana reluctantly agreed to the bus ride, which meant taking four buses per day. She brought to Afshin's attention that men were staring at her.

"You're the only woman without *hejab.* You also have this European face, which makes them think you're a foreigner," he explained.

After a week of bus rides, Afshin realized that he couldn't tolerate dozens of men staring at his wife, so he told Roxana that she could take her usual routine taxi, but he continued riding the bus himself. So every day Roxana went to work alone and returned home alone. She had to wait for an hour for Afshin to show up.

Afshin's money issues surfaced once again when she went grocery shopping in Zafar's supermarket. He preferred shopping in *Amirieh.* "Everything is ten times cheaper than here," he said.

"That's deep downtown Tehran, a two-hour trip by bus. Everything will be spoiled by the time you come home."

"You have a lot to learn."

Afshin reluctantly followed his wife to the Zafar grocery store. Every item she picked up he reminded her that he could buy it cheaper downtown.

Roxana noticed that many shelves were empty in the supermarket. There was not even one single box of American cereals, chocolates, or cookies. The economic sanctions and the war had changed the face of the Zafar supermarket.

After she picked up her needed items, Afshin pushed the shopping cart to the cashier, then left the line and waited near the exit door. She paid for the groceries.

He repeated the same action every time Roxana shopped. He shopped in downtown Tehran every two weeks when he visited her family, but he only purchased fruits and vegetables.

After a month of having dinner at her parents' home, Roxana felt guilty and started cooking at home. Afshin didn't like European, American, or Asian food, so she had to cook Persian food that would take a lot of preparation and time to cook. The man who had promised that he would help her with household chores sat in front of the TV, night after night, and listened to the lectures by different clergies, while Roxana cooked, cleaned, washed the dishes, and mopped the kitchen floor.

One evening, Roxana was exhausted. She had had a tough day at one of *Bonyad's* companies, so she didn't feel like cooking. "I'd like to go to a restaurant tonight," she suggested. "Since you've started taking your lunch to work, we haven't been to any restaurant together for a long time."

"Restaurants are very expensive in this neighborhood."

"Are you suggesting we should go downtown to eat?"

"You wanted to live in a rich neighborhood. Everything is expensive here."

"I've spent most of my life in this area. Did you expect me to live in *Amirieh*, where every woman wears black *chador*?"

Afshin didn't respond. Roxana went to the kitchen, and started peeling some eggplants, but she was so angry that it looked as if she was stabbing the vegetables. After she finished the peeling, the skins she threw away weighed more than what was left to cook. She remembered a movie directed by Lina Werthmueler—a Dutch director. The female character was married to an Iranian man. She also attacked the vegetables when she peeled them. She tried to remember the ending of that movie, but she couldn't.

After two hours of labor in the kitchen, she prepared a delicious *khoresht-e-gheimeh* with rice. She set the table for one. She had no appetite or any desire to dine with Afshin.

When Afshin started eating, she positioned herself to face him. She said calmly, "Since there's no credit card in Iran, I believe we should designate a box and put money in it, and also write down our expenses in a small notebook. At the end of the month, we can look at it and see whether we are spending too much money. If we are, then we can cut our expenses."

Roxana left the kitchen without waiting for a response.

"Where are you going?"

"To sleep. I have a difficult day tomorrow."

She went to bed feeling hurt. This was not the marriage she had pictured. She was a newlywed, expecting love and affection from her husband. But he was too busy acting like an accountant. She pressed her face on the pillow and remembered what her married American friends used to say: "You have to work on your marriage."

Chapter 47

She had a meeting to attend at the Ministry of Budget and Planning in downtown Tehran. Like the National Iranian Oil Company (NIOC), this ministry was also considered as one of the most significant government entities.

She was supposed to meet with one of the deputy ministers. It was raining, so she was happy that her long, loose raincoat covered all of her body. She fastened her flimsy beige scarf around her neck and felt she had enough *hejab* to enter the government building. She was stopped at the gate by a young security guard. "You can't come in. You don't have proper *hejab*," he said.

A young woman cloaked in *Maghnaeh* and black *chador* said, "You're also wearing makeup."

Roxana took a tissue out of her briefcase and rubbed against her cheek. She showed the tissue to the woman and said, "See, there is no makeup. When I walk fast, I get flushed."

The woman took the tissue from Roxana and rubbed it hard against both her cheeks. She saw no trace of any makeup on the tissue. She told the guard, "She doesn't have any makeup on."

"She still can't go inside with that little scarf."

Roxana gave the guard her business card and the name of the deputy she was supposed to meet. "Please let the deputy know I'm here."

The guard started dialing the deputy's number while Roxana sat in a chair feeling like she was in a foreign country. *What happened to the kind people who used to live in this land?*

"*Khanoom,* Dr. Ramsy," a man called out. She stood up and turned in the direction of the voice. The man had come to take her to the deputy.

The deputy was a young man in his thirties. He wore a very chic suit but without a tie. He looked freshly shaved. Unlike many government authorities Roxana had met, the deputy looked at her when he talked. "I apologize for the delay at the gate. Some of our young revolutionary men and women go overboard sometimes," he said as he pulled up a chair for her.

"It's okay," Roxana said.

After listening to the minister's explanation about their legal issues, she realized that the ministry's legal problems were similar to those she had handled for several of *Bonyad's* companies before. The only difference was the price tag attached to each contract. All of the ministry's contracts with foreign companies were multimillion dollars.

After reviewing many files, she went through her routine, categorizing the contracts by their dispute settlement clauses and putting them in separate piles.

The deputy watched Roxana's action as if he were watching a sorcerer. "How could you do this so fast?" he asked.

"I've done this for many *Bonyad*-controlled companies."

"Can you come and work for us?" The deputy smiled.

"No, thanks."

"You know I have more power than the *Bonyad's* chief. I can ask them to transfer you here."

"I'll draft some sample letters for you to send to your foreign companies, but I feel more comfortable working at my office."

The deputy thanked Roxana again. "I'll wait for those sample letters."

When Roxana returned to her office, two pleasant surprises were waiting for her. A note from Afshin indicated that he had to travel to Ahwaz to check on some of the company's heavy equipment. After what had happened the night before, she was not really in a mood to talk to him.

The second surprise was Lili's unexpected visit.

"I haven't seen you since *Noruz* holidays," she said. "Where is *Agha*?"

"Don't call him that," Roxana admonished her. "He's not my master."

"Doesn't every Iranian man become a master when he gets married?"

"That's not gonna happen in my home."

Lili's visit made Roxana feel that her marriage had not trapped her like a prisoner. She still had her friends, her books, and Adamo's music. She had already decided to ignore Afshin's stinginess. She was making so much money that she didn't need any of his. As for household chores, she remembered she had to do all of that in New York for herself, so she decided to consider Afshin as a lazy roommate.

"So how is your sex life?" Lili asked excitedly.

"You're not supposed to ask that question. We are Persians, remember?"

"I'm half British, so I can ask that."

"Haven't you heard the British motto, 'Don't talk to us about sex, we're British'?"

"Forget about my Britishness or your Persianness. How's your sex life?"

"Our sex life is fine. It's Afshin's stinginess and laziness that bother me."

After hearing different stories about Afshin's behavior, Lili was angry. "What happened to all his promises?"

"I honestly don't know. He has changed so much after the marriage."

"I think every Iranian woman is a princess in her father's home until she gets married. Then she has to serve a king."

Roxana changed the subject and talked about her experience at the Ministry of Budget and Planning.

"Why are you helping them when their security guards humiliate you?"

"Lili, I'm like a surgeon. If I see someone bleeding, I have to stop it. If I see him dying, I have to operate on him. I can't question his political views or his opinion of me."

"A true Dr. Zhivago!"

Chapter 48

"You feel nauseated and bloated because you're pregnant," the doctor said.

"That's impossible, Doctor!" Roxana said, moving nervously in her chair. "I got off the pill last month because it made me feel queasy and drowsy in the morning, but I was careful."

Roxana's feet were nailed to the ground. She couldn't move. She turned her head toward the window and gazed into the sky. She didn't want the doctor to see her teary eyes.

"If the baby's going to create a problem, maybe you should talk to your gynecologist for—"

"I'm not gonna have an abortion," she interrupted, "but I don't know whether I have the right to bring a baby into this world when we have this awful war going on."

She left the doctor's office. It was five o'clock already. She took a cab and went home. Afshin had a meeting at *Bonyad*; she expected him to come home late.

She went to the kitchen and started chopping chives, parsley, and onions to make *ghormeh sabzi*, one of Afshin's favorite *khorosht* over rice.

Her feeling about the baby was ambivalent. On the one hand, she always loved the idea of having a child. On the other hand, she didn't know how to raise a baby under Saddam's bombs. And what about all the problems she had with Afshin? As she cooked the dinner, she convinced herself that fatherhood would make him a more responsible person and maybe even a more attentive husband.

She greeted him warmly when he came home. She served him his meal more like a waitress in a restaurant. She needed to have him in a good mood before breaking the news. As usual, after the dinner, he went to the living room to watch TV.

She washed the dishes quickly and came back to the living room. She felt a swarm of butterflies in her stomach. She sat next to Afshin, took his hands, and said, "I have something to tell you—"

He interrupted her, raised both of her hands, and looked at her fingers. "Your fingernails look so grayish. You don't wash your hands anymore?"

"The dishwashing liquid doesn't clean them, so after I wash the dishes, I have to brush underneath my fingernails for a few minutes every night. I didn't have time tonight because—"

"Look how white and clean my fingernails are." He extended his hands to show her his clean fingernails.

Roxana looked at his fingernails and said with a bit of humor, "Listen, my dear. If you had washed dishes every day, your fingernails would have gotten dirty too."

He pushed Roxana's hands away, turned back to watching TV, and said in an angry voice, "This is it. If you want to nag, end this marriage now. I can't put up with this nonsense anymore."

She was speechless. She felt as if her heart had stopped for a second. She got out of her chair, went to the kitchen, and started brushing her fingernails, letting the water run in the sink. A shrill cry inside her was desperately trying to get out. She took a deep breath and suppressed the scream in her throat. She sat at the kitchen table, covered her face with both hands, and let her tears wash away the humiliation she had felt. She saw images in her head, images of a beautiful woman in a white satin wedding gown who was digging in the dirt. The woman dug a hole the size of her body and crawled inside. She needed to hide. All that could be seen of her now was her hands with long fingernails. A man shoved dirt into the hole, but he could not cover the woman's hands. The hands were extended toward the sky as if they were praying.

She saw Lili dressed in black standing on top of the grave delivering a eulogy.

"This woman was murdered by her husband three months after her wedding. No one called the police. There was no arrest and no trial because the husband didn't use a knife or a gun. He only used words, poisonous words!"

She went to bed wondering how many millions of women were murdered every night by their husbands' words—*a silent murder. That would make a good title for a novel*, she thought.

It was painful for her to admit that her father was right. Had she demanded a multimillion-toman *Mehrieh,* Afshin wouldn't have dared to talk about divorce. Had she not been pregnant, she would be the one seeking divorce. The thought of fighting custody in an Islamic court that always favored the father sent a chill to her spine.

She put her arms around her stomach as if she was hugging the baby. "Forgive me, sweet baby, for choosing a wrong father for you."

* * *

June 1981 was an eventful month not only for Roxana, but also for the country as a whole. She witnessed how Tehranians applauded Israel when, on June 7, 1981, it attacked the Osirak nuclear facility near Baghdad. People were celebrating in the privacy of their homes and saying, "Thank you, Israel," as if Israel could hear them.

Roxana was surprised when she read the June 19, 1981, UN resolution. The Security Council, which had kept quiet about Saddam's war for ten months, condemned Israel for its attack against Iraq. The resolution had specifically recognized that Iraq had an "inalienable sovereign right . . . to establish programs for technological and nuclear development to develop their economy and industry for peaceful purposes."

Apparently Saddam's brutal war against Iran did not create any conflict with his "peaceful purposes." The world realized how peaceful Saddam was when he used chemical weapons against Iran and the Kurds.

On June 28, 1981, Roxana was cooking in the kitchen when Afshin shouted, "Come quick and watch TV."

She rushed to the living room, assuming that Saddam had destroyed another city in Khuzistan. "What now?"

"Look, *Mujahedin* bombed the headquarters of the Islamic Republic Party and killed seventy people, including Ayatollah Beheshti and the prime minister."

She couldn't watch the footage of the devastating act for more than a few minutes. She turned away from the TV and asked Afshin, "Why?"

"This is *Mujahedin*'s retaliation."

"Retaliation for what?"

"President Bani Sadr's impeachment and the fact that the regime had executed a lot of their members. Khomeini dismissed them as 'Marxist' and *Monafegh* (hypocrite) and *Kafar* (nonbeliever) right from the beginning of the revolution."

For two days, Roxana kept hearing rumors about an inevitable coup d'etat.

The government's response to the bombing was hundreds of new arrests and dozens of executions.

After a three-day official mourning for the victims of the *Mujahedin*'s bombing, the government offices and private companies opened again.

When she entered her office building, Roxana saw Kazem in the security room. She was so thrilled to see him alive that she was about to give him a hug. "Welcome back! I'm so glad to see you again," she said.

Kazem smiled. He walked toward Roxana with a limp in his right leg. "I'm happy to be back."

While hearing Kazem's description of the war and his injury, Roxana felt like a coward. She went back to her office. She noticed two letters placed on top of her desk calendar. One was the updated circular advising female employees to wear the *hejab*. She discarded the letter as she always had in the past few months. The second letter was addressed to her. It was from one of *Bonyad's* high-ranking officials, thanking her for the legal services she had provided to the company and informing her that her services were no longer needed.

She felt numb and couldn't believe the words she had read. She was struggling to sort out the conflicting thoughts in her head when Afshin walked in. "You read your letter?" he asked. "I told you that if you solve all their problems, they wouldn't need you anymore."

"Why are you so angry? I'll find another job."

"Look, I can understand why they fired me—"

"They fired you too?"

"Yes. I don't have a job because all their machinery and equipment in the south have been either destroyed or damaged by Iraqi bombs. But you, how dare they?"

Afshin left the office. As part of his last office duties, he was supposed to travel to Ahvaz and take an inventory of the company's damaged vehicles.

Roxana started packing her stuff and organizing the files she had worked on. She was surprised when she opened the last file. It contained only a one-page letter to Mr. Kasravi informing him that as a result of the hostage agreement, a litigation office was about to be established to handle the claims of the American companies. The letter had encouraged all the directors of the *Bonyad*-controlled companies to provide the lists of their American claimants to Mr. Nasser Hedayat.

She took Mr. Hedayat's address, thinking that the new litigation office could have used someone with her expertise.

As she was cleaning up her desk, she heard her mourning dove's cooing. *Does the bird know I'm fired?*

Chapter 49

She couldn't figure out why Afshin was so kind that evening. Was it because he felt the firing of his wife was unjustified, or was it because he was leaving for Ahvaz the next day? Ahvaz, a city near the Iraqi border, was heavily bombed on a daily basis. Maybe he was not sure that he would come back alive.

He took Roxana to a nice restaurant a few blocks away from their home.

The restaurant owner had lived in California for many years. Inside, there were dozens of large pictures of Hollywood stars, including sexy pictures of Marilyn Monroe, Rita Hayworth, and Shirley MacLaine. Roxana was surprised that the neighborhood *Komiteh* had not raided the place or torn up the female pictures.

As the two were waiting in line to be seated, she felt something was pulling her skirt. She looked down and saw a beautiful little girl wearing a scarf trying to get her attention. She squatted. "Hi. What's your name?"

"Neda."

"How old are you?"

"Five years old. I came to say you're very pretty," the little girl said, and smiled shyly.

Roxana fought her tears. She hugged the girl and asked her where her parents were. She pointed to a woman who was wearing a light-colored, flower-patterned *chador*.

"Did you have to frighten that little girl?" Afshin asked. "And why are you so emotional these days?"

"Even the most religious Moslems don't cover their daughters' hair until they are seven. I'm crying because she could be mine! I'm pregnant," she blurted out.

There was a long pause. "The baby might be a boy," Afshin finally said. "Then you don't have to worry about the veil."

Roxana realized that Afshin was not that happy about the pregnancy, but she appreciated the fact that he didn't start a new fight. *He's nice because I lost my job.*

After they left the restaurant, they took a stroll on a quiet street leading to their home. Afshin was holding her hand. "Sometimes I wonder whether I know you or not," he said. "This morning you got fired. You stood there and took the news like a man. But this afternoon, a little girl in a scarf makes you fall apart."

"Her scarf is more important than my job because it affects every woman—"

She was interrupted by a thunderous chant of *Marg bar behejab* (death to women with no veil), coming from a passing tour bus. The black *chador*-cloaked women had their arms extended out of the windows chanting with their fists closed in a threatening manner. She looked at Afshin with a bitter smile. "That's why the little girl's scarf mattered."

* * *

Puri started dancing and thanking God all at the same time when she heard the news about the baby. She didn't look surprised when she heard about her daughter being fired. "That's their way of punishing you for not wearing *hejab*," she said. "But no bad news is going to ruin my happiness. I'm gonna be a grandma!"

Roxana called Lili and told her about the baby, losing her job, and Afshin's trip. "I'd like to get away for a few days," she said. "I'm going to call Nina to find out about her schedule. Would you come to Shiraz with me if she's free?"

"Of course," Lili said. "I miss her too."

Chapter 50

Nina was thrilled when she saw her friends in Shiraz. She was elated about Roxana's pregnancy. She talked about her busy surgery schedule. "I'm a knee surgeon, but due to the shortage of doctors and surgeons, I've done every kind of operation you can imagine."

"How successful are you?" Lili asked.

"Thank God, I haven't killed anyone yet," Nina said with a laugh. "My only problem was the scarf. I've gotten used to it now. I consider myself an engineer who has to use a hard hat every day."

When Roxana and Lili heard about Nina's work at the refugee camps, they asked her if they could do some volunteer work.

"Of course you can," she said. "We welcome any kind of help. I'll take you to our medical camp where the soldiers are recovering. We need volunteers to help them with their exercises. Sometimes they just need to have some visitors talking with them."

"How come they are not in the hospital?" Lili asked.

"We don't have enough rooms or beds in our hospital for the injured soldiers who need physical therapy."

Roxana told her friends about Kazam coming back from the war with a limp and about how cowardly she felt when she talked to him.

"First of all, your country doesn't draft women, so you're not avoiding your military service," Nina said. "Second, we're trying to do our best. If I volunteer and go to the battlefield, I'll get killed. But as a doctor, at least I'm helping our wounded soldiers."

"Nina's right. You helped your country with its international litigations. You've saved us millions of dollars," Lili added.

"Thanks for making me feel better, but I still feel Kazem's the hero, and I've only acted as a lawyer."

"Hey, listen, you've got to concentrate on that baby you're carrying now, not the war," Nina said. "Once you're a mother, you'll see that your kid becomes your number-one priority."

That evening after dinner, Roxana went to the kitchen to help Nina wash the dishes. Lili was chatting with Bijan in the living room while Nina's sons were playing with their games. This was the best opportunity for Roxana to talk to Nina about Afshin and his behavior out of the presence of Lili and others.

"I'm sorry to hear that," Nina said after hearing Roxana's marital problems. "The only thing I can think of is his age. He's still acting like mama's boy."

"So I was right when I ignored his proposal for all those months."

"Where does the stinginess come from?"

"His family was poor when he was growing up, but after he left for the United States, his father's business took off, and the family became rich. I think he still remembers the time they struggled financially."

"Every couple goes through a period of adjustment during the first year of marriage. Let's hope Afshin becomes more responsible when he's a father."

The next day, Nina drove her friends to the refugee camps. Roxana was surprised when she saw the size of the camps. "Where are the wounded soldiers?" she asked.

"They're in our medical camp. These camps over here house thousands of the Shiite Iraqis. Saddam has expelled them because he considers them Iranians."

"But these are Iraqis whose Iranian ancestors had lived in Iraq for generations."

"So much for your international law. Where is the United Nations' condemnation of Saddam's actions?" Lili asked Roxana.

"The United Nations is an instrument of the government members. I agree with Solzhenitsyn when he suggests that it should be called 'United Governments Organization' because it protects the rights of the governments, whether they are democratic or authoritarian."

Nina took her friends to the medical camp and introduced them to two soldiers. She had operated on their knees. She taught Roxana and Lili how to help them with their physical therapy.

After a long day of volunteer work, Roxana and Lili were ready to go home, but Nina wanted them to visit one last tent. "We have a dozen soldiers in this medical tent who are depressed and nonfunctional. We have a psychiatrist who visits them once a week and prescribes medication for them, but nothing seems to help."

When Roxana looked at the faces of those soldiers and their hospital robes, she felt for a moment that she was watching an Iranian film version of *One Flew over the Cuckoo's Nest.* She had never seen so many depressed faces in one place. She remembered how Jack Nicholson's character took the mental patients on a boat trip, which made them jovial. It was impossible for Roxana and her friends to duplicate the act. Wishing for a boat and a river in the middle of a desert was something that only a genie could fulfill. "Nina, let's ask them what they like to do to cheer them up," Roxana suggested.

"That is a very risky question. We are not allowed to give them even a deck of cards to play."

"Maybe there is a game other than cards they like to play," Lili said.

Nina walked to the middle of the large tent and said, "Gentlemen, my friends would like to know whether there is a game you like to play, just for fun."

Some men mumbled, some ignored Nina, but one raised his hand and said, "Could you please play for us some of Googoosh's songs?"

"We are only allowed to play revolutionary songs for you."

"We're sick and tired of the revolutionary songs," one of the soldiers said.

"Is the camp security guard coming to this tent?" Roxana asked Nina.

"No, from now until morning, the night duty nurses check on patients in this particular tent."

"Okay, then, we can sing some Googoosh songs."

"But Googoosh songs are all sad. Maybe we can perform the Andrews Sisters' 'Boogie song,'" Lili said.

"First, let's see if the Googoosh songs can cheer them up," Nina said.

The three friends consulted with each other to see whether they could find a happy Googoosh song, but they failed. Even the songs that were composed specifically for Persian dancing had sad lyrics. So each sang a Googoosh song she knew.

The songs made the soldiers more depressed. Some were crying, including the one who had requested the Googoosh song. The others just stared at them with a blank expression.

"I told you, Googoosh songs are sad," Lili said. "Let's do the Andrews Sisters' song."

The trio took their scarves off, folded them into a triangle shape and wrapped them around their heads, making a bow on the top. They looked like Lucile Ball when she cleaned her house. Nina, with her white doctor's uniform and white pants, looked funnier than Roxana and Lili, who both wore a long raincoat-like *hejab*.

Before performing, Nina informed the soldiers that the Andrew Sisters' famous song was popular in the forties with soldiers who fought in Europe.

Pretending to be the Andrews Sisters, the three started singing:

"He was the top man at his craft . . .

He's the boogie woogie bugle boy . . ."

As the song was near the end, the soldiers were clapping, laughing, and trying to repeat the 'boogie woogie bugle boy' line.

The singing and the laughter stopped when there was an earthquake-like sound followed by the roar of the Iraqi Russian MiGs in the sky. Roxana heard the sound of an explosion followed by sirens wailing.

"Hurry up!" Nina said in a frightened voice. "Turn your scarves around. I've got to go home to my kids. The MiGs are gonna scare Yerem again."

The three friends fixed their scarves quickly and ran out of the tent.

There was chaos in the camp. The refugees were running away, and the Revolutionary Guards were chasing them and ordering them to go back to their tents.

The fire and smoke had covered the sky near the hospital area.

"Oh my God. They must have hit the hospital." Nina muttered. She asked one of the guards whether he knew which area was hit.

"The hospital, sister, the butcher of Baghdad doesn't even have mercy on sick people."

"Oh my God, my patients!"

Nina ran back to the medical tent, found a telephone, and called home to talk to Yerem while Roxana and Nina were anxiously watching her. They could tell that she was talking to her mother-in-law. After a few seconds, Nina shrieked, "Noooo." She fell to the ground, dropping the telephone receiver. Lili ran to her and helped her sit in a chair.

Roxana got the mother-in-law back on the phone while she trembled every time Nina screamed.

She learned that Yerem had got sick in the early evening, with a high fever. Bijan, who couldn't find Nina, had taken Yerem to the hospital.

Roxana felt her heart was jumping out of her chest. She whispered the information to Lili. The two of them held Nina's trembling body—they were all shaken.

A distraught nurse covered in ash came running toward Nina. "Dr. Hakopian, your husband has asked me to tell you—I don't know what to say."

Roxana approached the nurse and asked her about Bijan's message.

"I saw him in the parking lot walking toward his car. He was going to pick up his son, who was just being released from the hospital. A nurse and his child were waiting for him at the emergency entrance, but in a split second the MiGs flew over and dropped several bombs."

Nina screamed, "Nooo . . . Oh my God, nooo . . ."

Roxana ran out of the tent, stopping every military vehicle that passed by and asking the drivers if they could give them a ride to the hospital. The answer was *no*. They were in a hurry, but finally one driver agreed. Roxana went inside the tent and got Nina and Lili.

The hospital building was reduced to concrete rubble and twisted steel. Some vehicles near the building were still burning, their shells smoldering. Thick smoke and ash had covered the hospital and the surrounding areas.

Roxana was the first one who recognized Bijan. His face and his clothes were covered in ash. He was carrying his lifeless child. Yerem's body was mangled—one leg twisted unnaturally, one foot sandaled, the other bare. His clothes were torn and full of ash. There were a few men walking with Bijan, all looking shocked with blank stares.

Roxana asked the driver to stop the vehicle. As soon as Nina got out of the car, she screamed. She ran to Bijan and began hitting him in the face and chest. "You killed my baby; you killed my son." She snatched Yerem from Bijan, sat on the ground, and rocked him gently. She sang an Armenian lullaby and wept. Roxana knew the song. She had put Yerem to sleep many times singing that lullaby. She looked at her motionless five-year-old godson. *My sweet baby, you'll never be scared of airplanes anymore*. She killed a scream inside.

Chapter 51

Another burial and another trip to Behesht-e-Zahra Cemetery that Roxana had not anticipated. She felt that the entire country had turned into a cemetery. Everybody was dying. *Who's going to be next?* She remembered Iraj's funeral. At least he lived to be thirty years old. Why did Yerem have to go so soon and why was the world sitting so indifferently watching Saddam's brutality?

Nina and her family moved back to Tehran despite the plea by the hospital's director that he couldn't lose a surgeon.

"I'm sorry," Nina said. "I've given my martyr. I don't owe anything to this country anymore."

She had stopped talking to Bijan. She held him responsible for the death of their son. She and her older son moved in with Narges. She needed to talk to another mother who had lost her son. She needed to learn how to cope with her tragedy.

Roxana took on the role of a mediator between Nina and Bijan, trying to make them understand each other's point of view. "If you think Bijan was responsible for Yerem's death," she told Nina, "you might as well blame me and Lili. If we hadn't gone to the camp with you, Bijan could reach you on the phone."

"With or without you, I had to spend that day in the medical camp. He should've brought my child to me. I'm a doctor, for God's sake."

"He didn't know about your schedule, but he knew your fellow doctors would take care of Yerem. He had a fever and—"

"Roxana, I know you're trying to save my marriage again because without you this marriage wouldn't have happened. You're a good negotiator, but this time it's not gonna work. This marriage is dead, like my child."

She left Nina feeling brokenhearted. She went directly to her mother. She needed her love and wisdom.

Puri advised her that Nina needed time to heal, that she would not divorce Bijan because the Islamic court would definitely give custody of her older son to his father. "Once she gets over the anger, she will be grateful that she didn't lose Bijan," Puri said.

"By the way, I was so shocked about Nina's child that I forgot to tell you that a gentleman has been calling here a dozen times asking for you."

"A gentleman? Who?"

"His name is Mr. Nasser Hedayat."

Since the tragic night in Shiraz, Roxana had forgotten that she was pregnant, and she had a husband who was in Ahvaz—a favorite target city for Saddam's bombing. She realized that she had to be patient with Afshin. There was a war going on. She had to concentrate on the real enemy, Saddam. She also wondered what would have happened if the Iraqi pilots had bombed the camp. She and her baby would have been killed. What a sad story, "The Death of an Unborn Baby." She remembered Hemingway's short story, "Baby Shoes Never Worn."

* * *

She called Mr. Hedayat, as soon as she arrived at her home.

"I've been waiting for your call for two days," he said. "Could you please come and see me right away?"

"It's a little too late. Can I come tomorrow?"

"Yes, of course, but plan for a whole day. You're hired."

"Without an interview? I don't even know what your office does."

"I've never seen a resume like yours. I've talked to your former boss and some people in *Bonyad*. You have the job as our in-house counsel. We are handling the American litigations at The Hague Tribunal in Holland."

Roxana started calling the directors of some of the *Bonyad* companies she knew to find out whether there was a job opportunity for Afshin. The first three directors said they had no knowledge of anything available, but the fourth person informed her that the

Tehran Bureau of Consumer Affairs was looking for someone with an MBA. Roxana took the address and telephone number. She couldn't help smiling. The bureau was located within walking distance from their home. *He doesn't have to ride a bus anymore.*

After three sleepless nights, Roxana fell asleep as soon as she went to bed. But an hour later she was awakened when she heard a noise in the hallway. Before she had a chance to get out of bed, the bedroom door opened and she heard Afshin's voice.

"Sorry I woke you up."

Roxana turned the light on, ran to Afshin, and gave him a big, long hug.

"I was the one who escaped death. Why are you trembling?"

"What death?"

"As we were driving out of Ahvaz, one of Saddam's scud missiles hit one of our trucks. I was supposed to be driving that truck, but a few minutes before our departure, the maintenance man added another truck and asked me to drive that one."

Roxana began crying. Afshin put his arms around her and kissed her face. "Why are you so emotional?"

She told him about her horrible experience in the refugee camps and about Yerem's tragic death.

"We should be grateful we both escaped death," Afshin said as he held Roxana tight.

He was tired. He had driven more than a day and needed to take a shower. As he was heading for the bathroom, Roxana said, "I've some good news. You and I both have a job."

"What?"

"I'll tell you all about it after you finish your shower."

While she lay in bed and watched the moon through her window, she thought about the events of the past few days. She had survived Saddam's bomb, and Afshin's truck missed his scud missile. Maybe God had saved them because of their baby.

Chapter 52

Roxana was happy to see a taxi stand next to her new office building. However, when she entered the building, she realized that there was still construction work going on. She saw electricians, painters, and other workers running around, but the one room that seemed completed was the security room. The black *chador*-cloaked teenager who was sitting behind a large desk stopped her at the entrance. "You can't see anyone here. You have a see-through scarf."

Roxana didn't wish to talk about her *hejab*. "Please call Mr. Hedayat and tell him that I'm here," she asked as she gave her business card to the security woman.

Roxana was staring at the huge framed picture of Ayatollah Khomeini, when she heard her name.

"Dr. Ramsy. Good morning. Please come with me."

Before she could say anything, the young security woman said, "Mr. Hedayat, I still have to search her."

The woman patted Roxana down to make sure she didn't have any weapons. She then searched through Roxana's briefcase and pocketbook.

"I'm sorry. Since the *Mujahedin's* bombing in June, all government buildings have set this harsh security check," Mr. Hedayat said.

"That's okay."

Mr. Hedayat took Roxana to the third floor and showed her an empty room. "This will be your office. The contractors have promised me that it will be finished by tomorrow. For the time being, both of us have to sit on these large boxes."

"Can they hold the weight of a person?"

"Yes, these boxes all contain American pleadings. The minute Iran signed the Algiers Declaration, the ink had not even dried, they bombarded us with their claims."

"Which one has a deadline?"

"Merrill Lynch's. We have one week to respond to them. The thick file sitting on the big box over there is Merrill Lynch's." Mr. Hedayat pointed to a box near the wall.

"I need two days to respond. If you have a fast typist, it'll be ready before your deadline."

"Two days! Are you kidding me? Do you know how many lawyers have looked at these claims and told me that they didn't have any answer?"

"Don't worry; give me two days."

"Dr. Ramsy, I hate to leave you here, but I have to go back to my office and attend an important meeting. Could you please come and see me there tomorrow morning?"

After Mr. Hedayat left, Roxana checked her new unfurnished office once more. It was smaller than the office she shared with Afshin. It had a large window, but thick branches of an old tree mostly covered it. She picked up the voluminous Merrill Lynch claim and a few loose pages of Iran's counterclaims. She chose a big, sturdy box to sit on, pulled her pad and pen from her briefcase, and began reading. She couldn't help remembering November 4, 1979, when she sat behind her desk in her Wall Street office, gazing at the Hudson River. The huge Merrill Lynch skyscraper always blocked a portion of her view of the river. *I bet the Merrill Lynch attorneys didn't write their briefs sitting on a box.*

It was getting late, so she took the heavy file home to review.

At home, a jubilant Afshin greeted her; he had got the job. "The most exciting part of the job is that I can walk to work."

"I'm so happy for both of us. I got a fascinating job too."

"But why the long face?"

"I have to wear a scarf, a real one."

She fixed hamburgers and salads for dinner. She finished reviewing the Merrill Lynch brief as she ate. Afshin continued eating and watching TV.

After dinner, she searched in her closet and selected a long, loose, black skirt and a large long-sleeved black blouse. She had borrowed the ensemble from Uncle Parviz's wife to wear for Iraj's funeral.

She put on the swinging skirt first. It reached to her ankles. She then tried the large blouse, which covered her hips. She buttoned the blouse and put on the large scarf. It not only covered her long auburn hair, but it also made half of her face disappear. She then put a pair of thick, long, black stockings on. She looked in the mirror and couldn't believe the transformation. *Who the hell are you?*

She remembered some passages in *The Gulag Archipelago,* and Solzhenitsyn's advice to his fellow prisoners. She had to stop the fight. The sooner she would accept the *hejab*, the sooner she could get on with her life. Solzhenitsyn was right, "You will never return to your former world."

* * *

Mr. Hedayat's office looked like a warehouse full of boxes. There were so many folders on his desk that one could hardly see his whole body. He greeted Roxana with a big smile. He looked at her outfit and said, "Thank you." Roxana knew why he was thankful—her ridiculous outfit was very Islamic.

He pulled up a chair for her and moved his own around his desk so that he could sit closer. He handed her two separate documents. "These are the two Algerian Declarations," he said. "One is the General Declaration; the other is the Dispute Settlement that we signed on January 19, 1981. We refer to them collectively as 'The Algiers Declarations.' There is an Iran-US Tribunal presently being established in The Hague, but for the time being, we are responding to the American claims from my office. Our office in Holland doesn't have enough lawyers or staff to handle the enormous litigations we have. Could you please take a look at these two documents and let me know about our strengths or weaknesses. I'll come back in the afternoon to hear your views," he added.

"You don't need to leave. I was lucky because someone had left the Algiers Declarations in the middle of the Merrill Lynch brief. I've read them. In fact, I've written a report analyzing every article for you."

"Boy, you're a godsend gift. So what do you think?"

"On the surface, it looks like a fair document, but if you weigh every legal word and phrase, you'll see that it's a very one-sided document favoring the Americans. I assume that the Iranian negotiating team didn't have a lawyer familiar with the American legal system to object to some of those provisions."

"No, they didn't."

"When the document states 'according to US laws,' and 'based on US court decisions,' you can be sure that the outcome is not going to be favorable to Iran."

"What about when it says, 'according to international law'?"

"There is a little hope there, but the vast body of international law and customary international law was codified when the United Nations had only a few dozen member states. They are for the benefit of the superpowers."

"So we're gonna lose all of these litigations?"

"No. When a contract refers to the Iranian law, even an international arbitration tribunal has to follow. In my report, I have also found some provisions that can be interpreted favorably for us provided that the neutral arbitrators interpret them the way we do."

Roxana submitted several folders to Mr. Hedayat, including the response to Merrill Lynch's claim.

"You finished that? I can't believe it!"

"I didn't have all the facts. The agencies involved should look at it and fill in the gaps."

"Thank you so much. We have hundreds of claims. Which ones would you like to look at, the defense cases, airlines, or communications?"

"The defense cases have to be resolved through political channels, but I can look at your other cases."

Mr. Hedayat gave several heavy folders to Roxana. "These are claims against the Ministry of Communications. Sorry, I have to attend a conference. You can use my office if you want."

"No problem. I only have a request. I have two friends who work here. If you are forming a litigation office, they are perfect for working on frozen Iranian assets. Could you please take a look at their resumes and see whether you can benefit from their expertise."

"Who are they?"

"They both have PhD's from London's School of Economics. Their names are Kayvan Panahi and Lili Cohan."

"I went to the same school. I'll look them up."

Chapter 53

Roxana was delighted when Mr. Hedayat recruited Lili and Kayvan. Apparently he was impressed with their educational background and work experience. It was a dream come true for the three friends to work together. However, they were all still sad and concerned about Nina. She had refused to see or even talk to Bijan for weeks now.

"She cries all the time; she's not getting better," Lili said.

"So being with Narges didn't help?" Roxana asked.

"No. Actually she has got Narges so depressed that now she is crying as much as Nina does. It's like Iraj has died all over again."

"Can you bring Nina to my house for dinner tomorrow night? I have to get them talking again."

"She's not gonna come if Bijan is there."

"She won't know. Tell her I've fixed the baby's nursery. I need her advice."

"Okay. By the way, did you find another job for Afshin?"

"Yes."

"Is this the third or the fourth job you have found for him?"

"This is the fourth one. He left the first three jobs because they were asking him to do various things, and he had no specific position, but now he's an economic advisor to one of the deputies of the Ministry of Budget and Planning—the same deputy I helped with their American litigations."

* * *

The next day Roxana tried to finish her work fast and leave the office early.

She was clearing her desk when she heard a familiar cooing. At first she thought she was imagining it, but the cooing continued. It was her mourning dove. She looked out the window, but again, like always, the thick branches of the tree hid the bird. *What took you so long?*

That evening, Roxana talked to Bijan for a long time before Nina's arrival. She was surprised to see that he was furious with Nina as well. "He was my child too. I'm hurting as much as she does. How dare she accuse me of killing my own child." He fought his tears.

"Everyone knows that, but she's a mother. Look, I'm pregnant. I haven't even seen my baby; yet, this baby's my whole life. Please talk to her nicely. You're both suffering. You need each other more than ever now."

"I love her. We have another son to worry about."

She took Bijan to the nursery. She had put a small round table in the room and had set plates and silverware for two people. "I have ordered her favorite dish, *chelo kabob*. When Lili brings her here, she'll be hungry. She has to eat. I'll keep the door locked until she talks to you."

Roxana heard the doorbell. Lili and Nina were on time. She hugged them both and let them in.

Nina had not seen Roxana's new house, so she walked around the yard for a while, looked at the trees, and smelled a few roses in the garden. "Not bad," she said, "but if I were you, I would leave this country as soon as possible. Don't let them kill your child the way they killed mine."

"Nina, don't say things like that; that's mean," Lili said.

"Look, you have a leader who doesn't feel anything. Remember what he said to Peter Jennings, that American reporter who flew with him to Tehran?" Nina asked. "Jennings asked him how he felt returning to Iran after being in exile for so many years. He said, 'Nothing.'"

"Saddam killed your child, not Ayatollah Khomeini. Let's not forget that," Roxana said.

"Oh, so you didn't hear what he said about Iran. He said, 'We do not worship Iran; we worship Allah. I say, let this land burn. I say, let this land go up in smoke, provided Islam emerges triumphant in the rest of the world.' I'm sorry. I'm not a Moslem; I am an Iranian. But if he wants to burn my country, then I don't want to live here."

"Let's go inside," Roxana suggested.

As she was leading her guest to the living room, the entrance door opened, and Afshin walked in. He greeted Roxana's friends warmly. He extended his condolences to Nina. "I was in Ahvaz, otherwise I would've been in Behesht-e-Zahra."

"Thanks. I know. Now let's see the nursery."

Roxana led everyone toward the nursery, but as soon as Nina entered the room, she turned on the light, closed the door, and locked it. She ignored Nina's screaming. "Open this door immediately," Nina said, repeating the phrase as she banged on the door. "Stop this silly act."

Roxana turned the record player on and played Tchaikovsky's *Symphony No. 6.* She made it so loud that Nina's yelling was barely heard in the living room. She tiptoed toward the nursery and heard Nina's voice again. "Come on, Roxana. You've been a reasonable person all your life. Stop this nonsense! It's not gonna work."

When Roxana heard Bijan say, "Nina, please talk to me," she went back to the living room.

Afshin seemed worried even though he knew about Roxana's plan, but Lili was full of smiles. They began eating their dinner. Tchaikovsky was so loud that no one could make a conversation. Roxana was happy that Lili was kind to her husband. Had she told her that Afshin had been seeking a divorce not long before, Lili probably would not have spoken to him.

She went behind the nursery door and heard Bijan telling Nina how much he had missed her and how much he wanted to have his family back.

Roxana came back, took off the Tchaikovsky record, and played the Righteous Brothers' "Unchained Melody."

"Why did you change the music?" Afshin asked.

"This song was the first song they danced to at their wedding," Lili said, smiling.

When the song finished, there was a long pause in the nursery. No one was saying anything. Then Roxana heard Nina calling her. "You invited me to dinner. What kind of hostess are you. I'm starving."

Hearing Nina's sarcasm, Roxana sensed that she may have forgiven Bijan, but she wanted to make sure that the couple had made up before opening the door. "Bijan, is everything okay now?" she asked.

"Yes, Roxana. I'm hungry too," Bijan said. "But we want to eat with you."

Roxana opened the door and let the couple out. As she was collecting the plates and the silverware from the small table, Nina leaned toward her and whispered, "Has God given you a mission to save my marriage every time it's in trouble?"

"No. I just want to see you happy."

After her guests were gone, Roxana started cleaning the dinner table. She didn't mind that Afshin was watching TV. She was so overjoyed seeing her friends back together that nothing would ruin her mood.

"Lili tells me that this is the second time you've saved Nina's marriage. What happened the first time?" Afshin asked.

"It's a long story. I'll tell you some other time. Right now I have work to do."

"How come you never invite my family here? My relatives have invited us many times, so naturally they expect us to invite them."

"Okay, next Friday, invite anyone you want."

"You mean it?"

"Yes."

For three days Roxana worked several hours in the kitchen after returning from work to prepare for the Friday dinner party. On Friday, she served twenty-five members of Afshin's family and relatives, including the uncle who had offered them his villa in Ramsar for their honeymoon. She had prepared six hors d'oeuvres and ten different dishes, including filet mignon, chateau de bryon, and poulet de touraine. When everyone was leaving their house, Afshin's uncle told him, "Your wife must have a PhD in the culinary field."

"Where did you learn to cook like this?" Afshin asked as soon as the guests left.

"Between writing my theses and essay papers."

Roxana had complained about pain in her legs to her gynecologist. He had told her that some women experienced that kind of pain during the first few months of their pregnancy, but that it would go away. Her doctor had also advised her to stay off her feet as much as possible.

She paid a price for disregarding her doctor's recommendation. She had pain in her legs for several days after the big Friday fiesta.

Chapter 54

Mr. Hedayat was waiting for Roxana in her office early in the morning. "Good morning. Sorry for occupying your office, but I need to talk to you," he said.

"What's the urgency?"

"First of all, we don't even have a name for our office. We keep calling it the 'Bureau of the Algiers Declaration,' which is not appropriate. Do you have any suggestion?"

"You know the Americans habit of creating acronyms for every long name. You should be careful with the name you choose."

"I was thinking of 'International Litigation Office,' or 'Office of International Litigation.'"

"That's my point. If you choose the first name, the acronym will be ILO, and that's the UN International Labor Organization in Rome. If you choose the second name, that will be OIL, and you can imagine how much fun Americans will have with that name!"

"You're right. OIL. That's funny. What would you recommend?"

"I was thinking of Bureau of International Arbitration, or BIA."

"I like that. Let's call our agency BIA for the time being."

"That's all?"

"No, this is our first international arbitration experience. We have thousands of claims to deal with. We have good lawyers here, but they are not experts in international law or international arbitration. Instead of interrupting you and wasting your time by asking you questions all day, I was wondering whether you would be willing to teach a seminar for a month or two. You know international law, as well as the American legal system. So, what do you think?"

"It's fine with me."

That evening, Roxana received a phone call from her mother wondering why she and her husband weren't there.

"What's the occasion?"

"Don't tell me you forgot your birthday again, two years in a row."

"I just went through hell with Nina's tragedy, and I've started a new job. Besides, I'm not a kid anymore. I'm gonna be a mother soon."

"You're still my baby. Get over here soon. We're hungry."

Afshin was happy to have another evening of feast, but he wanted to walk to his in-laws' home.

"It's more than two miles. I still have pain in my legs since Friday."

"The weather is nice. Let's walk."

Roxana agreed despite the cautionary remarks of her doctor. After the first mile, she felt the shooting pain in her legs again. She stopped and tried to negotiate with Afshin to get a taxi. There were dozens of taxis available on Zafar Avenue. As she was pleading with Afshin, a street vendor who was selling fresh-shelled walnuts approached her. "Four for four tomans."

She reached inside her purse and pulled out a five-toman bill to buy the walnuts.

"Put that back. That's too expensive. I'll buy it for you from downtown," Afshin said.

"It's less than fifty cents!"

"Your head is still calculating everything in dollars and cents?"

"I haven't had these fresh walnuts for ages. This is the only craving I've ever had."

"Here comes your taxi."

Afshin pulled Roxana's hand and hurried her to get into the taxi. She was still holding the five-toman bill in her hand.

Puri had prepared several of Roxana's favorite meals. There was a big cake and several gift-wrapped boxes on a small table in the dining room.

After serving dinner, Puri put one candle on the cake, Elli struck the match, and they sang the Persian happy birthday song. Roxana closed her eyes, made a wish, and blew out the candle. *God, please end this war.*

She was opening her first gift when Puri asked, "So what did your husband give you for your—"

"I haven't told him what I would like yet," Roxana interrupted her mother.

She started opening her gifts in a hurry to change the subject. Her father had followed his old tradition by giving her another Swiss wristwatch, and making everyone laugh.

Afshin was quiet during the taxi ride back to their home. As the cab was reaching the end of Zafar Avenue, Roxana told the driver, "Sir, if you could make a left turn here, this street will take us directly to our house."

Before the driver got a chance to make the left turn, Afshin commanded, "Continue your direction. You don't need to make a left turn."

Roxana turned to him and whispered, "I know that street. It's the best shortcut to our place."

He didn't answer. As soon as the taxi stopped, he got out and began walking fast. He didn't wait for Roxana to get out. Nor did he take any of the heavy packages she had. She paid the cab fare as she always did, because Afshin didn't believe in using cabs. She reached him while panting, "What's wrong?"

"F___ you and f___ your family. Don't you ever embarrass me in front of a cab driver again."

"I've lived in this neighborhood. I was trying to use the shortcut so that I didn't have to walk. I still have pain in my legs."

"Shut up. Shut your fat mouth up. I'll f___ your mouth if you keep talking. I'll f___ your whole family."

A few people stopped momentarily to see what was going on. She leaned against a large sycamore tree on the eastern side of Vali Asr Avenue. She gathered her gifts and tried to put them into two shopping bags. She felt as if a bomb had shattered her head and pieces of her brain were flying in the air. *Another silent murder in the middle of a dark night.*

* * *

It had been more than a year since Roxana had seen the front gate of Tehran University. Once inside the law school, she became emotional when she found out that she had to teach her seminar in the same classroom in which she had spent four years studying law.

She had come early to arrange her handouts and to draw a chart on the blackboard. On the outside, the faculty building for the School of Law, Political Science, and Economics had not changed. On the inside, however, many banners and pictures of Ayatollah Khomeini and other Islamic government leaders were hanging on the tall columns and walls of the law school.

She climbed to the second floor; she stood in the hallway for a few minutes and stared at the closed door of the Office of the Student Movement for the United Nations. She remembered how many times she and fellow members had lectured in Tehran high schools and other places promoting the work of the United Nations—the same United Nations that had kept silent about Saddam's war. She also remembered how many times during the shah's regime that office was shut down because it was considered to be *political.*

She left the handouts on a small table in the corner of the room. She then climbed to the podium and drew a chart on the blackboard describing the international courts in The Hague, most notably the International Court of Justice (ICJ) and the Permanent Court of Arbitration. She looked at her outfit, adjusted her scarf, and thought, *Thank God my belly doesn't show.*

Teaching at Tehran University was the dream of many of its graduates. To them, that university, the cradle of the Iranian intellectuals, was more prestigious than Harvard, Yale, Columbia, New York University, or the Sorbonne. To Roxana, however, the practice of law, not the teaching of law, was the most challenging part of the profession. "Enduring legal attacks by opposing attorneys and judges make an attorney alert all the time," she had always said. "Students don't have enough knowledge on the subject they're learning to challenge their professors," she added.

She never imagined herself teaching at Tehran University at such a young age, nor did she anticipate that her three hundred students would all be lawyers ages forty to sixty-five. If she needed any challenge, she had gotten it.

She looked at her students for a few seconds. She was surprised to see one of her former classmates in the front row—the clergy who had debated with her about polygamy and adultery during their first-year sociology course. He was wearing a regular suit.

"In case you're wondering what happened to me," the man said, smiling at Roxana, "I have disrobed myself."

Roxana smiled back. "Glad to see you here."

"Gentlemen, welcome," Roxana began the introduction. "My name is Roxana Ramsy. Mr. Hedayat has sent you some information about me. Don't let him mislead you. I'm here to learn from your expertise and wisdom as much as to share my experience with you. So please do not consider this seminar as a series of lectures; interrupt me anytime you have a question or comment."

Chapter 55

The international arbitration seminar was a success. Roxana's down-to-earth manner, sense of humor, and informal style of teaching had made her very popular. However, the long daily schedule did not leave her any free time to do grocery shopping, especially for milk, since there was a shortage of milk in Tehran. Roxana's family members were searching for milk in different parts of Tehran—Zafar supermarket was almost empty.

The third week of teaching coincided with the month of Ramadan. During the holy month of fasting, one could not eat or drink before *Iftar* (dinnertime). Islam, however, had exempted several groups of people from fasting. That included children, old and sick people, as well as pregnant women. But no restaurant was open anywhere until *Iftar*.

Roxana used to fix a small sandwich for herself and take it to work every day, but the security woman would always take it out of her briefcase and lecture her that she could not bring food to the office during Ramadan.

"I'm pregnant."

"You're not showing. How can I believe you?"

She brought a statement from her doctor to avoid the morning interrogation, but she was getting more thirsty than hungry. It was a hot summer in Tehran. By the time she finished her work at the office and arrived at law school at 3:00 p.m., her mouth was so dry that she couldn't talk. She needed an air-conditioned classroom, but instead she received enormous sun heat through the large windows.

One day shortly before the break, she excused herself, ran to the women's room, and took off her scarf. She felt the drops of sweat in every strand of her hair. She splashed cold water on her face, and then cupped her hands, gathered some water, and drank. When she turned around, she saw a young woman in black *chador* staring at her. "I'm sorry. I didn't mean to offend you by drinking water during Ramadan, but I'm pregnant. It's hot, and this scarf is killing me."

"You're Dr. Ramsy, aren't you?"

"Yes. How do you know my name?"

"I asked one of your students. You see, I was a third-year law student when they closed the universities. I miss school so much. Sometimes I just come inside the law school to remember the happy days we had. I hear the students' voices in my head and feel the excitement for a few moments. Then there is silence."

"How come the security guards allow you to come in?"

"I tell them that I'm writing a research paper, which is true, and that I need to talk to my professor. There are some professors at the university who still come to their offices and do research or other academic work."

"Are you a religious person, or—?"

"Oh, you're looking at my *chador*. This helps me get through the security office. I never wore the Islamic *hejab* before the revolution."

"Would you like to come and sit in my class?"

"Would I ever! I have to confess that sometimes I sit behind the door and listen to you. I love to hear your students' laughter."

"What's your name?"

"Parastoo."

"Beautiful name. Parastoo, don't get discouraged. When I was in law school, we didn't have even one female professor, and there were only ten women in my class."

Roxana dried her long, wet hair with a paper towel and put her scarf back on. She let Parastoo into the classroom and said to her students, "Gentlemen, we have a new participant today. Her name is Parastoo. For this hour, we'll be discussing nationalization, sovereign immunity, and state responsibility."

The next day when she went back to the women's room to splash water on her face, Parastoo ran after her. Once inside, she pulled out a small bottle of orange juice and a container of *olivieh* salad, and put them on the large edge of the window. "This is for you, professor."

"Thanks, but how did you smuggle the food and the drink?"

"I told the security guard this is for *Iftar.*"

Roxana took a sip of orange juice first, then ate some of the salad. "Thank you so much. I never imagined to see an angel in black *chador.*"

* * *

She was on the phone talking to one of the government attorneys when Mr. Hedayat walked into her office. He placed a note in front of her. "Please ask them to call you later. I need to talk to you right away."

She apologized to the attorney on the phone and then hung up. "Is there any problem with the seminar?"

"Oh no. Your students are crazy about you and your teaching style. One day, I'll show you some of the letters of appreciation they've sent me, but I'm here to send you to London."

"Aren't the borders sealed?"

"Yes, but not for us."

"What's happening in London?"

"We have a meeting with our British attorneys concerning the interest rate the Americans owe us on our frozen bank accounts."

"So what role do you want me to play?"

"The British lawyers know the banking laws, but I want you to write the brief using your international expertise. You should leave this Friday."

"That gives me only one day to wrap up my work. What about my seminar?"

"Don't worry; I'll cover it for you."

Mr. Hedayat left Roxana's office, but before she could absorb the news, he came back and said, "I forgot two things. Lili and Kayvan will join you at The Hague. You also need written permission from your husband for your exit visa."

She was excited about the trip, but getting her husband's permission to leave the country felt like a thorn in her eyes. The old rule that existed during the shah had continued despite the revolution. The interesting part was that the rule didn't apply to unmarried women. Roxana didn't need written permission from her father when she left Iran, but a decade later she had to get her husband's permission to leave the country. She negotiated the *right to travel* on behalf of Nina when she was just a high school graduate, but after years of legal practice, she didn't include that right in her own marriage contract. She couldn't help remembering her mother's remark, "You know how to defend everybody's rights but your own."

Chapter 56

Afshin didn't object to the trip. In fact, he proudly announced to her family members and relatives that despite the sealed borders, his wife was asked to go to London and submit a legal brief to the World Court.

Within a day, every relative and every neighbor who found out about Roxana's trip was calling and asking her to buy some over-the-counter medication for them. The popular request was for aspirin.

The economic sanctions on Iran and the war had made it difficult for the government to obtain the needed pharmaceutical products.

Since Roxana didn't have a car, Syrus volunteered to drive her to the Mehrabad Airport. The departure time was scheduled for 5:30 p.m. However, the airport authorities canceled the flight. They had been alerted that Saddam was planning to bomb the airport again.

She went back home. Then at 8:00 p.m. she received a call from Iran Air that the flight to London was rescheduled to leave at 9:30 p.m. She decided not to bother her brother; she called a taxicab.

There were only twelve passengers on board that Iran Air Boeing 727, mostly government employees. She was the only woman. When the plane took off, she looked out the window. There was nothing but darkness—a frightening darkness that had covered the city like a huge black *chador*. There was no sign of illuminated Tehran—the city Roxana had dubbed the "Sea of Diamonds."

The plane landed at Heathrow Airport at 3:00 a.m. local time. This was Roxana's third trip to London. During her previous trips, she always had a long list of to-do things in London, but this time she was there only to meet some lawyers and to write a legal brief. She then had to go back to her war-stricken country, where the rain of grief had soaked every soul.

Friends and relatives had envied her for being able to travel abroad because no one was able to get a passport or exit visa. She, however, didn't have any desire to walk in the streets of London wearing her Islamic *hejab.*

As the taxi traveled through famous residential areas of London, seeing the rows of illuminated white houses brought tears to Roxana's eyes. She felt she had landed on another planet. Earlier in the evening she had tried to find a trace of Tehran from the sky, but the city was buried under a black *chador*. Thousands of miles away, London sat like a queen on a diamond throne, and Londoners continued their gleeful lives. *They don't know Iraj committed suicide. They don't know Saddam killed Nina's child.*

She had a peaceful night of sleep. For more than a year, the sound of bomb explosions had rattled her every night. Sometimes she would wake up startled and pant for a long time before she could breathe normally again. She wondered whether the shooting of adrenaline to her heart and the fast heartbeat could harm her baby.

The modern books on babies and pregnancy indicated that babies could hear sounds. These books encouraged mothers to talk or even sing to their babies. She was sure that her baby could hear the horrifying sound of the bomb explosions, so she had started talking to her baby.

On her second day in London, after she finished a lengthy meeting with the British attorneys, she came back to the hotel, called for room service, and ordered a sandwich.

After lunch, she turned the TV on. It felt strange not to see a clergy with a black robe. Funny shows were on some channels, but they couldn't make her laugh. In her world, laughing was forbidden by unwritten laws. Everybody was angry. Her office coworkers in Tehran no longer started their mornings with popular jokes. Everyone had a grim face. Everyone was shouting. One of the last shouting arguments, which still echoed in her head, was her conversation with a man on the phone. The night before her departure, she had tried to call Lili, but due to the telephone company's technical problems, the dialing fell on someone else's number. At first, the man at the receiving end said angrily, "Wrong number!" and hung up. The second time, before Roxana could explain what number she had dialed, the man shouted, "Are you blind or deaf?" The third time, he shouted louder, "You stupid ass." Nobody had said those words to Roxana before. What had happened to the people who were famous for their hospitality and *taarof*? She wondered.

The war had changed people's lives so much that they couldn't tolerate the least inconvenience. People were basically angry with their government, but they couldn't manifest their anger. After the war, people didn't dare to criticize the government, because any simple outcry would label the complainant as antirevolutionary and send them to jail.

The decision-makers in the west had calculated that Saddam would destroy Iran's oil industry, flatten its cities, and get rid of the Islamic regime. They were wrong. The war strengthened the regime and its power more than ever.

Roxana put her hands on her belly, sang Adamo's "*Quand Les Roses*" song to her baby, and said, "I promise I'll protect you and make sure that you'll have a happy life." The baby moved! There was no one around to see her excitement. She mumbled, "The baby heard me."

She still had a few hours to kill before joining Lili and Kayvan in The Hague. Her hotel was located near Oxford Street, so she decided to spend some time in London's mecca for shoppers. At first, she felt awkward. She had never walked in London streets wearing *hejab* before. But after a short walk, she felt comfortable when she saw some Saudi women with their black *abayas* and *nigab*. Their *hejab* had covered them totally, even their faces except for their eyes.

As she was looking around to see people's reactions to the Saudi women and herself, she noticed that a young, bearded Iranian-looking man was behind her. She started window-shopping, but it became clear that the man was indeed following her.

She saw the sign of the Mother's Care store. All of a sudden she remembered that she hadn't bought any baby clothes yet. Her mother had already purchased everything she needed for the baby's nursery but not any clothes. She went to the maternity dress section first. She chose two loose dresses with no-cling A-line-shaped skirts. The swirling style skirt would make an ideal *hejab*. Her body's shape would disappear in either one, and that was exactly what she needed—to have no body to be noticed.

The young man who was following her entered the store and pretended he was shopping. He was looking at a table with piles of baby jumpers on sale. Roxana approached him and said in Farsi, "I can help you choose if your wife is not here."

"Oh no," the man said, startled. "I was just looking."

He disappeared when Roxana resumed her shopping. She didn't see the man again, but she felt that someone was assigned to watch her to make sure that she complied with the *hejab* code while traveling in Europe.

She went back to the hotel and ordered another meal from the room service menu. She didn't feel comfortable eating in a restaurant wearing her Islamic outfit. She couldn't help remembering how many times she had dined by herself in restaurants in major American and European cities either when she was on vacation or participating in a conference. Her problem during those trips was how to get rid of men who were chasing her, but her new problem was how to avoid people's stares.

Before packing, she decided to call one of her distant relatives in London. She dialed the number. A woman with a cockney accent answered the phone. "Sweetie, you dialed a wrong number."

She apologized and tried again. She got the same woman for the second time. The third time the woman said, "Honey, you got me again."

It was unavoidable for Roxana not to compare the words of her angry countryman who called her a "stupid ass" a few days earlier with the sweet words of the British lady.

When Lili called, Roxana shared the two encounters with her.

"Don't think for a second that the British are more civilized. I lived in London more than two decades. You should have been there when the transportation workers went on strike. People were climbing all over each other to get on the bus using curse words you never heard before."

"I still appreciate the lady's kindness. I dialed her number three times.

"Get a pen and write the hotel's address in The Hague. I'll meet you in the lobby."

* * *

She took a taxi from Amsterdam's Schiphol Airport to her destination. The Hague, also called Den Haag, was the seat of the Dutch government and was home to all the embassies of foreign countries. Amsterdam, however, was the official capital of the Netherlands. Roxana had never visited the city before. The first thing she noticed about the city was the row of houses with ornamental facades. She was impressed with the gothic and neogothic architecture of the buildings. The second interesting part of Den Haag was the baskets or vases of flowers displayed in the windows of many houses.

In the hotel lobby, she waited impatiently for Lili. When she saw her getting out of the elevator, she was shocked. Lili was not wearing any *hejab*. "What do you think you're doing?" she asked Lili anxiously.

"Hello to you too," Lili said, hugging Roxana. "Aren't you happy to see me?"

"Yes, I was until I saw you with no *hejab*."

"I'm sick and tired of it. This is Europe. I'm free here."

She took Lili to a corner of the hotel's lobby and told her in detail about the spy who followed her on Oxford Street. "If they have someone who could find me among millions of people in London, their spies can definitely locate you faster in a small town like The Hague."

She pulled a scarf from her carry-on bag and handed it to Lili, who wore it reluctantly.

Kayvan joined the two friends a few minutes later. After giving a warm welcome to Roxana, he carried her luggage to Lili's room.

Lili helped Roxana unpack. "I thought you wouldn't mind sharing a room with me," she said.

"Of course not. I can spend the money I save for all those bottles of aspirin I have promised friends and relatives." Roxana laughed.

It took two days for her to write the legal brief on Iran's first claim arising out of the hostage agreement. Lili and Kayvan assisted her in incorporating the data they had gathered on frozen Iranian bank accounts in the United States.

When the brief was ready, they took it to the International Court of Justice (ICJ). Although the Algiers Declaration between Iran and the United States had established a claims tribunal, the newly formed court did not have its own building or staff yet; so ICJ was accepting claims on its behalf.

Roxana couldn't hide her admiration when she stood in front of the Peace Palace. This was the building that housed the permanent Court of Arbitration as well as the ICJ. "This is where Prime Minister Mossadegh appeared in 1951 and argued the Iranian Oil Nationalization case," Roxana told her friends.

Chapter 57

Upon her return, members of the Revolutionary Guard interrogated Roxana at Mehranbad Airport for a couple of hours. They were suspicious of the twenty large bottles of aspirin she had purchased in Europe.

The next day, when Puri was distributing the bottles to relatives and friends, she let everyone know how the airport authorities had tortured her pregnant daughter for possessing so many bottles of aspirin.

Afshin liked his expensive London attaché case, and his mother flaunted to her relatives Roxana's expensive gift, a silk scarf from Harrods of London.

She finished teaching her seminar on international law of arbitration. Some of her students told her that it would take years of education for them to obtain the legal expertise they had acquired in only three months.

* * *

Roxana received two wedding invitations—one from Mara, her former secretary, and the other from Kazem. Ironically, both weddings were scheduled on the same date.

She realized she couldn't attend two wedding ceremonies simultaneously, so she attended Mara's reception, which was in the early afternoon right after the church ceremony, and Kazem's wedding celebration, which took place in the evening.

At Mara's reception, guests enjoyed live music, dancing, and alcoholic beverages. At Kazem's wedding, all women, including the bride, wore *chador*. Since men and women were segregated in two different rooms, Roxana couldn't understand why women, especially the bride, still had to wear *chador*.

She received royal treatment at both weddings. She didn't know what Mara and Kazem had told their respective families about her.

At Kazem's wedding, Afshin was in the men's section, so he couldn't interact with Roxana. However, at Mara's reception, he was sitting next to her. He seemed to enjoy the celebration, but he never invited his wife to the dance floor, even when the band played one of the songs they had danced to on their wedding night. She knew this was Afshin's revenge for the expensive gifts she had bought for Mara and Kazem. Afshin could not determine the price of the gold earrings for Mara, but he easily guessed the price of Kazem's gift—a Persian carpet worth $1,000.

"I put both of our names on the card. What's your problem?" Roxana asked.

"They know I would never spend that much money on their gifts."

When one of Mara's sisters invited Roxana to join the other guests to perform a group Armenian dance, she politely declined. This was the same group dance that Nina had taught the guests at Roxana's wedding. She knew the steps too well.

She enjoyed watching the guests dancing on the crowded dance floor. It was soothing to listen to the Armenian songs, but she couldn't forget the ongoing war, the changing phases of the Iranian revolution, and her troubled marriage. Invisible words were dancing in the air—it's against the law to be happy in Iran.

After they left Kazem's wedding, they had to walk a few blocks to reach a more popular road to find a taxicab. Roxana felt naked again, the same way she felt in London because everyone was staring at her. Kazam's ancestral home was located in the deepest part of southern Tehran, where every woman wore *chador*. A woman wearing a scarf in that part of the city resembled an alien from another planet. As she did in London, Roxana tried to ignore the stares.

"Didn't Kazem live in a mansion on Kakh Avenue?" she asked Afshin, trying to break his silence.

"That was a temporary arrangement."

She tried to make more conversation, but soon realized that Afshin didn't have any interest. She knew that she had to be punished. She had dared to buy expensive wedding gifts without Afshin's approval.

He finally hailed a cab. During the taxi ride, Roxana observed that at every intersection were several tables holding overblown pictures of young soldiers killed in the war. Some had displayed candleholders and served sweets usually offered at the grave site in cemeteries. The tables with a crystal chandelier lampshade, called *hejleh,* indicated that the young soldier had died before having a chance to get married.

She had a hard time falling asleep that night. Two weddings took place under the same sky, in the same land, yet felt so foreign and so far apart, as if one had happened in Sweden and the other in Sudan.

* * *

"So when are you going to Holland?" Mr. Hedayat asked Roxana the next day.

"Pardon me. I just came back from Holland."

"I mean permanently. The brief was fantastic. Kayvan gave me a copy this morning. Can't you see? I need you there, not here."

"I told you before, I've come back to live in Iran. I've lived abroad for too long."

"Okay, then, be ready to pack your bag and go to Holland every few weeks."

She wondered about living in Holland. The Hague, home to over one hundred international organizations, was the second most important city for the United Nations after New York City. It was a dream for an international lawyer to live and practice law in the judicial capital of the world, but she couldn't leave war-stricken Iran. She had to forget about the *city of peace and justice.*

Her train of thought was interrupted when Mr. Hedayat came back to her office again. "I want to talk to you about your friend Lili," he said.

"What about Lili?"

"She is a fantastic economist, but her disdain for *hejab* is gonna cost me my job. One day she wears her scarf like female characters portraying a harem scene in Hollywood movies. Another day she looks like Queen Nefertiti, and when she is bored with both styles, she wears her scarf like the genie in that American show, *I Dream of Genie*. Could you please talk to her?"

That afternoon, Roxana talked to Lili and emphasized that everyone's job was in jeopardy if Mr. Hedayat was fired.

Lili was not pleased to hear the remark. "So if we lose the war, are they gonna say we lost to Saddam because Lili didn't wear her scarf properly?"

Chapter 58

Roxana traveled to London and The Hague alone the second time; Lili and Kayvan were needed in Tehran, but during the third trip, in addition to her friends, Mr. Hedayat also accompanied her. This was the trip she almost didn't make. As she was boarding the plane, an airline security man stopped her. "You can't fly. You're more than seven months pregnant," he said.

She was embarrassed. Mr. Hedayat looked surprised. She told the security man that she had her doctor's approval for flying. The security man was demanding a written document. Mr. Hedayat got involved and explained how crucial Roxana's trip was. Then he turned to Roxana and said with a smile, "I thought you were gaining weight. Congratulations."

She was flustered. She didn't want to discuss her pregnancy with anyone, especially where a handful of people next in line were anxious to board the plane. "We always talked about legal issues. I was planning to tell you," she told Mr. Hedayat. "But I never found the right time."

She eventually got on the plane when Mr. Hedayat talked to the airport authorities. Despite the awkward scene at the beginning of her trip, Roxana enjoyed the third London trip. The city was decorated for Christmas. Every major store on Oxford Street had a Christmas tree in the window. Although Christmas was ten days away, Londoners and tourists were hurrying to the stores. She couldn't help remembering another city and its Christmas celebration—the stores on Fifth Avenue and the tall Christmas tree in Rockefeller Center. She was missing New York City.

The enjoyable part of the trip was not London's Christmas atmosphere—it was the cold weather. Roxana and Lili wore their chic long winter coats, which covered their Islamic outfits. Their tall leather boots, woolen scarves, and winter hats had totally disguised their appearances; yet, they had totally followed the Islamic dress code—only their faces were visible. Roxana was relieved when no one stared at them on Oxford Street anymore.

She attended two of the meetings with Mr. Hedayat in London in the morning, and had a free afternoon to spend with Lili.

She was concerned about Lili's smoking. She had never smoked in her life until their first trip to The Hague. So the free afternoon in London was a good opportunity for her to talk to Lili. She took her to a nice restaurant in Piccadilly Square where the large windows allowed them to watch crowded streets surrounding the square. After they ordered their meals, she noticed Lili was staring at a young couple embracing as they strolled outside the restaurant.

"This is your city. Why the long face? You can reclaim the life you had here."

"I can reclaim my life here as much as you can do yours in New York."

"There's a big difference. You're a British citizen, but I'm not a US citizen."

"I can't live thousands of miles away from Kayvan."

"You're not happy living near him, either."

"I'm gonna change that. Please don't lecture me for what I'm about to say. I have decided to sleep with him. He's Moslem. He can have up to four wives, so I'll be wife number two."

Lili stopped talking when she saw Roxana shaking her head in a negative way. Before she could comment, Lili talked again. "I know you're gonna point to those conflicting Koranic verses. I was in the classroom when you crucified that poor clergy classmate for advocating bigamy. I remember how you proved that Islam actually doesn't allow bigamy, but that's your interpretation. Thousands of Moslems have more than one wife. I can be his *sigheh,* concubine."

"Lili, do you hear yourself?"

"Yes, loud and clear. I've made up my mind. Don't be judgmental. I don't need your approval."

Roxana didn't say anything. She looked out the window and stared at young couples kissing or holding hands when they walked by. She thought about her own loveless marriage and the angry roommate she called *husband.*

"Whatever you're doing, I want you to be happy," Roxana told Lili after a long pause. "I don't want you to lose your free spirit. That's what's so unique about you."

That evening back in their room, Lili took a quick shower and blow-dried her hair. Unlike her usual ponytail, she let her long hair down. She wore a dark green silk dress that highlighted all her body's curves. The color enhanced her blonde hair.

Roxana was reading a document, but she was also aware of Lili's preparation for her big date. *He won't be able to resist her.*

She was ruminating why she couldn't approve Lili's romantic night with Kayvan. Was it her feminist side that was defending Kayvan's wife's right to know that her husband was cheating on her, or was it her friendship with Lili that compelled her to save her friend from a stressful relationship?

"Don't wait up for me," Lili said as she put her winter coat on and left the room.

Roxana finished reviewing her document. She was ready to go to bed when she heard a knock on the door. When she opened the door, she saw a young Iranian woman wearing a modern *hejab* standing in the hallway. She looked lost. "I'm sorry," she said. "I was looking for Mr. Panahi's room. The receptionist gave me this room number."

"I work with Mr. Panahi. May I ask who—?"

"I'm his wife."

Roxana killed a sigh inside and introduced herself. "Please come in," she said in Farsi. "I think he's out. Please have a seat. Let me find him for you."

"I can hardly wait to see him. I have such exciting news. I'm pregnant."

Roxana killed another sigh inside and said, "You're not showing, but congratulations. When did you find out?"

"A few days ago. I see you're pregnant too. When is your baby due?"

"Sometime in April. I'm curious how you could travel without your husband's permission. You know that ridiculous law. I have to deal with it every time I leave the country."

"I visit my aunt, who lives in Beirut, every time Kayvan travels. He has given me multiple permissions to travel. And my brother knows some people in the visa office."

Roxana hoped that Kayvan and Lili were not in bed. She dialed Kayvan's room number. She heard Kayvan's voice, but she pretended she was talking to Mr. Hedayat. "I'm sorry to bother you. Do you know where Mr. Panahi is? His wife is here waiting for him in my room."

She heard Kayvan mutter, "Oh my God," before he hung up.

"I'm sorry. He seems to be out. Can I get you something?"

"No, thanks. I'm so excited I can't eat or drink anything. You know, we've been trying for several years to have a baby."

In a short period of time, Roxana learned that Kayvan's wife was a graduate of Tehran University with a degree in history. She couldn't get a teaching job, due to the changes in the educational system. "They tell me that I studied during the shah's regime, so those history textbooks were all tainted."

There was a knock on the door. Roxana opened it and found Lili standing there, looking pale. She whispered, "Don't worry, nothing happened," then she said in a louder voice, "I couldn't find any Coke. The vending machine was empty."

Lili introduced herself to Kayvan's wife and shook her hand.

"I'm so happy to finally meet you. Kayvan can't stop talking about you. He thinks you're a genius," Mrs. Panahi said.

"Thanks. That's very nice of him."

There was another knock on the door; this time it was Kayvan pretending he was happily surprised. "What are you doing here?" he asked his wife.

Mrs. Panahi ran to her husband, gave him a big hug, and whispered something.

"What did she whisper in his ear?" Lili asked as soon as the couple left.

"I'll tell you tomorrow."

"No, I wanna know now."

"She's pregnant."

Lili ran to the bathroom and locked the door. She ran the water in the sink, but Roxana could hear her sobbing.

Chapter 59

The three-day trip to The Hague was difficult for Roxana. She found Kayvan's wife charming and likable. But she also saw Lili's pain. She had known that Kayvan had a wife living somewhere in Tehran, but now the wife was there—real and visible. The next morning, Roxana didn't talk to Lili about Keyvan's wife, but she did talk to her about her smoking habit. "If you don't care about your health, please have some mercy on my baby," Roxana blurted out. "I'm expecting the baby to start coughing any minute."

"You should worry about your baby's boredom," Lili said. "If the researchers are correct that your baby can hear you, the poor thing must be bored to death hearing your legal arguments all day."

"He or she is going to be a lawyer," Kayvan said, laughing.

"I can always use another lawyer," Mr. Hedayat chimed in. Everyone laughed. Roxana felt better when she saw Lili laughing too.

During the final night in The Hague, Roxana worked until 11:00 p.m. When she was ready to attach the exhibits, she realized that the conference table was not large enough. She sat on the floor and laid out all the pages and exhibits around her. When the monumental task was finished, she couldn't get up without Kayvan's help. She remembered her doctor's advice, "You have to reduce your workload. You need to rest during the last trimester."

Back in the hotel, Roxana called Afshin to tell him that she was flying back the next day. She found some irritation in his voice. "What's wrong," she asked.

"I lost my job today. They want me to create an economic plan for the whole country. I've given them some ideas, but apparently they're not impressed."

"Don't worry. You'll find another one."

She called Mr. Hedayat immediately. She explained Afshin's situation and his educational background and asked if there was any positions available at the bureau for her husband.

"Yes. Ask him to come and see me when I return to Tehran," he said. "We can always use an MBA graduate from an American university."

"The kingmaker," Lili said after listening to Roxana's conversation with Mr. Hedayat. "So how many jobs have you found for him so far?"

"I don't know, maybe five or six."

"Why does he keep losing jobs?"

"I don't know."

Mr. Hedayat needed another day in The Hague to finish his work. Kayvan decided to fly back with him. Roxana appreciated the fact that he avoided flying with his wife and Lili on the same plane. During the flight back to Tehran, she tried to keep Lili engaged in conversation. "Do you know that The Hague hosted the first peace conference in 1899, followed by a second one in 1907?"

"You don't have to entertain me. Come right out and say it, this is a doomed relationship. You've been telling me that since Paris."

"I'm not trying to be judgmental."

"Listen," Lili said suddenly. "These envelopes are for you. I was so shocked seeing Kayvan's wife that I forgot all about them." Lili handed a dozen opened envelopes to Roxana.

"What are they?"

"These are letters from Steve to Kayvan. You should read them. It's all about you."

"How come Kayvan's giving me these letters now?"

"He thinks you should read them. He feels bad for Steve. To be honest with you, I sympathize with Steve too. Like me, he loves someone he can never have."

Roxana looked at the envelopes. The oldest one had a post office stamp of October 1980, a month after Saddam's invasion of Iran.

In the first letter, Steve admitted how much he had missed everyone and all the places he had visited in Iran. The following letters were full of questions about Roxana and her marriage. Apparently Kayvan must have mentioned something about the unhappy marriage because in one of the letters, Steve wrote, "The minute I saw him, I knew that he was a wrong choice for her. How could an intelligent woman like her not see that?"

The last letter reflected Steve's frustration for not being able to get a visa from the Iranian government to travel to Tehran. "In the eyes of the Islamic regime," he wrote, "we're all CIA agents now. Please tell Roxana how much I love her. I'm a full-blooded American boy. I never imagined you could love a woman without sex. Now I'm surprised that I'm capable of loving her even thousands of miles away. Please tell her I can never forget her beautiful, speaking eyes."

After she finished the letters, she noticed that Lili was waiting for her reaction, so she put all the envelopes together and returned them to her. "Please thank Kayvan for sharing Steve's letters with me."

"And? Is that all you have to say?"

"And he can tell Steve that I'm a happily married woman now."

"Come on, be honest."

"How's this? She'll be a mother soon."

Lili put the envelopes in her purse, found a magazine in her seat pocket, and started reading.

Roxana's chaotic world had been shaken again. *Every time I try to forget him, he keeps appearing in my life. Doesn't he know I'm not a free woman?*

* * *

Two days after his return to Tehran, Mr. Hedayat hired Afshin. To Roxana's surprise, he never asked why some of Afshin's previous jobs had lasted only for a few days.

"They need you so badly, so they had to give him a job too," Lili commented.

Roxana's good mood changed quickly that afternoon when she found out that her US-educated gynecologist had fled Iran and had transferred all of his patients to another doctor.

During the first appointment with her new silver-haired doctor, she learned that he had studied in Germany and had practiced for thirty years. She was not impressed.

She began looking for another doctor. Some gynecologists were not accepting new patients; some had a two-month waiting list. Frustrated with her search, she called her friend Gelareh and sought her help.

"Why don't you go and see the best, the queen's doctor."

"Dr. Parham? Is he still in Iran?"

"Yes. He's under some kind of house arrest."

"It would take forever to get an appointment with him."

"They have turned his office into a public clinic. You go there, take a number, and sit until they call you."

Dr. Parham was the president of Tehran University when Roxana attended law school. He was also Queen Farah's gynecologist. He delivered Iran's crown prince.

Roxana had a picture with Dr. Parham when she was chosen as *Dokhtar-e-Urdu,* Miss Camp, for publishing the daily journal of Tehran University's summer camp, and for other activities. It was Dr. Parham who had handed her the camp's award.

She took the picture out of her family album and went to see him. She was surprised that his office was only a few blocks away from her previous workplace on Kakh Avenue. Once inside the office reception area, she saw at least twenty women in black *chadors* waiting their turns. She asked the teenage receptionist about the waiting time.

"I don't know. Take a number," she said.

Roxana took a number, sat in the only available empty chair, and started reading her book. Three hours later, her number was called. She was the last patient.

Dr. Parham did not resemble the man Roxana had met in the summer camp. Although still a tall man with broad shoulders and squared chin, he had grayish hair and looked very tired.

He was surprised to see a woman with a modern *hejab.* All his patients wore black *chadors.* "Where are you coming from?" he asked.

"Dr. Parham, *salam.* "You don't remember me because I was nineteen when we met in Ramsar, but this picture may remind you of the event. You gave me an award."

Dr. Parham looked at the picture and then looked at Roxana. The picture wiped away his sad expression. He got out of his chair, came around his desk, and gave Roxana a hug. "I remember that day well. You see this man in the picture?" Dr. Parham said, pointing to a tall, slim man in white pants and white polo in the photo. "This man was my dearest colleague and a family friend. They killed him." Dr. Parham struggled with his unexpected tears.

He told Roxana that due to the shortage of doctors in Iran, the authorities had decided not to imprison him, but he was supposed to come to the office and work every day, and see as many patients as they would have for him. He could not take any day off unless he was sick.

"I heard Moslem women couldn't see male doctors even for a regular exam."

"They don't have enough female doctors. The women you saw out there are either barren or have the most unusual female problems I've ever seen."

She explained the reason for her visit—her doctor's departure.

"I wish I could be your doctor, but I don't even have a nurse. I have some twenty new patients every day. You see, I have no control over my schedule. They may get mad at me and put me in jail next week. You're better off staying with your new doctor. You're young and healthy. Don't worry. Nothing will go wrong. Of course, you can always come and visit me if I'm here."

Dr. Parham asked Roxana some routine questions about her job, her health, and her pregnancy. Then he helped her get on the exam table. After a routine examination, he brought a tape measure and measured her stomach from different angles—a procedure that looked strange to Roxana.

"Your doctor is wrong about the April due date. This boy will arrive in mid-March."

"How do you know it's a boy?"

"I know." Dr. Parham smiled mischievously. "The only advice I have for you is to reduce your workload."

He hugged her and gave her a fatherly kiss on the forehead. "Thanks for coming and seeing me today. You really made my day."

Dr. Parham was not a politician. Why was he scared of being sent to jail? Roxana wondered. The man was too old to see twenty patients per day. *Was he punished because he was a bourgeois?*

Chapter 60

On March 14, 1982, Mr. Hedayat had scheduled a one-day seminar for Roxana to discuss their international litigations for three hundred participants, which included government attorneys, as well as Roxana's students who had completed the three-month seminar at Tehran University. She was to deliver the paper she had written on the status of the American Claims at The Hague Tribunal.

The day before the seminar, Mr. Hedayat caught her in the hallway carrying a heavy box full of handouts for the next-day seminar.

"That's a heavy box." He stopped her and grabbed the box. "Are you planning to have a forced labor?"

"Don't worry. I'm fine. I have three more weeks left."

"I need you to go to the Sheraton Hotel today. They have a case their lawyers cannot handle. Take the whole afternoon off. I'll see you at the seminar tomorrow."

She couldn't take the afternoon off. She had to wait for the secretaries to finish typing some of the additional handouts she had planned to distribute the next day.

* * *

Pressured by his parents and relatives, Afshin had bought a used Pontiac. They had told him that he needed a car. "You can't take your baby around in a taxicab," they said.

When Roxana heard their comment, she thanked them silently in her head. She knew that she couldn't drive with a big belly. Her father had offered to buy her a car many times, but she had declined. She didn't want to bruise Afshin's fragile pride.

She knew Afshin would be home, but she decided not to ask him for a ride. She took her routine taxi ride, got out at Vali-Asr Square, and started walking toward the Sheraton. The hotel was situated on top of a hilly area. The distance didn't seem that far at first, but by the time Roxana reached the hotel's entrance, her heart was pounding, and she was out of breath.

The meeting with the Sheraton Hotel managers and their lawyers lasted more than two hours. At the end of the meeting, Roxana asked them to send a copy of their contract and all relevant documents to her office. "These are service contracts. There are several good arguments strengthening your response. I'll write it for you."

When she arrived at home, Afshin was all dressed up waiting for her. "Where have you been? It's 7:00 p.m. We have to go and visit my grandmother in the hospital."

Roxana explained briefly about her lengthy day. "Could we please visit her tomorrow? I'm dead on my feet," she pleaded while collapsing into the big sofa in the family room.

"She's been there for two days. All my relatives will be there tonight. We have to go."

"Can I make myself a quick sandwich?"

"You can eat at the hospital's cafeteria."

When they arrived at the hospital, Afshin's relatives were all gone. He was upset but didn't say anything in front of his grandmother. The eighty-seven-year-old grandmother saw the pain in Roxana's face. She couldn't sit down or stand up.

"Afshin *Jaan*, take her home," she said. "I'm fine. The doctors are going to release me tomorrow. Your wife is the one who's in pain."

Outside the hospital, Roxana asked Afshin to take her to her gynecologist. "The pain is really bad," she complained.

After examining Roxana, her doctor concluded that her pain was the result of a stressful day, climbing a hilly area, and being on her feet for a long time. "But you should also prepare yourself. The baby may decide to come after midnight, as they always do," the doctor chuckled.

"Doctor, I have a very significant seminar tomorrow. Three hundred people will come to listen to me."

"Tell that to your baby."

"Can you delay the labor for one day?"

"No, I cannot." The doctor laughed loudly this time.

She was not amused. She thought her question was not funny at all.

Back in her bedroom, the pain got worse by 11:00 p.m. She called Afshin several times and even shook him in bed. He was fast asleep. She called her mother. "I'm sorry to wake you up, but I think the baby's coming. Afshin is fast asleep."

"Oh my God! Don't worry. Syrus and I will be there in ten minutes," Puri said.

* * *

They gave her a hospital uniform and took her to a room full of women in labor. Some were moaning; some were crying because of severe pain. Puri was allowed to sit by her daughter's bed.

Roxana kept talking about the seminar she had to conduct the next morning until Puri stopped her. "You have to relax and concentrate on your baby now," she said.

"Please ask Afshin to find Mr. Hedayat tomorrow morning and tell him about my condition."

When Puri left, Roxana noticed some of the women around her were in more serious pain than before. She got out of her bed and started talking to them. She found out that none of them knew about *Lamaze* breathing. As she was teaching them the deep breathing techniques, one of the nurses came in and advised her to go back to her bed. "You need your rest," she said.

As soon as the nurse left, Roxana resumed her teaching. The women thanked her for a little relief they got from deep breathing. But a young, tall woman was still screaming. The woman was a twenty-five-year-old gym teacher with an athletic look. She admitted that none of her sports activities had prepared her for labor pain. Roxana had read in a book that expectant mothers who exercise routinely could handle the labor pain better. *Sometimes a little brain exercise can work too.* Roxana's satirical thought brought a smile to her face, but before she could enjoy the fallacy of a scientific approach to exercise and pregnant women, she heard the familiar siren wailing, and the power went out.

There was chaos in the room and a lot of 'Oh my God' remarks. Roxana thought that she had seen the worst of Saddam's nightly bombing, but she had never felt so helpless. She could see and touch the panic in the dark room. A woman was cursing Saddam. "I hope God kills your children the way you're killing ours."

Another woman admonished her, "*Nefrin* is not good. Bad omen befalls into your own neck."

A nurse shouted, "Don't panic, we're trying to get the hospital's generator started."

Roxana's pain got worse, but she had gotten used to her physical pain. She was fighting some horrible images in her head—the images of the Shiraz hospital bombing and Yerem's dead body. *God, my baby is not even born. Please help me. Help all of us here.*

The electricity was restored, but once the lights came on, Roxana could still see the horror on the faces of all the expectant mothers. The continued sound of antiaircraft artillery reminded them that Saddam's MiGs were still bombing some parts of Tehran.

Puri found Roxana's doctor and demanded that she be given some medication to reduce the pain. The doctor examined Roxana for the last time. "She is not dilating. We have to perform a C-section immediately."

Roxana was relieved, but to her surprise, she learned that there was no operating room available. Several women were ahead of her—she had to wait.

Afshin was allowed to come to the room for a few moments. A nurse led him in and advised him not to look at other women because they didn't have *hejab.*

"Why is it taking so long?" he asked Roxana with a criticizing tone as if the delay was Roxana's fault.

"I haven't come to a beauty parlor to have my hair done," she said humorously. "I'm going to have a C-section."

"My mother says doctors in affluent sections of Tehran always perform unnecessary C-sections because of the money. Each one costs 20,000 tomans."

Roxana was furious with Afshin and his obsession with money, but she didn't want to have another dispute with him over money in front of strangers. "Please tell Mr. Hedayat tomorrow I'm so sorry for not being there."

It was about 8:00 a.m. when they took her to the operating room. She realized Dr. Parham's prediction was correct. The baby was due in mid-March, not early April.

She felt the needle in her vein and the mask over her face. Shortly thereafter, she saw she was running with hundreds of squares in rainbow colors. Moments later, she became a square herself.

* * *

"She's opening her eyes." Roxana recognized her mother's voice. The impact of the anesthesia was wearing off. She looked around. Her family members were all there, smiling, but Afshin was missing. "Maman, the baby—"

"You have a healthy baby boy, ten fingers, ten toes, and a beautiful face."

She smiled. Dr. Parham was right again in predicting the baby's gender. She always dreamed of having a little girl, but on that day, all she was thinking was that her child didn't have to wear *hejab.*

The baby was asleep when the nurse brought him to the room. Despite the pain in her body, when she felt the baby in her arms, Roxana tasted a joy she had never experienced before—a beautiful baby, what a prize. She wondered what she had done to deserve such a reward.

The baby had black hair like Afshin. She looked at his wide forehead, pink cheeks, and round face. The baby smiled in his sleep. She remembered what her grandmother Tala used to say, "When a baby smiles in sleep, that means an angel is talking to the baby." She didn't know how much to believe her grandmother's logic, but the baby's smile stole her heart. She kissed her baby's forehead, and then tried to hide her tears by lowering her head and kissing the baby's tiny fingers. When she raised her gaze, she saw her parents wiping their tears.

"He has his father's hair but your beautiful eyes," Puri said.

Afshin walked into the room. He didn't notice the baby at first. "The traffic was so bad—"

"Forget about the traffic," Miremad interrupted him. "Look at your beautiful baby."

Puri took the baby away from Roxana and put him in Afshin's arms. Roxana saw his pride and a big grin, but he quickly gave the baby back to Roxana and asked, "Aren't you gonna ask me about the seminar?"

"What seminar?"

Everyone in the room laughed and stared at Roxana as if she was joking. Finally, Elli and Syrus both said, "Your seminar, your speech."

"Oh yeah. I forgot all about it. What happened?"

"I told Mr. Hedayat that you were in the hospital. He panicked for a moment, but then he took the microphone and said, 'I have an announcement to make. Our speaker is in the hospital today.' He couldn't finish because the audience began applauding for a long time. They had guessed you were having a baby. You've a lot of fans out there. When Mr. Hedayat introduced me, they applauded for me too. As I was leaving the large conference hall, everyone who was close to me shook my hand and asked me to convey their best wishes to you."

"Did Mr. Hedayat cancel the seminar?"

"No. He, Lili, and Kayvan covered for you. Basically, they read your paper and went over the handouts."

She looked at her baby and was amazed at how fast her priorities had changed.

The nurse came to take the baby for bottle-feeding. "You can breast-feed the baby tomorrow," she told Roxana. "The doctor wants all the medications to be flushed out of your body before you start nursing."

When the nurse was taking the baby out, she turned to Puri and said, "I'm sorry that your daughter had to go through surgery, but look at your grandson—a perfect C-section head. He's unharmed because he didn't have to go through a bumpy road."

Everyone except Afshin left Roxana's room to give her a chance to rest. He was waiting for his family and relatives to come in the afternoon. As soon as his in-laws left the room, he turned the TV on. Roxana had requested a private room to avoid a potential noisy roommate. She was in pain and needed rest. She asked Afshin to turn the volume down. She closed her eyes and tried to remember her baby's beautiful face.

Because of her pain, she pleaded with her doctor to allow her to stay in the hospital a little longer. "Even simple coughing hurts," she complained.

"I'm sorry, but we don't have space for anyone more than three days unless there are serious complications."

"Doctor, I just had surgery. Why is everyone treating a C-section as a regular childbirth? I can't stand up straight."

"It's because of the stitches. We used to purchase the best stitches from Switzerland. Now the government gives us whatever cheap stitches they can buy. They're like a rope and don't heal well."

* * *

Fatherhood didn't change Afshin as Roxana had hoped. In addition to everyday house chores, she now had full-time responsibility to care for her baby. She was grateful, however, that Afshin didn't argue over the name. She named the baby Darius, like the famous Persian king—Darius the Great.

She was released from the hospital six days before *Noruz*. Everyone was busy preparing for the Persian New Year celebration, but Roxana was not. She had assumed that the baby would come in early April as her original doctor had predicted. She was always excited for *Noruz* celebration, but after her surgery, she had lost her energy.

On the first day of *Noruz*, as Roxana was struggling to bathe the baby, Afshin was nagging that his family expected them to go for *Eid didany* (visiting relatives).

"How can they expect me to go for a *Noruz* visit when I'm in so much pain? I just got out of the hospital. I cannot even lift up my baby. Please tell them if it weren't for the war and a shortage of beds in the hospital, they would've kept me there for ten days."

"It's disrespectful. They're older. It's our tradition to go and see them first. Do you expect them to come here for *Eid didany*?"

"No, no. Please, no guests here until I can get my strength back to serve them. Your mother criticized the fruits and the cake my mother served them in the hospital. How can I please her in my condition?"

Roxana realized that no logical explanation would satisfy Afshin, so she told him that he was free to go for *Eid didany* of his family and relatives. And he did. He left his wife in pain to take care of a newborn baby.

That afternoon, Roxana had a pleasant visit. Her family came over with gifts for everyone. There were a total of twelve gifts for Afshin,

Roxana, and the baby. Roxana's mother shook her head in disapproval when she heard that Afshin was out to have fun with his family. Her father kept quiet. Elli was all over the baby. "It feels so wonderful to be an aunt," she said.

Roxana slept for two hours and let her family take care of the baby. When she woke she saw that her mother had cooked meals for her that would last for several days.

She was waiting to have dinner with Afshin, but there was no sign of him. She heard the doorbell and thought he had forgotten his key. She walked slowly to the door, since the pain from the incision area wouldn't allow her to move quickly. There was a big surprise—Lili and Nina stood behind the door. They had brought flowers, *Noruz* gifts, and food.

After hugs and *Eidet Morbark* (Happy New Year), Lili and Nina rushed to the nursery. The baby was asleep. They had seen the baby in the hospital once before, but they couldn't get enough of staring at him and watching his moves while asleep.

"He's so beautiful," Lili said.

"Yes, he is," Nina said. "But, hey, look at Roxana. She's back to size two again."

After watching the baby for a while, the three friends sat at the small, round dinner table in the kitchen. The trio ate and talked about motherhood. Even Lili, who had no interest in having children, participated in the discussion. Roxana didn't burden them with her marital problems. She only asked Nina for some medical advice.

"Caesarean is a serious operation, but a male-dominated medical society treats it like a normal childbirth," Nina said. "When a man is operated on for his hernia, no one expects him to cook, clean, and lift heavy items. Your baby weighs four kilos, and that's the weight you feel in the incision area anytime you lift him up."

Afshin came home around 10:00 p.m. He claimed he was tired. He kissed the baby and headed for the bedroom. As he was leaving the nursery, he noticed many boxes of unopened gifts. "Your parents continue their bourgeois tradition despite the revolution and the war, don't they?"

"The same way your parents follow their *Eid didany* tradition."

* * *

The next day, Afshin dressed up for more *Eid didany.* He left the house without asking his wife whether she needed anything.

After bathing the baby, Roxana didn't put the baby in his crib. She held him in her arms instead. The baby's warmth against her body gave her confidence that she would get through the difficult time.

She was admiring her baby's beautiful brown eyes when she heard the first blast. Her heart began pounding. She heard additional explosions and the rattling of the windows. She held the baby tight, and then started running from the nursery to the end of the living room. She repeated that several times while shielding the baby with the upper part of her body. She ran to the telephone and dialed her mother's number. "Maman, did you hear the bomb explosion?" she asked frantically.

"No. There was no bomb explosion here. What's going on?"

"I think Saddam is bombing our area."

"He never bombs Tehran in daylight. He likes to terrorize people at night."

She said a quick good-bye to her mother and hung up the phone. She put the baby back in his crib and ran outside. She saw fire and smoke in the sky. The red flame was moving like an ocean wave. It looked as if someone had ignited the clouds. Roxana forgot that she wasn't wearing her *hejab*, and that she was bleeding heavily. She ran toward some neighbors' houses. She knocked on the doors of several neighbors, but there was no answer. She panicked even more. She thought that the neighbors were informed about the bombing, and they had left their homes.

As she was running from one house to the next, she saw a small-framed man entering the cul-de-sac. "What's happening?" she shouted. The man was too far to hear her. She shouted again.

"There was a huge explosion in the pharmaceutical company a few blocks away," the man responded.

She returned home soaked in sweat, her heart still pounding. The baby was asleep now. She decided to take a shower, but she heard someone opening the door. It was her mother using her key. "We heard it on the news," Puri said. "Are you okay?"

"Yes, I am."

"We're such a bomb-oriented nation that even when a tire blows out, we think that Saddam is bombing again."

* * *

Roxana took a thirty-day maternity leave, calculating that by the end of his first month, the baby would've learned about the rhythm of feeding and sleeping. She was wrong. It was she who had to learn about the baby's schedule. He called the shots. After all, this was the baby who decided to enter the world exactly on the date and at the time his mother was supposed to deliver a speech before three hundred people. He continued ruling Roxana's life. He refused to be breast-fed or to sleep at night.

When Roxana visited her doctor to have the stitches removed, she also asked him to give her the injection that would stop the flow of the milk. That decision faced the disapproval of her mother-in-law, as well as her own mother. One day she got mad at Puri when she was explaining why the baby refused being nursed by her. "I did my best. I'm not a milking cow," she said.

Roxana slept on a sofa bed in the nursery and took care of the baby the entire night. But she realized that she could not continue the same routine once she was back at work. The baby was keeping her awake several hours every night. She was exhausted, and the fatigue showed on her face every morning.

Two weeks after her release from the hospital, her father visited her and the baby. She was so busy washing the baby's bottles and his clothes, and cooking at the same time, that she didn't notice she had spent the entire time in the kitchen while her father was caring for the baby.

"Why don't you let me hire someone to help you out?" Miremad asked his daughter before leaving.

"I can hire someone myself, but Afshin will not accept it. He cannot stand having anyone else in his home."

That evening, Roxana brought up the subject of finding some help. Her prediction was correct. Afshin opposed the idea strongly without providing any valid reason.

"So we have to divide the night into two shifts," Roxana said. "You can care for the baby for a few hours; otherwise, I won't be able to go back to work."

"I have to go to work too."

"You don't let me hire a nanny, yet you expect me to work and make money. How's that possible?"

Afshin agreed reluctantly to care for the baby between 3:00 and 6:00 a.m.

Puri volunteered to care for Darius when Roxana went back to work.

Chapter 61

Roxana was surprised when she saw the number of files and documents in her office. As she was dialing Mr. Hedayat's number, she saw him walking into her office. "Hi. I'm sorry I wasn't at the reception to welcome you this morning," he said as he pulled up a chair and sat down.

"Mr. Hedayat, I'm only five feet five." The piles are reaching the ceiling. I'm going to need a ladder to reach the ones on the top," Roxana said humorously.

"Don't worry. We only need your final approval. These are the work of your students. They need to know whether their briefs are ready to be filed with The Hague Tribunal."

"Could someone at least sort them out based on their deadlines?"

"We will, but I'm really here to talk about our three most significant cases—the defense cases, the shah's assets, and the United States' violations of the hostage agreement. In your absence, I have talked to some of our attorneys. Unlike you, they believe we have a great chance to win the shah's case, but not the US violations case."

"I respectfully disagree. You won't get the Defense Ministry's assets through litigation. The Hague Tribunal is not going to order the Americans to return to Iran the Boeing jets or the missiles, which the shah had purchased."

"Okay, I see your point. But why are you so pessimistic about the shah's case?"

"Please read the Algerian Declarations again. The words are so carefully chosen that it makes the return of the shah's assets impossible. They're using the term *will* rather than *shall.* In any treaty, when you use the word *shall,* that creates a real commitment for the party that has signed it. Procedurally, they are imposing an impossible task on you. First, you've got to locate the assets, which may be in Switzerland or under the control of some dummy corporations you don't know about. Second, here—" Roxana pointed to an article in the second Algerian Declaration, "the article says that 'when the shah or any member of his family has been served as a defendant.' Do you know how difficult it is to serve them as defendants? There are jurisdictional issues involved here. If you locate the relatives of the shah in Europe and name them as defendants, the American courts cannot exercise jurisdiction over them. Also, beware of any document that says, *according to US laws,* because US laws are complicated. They don't have a fixed code system like the Europeans. You may use a provision of a specific code, but the US court involved is the one that *interprets* whether you're right or wrong."

"So it's hopeless."

"Look, Iran was caught in these hostage agreement negotiations without any prior experience. Americans, however, had dealt with several revolutions, such as the Russian Revolution of 1917 and the Cuban Revolution of 1959. They froze their assets too. So when they negotiated with Iran, they brought all of their previous experience to the table."

"Where were you when we needed you?"

"Right here in Tehran."

"How about the US violations of the Algiers Declarations?"

"Those claims can be made in one case categorizing different violations. You'll have my outline and the summary version of it this afternoon."

When Mr. Hedayat left Roxana's office, she heard her mourning dove's cooing. The bird was welcoming her. She got out of her chair, went to the window, and tried to locate the bird. It was hiding as usual.

That evening after she put the baby to sleep, Roxana realized that she had not informed any of her American friends about the baby. She took a paper and started writing.

> Dear Ellen,
>
> I hope you're doing well. I feel guilty for not having written to you for so long. Please share my letter with our mutual friends. They must have told you that I'm married now.

In her last letter to me, Cathy had asked me about my latest achievement. Please tell her his name is Darius, or Daryoosh, as we call him in Persian, and he's gorgeous.

I wish I could live near you and talk to you about my feelings. You're a lawyer, also a mother. I don't know whether you went through the same emotions that I'm experiencing. In the morning, when I wake up, I still see myself as Attorney Roxana Ramsy, not someone's mother or wife. I still feel lots of commitments toward my work, but sometimes I wish that the whole world would leave me alone with my baby. I love to spend endless hours watching every move and every sound that he makes. I never thought you could love someone that much.

I think he loves me too. At night during the three-hour night shift that his father has begrudgingly accepted, he cries a lot until I wake up. I take him in my arms and sing him an Adamo song. He sleeps immediately. His nightly cry tells me he needs to hear my voice and to feel my love.

My husband resents my devotion to our son. He thinks he has lost me because of the baby. He doesn't know that he had lost me long before the baby was born. I'm sure our friends have told you about my revolutionary marriage.

These days, I cannot help remembering a World War II movie starring the Italian actor Vittorio DeSica. As a military commander, he evacuates some Italian villagers. One female character is shown carrying her baby. At the beginning of the journey, she is worried only about her baby, but after miles of walking, she drops the baby without noticing it. Shortly thereafter, she collapses herself.

The revolution, the war, and the baby have exhausted me so much that sometimes I feel like the character in that movie.

Because of the war and the American sanctions on Iran, we have to spend endless hours waiting in different lines to purchase rationed food items. These days even the wealthy Iranians taste poverty and a sense of helplessness. They have the money, but they can't find the items they need.

Love,
Roxana

Chapter 62

In order to complete her brief on the US Violations case, Roxana needed information on the status of pending litigations against Iran in the US courts. She informed Mr. Hedayat that the bureau had to retain an American attorney. She provided a list of names of lawyers and law firms, including her former law firm of Rubin & Stein.

A few days later, Mr. Hedayat came back and stated that his boss had rejected those attorneys. "They're all Jewish," he said.

"Most good lawyers in New York are," Roxana said, looking disappointed.

"Why can't you work with our British or French lawyers?"

"They don't know the US laws like American lawyers do."

"I'm sure if you go and live in Holland, where you belong, you can find all the data you need."

"I told you I'm back here to live at home. Besides, I've got a baby now. I need my mother's help here."

Mr. Hedayat and his bosses approved Roxana's final candidate. They retained Attorney Alfred Keller, an American Catholic who also taught law part-time. He and Roxana had attended several international law conferences together.

Mr. Keller was a blue-eyed man with grayish hair, in his late sixties. He worked as a senior partner at a New York law firm that practiced corporate law, international law, and litigation.

After exchanging numerous telexes with Attorney Keller, Roxana finally finished the first draft of the US Violation case, referred to as *Takhallofat* by everyone at the bureau.

Mr. Hedayat arranged a meeting for Roxana and Attorney Keller in London. He was also flying to London to work with a group of attorneys who were working on the shah's case. Lili and Kayvan were to accompany the group to provide assistance with respect to monetary aspects of the case.

Roxana took a taxicab directly from her office to her ancestral home. She needed to talk to her mother about the London trip. When she arrived, the baby was asleep.

"Why are you so early?" Puri asked.

Roxana told her mother about the London trip and the fact that no one could handle the meeting with the American attorneys but her.

"Don't worry. I'll take care of the baby. Go."

"I'm sorry for imposing Darius on you. I don't trust Afshin. Our neighbor was telling me the other day that she hears him yelling at the baby when he doesn't go to sleep."

"I wouldn't leave the baby in his care either. I love Darius. This is no imposition."

Puri drove Roxana and the baby to their home. She also gave her two containers of milk, a box of twenty-four eggs, and a whole cooked chicken. She knew her daughter didn't have time to stay in lines to buy food.

After Puri left, Roxana played with her baby for a while. She sat on her comfortable chair and laid the baby on her lap facing her. She moved the baby's arms like the wings of a bird several times. As she did so, the baby stared at her as if he was trying to record her face in his memory. "What am I gonna do with you?" Roxana said. "You have exhausted my mother, and your father is angry at me. Can you help me out by sleeping a little more at night?"

Roxana's monologue was interrupted by a knock on the door. She prepared herself to face the complaining neighbor. She had predicted correctly. The neighbor was on the other side.

"Oh my God, he's so beautiful," she said as soon as she saw the baby. "I hope you don't mind my talking with you about the baby's crying."

"I'm sorry he wakes you up."

"No, no. I'm not here to complain. I'm a retired nurse. Look at my white hair. I took care of babies all my life. I love babies. I came here to tell you—" The neighbor stopped talking and began playing with the baby. "Look at this *moosh-e-kuchulu*, a little mouse. He's listening to me like a grown-up, like he understands what I'm saying. He interrupted my train of thought. What was I saying?"

"The baby's crying—"

"Oh yes. I think your baby is a colicky baby. If your husband holds him upright, and lets him burp, he's gonna be fine. You let him burp when you're singing to him; that's why he sleeps well."

"I'm sorry for my singing. I thought I was whispering."

"Don't be sorry. The walls are thin. I love to hear you and the baby. It's better than the sound of Saddam's bombs."

* * *

After serving Afshin's dinner and feeding Darius, Roxana played and talked with him for a while in the nursery. Then she opened her briefcase, took out the rough draft of her legal brief, and began reading.

The telephone rang. She let Afshin answer it. She couldn't hear the conversation but noticed that it was short. Shortly after the call, Afshin appeared in the nursery. He told Roxana that his brother had moved into an apartment ten minutes' drive from their house. "My family and relatives expect to see us there."

"I have to work on my brief. Can we do this another time?"

"If we don't go, they'll consider it rude."

"Afshin, I have to finish this legal brief tonight and talk to Attorney Keller on the phone tomorrow. I don't have time. Mr. Hedayat wants me to go to London next week."

"This is not your Wall Street law firm. People chat and drink tea half of the working day at the bureau. You're the only one who works all these crazy hours. No one can understand that. How am I gonna explain to my family that we cannot see them even when they're only ten minutes away?"

"Okay, Afshin. One hour. After that, please bring me and the baby back. Then you can go back and have fun with your family all night."

Afshin had promised that after one hour, all three of them would return home. But as soon as they arrived in his brother's new apartment, he forgot all about Roxana and Darius. Ramin had invited some of Afshin's high school friends to surprise him.

His father took the baby from Roxana's arms for a minute but returned him to her as soon as he cried. His mother approached Roxana and said, "How's our runaway daughter-in-law doing these days?"

"Very busy, Mrs. Imani. The baby doesn't let me sleep."

"My son tells me he helps you at night."

"Only from 3:00 to 6:00 a.m. I'm up until 3:00 a.m."

"Well, raising a baby is the mother's job."

Roxana didn't respond to the remark of the woman, who had not worked a day in her life.

Darius started crying. She began walking and rocking him, but he wouldn't stop crying. Afshin's mother instructed Roxana to take the baby to a room at the end of the hallway. That recommendation sounded familiar. This was Mrs. Imani's idea of seeing Roxana and her grandchild. She always nagged that she was not seeing Darius enough, but anytime Roxana accepted her invitation, she would direct her to a room to care for her baby. She never held the baby or offered any help.

She bottle-fed Darius and looked at her watch. It was 10:00 p.m. Afshin was enjoying himself, talking and joking with his high school friends in a different room. Not only had he totally forgotten about his promise to Roxana, he was ignoring his baby's nonstop crying.

Roxana asked her brother-in-law Ramin to remind Afshin that it had passed the baby's bedtime—8:00 p.m. "Please tell him that I just need a ride. He can come back and enjoy his friends as long as he wants."

Another thirty minutes passed. Finally, Afshin appeared in the room and told Roxana he was ready to go home.

When Roxana sat in the backseat of the car with the baby, he started the car and drove off without waiting for Roxana to fasten her seat belt. She was jolted, and her head bumped into the front passenger seat as the car jerked forward. She managed to shield the baby.

"You promised one hour. This is three and a half hours later," Roxana said calmly.

"Do you know what my older brother told me when I was saying good-bye?" Afshin shouted. "He asked me, 'Is she your wife or your husband?'"

She realized that Afshin was too angry to listen to any rational explanation. He didn't care about his baby's bedtime or the fact that his face had turned red after hours of crying. She kept quiet, but Afshin was still venting. "And what's wrong with that baby of yours anyway? I've never seen a baby crying that much."

She did not respond to any of Afshin's ranting. The ten-minute trip seemed like an eternity. They finally arrived at home. The baby was asleep now.

After she put Darius in his bed, she began reviewing her legal brief. She finished revising the brief at 1:00 a.m. and went to bed.

She was awakened at 3:00 a.m. by the sound of the baby's *eh eh.* Before the baby could develop a loud cry, she immediately prepared his formula. She held the baby, got him to burp, and put him back in the crib.

She woke up again at six thirty by the sound of the running water in the bathroom sink. The door was half closed, but she could see Afshin brushing his teeth. He couldn't see her. She went to the nursery. Darius was awake and playing. She kissed him and looked for his bottle. When she couldn't find it, she went back to the bedroom, stood at the bedroom door, and asked Afshin whether he had given the baby's 6:00 a.m. milk. She didn't hear any response. She thought that he probably didn't hear her because of the sound of the running water. She repeated the question—this time louder.

She left the bedroom when Afshin ignored her. As she was heading toward the nursery, she heard Afshin's hurried footsteps. She turned around. Before she could say anything, she saw Afshin's hand raised to her. He slapped her in the face several times before she could open her mouth. "What are you doing? Please stop it. Stop it!"

He kept hitting her in the eyes with an open hand while kicking her in the legs and the abdomen. She had never been attacked in her life. She didn't know what to do except plead with her husband. "Please stop. Why are you doing this? What have I done?"

When the hitting got worse, she guarded her eyes with the back of her hands and arms. Since he couldn't hit her in the eyes anymore, he threw several punches, hitting her in the ribs and abdomen. He stopped when he heard the baby cry. Roxana rushed to the nursery. Shortly after, she heard the screeching sound of his car speeding off.

She cried loudly for the first time in her life. She had gone to sleep many nights pressing her face against the pillow and crying quietly, but this time, it was the moaning of a shocked woman who had witnessed a crime—a crime that she couldn't report to the police. In the Islamic Republic, the police wouldn't get involved with domestic violence cases. Those were family matters.

She called her mother. When Puri asked what had happened, Roxana burst into tears. "Please don't ask. Just come and take me and Darius out of here."

While waiting for her mother, she fed Darius. She gathered clothes for herself and the baby and put them in a suitcase. She then went to the bathroom to wash her burning face. She stood shocked in front of the mirror. Her face was puffed up and red. There were wide purple areas and there was swelling around both eyes.

Puri gasped when she first saw her daughter. She picked up Darius and held him in her arms. While fighting her tears, she whispered in the baby's ears, "I should die for your *mazloom* (wronged) mother. How can my innocent angel be victimized like this?"

Roxana took off her wedding band and put it on a saucer. She laid the saucer on top of the TV. *He cannot miss anything on top of his beloved TV*, she thought.

She sat down with her baby in the backseat of the car.

She looked at the house once more as her mother drove away. She knew that she would never live in that house again.

Chapter 63

Puri told her family that Roxana had developed a skin rash and needed her help to get rid of it before her London trip. Everyone believed her, but Elli recognized the evidence of domestic violence—bruises around her sister's eyes. One of her coworkers used to come to work with a black eye or injured lips every few weeks. She knew that Afshin had injured her sister, but she kept quiet.

Puri breathed easier when the men in the house didn't ask any questions about the bruises. How could they have possibly guessed? This was Roxana, the champion defender of battered women. Puri also told everybody that Afshin was on a business trip.

Roxana felt strange to be back in her old room. The last night she had spent in that room was filled with excitement and happiness. She was marrying the next day, a man who worshipped her—a man who had told her with tearful eyes that he couldn't live without her anymore.

Three days before her trip, she found out that Darius had only one container of powdered milk left. She panicked. This was a British-made formula that didn't hurt Darius's stomach. When the government stopped importing the formula, Darius got sick. After each London trip, Roxana brought several containers of the formula with her, but now they were all finished except for one container.

As usual, her family members and some relatives started checking the pharmacies in different neighborhoods in Tehran to find the formula, but they failed.

Two days before her trip, a neighbor, who knew about Roxana's search for powdered milk, came to her door and told her that a

Komiteh van at the entrance of their cul-de-sac was selling dry milk formula. Roxana said a quick, "Thank you," went to her room, put on her *hejab*, and left the house running.

She saw a young, bearded Revolutionary Guard standing on top of a van selling baby formula. "I just sold the last one," he said in response to Roxana's inquiry.

"Is there any other place that I might find some?"

"No. We won't import this stuff anymore. They are expensive. We have a war going on. People should stop using this fancy foreign stuff."

"But *Sarkar*, I have a four-month-old baby whose stomach only accepts this milk. The last time we replaced it with a different formula, he almost died."

"*Beh Jahanam*, the hell with your baby. Hundreds of our courageous soldiers get killed on the battlefield every day, and you talk about your baby."

"Excuse me?"

"Whose life is more important, a twenty-year-old soldier who is sacrificing his life for his country, or your four-month-old baby?"

She stared at the man for a few minutes. She fled as if she had seen a zombie. *What happened to the compassionate people who used to live in this country?*

The next day at 7:00 a.m., Roxana appeared in Mr. Hedayat's office.

"You're wearing sunglasses. I hope you're not canceling your London trip because of your allergy."

"No, I'm not."

"Then what's the urgency of coming to work so early?"

"Do you still want me to work in Holland?"

"Yes, of course. I've been begging you for months."

"I'm ready."

"What changed your mind?"

"Long story. I'll tell you someday."

"I couldn't be happier. So why don't we arrange for you to go directly from London to The Hague?"

"No, I can't do that. I have to come back, settle my lease, and a lot of other things."

* * *

When the plane took off, Roxana felt that she had left a part of herself in Tehran. She sensed the weight of the pain on her chest. This was the first time she was leaving Darius behind. It took a long time for her to get used to being apart from the baby during office hours. But this time, it was different. She couldn't see her baby at the end of the day.

Lili, who was sitting next to her on the plane, realized that her friend had been looking out the window silently for over an hour. "Don't you think you've been brooding enough? Aren't you happy that I'm going to The Hague with you?"

Roxana wiped her tears and turned toward Lili. "I'm sorry. It's hard to leave a four-month-old baby behind."

"Your mom is there. His father is there—"

"Darius doesn't have a father!" She broke her silence and told her friend the story of her life. She began with Afshin's family, his stinginess, his anger, his behavior at home, and, finally, the beating. She took off her shades and showed Lili her bruises.

"Bastard! That son of a bitch!" Lili repeated. "If he were near me right now, I would've punched him in the face."

Bank Melli's London branch had made two large conference rooms available to Mr. Hedayat. While Roxana and Attorney Keller were working on the US violation case, next door, Mr. Hedayat, Lili, Kayvan and five attorneys were working on the case regarding the shah's assets in the Unites States.

One day, when Roxana poked her head through the door to ask Mr. Hedayat a question, several members of the group pleaded with her to stay. "We could really use your thoughts on this case too."

"Thanks. I'd rather interpret the Algerian Declarations," Roxana said, smiling.

She called Tehran every day. After talking to her mother, she also talked to Darius. She wanted him to hear her voice.

She finished her legal brief and decided to do some shopping for baby clothes. She also bought several containers of HMS powdered milk to take to Tehran. She mailed half of them.

For her next exit visa, she needed two photos. She took four instant passport photos in an Oxford Street photo shop. She had adjusted her scarf to cover her bruises, yet the black and white photos still showed some grayish marks in the outer corner of each eye.

She saved two photos for the exit visa in the shop's envelope. She threw away the third one but placed the last photo in her wallet. She needed some tangible evidence to show to Afshin—to explain why she was seeking a divorce.

Chapter 64

After her luggage was checked by customs at the Mehrabad Airport, she rushed outside. She kept looking for her brother or uncle, but she couldn't find either. In the past, the two had taken turns to give her a ride. She was looking for a taxi when she heard someone calling her name. She turned toward the voice. It was Afshin. "I'm here to pick you up."

"Who told you about my arrival time?"

"Your mother."

"She had no right to do that."

"Look, I'm taking you to your family home, not our home."

"There is no *our home* anymore."

"We have to talk."

"I have nothing to say to you."

"Let me take you to your family, and then I'll leave."

There was no taxi available. She followed him reluctantly. She refused to let him carry her suitcase. She sat in the backseat of the car and did not say a word during the entire thirty-five-minute trip. She was angry, and she felt the urge to scream, "How dare you to get near me?"

When she arrived at her family's home, she went directly to the baby's room. The baby was asleep. She stared at her baby for a long time, then kissed him, and left the room to find her mother.

She found her busy cooking in the kitchen. "How could you do that to me?" she complained.

Puri turned around, put her arms around her, and hugged her. "Welcome home."

"You didn't answer my question."

"Please have a seat here. Let me explain."

Puri gave the detail of how Afshin had approached her, how he had cried, and how sorry he was. "I told him that if he wanted to beat his wife, he should have married a villager in remote areas of Iran, not a city girl."

"That's not good enough for me."

"Listen, your baby misses him. When Darius saw his father, he jumped into his arms."

"Impossible."

"Obviously he loves you more than his father, but your baby's smart. He had realized his father was missing."

Puri also talked about the family court and reminded her daughter that the Islamic court always gave custody to the father, and if he were dead or in prison, they would still give the custody to the father's relatives. "I will die if Afshin's mother ends up raising my precious grandchild. I will die if she doesn't give me visitation rights."

Roxana left the kitchen and went to her room. The baby was awake now. She was amazed how much he had grown in just ten days. He had more hair and thick eyelashes now. The baby was staring at her and listening to her as if he was trying to absorb every word.

"So you missed your father, huh?"

She showered her baby with kisses and whispered in his ears, "What am I gonna do? I can't live with an angry man."

Puri reminded Roxana that her father and brother didn't know anything about the fight.

During dinner, Roxana pretended everything was fine in her marriage. She was relieved when her father asked about the Falkland Islands war. Miremad had talked to his daughter about politics since she was seven years old. He would put her on his lap and read Tehran's daily newspapers to her. So it didn't surprise anyone when one day he proudly announced that his seven-year-old could read the newspapers.

"BBC is still talking about it," Roxana said.

"But those islands belonged to Argentina. How can the British claim islands located thousands of miles away from their coast?"

"They claimed Bahrain, which belonged to Iran," Afshin chimed in.

"You're right. Bahrain was also thousands of miles away," Miremad agreed.

After dinner, Roxana told her family about her decision to move to Holland earlier than she had planned. Although everyone was happy that she was leaving the war-stricken Tehran, they were sad that it had to be so sudden. They had hoped to see her and the baby for another month.

She used the early trip as an excuse to stay in her family's home. "The baby will have to get used to another environment soon. I don't want to mess up his sleeping pattern," she said.

Afshin asked Roxana to give him a chance to talk for a few minutes. She reluctantly agreed. They went to the garden and sat at a table.

He had a sad face and an apologetic tone of voice. He assured her that what had happened between them would never happen again. He told her how much he loved her and their baby. He blamed his brother for provoking him.

"Do you love me enough to let this marriage work?" she asked.

"Yes," he responded immediately.

She didn't believe him, but she remembered all the problems that her mother had discussed with her. She couldn't imagine living without her child.

Afshin could also prevent her from going to Europe by not giving his consent for the exit visa. *How humiliating.*

"And are you ready to leave your family behind and live in Holland?" Roxana asked.

"Yes. I'm sick and tired of this war too."

The next day, Roxana had prepared herself to talk to Mr. Hedayat about Afshin's job transfer to Holland.

She found him in a very good mood. He offered her a cup of tea and pulled up a chair for her. "Please have a seat. First of all, let me thank you for that brilliant legal brief. I read it when I was flying to The Hague. It was fantastic, beautifully written, and full of amazing arguments."

"Let's not forget Attorney Keller's contribution."

"I know. But I know your writing style. You'll get a reward for that legal brief. I have got *Bonyad* to agree to send your mother with you to Holland, as long as you need her. We have already rented a two-bedroom suite in a hotel near the bureau. We'll pay for your moving expenses. You will also get two months of your salary in advance."

Roxana was speechless. She thought she was dreaming. This could've only happened in the United States when a company moved an employee to another jurisdiction. As she slowly grasped the reality of what was happening, she remembered why she had come to see her boss. "What about my husband?"

"Don't worry, I'm working on it. He'll join you a month later."

* * *

At Mehrabad Airport, before entering the terminal, she took Afshin away from her mother's earshot and said, "I have one request before I leave." She got closer to him and pointed to the corners of her eyes where one could still see small, pale purple bruises. "I got a severe headache after the beating. I went to a doctor here in Tehran who gave me a penicillin shot and told me I had developed sinusitis. He kept asking me whether I was hit by something in my sinus areas. I didn't want to believe what he was telling me, so I went to another doctor in London who confirmed the Iranian doctor's diagnosis. Because of your beating, I now have developed sinusitis. So my request is, please come to Holland as a different man. Leave your anger behind. I *cannot* live with an angry man."

She was tearing up. She left Afshin and walked fast toward the terminal to join her mother and the baby. She didn't look back.

PART 3

Chapter 65

Roxana was worried about her baby's first flight. Darius once had developed a bad earache. She consulted with his pediatrician for advice. The doctor recommended two short flights instead of a lengthy nonstop flight.

She picked out Athens for a one-night stopover. The short flight went smoothly; Darius didn't have any earache.

After a nice breakfast, she realized that they still had six hours before their flight to Amsterdam. "We'll have a little tour of Athens," she told her mother.

"Look. It's summer. Women are wearing shorts or tube tops. They'll laugh at our outfits," Puri said.

"We're not going with a tour bus," Roxana said while pushing Darius's stroller.

Outside of the hotel, she approached a group of cab drivers standing together and chatting while waiting for passengers. "Does anyone speak English?" she asked.

"Yes," one of them responded.

She told him that she had an afternoon flight and needed a cab to take them to the airport. She also desired a private tour of Athens in exchange for $100. The man's eyes got wide. He smiled, and said, "Which area do you want to start in first?"

"The Acropolis and Parthenon first."

The driver, who was looking at their scarves through his rearview mirror, asked, "Are you Turkish?"

"No. We are Persians."

"We don't like Turkish people. They had a war with us in 1972, you know."

"I know. But I'm sure Turkish people hated that war as much as you did."

"How do you know?"

"Right now we are at war with Iraq. Do you think the Iraqi people like that? No. It was Saddam's decision to attack Iran, not the Iraqi people's."

"Maybe you're right, but anyway, we like Persians. In Greece, we believe that the great Persian civilization was destroyed when Moslem Arabs attacked Persia."

Roxana didn't need to hear that remark; a Greek diplomat friend at the United Nations had once made a similar statement. "Religion destroyed Persia," he had said.

She started talking in Farsi with her mother, explaining that the Parthenon was the remains of a temple dedicated to the Greek goddess Athena.

When they reached the Acropolis, the driver stopped and let them walk over the hill and see the city of Athens spread out below them.

The driver then took them to Syntagma Square, where the Greek parliament building was located. Roxana asked him to take them to a quiet beach on the Mediterranean, which he did.

She sat in the cab and encouraged her mother to walk on the beach for a while. Although it was summertime, there was a breeze that Roxana was avoiding. Darius didn't have sufficient clothes. After Puri came back, it was Roxana's turn to walk along the beautiful beach. She remembered her interrupted honeymoon in Ramsar and the promise she had made to herself to go back to the Caspian Sea.

The beach at the Mediterranean Sea was scenic, but it was not the Caspian Sea—her Caspian Sea.

* * *

As Roxana was leaving Schipol Airport, she saw a reddish-haired young man with a sign bearing her name. The name was written in Farsi. She approached the man and introduced herself. "Are you looking for me?"

"Salam," the man said. "Dr. Ramsy, I'm here to give you a ride."

"Who are you, may I ask?"

"I'm the bureau's driver. My name is Behzad."

As Behzad was driving from Schipol Airport to The Hague, Puri took advantage of a Farsi-speaking countryman and asked him many questions.

Roxana played with Darius, who was awake now and looking out the car window. The expression on his face showed that despite his young age, he had noticed he was in a different environment.

Behzad offered Puri information about himself. He was a permanent resident in Holland. He studied at Utrecht University and was living with his Dutch girlfriend.

Roxana had to ask a burning question. "Does your boss at the bureau know about your lifestyle?"

"They can't force their will on me. I'm a permanent resident here. I speak Dutch, English, and, of course, Farsi. They need me. They have only asked my girlfriend to wear a scarf when she comes to the bureau."

Oh, the magic scarf. If every woman wore a scarf, there wouldn't be any problem in the world.

After checking into the hotel, Roxana sought the help of Behzad and his girlfriend to purchase a crib and some other items she needed for Darius.

She was amazed seeing daylight in The Hague at 10:00 p.m.

Their hotel suite resembled a one-bedroom apartment. The living room opened to a small backyard with a nice garden. That gave Puri the feeling of living in a house rather than in a hotel suite. It also had a partition that could separate it from the dining room and the kitchen area.

Chapter 66

Roxana was sent to the Holland branch of the Bureau of International Arbitration to replace a former law professor in the bureau's research department, but when she arrived, the professor pretended that he was not aware of the director's decision in Tehran. He was a pleasant man, twice Roxana's age, and with a great sense of humor. The research department consisted of one small room with only one desk for the professor. Although he had four research assistants, they were working in the secretaries' room.

There was no chair or desk for Roxana to use, so she did most of her research in the conference room. When the conference room was occupied, she used the library of the International Court of Justice at the Peace Palace.

Despite hectic days at the office, she spent her evenings interviewing babysitters and searching for an apartment. She followed her mother's advice and found an apartment only five minutes away from work. When the real estate agent told her that the building was new—only sixty years old—she killed a chuckle. She thought that the place would fall apart in a year, but she soon learned that Dutch engineers and architects built indestructible buildings.

The Dutch babysitting agency sent Roxana a dozen young girls ages eighteen to twenty. After many interviews she was about to give up and place an ad in the local newspaper when the last candidate showed up. She said a quick "Hello" and went directly to the crib. She picked up Darius and started playing with him. Puri nodded and made a gesture that said *she is the one.*

Maria was a twenty-eight-year-old woman from Athens. Her husband was getting a PhD from Utrecht University. She resembled a typical Persian woman—dark-haired with brown eyes. Roxana had an immediate feeling of connection.

After moving to the new apartment and hiring Maria, Roxana had more time in the evening to concentrate on her work. A new director from Tehran had arrived. He made significant changes in The Hague bureau, including appointing Roxana as the director of the research department and allocating two large rooms for her staff. She finally got a spacious office with large windows overlooking a nice park. The bureau also hired two recent law school graduates and two college graduates to work as her research assistants. She was proud that three of her research assistants were women.

She was the only female attorney working with a dozen male attorneys at The Hague bureau. In the beginning she faced a hostile reaction from her colleagues, all of whom were much older than her. Those who had a PhD in law from European countries didn't think they needed her help at all.

The attorneys met several times a week. During each meeting, they challenged Roxana's recommendations, even on issues related to American laws. She sat through those meetings patiently and listened to some of the most untenable legal arguments in international law.

She categorized and summarized all the pending legal issues before the Claims Tribunal. She added the potential legal arguments that could be raised in the future. Then she researched each topic the attorneys needed and wrote a paper for each one of them.

As the research papers piled up on the attorneys' desks, they realized that Roxana had gathered and analyzed exactly what they needed to incorporate into their legal briefs. Some of those topics included sovereign immunity, state responsibility, force majeure doctrine, and expropriation cases.

It didn't take too long before the attorneys' hostility turned into praise for her work. So the good old boys finally accepted Roxana into their exclusive club.

She worked from 8:00 a.m. to 4:00 p.m. six days a week, and sometimes at home, as late as midnight. The bureau's director expected her to assist him in a lot of nonlegal matters as well. She once called Mr. Hedayat's office in Tehran to inform him of her enormous responsibility. She was shocked to learn that another director had replaced Mr. Hedayat. He was the one who was supposed to facilitate the transfer of Afshin, Lili, and Kayvan to The Hague.

One day in August, Roxana came home late. She smelled the aroma of *ghormeh sabzi,* her favorite Persian dish, as soon as she stepped out of the elevator. She thought her mother was rewarding her for long hours of work. She had done that many times in the past.

When she entered the apartment she was surprised to see that her mother had arranged a birthday celebration for her.

When she tried to blow out all the candles at once, her gesture made Darius laugh loudly—his first grown-up-like laughter.

Roxana forgot about the cake and kept repeating, "Did you hear that *Maman*? His first loud laugh." She sat in a chair near the window and positioned the baby on her lap with his back leaning toward her chest. She took the baby's hand and motioned toward the tree. "That's a tree," she said.

"The baby's first word is usually Mama or Dada," Puri said, laughing. "You should be teaching him Mama or Mommy, not *tree.*"

As Puri was educating Roxana, the baby muttered *Mama* several times. Roxana screamed. Puri's jaw dropped. "Didn't I tell you? *M* is an easier letter."

She kissed her baby. She thought this was the best birthday gift anyone could have given her. She remembered how Afshin had ruined her last two birthdays. The first one, she was pregnant when he had a fight with her in the middle of the street. The second birthday, thanks to his beating, she had gotten bruises followed by sinusitis.

She was happy that Afshin wasn't around this year. She didn't have any gifts because Puri didn't know how or where to shop in a new town. But Darius gave her the best gift ever—he uttered the word *Mama*.

She looked outside the window. The long summer days meant there was still daylight. It was 8:00 p.m.—time for the baby's last bottle. As she was leaving the room with the baby, she heard a familiar sound coming from the window. At first she thought she was imagining, but when she heard the cooing, she knew there was no mistake. *The bird has found me.*

* * *

Bahram, Roxana's brother, flew from the United States to visit his family in Holland. Darius fascinated him, so he spent most of his time playing with him.

Seeing her brother's interaction with Darius, although enjoyable, made Roxana sad. She had never seen Afshin spend any time with his son.

Bahram took his mother for a tour of Amsterdam. They spent two days visiting popular tourist attractions. At the end of each long day, Roxana would hear about interesting places in Amsterdam—the Venice of the North.

Bahram told his sister that there were hundreds of kilometers of canals, ninety islands, and fifteen hundred bridges in Amsterdam. The three famous bridges of Herengracht, Prinsengracht, and Keizersgracht, built in the seventeenth century, had impressed Bahram, an engineer.

The last day of their tour in Amsterdam, they visited two museums that Roxana had dreamed of visiting even when she lived in New York—the Rembrandt and the Van Gogh museums. Bahram also took his mother for a tour of The Hague.

Roxana felt jealous when she heard her mother talking about Mauritshis, the art museum that displayed Rembrandt's famous masterpiece, *Anatomy Lesson*, and Vermeer's masterpiece, *The Girl with Pearl Earrings.*

Roxana didn't know whether she could ever visit any of those museums. She didn't like to be the object of stares because of her Islamic *hejab*. The woman who had not missed even a Dadaists exhibition now had to hear about Dutch museums from her family.

Chapter 67

The last week of Puri's stay in Holland coincided with the death of Princess Grace Kelly of Monaco. She told Roxana how much she had enjoyed the trip and how much she needed to be far away from the war. But the death of Princess Kelly had stirred all of her concerns.

"*Maman*, don't let this ruin your good memories of the trip. She had a good life. She lived like a princess even before she officially became one."

"I know," a tearful Puri responded while watching the funeral on TV. "But I'm thinking of her kids. You need your mother no matter how rich or how old you are. I'm wondering all of a sudden about my own kids. I haven't seen Neghar for four years now. Once I go back to Iran, I may never see you or Darius."

Roxana put her arms around her mother and said, "You have survived Saddam's worst bombing. You'll be just fine. As for Neghar, you've got a green card. Once the relationship between Iran and the United States gets better, you can travel and visit her."

She felt a void in her heart when her mother left. She sensed that even Darius knew that a familiar face had suddenly disappeared.

Afshin arrived in The Hague a week after Puri's departure. Roxana had Darius in her arms when she opened the door for him. He was excited to see his wife and his child. He gave them a quick collective hug and then said, "My God, he has grown so much. He's smiling at me, so he hasn't forgotten me."

As Afshin was talking, Darius opened his arms and pulled his body toward him, showing his eagerness to be held by him. Roxana gave Afshin the details of finding an apartment and buying all necessary furniture.

"We need a car. I waited for you to come and choose one."

She was anxious to hear about the war, the people, and the universities. Afshin was full of information and eager to share. Universities had finally reopened. Sadegh Ghotbzadeh, a former foreign minister, was executed for allegedly plotting to overthrow the Islamic Republic. Iran had liberated all the Khuzestani cities that were occupied by Saddam. They had also captured tens of thousands of Iraqi soldiers and several Iraqi oil export terminals. France and the Soviet Union were competing with each other to arm Iraq with the latest military supplies and higher-technology equipment.

"By selling five AWACS aircraft to Saudi Arabia, the United States is indirectly helping Iraq," Afshin said. "The CIA has been routinely providing intelligence to Saddam. They have even pressured the Export-Import Bank to provide Iraq with financial aid and loans."

"Now I can understand why the last two UN resolutions were pressuring Iran to stop the war and negotiate peace," Roxana said. "Here in Europe, the media gives the impression that it's Saddam who is winning."

* * *

She had a normal marriage for the months of November and December of that year, 1982. The four-month separation had affected Afshin. He wasn't disputing every trivial thing the way he used to. He showed more love and affection for Roxana. For a while she felt this was the honeymoon she never had. Afshin was now living in a peaceful city far away from the war, with a high-paying job.

Roxana resolved the nightly care of Darius by sleeping in his room the entire night.

Despite her request for a suitable family car, Afshin bought a cheap hatchback used car. The car was too small, and the harsh North Sea wind shook it hard every time it was driven.

Roxana taught Afshin some words in Dutch. "Despite their incredible English, the Dutch prefer hearing 'Dag,' instead of 'Hi,' and 'Goede morgen,' instead of 'Good morning,'" she said.

Roxana was not aware that there was a Turkish market in Den Haag. However, the frugal Afshin learned about it quickly. Now he was postponing grocery shopping until he could go to the Turkish market on Saturdays, the same way he did in Tehran, preferring to shop in his old family neighborhood. He had found his *Amirieh* in Den Haag, where grocery items were cheap.

She had no one to help her when shopping for baby food and other items Darius needed. At least the bureau's cafeteria saved her time and energy. The new director had brought a chef from Tehran. He cooked a variety of delicious Persian dishes that one could only enjoy in fancy Tehranian restaurants. Roxana didn't have to spend endless hours preparing Persian meals anymore. In the evenings, she would prepare American or Italian food that would take no more than forty-five minutes of her time.

Afshin was eager to discover The Hague, but Roxana refused to go to places that would invite people to stare at her—places such as Scheveningen beach. Luckily for her, Holland had the second-largest Turkish immigrant population in Europe, right after Germany. The Turkish women wore their regular clothes, thick stockings, and small scarves. She was considered as another Turkish immigrant until she spoke English with an American accent. Turkish immigrants only spoke Turkish or Dutch. Then people would ask her where she was from.

Afshin was not interested in museums, so she was relieved. Puri had told her that she hadn't seen any women with a scarf in the Rembrandt or Van Gogh museums. Roxana agreed to accompany Afshin to the shopping malls and the parks, where there were many Turkish women.

Afshin was fascinated by the Dutch shopping malls—especially how the stores would seem ordinary at their entrances, but they would suddenly open to the sea in the back.

* * *

Roxana's short-lived normal marriage was shaken when the bureau's general director came to The Hague with a long list of reforms. The one that affected her the most was the drastic reduction of Afshin's salary. The new rule put a cap on the combined salaries of the couples that worked for the bureau. Some of the wives of the employees were hired in Holland to do secretarial or other administrative work. The director's goal was to eliminate the spouses' work.

Afshin packed his suitcase and was ready to go back to Tehran. "They are treating me like a secretary. They've cut two thousand guilder from my salary, I can't stay here."

"You just got here. Now you're ready to go back!"

"I cannot let them humiliate me like this."

She made an appointment with the director. He greeted her warmly.

"How could you treat my husband like this? He has an MBA and almost a PhD in economics."

"Well, with all those degrees, he definitely can go find a job."

"This is not the United States. This country has a population of only fourteen million. It has immigrants from Turkey, Indonesia, Morocco, and elsewhere. How can he compete with the Dutch citizens and those immigrants who have been here for years?"

"I don't know. I can't make an exception."

"My husband was hired at the Tehran bureau, but the wives of the employees were hired here. He should not be categorized in the same group."

"I can't bend the rule. He's a spouse too."

Roxana stared at her boss for a while. For a moment she considered resigning, but she remembered her struggle in Tehran to find Darius's milk formula. She also remembered how Darius jumped into his father's arms when he came from Tehran. How could she separate him from his father again?

She was about to leave, but before she reached the door she turned around and came back toward the director's desk. "Would you kindly take two thousand guilders out of my salary and add it to my husband's?"

"Are you sure you're not gonna regret this?"

"Yes, I'm sure. I cannot separate my child from his father."

Chapter 68

Afshin unpacked his suitcase when he learned that the bureau had accepted Roxana's suggestion by adding a portion of her salary to his, but his good mood had changed. He was getting irritated and angry again.

In February, she suggested that they visit Brussels; the Belgian capital was less than a two-hour drive from The Hague. She was trying to cheer up Afshin, but she also needed to forget two unhappy incidents that had occurred earlier that week. One day she needed to purchase certain kinds of baby clothes. She took the streetcar that had a stop in front of her office building. Finding a parking space in downtown shopping areas was almost impossible, but the tram would take her there in only five minutes. She did her shopping in a hurry because she had to do some research at The Hague Academy of International Law that afternoon.

The streetcar was passing through beautiful streets of Den Haag, but Roxana was miles away. She couldn't get the image of Afshin and his packed suitcase out of her mind. *He was ready to leave his child.*

She also couldn't forget about his big fight over money—his salary.

Roxana's train of thought was interrupted when a uniformed police officer addressed her. "You didn't punch your fare card," the officer said. "I have to give you a ticket."

She looked at the fare card in her hand. "Officer, I'm sorry. I was so preoccupied. I forgot to punch the card. As you see, the card is worth more than forty-five guilders, and it has many punches on it."

The officer wasn't interested in any explanation. He wrote his citation and handed it to her. She didn't even look at the amount. She took a one-hundred-guilder bill out of her purse and handed it to the officer. She put the money she got back in her purse without counting it. *He would have believed me if I didn't wear this crazy hejab.*

Still upset about the humiliation she had felt earlier, she drove toward the Peace Palace. About a block away from her destination, she made a left turn to Carnegie Plein. The Peace Palace appeared in front of her. She was driving straight toward the palace, when her car was hit hard by a large American Chevrolet. The car was truncated between the cars parked to her left and the Chevrolet on her right. As she struggled to step out of the car, she noticed that the driver of the car that had hit her was already out looking at her angrily. She was a tall, good-looking blonde teenager. The first thing she said to Roxana was, "Do you have a driver's license?"

Roxana pulled her wallet out of her pocketbook and showed her licenses from Tehran; Washington, DC; New York; Paris; and Holland. "Which one are you interested in?" The teenager shrugged and walked back toward her car. When the police arrived, Roxana was still holding her various licenses in her hand. She explained to the police that she was in her lane going straight when she was hit on the right side. The teenager spoke to the officer in Dutch. Despite her limited knowledge of the Dutch language, Roxana understood what the teenager said. She practically admitted that she had panicked when she found herself between a bike path and the tram track. She had no choice but to drive to her left. That's how she hit Roxana's car.

The officer went to his car to get some forms. The teenager was crying now. Roxana approached her and said, "It's okay. You're safe. I'm safe. This is just property damage. The insurance will pay."

"This is my father's car. I don't have a permit. I'm fifteen. He's gonna kill me," she said, still crying.

"I'm sure he'll be happy to see you safe."

The girl looked at Roxana's outfit shyly and said, "I'm sorry for doubting that you had a driver's license."

"Don't worry. I just got a ticket because of this *hejab*."

The accident turned out to be a blessing after all. The insurance company considered the car "totaled." With the money they paid, Afshin bought a nice, large family car.

After those two incidents, Roxana needed to get away from the city for a few days. Brussels seemed like a next-door Paris.

* * *

She had visited the city in the early '70s. She had seen all the tourist attractions, including the Galeries Royales Saint Hubert, Palais Royal, Royal Museums of Fine Arts, and Eglise du Beguinage and Gudula cathedrals. She knew that her husband was not interested in any museum, so she thought he would enjoy visiting the Grand Place. This was Brussels's historic market square. The splendid guild houses and the gothic town hall had turned the place into one of the most impressive town squares in Europe.

Afshin did enjoy visiting the Grand Place, but the baby was getting restless. Roxana wanted to go back to the hotel, but Afshin was still eager to do more sightseeing. He drove aimlessly in the streets of Brussels. As they passed through a street with several theatres, Roxana saw a sign with Adamo's pictures. He was in town and had a concert for a few days. She sighed unintentionally and kept playing with her baby until she heard Afshin complaining. "I think we're lost!"

She looked out the window. "Oh my God," she said in a panicky voice. "We're in the Red Light Zone."

He had mistakenly driven to the area where women sat naked in the windows to attract customers. She had heard about the Red Light District in Amsterdam, but she didn't know that Brussels also had one. "Please get us out of here," she begged. "If someone from the bureau sees us here, we'll be fired."

"No one from the bureau is here. Besides, you're wearing your *hejab*."

"The more reason to run from here. People will laugh at me."

"I'm trying, but this is a congested, narrow street."

The next day, Afshin wanted to visit the shopping malls in Brussels. Roxana refused. "You'll get lost again. You don't ask for directions, and you don't follow the map. So why don't you discover the city on foot?"

Because he persisted, Roxana took the baby and reluctantly accompanied him.

Many parking places were available, but he was looking for a free one. He found it, but it was far away from the shopping mall. It was cold and windy. Roxana was concerned about her baby. He took Darius in his arms, and she walked behind him carrying the baby's bag. The wind was bothering her eyes. After twenty minutes of walking, she started complaining. Her eyes were itching severely now. It was also the time to feed Darius.

Afshin forgot where he had parked the car. Fortunately, Roxana had memorized the name of the street. She asked a passerby how to find the street. When they reached the parking area, she noticed immediately that their car had been vandalized. Someone had broken the backseat window and had taken Roxana's expensive leather boots. Before heading toward the shopping mall, she had changed her boots to a more comfortable pair of walking sneakers.

Afshin obtained a piece of plastic from a gas station and covered the broken window.

She had to cover the baby totally to protect him from the harsh February wind entering the car. During the entire two-hour drive, she felt like screaming many times but kept quiet and didn't say a word.

Afshin's stinginess in paying for parking and his reluctance to ask for directions ruined Roxana's future trips to Amsterdam and Rotterdam. Thereafter, anytime he suggested visiting another city in Holland, she told him he should travel by himself.

* * *

She celebrated Darius's first birthday in March. She decorated the living room with fancy balloons and other birthday decorations. It was an emotional day for her because the only guest present was Maria, Darius's babysitter. Afshin had forbidden her from inviting anybody from the office. "I don't like to socialize with them," he had said.

Darius now uttered ten words in Farsi and Dutch. Roxana was adamant to teach him Farsi—the language of Hafez, Omar Khayam, and Rumi. It was not surprising, however, that he would pick up some Dutch words because Maria spoke with him in Dutch. Afshin didn't make any effort to teach his son anything. He was always busy watching TV. At first, Roxana tried to get his attention whenever

Darius did or said something new. "Look, he said . . ." "Look, he is walking now . . ." but she eventually gave up. However, each time Darius said a new word, Roxana kissed him and encouraged him. "I'll remember this moment forever," she whispered in his ear.

The arrival of Lili and Kayvan brought excitement to Roxana's life. "I'm so thrilled to see you," Roxana said as she hugged Lili. "These past eight months I felt that something was missing here. Now I know it was you."

"You have no idea how happy I am to be out of Tehran," Lili said. "The lines for buying rationed food are getting longer. The modesty squads are still harassing women in the streets of Tehran, to make sure they comply with the *hejab.* Many people are having heart attacks. In our neighborhood alone, heart attacks have killed more people than Saddam's bombs."

Lili talked about Kayvan and her relationship with him. Roxana learned that Kayvan's wife had had a miscarriage. As the only child, she didn't want to leave her parents, especially since her father had had a stroke, so she allowed Kayvan to come to The Hague alone.

Roxana told Lili about her trials and triumphs at the bureau, her never-ending research, and how the director had cut Afshin's salary.

"There is something you should know about Afshin. Kayvan and I worked with him on a case. He has all those degrees, and he is good in an academic setting, but he cannot apply his knowledge to a given problem. Also, he leaves the project when the office hours are over. He doesn't believe in working overtime unless he's paid for it. Maybe that was the reason behind the director's decision."

After hearing Lili's remarks, Roxana worried whether Afshin would lose his job again.

A second interesting event in March was the arrival of a new director. His name was Dr. Rohani. With his green eyes and reddish hair, he resembled a European more than an Iranian. During their first meeting, he told Roxana how much he had appreciated her research and the legal advice she'd provided to various government entities. "But we need you at the tribunal," he said. "The government attorneys or representatives who come from Tehran not only do not speak English but also don't have any experience with an international tribunal. Legal arguments can easily get lost in simultaneous interpretation."

"I have a few more topics to research. When I finish, I'll be happy to go to court."

"There are 2,884 small claims under $250,000 filed by the Americans. There are 960 big claims and some ninety government claims. I'm going to assign seventy-five of those cases to you. I know that you're already handling the US violation case."

"Do you know that there are 242 claims within one of the sections of that case?" Roxana smiled.

"Yes, Mr. Hedayat has told me all about that case. He has also told me that the case is older than your son, and you know every argument by heart."

Roxana found a lot of similarities between Mr. Hedayat and Dr. Rohani. The two men knew about the seriousness of the cases pending before the tribunal. They knew that revolutionary rhetoric would not sway the non-Iranian arbitrators, but good legal arguments could. Mr. Rohani also understood the need for a computer programmer Roxana had asked for. He hired someone from Tehran to help Roxana, but the man couldn't help because he was not a programmer. Following Roxana's suggestion, he allowed Attorney Keller to provide the needed technical support to the bureau.

While the nine arbitrators heard cases in three different chambers of the Claims Tribunal, there were ongoing out-of-court settlement negotiations between the American companies and the Iranian government agencies. The settlement agreement would then become an award and, once signed by the arbitrators, would be paid out of the security account established by Iran. According to the Algiers Declarations, Iran was obligated to maintain a minimum balance of $500 million in the account for the purpose of paying the American companies' awards.

Roxana had heard that both the American companies and the Iranian government agencies preferred amicable solutions to their disputes. Taking advantage of Dr. Rohani's open-door policy, one day she took a copy of Afshin's resume and knocked on his door. She gave him the details of how he didn't have any specific job and, most importantly, of how his salary was cut by two thousand guilders. Once she saw Dr. Rohani's sympathetic reaction, Roxana indulged herself to suggest that Afshin would make a good negotiator in the Settlement Division of the bureau.

Dr. Ronhani looked at Afshin's resume and said, "You're right. With his educational background and job experience, he belongs to the Settlement Division."

She thanked him, and as she was leaving his office said, "Please don't let him know I talked to you about this."

Chapter 69

Noruz arrived, and the bureau closed for one week to celebrate the Persian New Year. Roxana had promised herself that she would not travel with Afshin anymore, but she couldn't waste a week of vacation in a cold and damp city like The Hague. She felt as if she was living in a snow globe on an Iranian enclave. Everyone could see her in the globe with her Islamic *hejab*. The globe could be shaken at any time, and she could be sent back to war-stricken Iran.

Afshin was in a good mood those days; his job at the out of court settlement division of the Bureau had given him the career boost he needed. Although he was still nagging about his salary, most days he came home and boasted about how he had finished a multimillion-dollar settlement with a big American company. Roxana always commented, "That's wonderful. Congratulations."

She took advantage of Afshin's good mood and told him that she wanted to go to Paris. Afshin had never been to Paris, so he agreed to drive.

She purchased a road map and the city map for driving in Paris. She made reservations for one week in a Quartier Latin hotel. Before driving to Paris, she sat at the dining room table, opened the travel map, and drew arrows on it. She also told Afshin that there were different gates entering Paris and found the one that would lead them to Champs-Élysées. "Once you reach Champs-Élysées, I can direct you to our hotel."

She was reading a children's book to Darius but occasionally would look out the window to make sure that Afshin was driving on the right highway. Everything seemed to be going smoothly until she noticed that the car had stopped.

"We're lost," Afshin said.

"How is that possible? This was a simple direction."

Afshin picked up the big unfolded map, tore it up, and said, "This is good for you, not for me."

She looked around. They were in a cobblestone square with a small fountain in the middle. A man was sitting on a stone bench near the fountain reading *Le Monde*. Roxana took the map and walked over to him.

"Pardonnez-moi, monsieur. Nous sommes perdu, Je sais Francais. Mais maintenant je suis tres furieux. Je peux parler seulment en Englais."

She asked the Frenchman directions to Champs-Élysées. The man took the map, drew some arrows and explained to her in English how to get to the right gate.

When she returned to the car, she handed the map to Afshin. "Where are my American friends who always say French people are rude and never speak in English? I just told him that I'm too angry to speak in French, and he gave me the direction in English."

By the time they reached Champs-Élysées, it was dark, but the lights were on, and the streets were illuminated. Darius woke up, looked out the window, and said in Farsi, "Bah-bah" (nice).

Roxana almost screamed inside. That was a grown-up term Darius had heard from his grandmother Puri—every time she referred to something nice.

She decided to forget about another episode of getting lost with Afshin. She tried to see Paris through the surprised eyes of her one-year-old son.

* * *

She stayed in the hotel most of the day caring for her son. She gave Afshin information about sightseeing in Paris and encouraged him to explore the city on his own.

During the day, her share of Paris was the limited view of the streets from the hotel's windows. At night, she directed Afshin to drive to the best parts of Paris. She didn't get out of the car, as if she was hiding from Paris. She didn't want Paris to see her in veil.

One day, feeling guilty that Roxana had stayed at the hotel almost every day, Afshin volunteered to care for Darius for a while. "This is your Paris. Go and enjoy it. Nobody from the office is here."

Roxana took advantage of his generous offer. She wore her tall boots and long raincoat because it was raining. She covered her hair under a rain hat. Although she looked very European, her outfit passed the Islamic criteria. She was totally covered.

She walked in the streets of Quartier Latin, feeling like a stranger. She remembered how much she had enjoyed Paris three years earlier after she ran away from the hostage crisis. Her friends were right. To her, Paris was like a mistress. She made Roxana forget about those miserable days in New York City. Paris was still a friend, but Roxana didn't have any desire to talk to her friend. She was devastated by Saddam's war and her own domestic war. She didn't want her friend to see her wounds.

She had left Tehran behind, and she was ready to say good-bye to Paris too. Why was she saying good-bye to every city she loved? She remembered her long and torturous good-bye to New York City. Lately she had been missing that city a lot. The Dutch TV channels often showed American movies. The last one had a scene in a diner where characters were seated in a booth with red-and-white-checkered tablecloths. Roxana wondered if she would ever see an American diner again.

* * *

The *Noruz* celebration was over, and everyone was back at work.

"So how was Paris?" asked Lili.

"I don't know. Either this was another Paris, or I took the wrong Roxana with me. How was London?"

"I didn't go to London. I went to Tunisia."

"Why Tunisia?"

"Because it was warm and sunny and . . ." Lili paused, "the best place to get married. Kayvan and I are married now."

"You what?" Roxana gasped.

Lili extended her left hand and pointed to her ring finger. She wore an oval ruby gold ring trimmed with diamonds.

Roxana wanted to shout at Lili, "Are you nuts?" but she had never seen her friend that happy.

"I fell in love with him all over again. You witnessed my struggle to stay away. But I couldn't. I'm his *sigheh,* concubine. We found an imam in Tunisia who performed the marriage. You're looking at a concubine with a PhD. Yes, I'm Kayvan's concubine for ninety-nine years."

Lili left Roxana in a state of shock. She tried hard not to be a righteous, judgmental friend, but something was bothering her deeply. At the end of the day, she recognized the nagging voice—a feminist, a woman's advocate. *Kayvan's wife had the right to know.*

For the next three days, Roxana had a case scheduled before every chamber of the tribunal. She won the first two cases easily. At the end of the third day, during a break when she was waiting for a call from the bureau at the tribunal's reception desk, she was approached by one of the American arbitrators. "I believe you're from my neck of the woods," he said.

Roxana knew the arbitrator was from New York. "I believe so."

"Where did you get your JSD?"

"NYU."

"The best school for international law, I hear."

Roxana was trying hard to avoid talking to the American arbitrator. Her call didn't come through, and the eyes and ears of the bureau were watching her. She excused herself by saying, "Your Honor, I don't mean to be rude, but I have to go back to my hearing." She hurried back to the arbitration court.

The claimant in the case, represented by a famous law firm, was an American company that had entered into a verbal agreement in 1978 with an Iranian company to build a hotel for them in Shiraz. The agreement consisted of a few letters, with no additional activities before or after the revolution.

After half a day of arguments, it was Roxana's turn to respond.

"Your Honors," she started, "the claimants are asking an award for millions of dollars for breach of a *contract* that didn't exist. They have failed to prove to this honorable tribunal that they entered into any agreement. We argue that the exchange of a few letters doesn't establish a contract. The claimant didn't contact the hotel in Iran in 1978—one year before the revolution. They never sent any drawings or any design, and they never visited the site. I will not be discussing the *frustration of purpose doctrine,* or *quantum merit*, because there was no contract."

After Roxana finished her argument, there was a long pause by the chambers' neutral arbitrator, who happened to be a well-known Swedish jurist. He looked at Roxana as if he wanted to hear more. Roxana saw a glimpse of admiration in the neutral arbitrator's eyes. She didn't pay attention to reactions by the American or the Iranian arbitrators, primarily because she knew that in most cases the American arbitrator would vote for the American claimant, and the Iranian arbitrator for the Iranian side. So, it was important if the neutral arbitrator was moved by her argument.

When she came out of the court, Lili was waiting for her. "So you won the third case too?" she asked.

"They're deliberating now. We'll probably hear from them by the end of the day."

* * *

Lili invited Roxana to lunch to celebrate her triumph. She wanted to take her to the Kurhaus Hotel restaurant, which had a panoramic view of the sea.

"Are you crazy? Go to the Scheveningen beach area? Everyone will stare at us."

"Look, with your chic, tall leather boots, knee-length skirt, and that American business jacket, you look like an American lawyer."

"Did you forget that I'm wearing a scarf?"

"Even your scarf looks chic since you're knotting it under your ear."

"I don't mean to make a fashion statement, but after a year of wearing a scarf, and having my head down researching, the skin under my chin has developed some kind of rash, so I have to move the knot to the left side of my face."

"Still, it's very fashionable."

Lili, acting like a happy newlywed, convinced her friend to go to the Kurhaus Restaurant. She turned the radio on as she was driving toward the restaurant. She changed the station to the one that played American music. When the station played "Stayin' Alive," by the Bee

Gees, the two friends, who were in a celebrating mood, forgot about their *hejab* and began moving their arms and the upper parts of their bodies as if they were doing the hustle on a dance floor. When Lili stopped the car at a red traffic light, Roxana noticed that people in the cars around them were staring at them. She couldn't help laughing when Lili stuck her tongue out, made a funny gesture, and sped off.

At the restaurant, Lili continued talking about her happy life, but Roxana was watching the grayish sea. The North Sea was blue on sunny days; unfortunately, there were only a handful of sunny days per year in The Hague. She longed for the greenish blue color of the Caspian Sea.

"May I join you two lovely ladies?" a voice asked. Roxana turned around, and her jaw dropped. There stood Steve Radcliff, looking at her with the familiar love in his eyes.

Chapter 70

"You look so beautiful even in a scarf," Steve told Roxana.

"Who's the chief conspirator here?" Roxana asked, looking at Lili.

"I am," came a familiar voice. "I invited him."

Roxana looked back and saw Kayvan. "Don't you think it's a little risky for you and Steve to show up here?" she asked.

"Don't worry. He's a journalist. We can always say he was going to interview you," Kayvan answered.

Kayvan and Steve joined Lili and Roxana and ordered some appetizers.

"Why're you here?" Roxana asked Steve after staring at him with a smile.

"Unlike the Iranian authorities, who've refused to issue me a visa, the Dutch immigration office has given me a one-year visa."

As Lili and Kayvan were looking at the menu and talking to each other, Steve pulled his chair closer to Roxana and gazed into her eyes, saying the unspoken words, *I missed you. I still love you.* "Are you happy?" he asked.

"Yes, I am, because I'm in love."

"With a man who has nothing in common with you?"

"No. I'm in love with a little guy. His name is Darius."

Roxana pulled her wallet out of her purse and showed Steve several pictures of Darius. He looked at each one, and paused for a few minutes. "He's beautiful. He could've been mine."

She pretended she didn't hear Steve's last comment. She stared at the sea. Finally, she asked, "So what are you doing these days?"

"I'm writing my book about Iran's revolution, as I told you before, and I've also started covering news about this tribunal, so you'll be seeing a lot of me in Den Haag."

"I hope you're not seeking me out. Den Haag is not a large city like Tehran. Those who work at the bureau and the tribunal keep bumping into each other all the time."

"Don't worry. I won't be causing you any trouble. I just want to see your beautiful face and to hear your voice from time to time. Boy, I missed you so much."

The foursome ate their meals while talking and catching up with each other's lives. Roxana remembered their trips to Paris and Rome. She regretted how she had worried about the revolution instead of enjoying herself. She was a free woman, like a bird who could have flown anywhere, but now someone had cut her wings. She was in a cage.

That afternoon, Dr. Rohani was full of smiles. "I told you we need you in court," he said as soon as Roxana entered his office. He then asked Roxana to write a report on the tribunal's procedural rules. "I heard that you made suggestions on . . . what's the name? I forgot."

"It's a long name," Roxana said. "The United Nations Commission on International Trade Law, or UNCITRAL."

"Yes, that's it. I need to read your comments on that. Also, before I forget, there is a seminar on international law that will be held in the Peace Palace in July and August. Make sure you're there."

"I'll send you the report right away," Roxana said as she walked to the door, but before she left the office, Dr. Rohani addressed her. "Dr. Ramsy, one more thing. Thanks for the three cases you won."

That night, Roxana couldn't forget the lunch. She thought about Lili and Kayvan, two people who were deeply in love, yet they had to go through a bizarre marriage to give legitimacy to their relationship. She thought about Steve, who had accepted a one-sided love. And then she thought about herself, someone who lived with a stranger in a loveless marriage.

For days she couldn't forget the sad expression on Steve's face or his words when he looked at Darius's pictures, *He could've been mine.*

* * *

The seminar that Roxana participated in was sponsored by The Hague Academy of International Law and was located at the Peace Palace. Roxana had taken part in many seminars and conferences before; this seminar, however, resembled a mini-United Nations. At first she felt awkward. The participants included hundreds of men, but only dozens of women. She was the only one wearing a scarf. During the first few days, she tried to enter the seminar hall quietly, pretending that she didn't exist. But when the professors and the instructors talked about the Iran-US Claims Tribunal, and misinterpreted the tribunal's decision or Iran's position in a pending case, she had to speak. The students and the professors soon recognized that the woman in a grayish business jacket and pearl-gray scarf had a lot to say about the Iran-US Claims Tribunal. During the break, attorneys from different countries surrounded her. She met many interesting people, most notably a young woman from Finland who enjoyed the rainy days of Holland because she felt at home. She also met a warmhearted, smiling Egyptian woman who was tired of the rain and longed for the sunny days back home in Cairo.

During the last week of the seminar, Roxana learned that every year there was an exam for the lawyers who had applied to receive the academy's diploma. When she found out that during the fifty years of the academy's existence, no Iranian lawyer had ever received the degree, she signed up. To participate in the exam, a lawyer had to have a minimum of a master's degree in law. Many participants held doctoral degrees.

That night, when she brought up the subject of the academy's award, Afshin said sarcastically, "You just saw another challenge and couldn't resist it, huh?"

"What's your objection? I just want to participate because no one from Iran has ever earned this award. Don't worry; it's a tough exam. I'm not gonna win."

"Have you ever failed in anything in your life?"

"Yes, my marriage."

* * *

She entered the huge exam room and found her assigned seat. She hated that her heart was beating so fast. She had left student life behind. She didn't need the anxiety of taking another test. The proctor announced that this was a three-hour written exam. At the direction of the proctor, all participants opened their booklets. Roxana debated whether she should leave the exam room. At least she could claim she didn't participate. But she decided to look at the question. There was one topic, "The Freedom of the High Seas." Roxana smiled and began writing. After two hours and fifteen minutes, she put her pen down, closed the booklet, and left the exam room. Lili was waiting for her outside. "How did it go?"

"I don't know. I wrote seventy-five pages. But look at the number of participants!"

"I'm sure you did well. Let's go and eat. They have a cafeteria-style luncheon for you."

To her surprise, Roxana was one of the eleven attorneys who had won the written test. The oral test was to be held the next morning. She heard from other participants that a panel of four to five judges would test the candidates. The judges had the right to ask any question related to international law.

She read a book for Darius and waited for him to fall sleep. She went to bed but kept reviewing famous international law cases in her head. She admitted she didn't need this tension in her life. *Why did I have to participate in such a difficult contest?*

The next morning, when she entered the large auditorium, again she doubted her ability to pass the oral exam. The auditorium was packed with spectators, mostly the candidates who had failed the written exam, as well as other participants in the seminar.

She was told to stay outside until her turn. She studied the faces of her competitors. They were in their thirties, forties, and fifties. She was one of the few young contestants.

She was the fourth candidate escorted to the auditorium. She was directed to sit in the candidate's seat at a large, oval conference table. A panel of five judges was seated on the opposite side of the table. Roxana said, "Hello." She immediately recognized one of the judges of the ICJ. She also knew Professor Rideau, a well-known French jurist. The third judge was an Egyptian professor who was one of the instructors at the academy's seminar. She didn't recognize the other two judges.

The judges asked her questions after making some hypothetical cases. She was supposed to recognize the fact pattern, name the real case, and analyze the decision made by the ICJ or other international courts.

She was successful in remembering all the names and legal opinions of the ICJ or other international tribunals. However, she paused when the ICJ judge gave her his hypothetical question. She didn't recognize the case and had to improvise. When her oral exam was over, the French professor, who seemed agitated, asked the ICJ judge, "What was that all about?"

"I just made up a case. I was looking for a futuristic approach," he responded, acting victorious.

She came out feeling terrible. She was certain that her last answer had ruined all the previous good answers. As she was walking away from the auditorium, a young woman ran after her. "Please wait."

The woman gave Roxana a hug. "You were wonderful out there. You had the best answers."

"Thanks," Roxana said. "Do I know you?"

"No, you don't. My name's Pamela Norton. I'm a law graduate, but my husband is one of the lawyers who represent the American companies at the tribunal. I've been watching you during the two weeks of the seminar. You were magnificent there, and you were terrific today."

"Thanks for the words of confidence, but I really messed up with my last answer."

"No, you didn't. You're gonna win."

She left the area feeling certain that she had lost. As she was about to leave the building, she saw Lili running toward her. "I'm sorry I couldn't be here. I got a last-minute assignment. How was it?"

"Awful," Roxana said.

She described her encounter with Pamela Norton and the fact that her husband was one of the attorneys suing Iran. "You're wondering why I like the Americans. That's your answer. After the hysteria created over the hostage taking, that woman should consider me as an enemy, yet she genuinely wants me to win."

"Enough about the Americans. Let me buy you a cup of coffee."

After Lili left, Roxana called Afshin and told him that the result of the oral exam would be out in ten minutes. "Please come and pick me up."

She saw several of the seminar's participants as she was heading back toward the Peace Palace building. One of them was her Egyptian friend. "Where are you going?" she asked Roxana.

"Getting the results of the oral exam."

"I know the result."

"Who won?"

"Well, there was a Sorbonne graduate from Africa. Then there was a French lawyer, and then there was this wonderful woman I know . . ."

"Who?"

The Egyptian woman came closer, hugged Roxana, and said, "You. Congratulations. You won."

"Are you sure?"

"Yes."

She was soon surrounded and congratulated by a group of lawyers who had participated in the contest.

* * *

She ran toward the gate at the Peace Palace when she saw Afshin and Darius entering the gate.

"I thought at the end of this long day, Darius's face is the one you'd like to see," Afshin said.

Roxana kissed her son. Indeed this was the face she wanted to see. "I won!" she blurted as she embraced Darius.

"Really?" Afshin asked. He smiled proudly as if he had won the award.

Roxana nodded. "I have to attend a reception, but I'm going to make an excuse and come back. Don't go too far."

She gave Darius back to Afshin and walked to the reception room. There was a long table full of food, drinks, and pastries. She was going to thank the academy's hostess when the ICJ judge and the Egyptian professor who had tested her earlier stopped her. "Congratulations," they both said simultaneously. They extended their hands to shake Roxana's hand. She stepped back and apologized. "I'm sorry, Your

Honors. The Islamic protocol doesn't allow me to shake hands with men."

She practically rushed out of the reception room and ran toward their car. Afshin was already in the driver's seat, and Darius was seated in the backseat.

"That was quick!" Afshin commented.

"I've never felt so humiliated in my life. Two of the academy judges wanted to shake hands with me as they congratulated me, but I had to excuse myself. They must think all Iranians are going nuts."

"This was a big win—like the Nobel Prize in the legal field. You should be happy."

"That handshake moment ruined it for me."

"Let's go and celebrate your birthday."

Afshin took her to a gift shop in downtown Den Haag and asked her to choose a gift she liked. She was surprised. Afshin didn't believe in celebrating birthdays or buying gifts. She felt this was his gift for winning the academy's diploma and not for her birthday. She picked out a gold-tone brass bracelet that cost only one hundred gilders (fifty dollars). It wasn't gold, but it shined like gold. She never liked gold jewelry, but she thought for the first time that she could show that bracelet to friends and relatives and say, "My husband's gift for my birthday." The only gifts Afshin had ever given her were an engagement ring and a wedding band.

They had a nice, relaxed dinner at a Chinese restaurant in downtown Den Haag. She was happy that the long day was over, so she didn't mind people staring at their table. Before she had a baby, people were staring at her *hejab*, but after Darius was born, she discovered that the Dutch were crazy about children. People would not talk to her, but they would walk directly to Darius and speak to him in Dutch. Darius's large brown eyes and thick eyelashes attracted the Dutch every time.

After they left the restaurant, Afshin suggested that they walk in downtown for a while. Despite Den Haag's unseasonable heat and despite her reluctance to walk wearing a *hejab*, she agreed. They had not walked more than fifty feet away from the restaurant when a young man who was walking with his girlfriend stopped Afshin. "Excuse me, sir," he said as he held Afshin's arm with a friendly smile. "You see how hot it is. Look at my girlfriend. She is wearing a short and a strapless top. Why are you putting your wife under that long dress and big scarf?"

Afshin was surprised. He had never been confronted by anyone like that. He struggled explaining that the Islamic tradition dictated the wearing of the *hejab* for women. The Dutch man suggested that he should break the tradition. Roxana was enjoying this, but Afshin was getting frustrated. At one point, he turned to her and said in Farsi, "Can you help me out here?"

"I'm sorry. You're on your own."

She couldn't help remembering her honeymoon in Ramsar, the Caspian Sea beach town where one of the locals stopped Afshin and asked him why he wouldn't impose *hejab* on his wife. She would've liked to see the man from Ramsar and the Dutchman from The Hague debate the issue.

After hearing the Dutchman's lecture for a few minutes, Afshin finally walked away.

"So, what happened to the brilliant legal mind who just won The Hague Academy's award? Couldn't you just come up with an argument justifying the *hejab*?"

"There's no justification for the *hejab*."

* * *

Roxana's family was proud when they heard the news.

"This is like Iran winning the World Cup," Syrus said.

After praising her daughter, Puri told her that her father had developed a kidney stone and needed an operation. "We don't have good doctors or good medications here anymore. I can't send him to the United States because he can't get a US visa."

Roxana detected the anxiety in her mother's voice. After what she had gone through with her own C-section, she believed her mother was right in sending her father to Holland for the operation.

Chapter 71

Miremad had to take care of many urgent business matters before traveling to Holland. That gave Roxana enough time to search for the best doctor in The Hague to operate on her father. He arrived two days before Christmas 1983. The Dutch doctor agreed with the Iranian specialist that the stone was too big and couldn't be shattered by medication. He scheduled the surgery two weeks after his first consultation.

The waiting period gave Roxana an opportunity to take her father to visit interesting places in The Hague and other cities in Holland. The first place he wanted to visit was the Peace Palace. Before entering the building, he stood in front of it for a while and admired the architecture. "Prime Minister Mossadegh came here and argued about Iran's rights to its oil resources," he said. "And some thirty years later my daughter comes here and gets a postdoctoral degree. How about that!"

"It's not a big deal; 179 other people have received this degree before me."

"Yes, but this is the first time for Iran. You should be proud of yourself. I remember when you were ten years old, I told you to be humble, but not this humble."

Roxana remembered the day her father talked to her about humility. His words had stayed with her all her life. Whenever she came up with the best legal arguments, she made everyone believe that it was a team effort, not hers alone.

She thought that this might be her father's only visit to Holland; she had several special places to show him. She took him to the Rembrandt and Van Gogh museums. Because of her father, she didn't mind being the object of stares. She also showed him the boathouses floating in the canals and the famous Dutch windmills, monuments, and palaces.

Miremad had fun with his grandchild when they visited Madurodam, a miniature city that had replicas of all the major buildings in Holland, including a mini-Peace Palace.

She noticed that her father was disturbed by the fact that every time they went to a restaurant, Roxana was the one who paid for the meals. He didn't have enough guilders, but he had brought thousands of dollars with him. He would put some of his dollar bills on the table, and Roxana would put them back in his pocket. Afshin was acting as if this was a *Taarof*, between a father and his daughter. He didn't feel any obligation to pay for the meal of his father-in-law, a man in whose house he had dined a thousand times.

She also noticed the pain in her father's face anytime Afshin had a disagreement with her. She was hiding all the disputes from her father by letting Afshin vent during office hours. At home, she was careful not to do anything or to say anything against Afshin's wish, but he would still find an excuse to argue or disagree with her. Miremad never advised Roxana about her marriage. Nor did he comment about Afshin's behavior. But one day when Roxana took him to the window to show him the tree and to talk to him about her mourning dove, he interrupted her. "You shouldn't have come back to Iran."

"But you encouraged me to come back home."

"I was wrong."

She didn't continue the conversation. Her father had recognized that she was in a cage—an outdoor cage created by her government dictating her to wear the mandatory *hejab*, and an indoor cage at home where her husband controlled her actions and words. She was hurt by Afshin's behavior, but she didn't know what to do. *I have to put up with him until my father leaves.*

A few days before his admission to the hospital, Miremad told his daughter he needed to do some shopping. He wanted to buy gifts for his family, relatives, friends, and his employees.

By the time he finished his shopping, he had two large suitcases full of gifts. He had even bought a gift for an old porter who occasionally moved clothes for him from one store to another—one hundred feet apart.

"You'll end up paying a lot of money to customs," Roxana said.

"When my father traveled on business to Russia, he bought gifts not only for family and friends, but also for the entire neighborhood."

* * *

The surgery was successful. The doctor wanted Miremad to stay in the hospital for one week. Roxana visited him twice a day, before going to work and after work was finished. Afshin was with her during most of the visits. One day Roxana was surprised to see that he had bought a transistor radio for her father. Miremad was pleased to listen to the Iranian radio stations speaking in Farsi, but after a few days, he gave the radio back to Afshin. "They only talk about the war," he said. "It's sad to hear how many people are dying every day."

Roxana found a Turkish orderly in the hospital, paid him one hundred guilders and asked him to check on her father a few times a day. "He speaks Farsi, Russian, and Turkish," she said.

On January 15, 1984, Roxana had an important meeting with an Indian professor at the bureau. She had invited him to come to The Hague to discuss some of the legal issues raised at the tribunal.

She had met Dr. Nematollah, a Moslem scholar, at a conference in New York City. He was the perfect individual to work on some of the expropriation cases for Iran.

When the professor arrived at the bureau, some other attorneys also showed interest in meeting with him. Roxana was anxious to finish her work early and go to the hospital on time. Her father was supposed to be released at 3:00 p.m. Earlier that morning, when she visited him, he was walking outside his room impatiently. "Why can't I go home now?"

"Your doctor wants to examine you one more time. He has to sign your release."

She hugged her father and told him that she would return at 2:00 p.m.

After introducing Professor Nematollah to the bureau's attorneys, Roxana encouraged them to share their specific legal problems with him.

It was 11:00 a.m. when a secretary came in and whispered in Roxana's ear, "The hospital has called. They need you there."

Roxana apologized to the professor and the other attorneys, picked up her briefcase and rushed to the garage.

As she was driving, she wondered why the hospital had called her. *Maybe he had asked them to release him earlier.*

Roxana parked the car and ran to her father's room on the third floor. Her father's bed was empty. A nurse showed up and took her to the end of the hallway. She offered Roxana a seat and said, "Your father is there," pointing to a room. "They are operating on him."

"Operating on what? Was he bleeding?"

"No. He had a heart attack."

"What are you talking about?"

"According to his roommates, he was drinking his soup, and then he lowered his head. One of his roommates called me. We took him immediately . . ."

She wasn't hearing the nurse anymore. She started pacing in the hallway. *Another operation. That means more days in the hospital. He's gonna hate that.*

She gazed into the grayish sky and wondered how her father would handle the new heart problem. He was a healthy man who never needed to take any medication. The kidney stone was his only major medical problem.

A silver-haired Dutch doctor approached Roxana and tapped her on the shoulder.

"We tried to revive the heart, but he was gone the minute he had the heart attack. We tried everything. I'm so sorry."

Roxana's heart stopped. "No, that can't be possible. He can't die. Please do another operation."

"I'm sorry. We did all we could."

"Oh my God! Oh my God!" Roxana moaned as she covered her face with both hands. She felt feverish. Her clothes felt tight. Her heart was racing. She leaned against the window trying not to collapse. She didn't know what to do. The doctor left. The nurse led her to a chair and asked her if she had someone to take her home. She gave her Afshin's number. She asked the nurse if she could see her father.

"They have to clean him up and take him to the morgue," the nurse said.

She looked out the window and cried quietly; her father's life played in her head like a movie.

He was born to a rich, well-known family in Azerbaijan. He lost his mother at age two, and then his father at age six. His father had taken him along on his last business trip to Kiev, Russia, when he died of a heart attack at age thirty. Miremad witnessed how his father's employees rushed to his vest and jacket pocket and stole his gold jewelry and money. Then there was a custody battle between his paternal and maternal uncles. The two men were rich, but Miremad's father was richer, so each would benefit from his wealth by caring for his only child.

The maternal uncle won the custody of his nephew when Miremad preferred to live in his town, but the uncle was a gambler, a womanizer, and a drunkard most of his life. By the time Miremad reached age fifteen, his uncle had gambled away all of his land—the land that had comprised half of the real property in town—his father's crystal store, and other businesses.

When Miremad was six years old, his father had shown him a stash of gold and diamonds buried in their garden under a bush. "If I'm dead, and you lose all my wealth, remember this stash."

When his uncle lost all of his father's wealth, the fifteen-year old Miremad found the stash of jewelry and headed for Tehran. After some odd jobs and serving his two-year military service, he established a successful business manufacturing men's clothes.

Someone shook Roxana. It was Afshin, trying to hold back tears. "What happened here?"

"He's gone."

"He can't die; he's only fifty-nine."

The nurse came and led them to the morgue. Roxana couldn't believe that a vibrant man full of life and passion could be dead. She kissed her father's forehead and whispered, "You were supposed to return to Tehran. Why did you change your plan?"

Miremad died in *ghorbat,* a land he didn't know, just like his father did. He loved people and found something to admire about every nation. He loved the Americans for their courage and innovative lifestyle. He praised the Germans for building a technologically advanced nation on the ruins of their country after the war. He liked Iran's neighbors, but when someone asked him where he wanted to live, he always said "Iran" with no hesitation. So Roxana took Miremad to his beloved Iran. Afshin offered his help to accompany her and Darius to Tehran, but she thanked him and declined. She was not in any mood to tolerate Afshin's disagreements or unexpected bursts of anger.

During the entire trip, she kept hearing her mother's moaning on the phone. "I was preparing to welcome my traveler, not his coffin," she sobbed.

She put Darius on her lap, hid her face in the back of his hair, and cried softly. *How many people have traveled with the coffins of their fathers?* she wondered.

Chapter 72

The Lufthansa plane landed at Mehrabad Airport at 8:00 p.m. Standing in the long passport check-in line, she felt a twinge in her heart. She had experienced the sharp pain several times since her father had passed away. She wondered whether she could survive the sad days ahead.

As she waited in line, Darius pulled her skirt and said in Farsi, "Look, Mommy, P-A-S-S-P-O-R-T. Passport." He motioned to the passport sign. Roxana was surprised. She had been reading children's books in English to him, but had never taught him English. A woman behind her in line heard Darius and said, "Oh my goodness. He can read English this young?"

"No, no," Roxana replied. "I said the word, so he's imitating me."

Darius distracted her only for a minute. She continued rehearsing in her head what to say to her mother. She felt responsible for her father's death. *If I had taken a week off and sat by his bedside, maybe he wouldn't have died.* She was going through a list of "ifs" in her mind when she saw her uncle Parviz making his way through the crowd to reach her.

"Daii *Jaan* Salam. Can you believe he's dead?" Roxana threw herself into her uncle's arms. Parviz hugged her and wiped her tears. He then kissed Darius, took him in his arms, and said to Roxana, "I know you've been brave throughout this whole ordeal, but you have to continue being brave for your mother. Puri is devastated."

Puri and Roxana cried in each other's arms for a long time. Then Roxana spent time consoling her siblings. There was no smile on Elli's always smiling face, and Syrus wore a blank expression that reflected his grief and shock.

Puri was the first one to notice Darius. During the entire car ride to the house, she played with her grandson. She was surprised how much he had grown and how well he was speaking Farsi. "He's only twenty months old, and he communicates with me perfectly," she said.

Roxana had promised herself several times that she would never go back to *Behesht-e-Zahra*, but each time, shortly after such a promise, she found herself back in the cemetery attending the funeral of a loved one.

She never expected to see such a crowd at her father's funeral. The businessmen who manufactured men's clothes had closed their businesses in Tehran's Bazaar for the entire day to honor Miremad's memory.

Puri was distraught; Roxana had to take her mother away from the coffin when they started lowering her father's body into the ground.

The family fed relatives, friends, and the poor for three days. They visited the grave at the cemetery on the third and the seventh day of the burial, following the Persian tradition. Nina accompanied Roxana each time she went to the cemetery, and then she walked to Yerem's grave and mourned her son's death as if he had just died. At the end, it was Roxana who would end up comforting Nina. The same was true with Yahya and Narges. A visit to *Behesht-e-Zahra* cemetery would remind them of losing Bijan all over again. And every time Roxana went to the cemetery, she saw the mother of the young soldier who had died in the war, still staring at her son's picture.

For ten nights, Roxana tiptoed behind her mother's bedroom door and listened to her moaning and crying until she fell asleep.

She had brought two suitcases full of gifts her father had purchased in Holland. The opening of the suitcases proved to be another emotional event. She didn't know that her father had neatly folded and wrapped every gift and left a piece of paper bearing the name of the recipient.

Puri thanked Roxana for bringing Darius to Tehran. "He saved my life. Before you came, I couldn't breathe. I didn't want to live, but Darius gave me a reason to go on. I want to live now and watch him grow."

* * *

Nina insisted that she drive Roxana to the airport. During the long ride she talked mostly with Darius, but when he fell asleep, she told Roxana about her terrible life in Tehran. "I know you've a lot on your plate these days, but you've got to help me get out of here."

"How can I help you when the government doesn't even issue a passport for you?"

"I don't know. All I know is that I have got to get out of here. Sometimes I even consider wearing a sheepskin as a disguise to escape through Turkey like some other people."

"Please don't do anything irrational like that."

"You have no idea how terrible life is here. Did you hear about the woman who hid in a suitcase to go to the United States? By the time she reached US soil, she was dead. People are so desperate to leave Iran that they are willing to risk their lives."

"Please don't even think about any risky way of escaping the country."

When the plane took off, Roxana had a strange feeling that this would be her last trip to Tehran. This was not the city she once knew. Tehran had turned into a large cemetery. She only heard the voices of clergies reading the Koran and reciting religious rituals to bury the dead.

She looked out the window; the city had now disappeared from her view. She felt she had left a part of her buried in *Behesht-e-Zahra*.

* * *

Back in The Hague, Dr. Rohani held a memorial for Roxana's father at the bureau. He invited not only all the diplomats and employees of the Iranian Embassy, but also some diplomats from other Moslem embassies in The Hague.

Several speakers praised her father. She recognized that Afshin must have provided the speakers with all the information they needed. Under normal circumstances, she would have objected to his action because she was a private person, but the kind gesture of Dr. Rohani was so overwhelming that she couldn't comment on any part of the ceremony.

She hid her face and her tears behind Darius, who was sitting on her lap.

"He's truly your son," Lili commented after the ceremony. "He just sat there and listened like a grown-up." Roxana flashed a half-smile.

She thanked Dr. Rohani and the other bureau's staff who had arranged the memorial for her father. She then left.

When they returned home, Darius rushed to the room Miremad had been using during his stay, opened the door, and yelled, "Mommy, where's Grandpa?"

Chapter 73

Like an uninvited guest, pain had entered Roxana's life. Like her shadow on the wall, it followed her. As the days passed, that pain grew more and more into a monster. That monster was now stabbing her in the heart, drinking her blood. The woman who was nicknamed *Smiley* couldn't smile anymore.

Two days after her father's memorial, she received a phone call from Dr. Rohani. He wanted to know whether she was interested in becoming an arbitrator in a case. "I know you're mourning your father's death, but this is not an immediate thing," he said. He described the nature of the dispute between an American airline and Tehran International Airline. He emphasized that the dispute existed even before the revolution.

"Don't the airlines usually resolve their disputes through a clearinghouse in Ottawa, Canada?"

"*Marhaba,* bravo. You know these laws; that's why we need your expertise."

When she was assured that there was no immediate hearing, she accepted the assignment.

There was a knock on the door; it was Lili checking on her friend. She had been stopping by every day to make sure that Roxana was not drowning herself in her tears. "What's the matter?" she immediately asked. "You look like someone who has seen a ghost."

"They just appointed me as an arbitrator for a multimillion-dollar airline arbitration."

"So?"

"Have you forgotten that Islam doesn't allow women to be judges?"

"Oh, I forgot about that. I bet Dr. Rohani must have twisted some arms to get you this appointment."

Lili kept moving toward the window, playing with some of the items on Roxana's desk. Finally, she stopped and said, "I have to ask you a favor."

"What?"

"Kayvan wants to come and extend his condolences, but he knows how you feel about our *sigheh* marriage. Could you please go easy on him?"

"I won't say a word unless he talks about it."

"Thanks."

That afternoon, as Roxana had expected, Kayvan showed up in her office. He extended his condolences and asked Roxana to rely on him for anything she needed. "You're more than a friend to me. I know that I have lost your respect after my marriage to Lili, but—"

"Hold on," Roxana interrupted. "You haven't lost my respect. I'm only disappointed because you have lost your 'Persian-ness.'"

"What does that mean?"

"You see all those ayatollahs who are running the country. Unlike some other Moslem leaders and despite their religious beliefs and strict adherence to the Islamic law, they don't practice bigamy. That's the Persian-ness I'm talking about. Each one has only one wife."

Kayvan turned around to leave Roxana's office, but before reaching the door, Roxana talked again. "You may not believe this after what I just said, but I still love you like a brother-in-law."

She had an important case scheduled at the end of the week before Chamber Three of the tribunal. The neutral arbitrator was Professor Rideau, the same French professor who also sat on the panel of The Hague Academy, the panel that unanimously voted for Roxana to receive her diploma.

She was nervous before the hearing for two reasons: first because she had to appear before Professor Rideau, and second because she had made a risky decision to attack the case only on jurisdictional grounds.

The five attorneys for the American claimant spent the entire morning making legal arguments and submitting exhibits and charts to prove their claim. When they rested their case, Professor Rideau was about to announce a lunch break when Roxana addressed the tribunal. "Your Honor, my argument will be short," she said.

The chair allowed the hearing to continue. Roxana addressed the tribunal.

"Your Honors, I will not discuss the merit of the case because I believe it's not necessary. I will not submit any evidence because this honorable tribunal lacks jurisdiction to hear the case."

There was a whisper at the American claimant's table. Roxana had gotten the arbitrators' attention now. They were all staring at her, including the Iranian arbitrator, who wore a worried expression.

"Your Honors, all the evidence that the claimant has submitted in this case proves that the company that owed the claim ceased to exist before the signing of the Algerian Declaration of January 19, 1981. The newly formed company doesn't have any shareholders of the old company, nor has it employed any member of its board of directors. In this case, we don't even have to worry about *piercing the veil* doctrine. Claimant itself has submitted documents that prove that this is a new company. Article VII, Section 2, of the Algerian Declaration defines claims as *claims owned continuously, from the date on which the claim arose to the date on which the Algerian Declaration was signed.* The claimant has failed to prove the elements of *ownership and continuity* of the claim in this case as required by the treaty. Therefore, the tribunal doesn't have jurisdiction to hear this case. With that I rest my case and thank the tribunal for its time."

There was a pause. The claimant asked for time to rebut the argument, but the request was denied. The chair announced that the hearing was adjourned and informed the parties that the arbitrators would deliberate in the afternoon and announce their decision.

Roxana gathered her papers and put them in her briefcase. She felt a tap on her shoulder. She turned around to find a smiling Professor Rideau extending his hand.

"I'm sorry, Your Honor. You know that the Islamic protocol doesn't allow me to shake hands with men." Roxana purposefully spoke in English for the benefit of the eyes and ears of the bureau, who attended every court hearing.

"It was a great legal argument," Professor Rideau said as he put his right arm around Roxana's shoulder and shook her warmly. She released her shoulder shyly and stepped back. It was an awkward moment. She saw that even the eyes and ears of the bureau chuckled as they turned their heads the other way pretending they hadn't seen anything.

Back in her office, Roxana described Professor Rideau's praise of her work to Lili, laughing. "I didn't expect the hugging after I told him I couldn't shake his hand."

"Frenchmen have a weakness in their knees when it comes to beautiful women," Lili said.

That afternoon, Dr. Rohani called Roxana and congratulated her for winning the case. "You made a precedent. I have assigned someone to dig out similar cases. You may have won fifty similar cases by winning this one."

* * *

She wore black for forty days to mourn her father's death. She would've liked to wear black for one year, which was the Persian tradition when a close family member dies, but she noticed that sometimes Darius looked at her differently.

Changing the black outfit didn't end Roxana's mourning. She was still living with a pain invisible to others. She didn't want her son to see her sad face, so to distract Darius she would take him to the large pond near their apartment building. She had taught him how to feed the ducks, and she breathed easier every time he laughed watching the ducks rushing to catch the food.

From where she sat by the pond, she could always see the window of her living room. Even from a distance, she could see the pale shadow of the woman who was in prison—the woman who lived with an angry cellmate called husband.

At home, after she served dinner and washed the dishes, she would sit in a chair by the window facing the large tree. She would place Darius on her lap and read books to him while Afshin watched his favorite TV programs. Sometimes she heard her mourning dove cooing. *Does the bird know that my father has died?*

On warmer days, she took Darius to his favorite place, West Broek Park, where she always found a place with no one around. She enjoyed disappearing in that park with her little boy.

One day, when she was driving back home after visiting the park, a few blocks before she reached their street, she saw a crowd in front of a building. She hadn't noticed that there was a concert hall minutes away from her apartment building. When she drove closer, she saw the name and the picture of the singer. Adamo was the featured entertainer at the concert.

That night, she put Darius to sleep by singing his favorite bedtime song, Adamo's "*Quand Les Roses*."

The following week, she had to visit the director of the visa office in Den Haag. A relative of one of the bureau's employees needed to extend his visa.

Mr. Drost, the director, was a pleasant Dutchman who knew a lot about the bureau and the Iranians in Den Haag. After providing Roxana with the information she needed, he said, "So I hear you just won our academy's latest award. Congratulations."

"How do you know?"

"It's my job to know who's doing what in my town."

She thanked Mr. Drost for his help and took the visa forms he had provided back to the office. A few days later, Mr. Drost called Roxana and said that he would like to meet with her and talk more.

She met with Mr. Drost at his office. He started the meeting with some pleasantries, and then he told her about the purpose for the meeting. "Because of all these international courts here in Den Haag, we meet some brilliant attorneys, and sometimes we are interested in keeping them here. I'm wondering whether you would be interested in establishing your permanent residency in Holland."

"That's very generous of you," Roxana responded, trying to hide her surprise. "I love the Dutch people, but I don't think I can live in a city that has only ten to fifteen really warm, sunny days per year. I wake up to a black sky many days. It feels like night. Do you know that *cloud* was the third word my son learned after Mama and Dada in both Farsi and Dutch?"

Mr. Drost explained that sometimes even the Dutch people get tired of the damp, cloudy climate. "The reason we are so tall is because we are trying to reach the sun," Mr. Drost said with a laugh. "I always use that joke when someone complains about our weather."

He stopped laughing, and his face turned serious. "I have some friends who'd like to meet you. You don't mind talking to some Americans, do you?"

"No, I don't have any problems with Americans. I lived with them for more than a decade."

Mr. Drost took Roxana to a conference room. There were three men in three-piece suits. The men were interested in the makeup of Iran's Bureau of International Arbitration.

"You get the attorneys' names on all the pleadings submitted to the tribunal, don't you?" she asked.

"Yes," one of the men said, "but we don't know whether those attorneys are living here or in Tehran."

"The bureau has fifteen attorneys here. The attorneys who work with different government agencies in Tehran write their legal briefs. Here we review them before they are filed."

The three State Department men asked more questions. Roxana was surprised about why they were asking her the information they already had. At 8:00 p.m., she stood up and said, "Gentlemen, it was nice meeting you. I have a little boy who's gonna get cranky if he doesn't see me soon."

The American men and Mr. Drost thanked Roxana for her time. As she was leaving the conference room, one of the State Department men said to her, "If you ever decide to go back to the States, let us know."

"Thanks." Roxana left quickly, hoping that no one from the bureau would see her leaving Mr. Drost's office. She still wondered why the Americans needed to talk to her. *I hope they're not from the CIA.*

Chapter 74

Dr. Rohani asked Roxana to help him arrange for an oil symposium in The Hague. Her research showed that the first oil well in the Middle East was discovered in Persia in 1901 by William S'Arcy. Prior to Iran's nationalization of oil in 1951, the foreign oil companies paid Iran 20-25 percent royalty, and kept the rest of the profits for themselves.

Iran introduced the concept of a service contract whereby foreign oil companies were paid for their technical and financial participation. During the decade of the '70s, many service contracts were signed by the National Iranian Oil Company (NIOC). However, they were canceled due to the revolution. As a result, NIOC had to respond to many claims brought by US oil companies at The Hague Tribunal.

With the help of Roxana and some other attorneys at the bureau, Dr. Rohani invited well-known professors from European and American universities. The goal of the symposium was to help the NOIC respond to its litigations.

Roxana had published an article on Persian Gulf oil in a prestigious American law review, so Dr. Rohani insisted that she should attend the symposium and write a report for him. She didn't like participating in an all-male conference, especially wearing *hejab*, but she complied because her boss had asked her.

For the first two days of the weeklong symposium, she sat and listened patiently to the participants. She heard old arguments of existing oil contracts and well-known oil arbitration cases.

When it was her turn to speak, she realized that two days had already been wasted and that no one had said anything to help Iran's oil litigations.

"Gentlemen, my colleagues from BIA and I came here to learn something new, but so far, all we've heard are reiterations of the old rules of international law. The Hague Tribunal is strengthening those old rules and formulating new rules of international law at the expense of Iran. And the amazing thing is that by paying billions of dollars to the American claimants, Iran is also unintentionally hurting the future of any other third world countries going through revolutions. I've been dying to hear a scholar in this forum say, 'Enough is enough. You cannot penalize a nation because it dared to have a revolution.'"

She felt relieved when the conference moderator announced the lunch break. She picked up her briefcase, left the conference room, and decided not to return.

Three days later, Roxana received a phone call from a Dutch friend, Rik Van Rijn, an attorney she had worked with in New York City. "There's an oil man who would like to meet with you," he said, laughing.

"Are you joking? What does he want?"

"I'm not joking, and I don't know what he wants. Apparently one of the participants in that oil seminar has talked to him about you. He's Lebanese. His name is Mr. Elkhouri. He has a small oil company and comes to Rotterdam a lot to sell his oil. Why don't you come to my party and talk to him?"

She decided to go to Rik's party, mostly because of Afshin. Since her father's death, he was nagging more than ever. She wondered whether this nagging was justified. After all, he had lost a cheerful wife who always found a way to make his life interesting.

Mr. Elkhouri was a charming man in his sixties who spoke English with an Arabic accent.

He had read Roxana's article on Persian Gulf oil and was impressed. "I'm going to attend a business meeting in London next week, and I have to familiarize myself with the data you have incorporated into your article. I need your help."

"So why don't you take the article with you?" Roxana suggested.

"Look, I'm a businessman, not an academic. That article is lengthy and complex. You have more than two hundred footnotes. I need you to simplify it for me and spoon feed me so that I can use it in my meeting."

Mr. Elkhouri offered Roxana a trip to London for three days all expenses paid, plus a consultation fee.

She asked Mr. Elkhouri several questions to make sure that he didn't have any dispute with any Iranian government entity.

"I like Iranians. Actually, I admire how Iran is standing against a superpower."

Roxana thought this was a godsend gift to entertain her bored husband for a few days; she accepted the offer.

Contrary to what she had expected, this was not a cozy dinner party to facilitate Mr. Elkhouri's meeting with Roxana. Rik had invited twenty other people. When Roxana, accompanied by Mr. Elkhouri, entered the dining room, Rik was talking with a group of Africans. He took Roxana around introducing her to his friends. He embarrassed her by mentioning The Hague Academy award every time she was introduced.

She almost froze momentarily when Rik introduced her to an Iraqi diplomat. She forced a smile, trying to find something to say. "How's your family?"

"They're all here. Thank God," the Iraqi diplomat said.

"Any relatives back home?"

"Unfortunately, yes. But they have all moved to the Kurdish province to escape the war."

She excused herself and went to the opposite corner of the room to find Rik. He was instructing the caterers to begin serving dinner. "How could you purposefully introduce me to an Iraqi?"

"Come on now. You're an intellectual. You know that man has nothing to do with the war."

"Still, it's an emotional thing to meet an Iraqi diplomat. I feel like a Jew meeting one of Hitler's soldiers. I know the soldier is carrying out orders, but that doesn't make me comfortable talking to him."

"Roxana, that Iraqi diplomat has as much power to stop the war as you have power to stop the *hejab*."

She stared at Rik, and then left him quickly. *No wonder everyone who's seeking justice comes to The Hague.*

Afshin was more than pleased with the royal treatment he and his wife received in London. Mr. Elkhouri had reserved a one-bedroom suite in the Ritz Hotel where he stayed himself. Afshin immediately calculated the paid expenses, which amounted to several thousands of dollars. "The nightly rate for this hotel suite is equal to a month's rent of our apartment in Holland," he told Roxana.

Roxana's meeting with Elkhouri took only an hour. She submitted a short, simplified version of her article to him and answered all his questions. When she took her briefcase to leave his suite, he asked about her consultation fee.

"Nothing, really. The travel expenses you paid covered everything."

"I insist. You spent an hour here not to mention traveling time."

"Okay, one hour should be sufficient."

"How much for that one hour."

"I'll leave it up to you."

Mr. Elkhouri took out a stack of bills from his heavy attaché and put it on the table. That's $3,000; I hope it's enough," he said.

"That's too much."

"You deserve it."

When she returned to their suite, Darius had just awakened. Afshin's eyes sparkled when he saw $3,000 on the table. "I'm not saying that you don't deserve it, but I doubt even the queen's attorney gets $3,000 an hour."

"This is your first trip to London. Take as much as you want, and do some shopping. I'll take care of Darius now."

Afshin took two one hundred dollar bills and left. She felt happy that she'd have several hours alone with her son.

* * *

There was no *Noruz* celebration for Roxana on March 21, 1984. Puri encouraged her daughter to travel to Geneva and visit some relatives. Both Roxana and Afshin had cousins studying in two colleges in Geneva, so it made sense to take advantage of a one-week holiday when the bureau was closed. Roxana was using any excuse to leave The Hague.

In addition to Geneva, the couple also visited Zurich and Bern. In Geneva, Afshin took some pictures of Darius playing with pigeons in a gazebo near a lake. Roxana had asked him not to take any picture of her, but he accidentally took a picture that showed her face. For the first time, she saw her grief-stricken face, a face that Darius had to see every day.

Her father had passed away almost three months ago now, but the twinge in her heart hadn't gone away. After her trip, she saw a cardiologist. He told her she was too young to have any heart problems. The pain she felt was all due to stress. She visited a second cardiologist, who informed her that aside from her emotional distress, little veins were breaking around her heart. "That's why you feel the twinge in your heart," the doctor told her.

In late March, Roxana met with the neutral arbitrator that was selected as the chair for the airlines dispute. The two drafted the procedural rules needed for the upcoming arbitration and sent them to the American arbitrator for his review.

She continued her weekend trips to European cities. She needed to be far away from The Hague as often as possible. She had not forgiven the city that had taken her father from her. Within the next two months, she had visited Luxembourg, Cologne, Düsseldorf, Bonn, and Frankfurt.

One day, Lili asked her about the trips. "Boy, you're never around."

"I have to escape this city and my life here."

"I have some news to cheer you up. You won't believe this. Aunt Narges is married!"

Roxana jumped onto her feet. "After all those years!"

"Yes, she was married to Iraj's father only for two years when they executed him. And after Iraj's suicide—"

"Who's the man who stole her heart?"

"He's a widower, a retired employee of the Ministry of Education. They met at the Behesht-e-Zahra Cemetery. The man's son, a soldier, was killed in a minefield two months after Iraj's death. He was buried ten feet away from Iraj. He and Narges ran into each other at the cemetery every week. After a few weeks, they started talking, and then started dating. Boy, who would've guessed you could find love in a cemetery?"

"An amazing story. I'm so happy for Narges."

"Enough about my aunt. Why are you escaping town every weekend?"

"It sounds crazy, but I feel this city took my father. I have to go away to forget my loss. Besides, I have to entertain Afshin. My marriage has become so painful."

"Why don't you send him back to school? That'll occupy him. I heard him talking to Kayvan the other day. He seems interested in learning computers."

"I'll look into it. Thanks."

Chapter 75

Roxana couldn't help thinking about Narges's life. It took thirty-seven years for her to finally find happiness. Unlike Moslem clergymen who warned people of God's anger and punishment, Roxana always believed in a compassionate God. He has to worry about billions of people, so sometimes it takes him thirty-seven years to shower one of his subjects with happiness, she thought.

She took Lili's advice and talked to Behzad, the bureau's driver. He informed her that Utrecht University had a good computer program.

Afshin embraced the idea of going back to school. Utrecht, a cultural and historic town, was the fourth-largest city in Holland. Utrecht University, however, was the largest university in the country. Roxana was impressed with the city's history. It had hosted a series of treaties among major European cities between 1713 and 1714.

When Afshin signed up for several courses, she breathed a sigh of relief. Now she could pay Maria overtime to stay with Darius while she was grocery shopping, cooking, or reviewing her cases.

* * *

In June 1984, Roxana had a difficult case before the tribunal. An American company had sued Iran for $42 million for breach of contract by a private Iranian shipping company. The claimant argued that because the Iranian company had to get the approval of the Ministry of Transportation for its contracts, it should be considered as an Iranian government instrumentality.

Roxana and three other attorneys from the ministry argued strongly against the concept of agency relationship between the ministry and the private Iranian company. The tribunal ruled in favor of Iran. The American claimant did not get its $42 million. Instead, it only received $750,000 for damages based on the theory of unjust enrichment.

After spending so much time and energy on that case, she needed a little vacation. She chose Copenhagen. When Afshin asked why Copenhagen, she told him an interesting story.

During her student years in the '70s, when Roxana interpreted for the State Department's Language Services, she had experienced an unforgettable day in one of those conferences. The participants were Asian and European drug enforcement officers. The European group included Denmark. One day, the American lecturer stated, "The reason kids use drugs is because their mothers are out working, so no one is at home to supervise them." Most participants agreed. However, the drug enforcement officer from Denmark raised his hand and stated, "Why does everyone think that it's the mother's responsibility to stay at home and supervise kids? Why not the father's?" Roxana couldn't believe her ears. She started clapping for the Danish participant.

During the coffee break, she talked to him more. His feminist views were a breath of fresh air. "I have got to visit a nation that has feminist cops," she said. And that she did.

They drove to Berlin, spent a night there, then drove their car onto a ship that accommodated passengers and their cars, and sailed to Copenhagen.

Aside from picturesque buildings and fishing boats towed along the canals, Roxana found her eyes drawn to the soft, long, velvety grass, and the way it danced in the wind.

She chose Tivoli Gardens for their first tourist activity because she knew that Darius would enjoy the gardens. They drove by the Royal Palace of the world's oldest monarchy. She was amazed that only two guards were in front of the palace.

Afshin had bought some sandwiches. He suggested that they have a picnic in one of the nice parks they had passed through. They stopped at the park and found a quiet area. They spread out their blanket, but before they could open the picnic basket, an attractive

Danish woman entered the area. She spread out her blanket near them. She wore a short and sleeveless T-shirt. As soon as she sat on her blanket, she removed her top and lay down to get a suntan. Roxana panicked. Every time they traveled in Europe, she was afraid that one of the bureau's spies might have followed them. She still remembered the man who followed her in London for a day. She also thought that the combination of a woman with an Islamic *hejab* and a topless blonde would create a tourist attraction. She gathered their stuff in a hurry and rushed back to the car.

* * *

When she returned to work, a pile of reports from the tribunal was on her desk, but before she had a chance to begin looking at them, she had a visitor. It was Afshin's boss. "Dr. Ramsy, I'm sorry to take your time, but there is something that I really need to discuss with you."

"Please come in."

"It's about your husband. Since he has started attending Utrecht University, all he does is sit at his desk and study his books. I supervise several other people, and if any one of them complains, I'll have to fire your husband. Could you please talk to him?"

That evening, she tried to delicately bring up the subject, but, as she had expected, Afshin exploded. "They're doing some negotiations that they don't want me involved in, so if I don't have an assignment, I study my books."

"Since you've gone back to school, you don't even do the little shopping you used to do for us. I'm not complaining; I was the one who encouraged you to go back to school, but you cannot expect your boss to have my patience."

"You stay out of my business. I know how to handle my boss."

She didn't say anything. She knew that one more word out of her would be like lighting the fuse on a stick of dynamite.

The next day, he drove her to work as usual, but after parking the car, he didn't wait for her but started walking fast toward the office building. When he stepped inside the elevator, Roxana was right behind him. He pushed the button and the elevator door slammed in Roxana's face. One of the bureau's employees saw that. "Did Mr. Imani close the elevator on you?" he asked.

"No," Roxana said with a smile. "Sometimes you want to push the *open* button but accidentally push the *close* button. I think that's what happened."

That afternoon when she finished her work, she didn't feel like going home. She expected another fight, but she couldn't leave Darius with an angry father. Besides, she missed her son. At the end of a long day, seeing Darius was the only joy in her life. When she reached their car in the bureau's parking area, she saw Afshin playing with Darius near the car. "What's he doing here?" Roxana asked as soon she took Darius from his father.

"I brought him here because I'd like to go to the Scheveningen and dine there tonight."

"You know I don't like to go to the beach area with this Islamic outfit."

"I'll buy some sandwiches. We can eat in the car."

She agreed. She thought maybe that was Afshin's way of apologizing for his fight the night before.

Unlike the usual rainy, cloudy days of Den Haag, that day was sunny and clear. The nice weather had brought more people to the beach area. Roxana stayed in the car, but when Darius started getting restless, she got out, put him in his stroller, and started walking up and down the street where the car was parked. More than forty minutes passed and there was no sign of Afshin. Darius was crying now. The shops and restaurants were inside the mall. At one point, she decided to walk to the huge mall and look for Afshin, but she didn't know where to start.

She waited for another fifteen minutes, tolerating stares from many people around her. She put her sunglasses on, wishing that they would make her disappear.

Afshin finally showed up. He was irate. "It was so crowded," he said as he was coming toward Roxana. "I got lost."

"How can you leave me here with this outfit and a restless—"

Before she could finish her sentence, Afshin began hitting her in the eye and the face with an open hand. "Shut up."

"What's wrong with you? It was your idea to come here."

Afshin continued hitting Roxana until her sunglasses broke. Several people gathered around them. When he noticed them, he got into the car. Roxana put Darius's stroller in the trunk, took him inside, and sat in the backseat. Afshin started driving; he was still enraged. She was trembling. "I hope someday you pay for all you've done to me," her voice cracked.

When she arrived home, she rushed to the bathroom, splashed some cold water to her burning face, and looked in the mirror. She saw the familiar bruises that she had seen around her eyes two years ago in Tehran. She didn't call the police, because she didn't want people in the office to know that her husband had physically abused her. She kept thinking about divorce and her freedom, but every time she came up with a new theory, she concluded that she would lose her child's custody.

* * *

In October 1984, Roxana received a phone call from her mother. Puri was sending Elli to Holland, hoping that she would get a visa from the American Consulate and travel to the United States. She thought that after losing their father, her children needed to comfort each other. Roxana panicked. She had not talked to Afshin for four months—since the day of the beach incident.

When Afshin came to Holland in 1982, Roxana gave him the master bedroom and its king-size bed. She preferred to sleep on a sofa bed in Darius's bedroom. Now that Elli was coming to The Hague, she had to sleep in the same bed with Afshin—as she did when her father visited her.

She had planned to move to a new place for some time. Her small two-bedroom apartment was full of memories of her father. Elli's trip was another reason to expedite the search for a new place.

Her real estate agent found her a nice three-bedroom townhouse in Kijkduin, The Hague's second famous beach in the southwest area. The beach was smaller and didn't attract tourists as much as the Scheveningen beach.

Afshin liked the place because the rent was three hundred guilders less than their two-bedroom apartment.

Roxana faced another problem—the new place would not be ready until a week after Elli's arrival. She knew that she had to start talking to Afshin. She didn't want Elli to know about the second assault. *What the heck, I can share the bed with him for one week.*

Chapter 76

Elli's trip brought a lot of unexpected joy to Roxana. The only problem was sleeping in the same bed with Afshin. One night, she gave up and let him have sex with her. She had denied him for six months. She knew that if she rejected him again, he would have made Elli's trip miserable.

She took her sister to major cities in Holland and Germany. At first, Afshin promised that he would drive them to every one of those cities, but he later declined—sometimes even a few hours before the trip. Roxana didn't allow him the satisfaction of destroying her plans. She traveled with her sister and Darius by train.

The American consul in Rotterdam refused to give Elli a visitor visa to travel to the States. "She is young and attractive. She'll go there and marry an American," he told her.

Roxana's reasoning that Elli had a job in Tehran and that she was still mourning her father's death didn't impress the consul.

Roxana was happy with all the comforts that the new place had offered her, but when Elli left for Tehran, she felt a void in her heart and started missing the old apartment. She couldn't determine why she longed for that small, uncomfortable place. After days of ruminating, she realized that it was not the place she missed; it was the memories of her father. Sometimes she found herself driving to the old neighborhood, walking toward the pond, and looking up at the window of the room her father had occupied for two weeks. Sometimes she had to fight the urge of knocking on the door of the old apartment and asking the new tenant to allow her to look at her father's room.

She had developed a great appetite for Danish pastries. She noticed she was gaining weight. Overeating seemed to be her new way of fighting her grief. Of course, with her loose Islamic outfit, no one noticed her extra pounds except herself, but when Afshin commented on her new eating habit, she wondered whether she had some health problems.

She made an appointment with their family doctor. Dr. Jansen examined her and took some urine and blood samples. He told her that he had to send the blood sample to the lab, but he could give her the result of the urine test immediately.

"Well, I don't think we need any blood test," the doctor said. "You're pregnant."

Roxana killed a sigh. "How is that possible? I've been having my periods regularly."

"It can happen. When did you have your last intercourse?"

Roxana remembered the night she had sex with Afshin during Elli's visit.

"Two months ago," she said after a long pause.

"So you're two months pregnant."

Dr. Jansen wrote the name and address of a gynecologist for Roxana. "You should be seeing Dr. Schwitzer from now on. He is the best gynecologist in Den Haag."

She thanked her doctor and left his office still feeling numb. What was she supposed to do? She had more than seventy-five cases pending before the tribunal, and she had to raise a toddler and continue a troubled marriage. The baby was going to complicate her life more than ever.

That afternoon when she was cooking in the kitchen, she looked out the window. As she was admiring her neighbor's garden, she heard a cooing. There was a huge tree to the right of her kitchen window, so she couldn't see the mourning dove, but she knew that the bird had finally found her. *Does the bird know about the baby?*

* * *

When she moved to The Hague, the first information she obtained was about doctors and pediatricians. Like many Dutch physicians, Dr. Jansen was making house calls. He informed Roxana about Holland's psychological services for children. "You can find a free child psychologist in every neighborhood in the city. They're paid by the government to monitor children's developmental behaviors."

Roxana found a child psychologist whose office was two blocks away from their home. Unlike most Dutch women, who were tall and slim, Darius's psychologist was short and overweight, but she was a pleasant woman with perfect English. She fell in love with Darius the minute she met him. She saw him once a month, gave him different toys, and observed his behavior during an hour-long visit.

After she found out that she was pregnant, Roxana became concerned about the age differences between Darius and the second baby. She made an appointment with Darius's psychologist and took him with her.

"By the time he's born, Darius will be three years and three months old," the psychologist said. "A perfect age difference. They're not too close in age to compete with each other and not too far apart to have a generation gap."

The psychologist spoke with Darius in Dutch. Roxana understood only a part of it. After she finished questioning Darius about his activities in day care, she talked to Roxana in English. "You may have a genius on your hands. He has graduated here. You don't need to bring him here anymore. Bring me the new baby when he or she is born."

She left the psychologist's office feeling better. She found a restaurant, and after they finished their meal, she took Darius to the pond near their old apartment building. She gave him a bag full of little pieces of bread and taught him how to feed the ducks. While he was feeding the ducks, Roxana stared at their old apartment building. Her gaze soon found the window of her father's room. She took a deep breath. This was the first time she didn't feel the twinge of pain in her heart. *Father, I'm going to have a baby.*

Her happy mood disappeared that afternoon when she was served with a summons to appear in court. She was shocked. She hadn't done anything wrong to be sued. But when she saw the name of the plaintiff, she recognized the name. Mr. Van Bruggen was their former landlord. He had asked for one hundred guilders to wash the carpet in the living room because of an orange juice stain he had found on it.

In a bitter fight, Afshin had forbidden Roxana to pay the one hundred guilders. "I'll talk to him myself," he had said.

She called her Dutch lawyer friend Rik and explained the situation. Rik recommended a landlord-tenant attorney he knew.

Roxana made an appointment with her for the next day. That evening, she put the summons in front of Afshin and said, "How could you do this to me?"

"I offered the man fifty guilders, and he refused; then I forgot about it. Don't worry; the judge will throw the case out."

"Do you know that the initial fee for our lawyer is three thousand guilders?"

"Why can't you defend our case?"

"I have reading knowledge of Dutch. I can't handle a court proceeding in Dutch."

When Afshin acted as if the court involvement was Roxana's responsibility, she lashed out. "Do you know how humiliating this is for me? I've never been sued before in my life. I don't even have a traffic ticket. I'm not supposed to have any stresses in my condition—"

"Are you talking about your heart again?"

"No, about the baby. I'm pregnant."

She hated Afshin's smirk and the expression on his face that said, *I know how to plant a seed.*

Roxana couldn't attend the hearing in the landlord-tenant case in the Dutch court because of the scheduling conflict with an arbitration case at The Hague Tribunal. She relied on her Dutch attorney to handle the case. The outcome was shocking, though. The court awarded Mr. Van Bruggen four thousand guilders for damages plus three thousand guilders in attorney's fees.

"The landlord claimed one hundred guilders to clean a carpet stain. How can a court award him seven thousand guilders?" Roxana asked their attorney.

"I don't know. I was surprised myself," the attorney responded.

That night, she put a ten-thousand-guilder check she had written for the payment of the court's order and the two attorneys' fees on the dinner table in front of Afshin. "The man asked only for one hundred guilders, $50, and you did not allow me to pay it. Now I have to pay $5,000. Is this how an MBA's brain functions?"

Despite all the miseries Afshin had created in her life, Roxana had never felt so much anger against him as she did after the court's decision. She knew that it was not the ten-thousand-guilder penalty. That was only the tip of the iceberg. She didn't know whether it was the pride of an attorney who had never been sued, the death of her father that had shattered her world, or the hormones that had invaded her pregnant body. She realized she needed some professional help to analyze her anger. She asked Lili for help.

"I need to see a marriage counselor," she said. "I went through one pregnancy fearful of Saddam's bombs, I can't go through this pregnancy with the anger I feel toward Afshin."

"You need to see a divorce attorney," Lili advised.

"Come on, Lili, I don't have any nexus with Holland. My divorce will be considered as a *personal matter* here, according to private international law. So they'll send me to the embassy, and guess what? The clergy in charge of the divorce will give the custody of my child to his father like an Islamic family judge in Iran. Besides, Darius loves his father. He's too young to understand what's going on between his parents."

"What do you want me to do?"

"Find me a marriage counselor. I'm so overwhelmed with work. I don't have time to search for one."

A week later Lili called Roxana and asked her to stop by her office. She had found a marriage counselor for her, an American woman who practiced in The Hague.

Roxana was thrilled. She ran to Lili's office. She quickly took the contact information, thanked her friend, and rushed to the door. When she opened the door, she was startled, not believing her eyes. Steve let himself in and closed the door. "I'm not a ghost," he said to Roxana. "Aren't you gonna ask me where I've been all these months?"

Roxana was speechless—she kept looking at Lili.

"This was not a conspiracy," Lili said. "I knew he was in town, but I didn't know he was coming here."

Steve sat in a chair and told them that his long absence was due to his father's death. As the only son and the executor of his father's will, he had to stay in Ohio and take care of the probate problems. He then turned to Roxana and said, "I heard that you lost your father too. I'm so sorry."

"I'm sorry for your loss too," Roxana said. "What are you doing here?"

"I have the permission of your director to interview several people here. I'd like to start with you."

"No, no. Count me out," Roxana said immediately. "I don't want anyone to know that I exist."

"You're the one who's winning cases, and you don't want to be interviewed?" Steve sounded disappointed.

"That's right. Please talk to other attorneys."

Roxana left Lili's office feeling guilty about the cold way she had treated Steve. The expression on his face showed that he still loved her. *Why does he ignore that I'm not a free woman?* She resented the fact she hadn't had any control over the events happening in her life since the hostage taking. In Paris, where she first met Steve, she was an idealist, captivated by the revolution. In Tehran, the revolution and the war shaped her thoughts. A near death experience was a turning point, changing her life forever. In The Hague she found herself in a cage. She wondered why Steve couldn't understand her complicated life.

She made an appointment with the American marriage counselor. Dr. Miller was a pleasant woman who made Roxana feel connected immediately. She listened to her as she hurriedly summarized her marital problems in twenty minutes. When she stopped, Dr. Miller looked at her, baffled for a minute, and then said, "Kick him out of your life."

"Excuse me?"

"You heard me. Kick him out of your life."

"I expected you to tell me what I was doing wrong."

"You're not doing anything wrong. He is. He is the one who is constantly arguing and yet doesn't believe in marriage counseling."

"During the time I lived in the States, I kept hearing that you have to keep working on your marriage."

"You have done that for more than three years."

Dr. Miller gathered more information in order to analyze Roxana's relationship with Afshin. In the end, she concluded that she should get a divorce. It didn't matter to her that Roxana would lose the custody of Darius. She believed that ultimately Roxana would get him back.

Chapter 77

The bureau was closed for one week to celebrate the Persian New Year in March 1985. Roxana needed a warm, sunny place, so she got Afshin's approval to visit some southern European countries. She made reservations for hotels in Madrid, Barcelona, and Málaga. The trips to Madrid and Barcelona went well, but Roxana's vacation in Málaga was ruined by the news from Iran.

She had chosen Málaga because it was the warmest spot in Europe during the winter months. As soon as they arrived in their hotel room, Afshin turned on his transistor radio to hear the news from Tehran Radio.

She had not even started unpacking when she heard that Saddam had bombed the Saltanat Abad area in Tehran. She dropped the bag she had in her hand and rushed to the telephone. Saltanat Abad was near her family home. She kept dialing her family's telephone number, but no one answered. Finally, on the second day, she found a relative in Tehran who informed her that her family had traveled to Shiraz for their *Noruz* vacation. For two days, Roxana's world had turned upside down. She had lost her father, and she was not prepared to lose the rest of her family. Saddam had purposefully intensified Tehran's bombing knowing that everyone was celebrating *Noruz*.

On their third day in Málaga, she tried to enjoy the city that was founded by Phoenicians. She was surprised to find many Dutch pubs and Dutch tourists in the city. She remembered Mr. Drost's statement, "Sometimes we get sick and tired of our cold and damp weather too."

She was tired of the war that lingered on—the war that followed her to Holland, and even to Málaga, thousands of miles away.

* * *

Puri traveled to The Hague to help Roxana prepare for the arrival of her second baby. Darius enjoyed his grandmother's visit so much that he hardly bothered his mother, but Afshin was resentful. Although he relished the variety of delicious Persian meals Puri prepared for the family every day, he didn't like the love and attention Roxana was receiving from her mother.

Puri had planned to stay with Roxana for one month after the birth of the baby, but one day she received a disturbing phone call from New Hampshire. Neghar's apartment had burned down, partially due to the negligence of her roommate.

The fire had destroyed all of Neghar's belongings and valuables, including significant documents such as her passport and birth certificate. Puri showed no emotion, but Roxana knew her mother well. She saw how sometimes Puri stared at an object, forgetting about the time and the place. She called Bahram and told him that she was sending their mother to the States. When she put Puri's ticket in front of her and explained the change of plan, Puri had tears in her eyes. "What about you here alone with another baby?"

"Don't worry about me. Neghar hasn't seen you for a long time. She needs you more than I do."

Despite her big belly, and against her doctor's advice, Roxana was still driving herself everywhere. She hated asking Afshin for any favors. She was happy when she learned about the baby's gender. As much as she would have loved to have a girl, she was relieved that her second child would not have to wear an Islamic *hejab* either.

When Maria didn't return from Athens, Roxana contacted her babysitting agency to find her a babysitter. The agency sent her a dozen names. She interviewed each and every one of them. They were all college students who were interested in a part-time job. Disappointed with the result of her interviews, she placed a detailed ad in one of Holland's popular daily newspapers.

The first Saturday after her mother's departure, Roxana worked late at the office to finish a legal brief. When she returned home and hugged Darius as usual, she noticed that he was burning with fever. She asked the temporary babysitter about her son's fever. She was not aware of Darius's fever. She asked Afshin, who was busy watching TV.

He shrugged. "He was playing all day. There's nothing wrong with him."

She called Dr. Jansen and described Darius's fever. He advised her to put cold compresses on his forehead and feet, but didn't prescribe any medication.

She followed the doctor's advice, but the fever didn't stop. On Sunday morning, Darius didn't have any appetite and looked pale.

She took him to the children's hospital. The attending physician ran some tests, which indicated that Darius had a stomach bug. They kept him at the hospital until 8:00 p.m., when his fever stopped. The doctor prescribed a liquid medication for him.

By the time she filled the prescription and came home, it was 9:00 p.m. Afshin was still sitting in front of the TV as if he hadn't left his chair. She put Darius in his bed, gave him his medication and sang one of his new favorite bedtime songs, "*Si la vie est ton cadeau.*" This was a winning song in one of Europe's annual music contests. A young woman from Luxembourg had won the contest when Darius was two years old. As she sang the song on TV, Darius imitated her. Later, anytime Roxana would start the song, Darius would continue it and put himself to sleep.

As she sang the song that evening, for the first time she paid attention to the meaning of the lyrics. "If life is your gift . . ." She found herself muttering, "What a torturous gift."

After Darius fell asleep, she realized that she hadn't eaten during the entire day. She tried to eat some cheese and crackers, but she didn't have any appetite. She was exhausted; she hadn't slept the night before. She desperately needed some sleep. She checked Darius's forehead again and made sure the fever was gone. She kissed him and went to bed. She kept tossing and turning; she was restless. After an hour of struggle in bed, she got up and sat on the edge of the bed. She looked at Darius's face. He was sound asleep. She felt pain on both sides of her body. She had noticed a dull pain all day, but she had ignored it because she needed to concentrate on her sick child.

By 11:00 p.m., the pain got sharper. She was familiar with that pain. She was in labor.

She panicked. She went downstairs to the living room. Afshin had fallen asleep in front of the TV. She shook him hard several times before he woke up. "I have to go to the hospital. I'm in labor."

"The baby's supposed to come three weeks from now."

"I'm sorry. He's coming now. Please get the car ready, and take Darius to Parvaneh, my assistant. Her house is five minutes away. Then come back and take me to the hospital."

"Why don't you ask Lili to help?"

"She's in London; she'll come back next week."

She packed Darius's bag hurriedly. After Afshin drove him away, she started packing her own clothes and the things she needed in the hospital. She called Dr. Schwitzer's answering service. The operator informed her that the doctor was out of town, but he would return on Monday. She advised Roxana to go to the hospital immediately. She waited for thirty minutes. There was no sign of Afshin. *He must be chatting with Parvaneh and her husband.*

She called a taxicab. She picked up her heavy suitcase and climbed down the staircase. She stood by the curb waiting for the cab.

When she arrived at the hospital, a nurse was already waiting for her in the hallway.

"You came alone?" she asked.

"Did I have to bring someone?"

"No, but usually a woman in labor comes with someone."

Roxana could have had the second baby through natural childbirth. She opted for the C-section because she didn't want to go through labor again. But now she had to wait for her doctor to return from his trip.

Afshin arrived at the hospital after midnight. He soon became bored because nothing was happening. Roxana told him to go home and sleep. She wrote a short note for the staff at Darius's day care advising them that he needed to have two more doses of his medication. "Please give this note to them," she said to Afshin, handing him the paper.

He left the hospital. The nurse came every two hours and gave Roxana two painkillers. She had a painful night, but she was grateful that this time she didn't have to worry about Saddam's bombs. She remembered her first childbirth; her whole family was at the hospital. But in Holland she didn't have anyone except Lili, who was away.

On Monday, at 9:00 a.m., when the nurse tried to give Roxana more painkillers, she lost her patience. "If Dr. Schwitzer is not coming back from his trip, please have another doctor perform the C-section. I can't take this pain anymore."

"He'll be here at noon," the nurse said as she was leaving.

There was no sign of Afshin. She assumed that he had probably gone to work. Roxana's eyes scanned her room. At that moment, she felt *gharib,* lonely. She needed to hold someone's hands.

* * *

An anesthesiologist came to Roxana's room at 11:00 a.m. and talked to her for a few minutes. At the same time, a nurse brought another woman in labor into the room. Helga, her roommate, was about to have a C-section too. Despite her pain, Roxana flashed a smile and greeted her warmly. The anesthesiologist left her and began talking to Helga in Dutch. She didn't understand most of the conversation, but she was surprised that it lasted for a long time. She wondered why the anesthesiologist talked to one C-section patient for just a few minutes and the other for more than thirty minutes.

The nurse took her to the operating room. They hooked her up to wires, and she felt a prick in her wrist area as they inserted an intravenous needle into her vein. They put an oxygen mask on her face, and she was gone.

She felt serious pain in her abdomen. She tried to open her eyes, but she couldn't. She tried to raise her right arm and ask for help, but her arm didn't move. To her horror, she realized that she was still in the operating room, and the doctors were still working on her. She heard a baby's cry and Dr. Schwitzer's voice, "Dat is heel goed." Then she felt the pulling of her skin and the stitches. She tried to moan or raise her arm to get the doctor's attention, but she couldn't. When the pain stopped, she was gone again.

She opened her eyes and found herself in a large room. Next to her bed was a baby crib and a baby. *Oh my God, my baby!*

She couldn't move; she was in pain. She buzzed for help, and a nurse came in. She asked her to put the baby in her arms, which she did. She kissed the baby, wiped her tears, and muttered, "Thank-you, God." She felt that God had given her a baby to stop her grief. Holding the baby in her arms gave her the same euphoria she had felt when Darius was born. She had forgotten about Darius for a day. *Oh my God, how can I forget about him? He was sick.*

She looked at the puffy pink face of her baby and his little fingers. "Is the baby okay?" she asked the nurse.

"Oh, yes. He weighs eight kilos and 320 grams."

"Are you assigned to care for my baby?"

"No, you'll care for him."

"But I just had surgery."

"In Holland, we don't separate babies from their mothers."

"But I don't have anyone to help me out. How can I feed him? How can I lift him?"

"We'll help you; just buzz us."

She learned from the nurse that Afshin had come around 1:00 p.m. He had looked at the baby briefly and then had left. He must have used his lunch hour, she thought.

Afshin had thirty days of paid vacation. Roxana expected him to take at least one day off for the birth of his child, but he was saving all of his vacation days to spend with his family in Tehran.

In the afternoon, the nurse moved her and the baby to her original room. Helga had half a dozen visitors. She introduced Roxana to her husband and her family. She then looked at the baby and said, "*Groot*, big baby." Helga's baby was a girl, born an hour after Roxana's.

When Helga's relatives left, her husband started kissing his wife and hugging her. Roxana thought that they would stop after a while, but the kissing got longer and noisier.

She got distracted when she heard Darius's voice in the hall. Moments later, he appeared in her room with his father. Afshin started complaining about Darius as soon as he walked in.

"His day care finished at 4:00 p.m.; it's 5:00 p.m. now. How can you complain after having him for only one hour?" Roxana asked, feeling frustrated.

"He asks for you all the time. I don't know what to do with him."

"Just read him a book. He'll be quiet."

Darius was anxious to see the baby. Roxana had talked to him during the last three months of her pregnancy. He knew that he was going to have a brother. She asked Afshin to put the baby in her arms. She then asked Darius to hop up on the bed. She let him touch the baby's hand. When Darius tried to kiss the baby, Afshin pushed him back. "No, you can't kiss him."

Roxana whispered, "Please don't treat him like that. You should feel lucky that he likes the baby. Some kids resent their newborn sibling."

"You've spoiled him rotten. He thinks that he can do anything he wants."

She was happy that Afshin was speaking in Farsi, and Darius couldn't understand many of the words.

Afshin's attention was drawn to Helga and her husband when the kissing got louder, and their body movements resembled two people making love.

"What the hell is wrong with those two?" he asked in Farsi.

"They're celebrating the birth of their baby."

"This is a public place, not their bedroom."

When Afshin left, Roxana called her staffer, Parvaneh, and asked her for help. "I hear you took care of my son the entire night last night. I'm so grateful. Is it possible sometimes after work to let him play with your son? He misses me so much."

"No problem. I'll take him home after work. Just ask Mr. Imani to come and get him before bedtime."

"I don't know how I can ever thank you. Lili is in London, I have no one—"

Roxana couldn't finish her sentence. She had a lump in her throat, and tears welled up in her eyes.

"Don't worry, Dr. Ramsy. I'll take care of him until you come home."

When Dr. Schwitzer came to check on Roxana, she told him about her experience in the operating room. "With my first C-section, I didn't feel any pain when they were operating on me. I think your anesthesiologist didn't give me enough drug to keep me asleep."

"The amount of drug is based on your weight and medical history, but sometimes when one goes through a second operation, anesthetic doesn't work like the first time."

Roxana didn't accept the explanation. Deep down she felt that the anesthesiologist had treated her like a foreigner. He talked to Helga for thirty minutes but finished with her after a few minutes.

That night, Helga's snoring didn't let Roxana sleep. Now this was the third night she hadn't slept. The next morning, she asked the nurse to give her a private room as she had originally requested. They found her a private room, far away from the nurse's station. The air-conditioning in the room was harsh, and she had only a sheet. She requested a blanket, which came a day later. It took a long time for a nurse to answer anytime she buzzed for help. She felt that she was being punished for requesting a private room. She visited Helga the next morning and explained why she had to change her room.

"You don't need to explain anything. I understand. It's tough not to have any family member to help you out. Sounds like your husband doesn't like this baby."

"No, he likes the baby, but he doesn't like for his daily routines to be disturbed."

Despite her repeated requests, they didn't put a telephone in her room. So, in order to make a phone call, Roxana had to walk through a long hallway to find a pay phone. She needed to interview potential babysitters that had responded to her ad.

The first five applicants were college students. That was a total waste of time. She was bleeding heavily, so she had to stop walking through the long hallway to make her phone calls. On the sixth day of her hospitalization, she decided to make one more phone interview. A young woman with a soft cockney accent seemed very excited about the job. Roxana asked her to come by and visit her at the hospital.

Caroline was a sixteen-year-old Londoner whose mother had married a Dutch man in The Hague. When she entered the room after saying "Hello," she immediately went to the baby's crib, lifted him up, and placed a soft kiss on his forehead. "What's his name?"

"Kurosh, which is Cyrus in English," Roxana said. "Like Cyrus, the Persian king."

"So I have a king in my arms," Caroline said, and chuckled.

"You seem to love babies, but you're only sixteen."

"Don't worry. I'm experienced. I'm the oldest of six siblings. My mother left us when we were young, and my father got married. I raised my brothers and sisters."

"You're hired."

Caroline was exuberant. She almost jumped with the baby in her arms when she learned about her salary. "One thousand guilders! That's too much. I'll do it for five hundred."

"You'll be caring for my precious baby. Nothing is too much."

She was released from the hospital while suffering from a serious case of laryngitis. She blamed the harsh air-conditioning in her room. Every time she coughed, she felt severe pain in her lower abdomen. She was scared that her stitches would be ripped. Dr. Schwitzer advised her to stay in the hospital a little longer, but she couldn't bear to be separated from Darius anymore.

She didn't ask Afshin for any help with their newborn baby. She had learned a hard lesson when Darius was born. She put the baby's crib in her bedroom and decided to take care of him all by herself. Afshin was pleased with that decision; he volunteered to care for Darius, knowing well that he slept uninterrupted throughout the night.

In Roxana's mind was a picture of a woman with two kids, taking a long journey. The road was bumpy, but the woman was determined to finish the long, arduous walk.

Chapter 78

Puri came to The Hague to look after her grandchildren when Roxana was preparing for her arbitration in Geneva. She got teary eyes when she saw Kurosh for the first time. "I should have been here when he was born. I'm sorry you had to go through a difficult time all alone."

"I survived."

Roxana realized that Kurosh was not only a gift to her, but also to her mother. Puri laughed wholeheartedly again just like the time her husband was alive. Now she was capable of forgetting her loss for a short period of time.

Roxana met with the Swiss arbitrator who was the chair of the airlines Arbitration Tribunal, and the two had a conference call session with the American arbitrator.

The arbitration between American International Airline (AIA) and Tehran International Airline (TIA) was held in Geneva to accommodate Dr. Legrez, the Swiss arbitrator, although the seat of the arbitration was in Paris.

Roxana had asked Dr. Rohani to allow Lili to assist her during the arbitration procedure. She explained that there were conflicting views on the amount of interest owed to TIA and the applicable interest rate. "I need Lili to calculate the amount of the interest for me."

During the flight to Geneva, Roxana explained to Lili that the TIA's claim against the American airline hadn't arisen out of the hostage taking of 1979. It was a claim based on a 1976 ground handling agreement between the two airlines where the Iranian airline was to provide all ground services to the American airline.

"Didn't you say once that the International Air Transport Association resolves airline disputes in Ottawa?"

"You're right. IATA does that through their Settlement of Account procedure."

The next day, Roxana was assisting Lili to sort out their documents on the arbitrator's table when the American arbitrator, Mr. Cunningham, entered the conference room. He was a partner in a prominent law firm in Atlanta, Georgia. He was in his midsixties and resembled the Hollywood actor Jimmy Stewart. As he talked to Dr. Legrez at the entrance of the conference room, a woman who had arrived with him walked to Roxana and hugged her. "I'm Mrs. Cunningham," she said. "I always travel with my husband when he has an arbitration. This is the first time I've seen a lady arbitrator. He has told me so much about you that I had to come and meet you."

"I hope nothing bad," Roxana said, smiling.

She was talking with Mrs. Cunningham when her husband approached her and extended his hand. "I see you've met my wife," he said.

Roxana stepped back and prepared herself for another humiliating moment. "Yes, we've met. I'm sorry, Mr. Cunningham, I cannot shake hands with you. The Islamic protocol doesn't allow me."

Mr. Cunningham came closer to her and opened his arms. "Shall we hug instead?"

The remark made everyone laugh except Roxana who was embarrassed. She couldn't help remembering that she had used the same line with the judges of The Hague Academy of International Law, and the French arbitrator at The Hague Tribunal. She turned around and told Lili in Farsi, "Now you see why the Americans have a special place in my heart. She hugged me like Pamela Norton, the American woman who wished for me to win the academy's contest."

The arbitration hearing lasted for two days, from 8:00 a.m. until 8:00 p.m. The three arbitrators heard the testimony of twenty-eight witnesses and reviewed dozens of documents that were brought to the tribunal in large boxes.

On the second night of their stay in Geneva, Roxana confessed to Lili that she had not had an uninterrupted sleep in months. "Last night, I slept for seven hours. The last time I had slept that long was before the hostage taking of November 4, 1979."

"I don't know how you do it—the kids, the career. Where do you find your energy?"

"The love I receive from my kids. Now tell me about you and your marriage."

"It's wonderful. Kayvan and I each have our separate apartment. We see each other three times a week. It's like a permanent engagement without the boring parts of the marriage like cooking, cleaning, and grocery shopping."

"Many marriages would last longer if couples lived in two separate homes."

* * *

On the last day of arbitration, Roxana spent five hours with the other arbitrators analyzing and arguing the two airlines' claims and counterclaims. At the end, it was obvious to Roxana that the neutral arbitrator was going to side with her. Now the next significant remaining issue was the amount of the interest to be awarded to the Iranian airline. The American respondent had argued that since interest was forbidden according to Islamic law, the Iranian airline was not entitled to anything. Roxana referred to the testimony of several witnesses who had testified that interest was paid to individual bank accounts in Iran, and were included in the judgments of the Iranian courts. She also referred to the well-known rule of international law that the issue of interest had always been *procedural* and not *substantive* law. She brought to the attention of the two arbitrators that because the seat of the arbitration was in Paris, the French procedural laws and not the Islamic law of Iran applied.

The American arbitrator disagreed with the amount of judgment, which was close to $2 million, as well as any amount of interest. He informed the Swiss arbitrator that he would write a dissenting opinion. Roxana also informed him that she would be writing a concurring opinion justifying the payment of interest.

On their way back to The Hague, as soon as the Swissair plane took off, Roxana bombarded Lili with figures of various claims by the TIA. Lili's calculation on interest rate and the total interest owed TIA came close to the amount of the original claim.

"If the Swiss arbitrator agrees with the 10 percent rate for seven years of unpaid debt," Lili said, "the interest will amount to $1.6 million. That means they will get a total of $4 million."

"It broke my heart to say good-bye to a sad Jimmy Stewart," Roxana said.

She was satisfied with the outcome of the arbitration, but she was eager to go home and see her kids.

Chapter 79

On her first day back from Geneva, Roxana received a call from the bureau's director, Dr. Rohani. He wanted to see her right away in his office.

"First of all, a very heartfelt congratulations on the airline arbitration," he said as soon as she entered his office.

"The claim of the Iranian airline was strong. I have to tell you, if the American airline had a legitimate claim, I would have had to vote for them. I could not compromise my position as an arbitrator, or be accused of bias. But they didn't have a prayer."

"Well, I'm glad they didn't, but look what the so-called neutral arbitrators are doing to us at The Hague Tribunal. They are mostly siding with the Americans. They're even citing the laws of the American states. In one recent case, they applied the laws of Idaho. Can you imagine a contract executed in Tehran and being decided by an international tribunal using the laws of Idaho? That's absurd."

"It's unfortunate that the individuals who signed those contracts in Iran didn't notice the *applicable law* provision of each contract."

"We're being beaten up by the dual nationality cases as well. Those Iranians who fled Iran are bringing their litigation to The Hague Tribunal claiming they have US citizenship. What about the Iranian law that doesn't recognize dual citizenship?"

"There is this famous Nottabom case that decides on dual nationality cases. The court should look into the real connection between the individual and the country of citizenship. I'll prepare a report for you on that."

Roxana admitted that some of the cases submitted to The Hague Tribunal were without merit.

One of the recent cases Roxana had won belonged to an American company that claimed its office was taken over by a group of unidentified revolutionaries. The only evidence submitted to the tribunal was a phone call received from the Iranian landlord. The tribunal denied the $47,000 claim and agreed with Roxana that there was not sufficient evidence to prove that any Iranian government entity was responsible for the act of an unidentified revolutionary group.

* * *

In October, Roxana asked her mother to leave the States and come to The Hague again. She had to handle several important cases during that month. She needed her help with the children. Puri felt blissful to have a chance to spend more time with her grandchildren. "Darius and Kurosh give me a reason to live longer," she had said repeatedly.

During the second week of her stay in Holland, Puri received news from Bahram that her applications to obtain green cards for Syrus and Elli had been approved by the immigration authorities in the United States.

On the day Syrus and Elli were supposed to fly to Amsterdam, Roxana heard on the Tehran radio that Saddam was again planning to attack Tehran's Mehrabad Airport. She kept the news from her mother. She called KLM Airlines and asked for more information. She was told that all flights from Tehran were canceled. She kept calling her siblings at home in Tehran, but no one answered.

She kept a vigil all night, praying that her siblings were safe. At 5:00 a.m., when she was half-asleep on the sofa in the living room, she heard some people talking on the street. She looked out and saw two individuals emerging from a taxicab in front of her house. She rubbed her eyes. She wasn't dreaming. She saw Syrus talking to the cabdriver near the trunk of the car. Then she saw Elli carrying small pieces of luggage.

She ran to the street barefoot, throwing her arms around her siblings; she hugged them tightly. "I almost died when I heard about Saddam's threats."

"I paid fifty dollars to the driver. Is that enough?" Syrus asked.

"Yes. Now tell me what happened."

"We went to the airport three times. It was a hoax," Syrus said. "This is Saddam's new game, to scare people without wasting his bombs."

She led them inside the house and took them to the living room on the upper floor. She told them that she didn't share the information with their mother because she didn't want to alarm her. She fixed breakfast for her siblings. They lowered their voices so as not to wake up anyone.

Roxana knew how eager her brother and sister were to see the baby, so she ran to the second floor and brought Kurosh to the living room. She expected Kurosh to cry as soon as he saw strangers, but, to her surprise, he smiled and let his uncle and aunt hug him.

When Puri saw her children in the living room, she froze. She hugged each child for a long time and then started crying. She hadn't seen Syrus and Elli for sixteen months.

Roxana was happy that Afshin was a heavy sleeper. He had an 11:00 a.m. settlement negotiation at the Tribunal, so she let him sleep late.

She didn't take Darius to his day care that day. She knew how much her family would enjoy having him at home.

The next day she was surprised to see a fancy bouquet of flowers on her desk. She immediately searched for the sender's card. She found it. It was from Steve. It read:

> Dear Roxana,
>
> Please accept my belated congratulations on the birth of your second baby. I had to go back to the States to handle my father's estate. I just got back and learned about your baby. Does this mean you have a happy marriage now? Please let me know.
>
> Love,
>
> Steve

She put the card in her drawer, called Lili, and asked her to take the flowers to her office. She smelled the flowers and muttered, "I don't have a happy marriage, but you'll never know."

Late that afternoon when Afshin came to drive her home, he had a smirk on his face. "I see that Roxana's international hotel is full again," he said sarcastically.

"I'm paying for their food, as well as yours. In fact, whenever any member of my family stays with us, you don't spend a penny on anything. Look at our expense book."

She took a day off to take her brother to Amsterdam. Although Puri and Elli had visited Amsterdam before, they decided to tour the city too. She felt at peace when she saw her brother laughing and enjoying life again. After his father's death, Syrus was crushed under the huge financial responsibility that was imposed on him. Not only did he have to deal with the emotional aspect of his father's death, he also had to run his business and protect his siblings' inheritance. He was a computer engineer who had sacrificed his career to save his father's legacy. *Syrus is a saint.*

Puri stayed behind when her children flew to the United States. She wanted to help Roxana during her difficult litigations at the tribunal.

When her court hearings were finished, Roxana took a few days off. She was invited to attend a seminar in Berlin. She had always desired to visit the Berlin Wall. Somehow she had the feeling that the wall would be torn down in the near future.

She asked Afshin if he would drive them to Berlin and if they could turn the two-day seminar into a minifamily vacation. Afshin, who was overwhelmed by Puri's kindness and spoiled by her delicious Persian food, agreed.

It took half a day for Roxana to obtain visas from the German Consulate. She made hotel reservations for two rooms and packed all the things her kids needed for a five-day trip.

On the morning they were supposed to leave, however, Afshin refused to drive. "I don't feel like going to Berlin," he said casually.

"But you agreed," Roxana pleaded. "What am I gonna do with two kids, two heavy suitcases, and a baby stroller?"

"You're smart; you'll figure it out."

She saw the sad expression on her mother's face, but she didn't hear any complaint.

She called Eurorail. Seats were available from Amsterdam to Berlin, so she made reservations. Roxana saw Afshin's shocked face when she helped her mother and kids get into the taxicab. *He thought he had ruined my plan.*

When the cab took off, Roxana looked at her mother's worried face. "Everything will be fine. We don't need him."

Chapter 80

After the seminar was over, Roxana bought two tickets for a tour of Berlin. It was cold outside, but inside the tour bus it was warm and comfortable. The first stop was the Brandenburg Gate. The tour guide said that the gate was built in the 1700s to represent peace.

They visited Schloss Charlottenburg Palace, Berlin's Jewish district, and many more tourist attractions. Then they arrived at the Berlin Wall. Roxana got out of the bus, stopped in front of the wall, read some of the graffiti, and took a few pictures. She explained to Puri that the wall, a symbol of the Cold War, was built in August 1961, dividing the two Germanys.

She didn't find any porter at the train station to help her with their luggage when they were returning to Holland. To her surprise, nobody extended a helping hand when she was getting Kurosh's stroller on board the train. But as soon as they reached the Dutch border, things changed. When she couldn't find her tickets, the Dutch inspector held Kurosh so that she could search for them.

"You see how lucky I am to live in Holland," she told her mother. "The Dutch are crazy about kids. Do you know that this small country pays one fifth of the UNICEF's fund?"

"No, I didn't."

During the train ride, Puri found an opportunity to talk to Roxana about her marriage. "I know it's difficult to live with him, but he's the father of your children. His problem is money. Just tell him he doesn't have to pay anything. You're Miremad's daughter; treat him like a guest."

"I've paid $35,000 for two babysitters, Darius's day care, and kindergarten. That's the price of a two-story townhouse in our neighborhood. I make four times as much as he does, but we have the same amount of savings in our bank accounts. That explains who is paying for family expenses."

"Don't worry. God will provide. He always has; he always will. Count on me if you need help with the children. I am always looking forward to coming back to The Hague."

Puri didn't know that the October trip to The Hague would be her last, and she would never see the city again. Two days after her arrival in New Hampshire, she had a heart attack. A tearful Syrus called Roxana telling her that their mother was in the hospital.

"What happened? She was fine here," Roxana asked frantically.

She learned that Puri was brooding over Afshin's behavior. She was also stressed out because of her husband's business in Tehran. After Syrus left Iran, Uncle Parviz took over Miremad's business. But he hadn't been able to sell the business. Besides, he and his family were planning to travel to Europe and live in Austria for good.

"Can I call the hospital and talk to her?"

"Not until her doctor says it's okay. I have to go now."

She held the telephone receiver in her hand for a while even though Syrus had hung up. A voice kept repeating in her head, *Not again, not another death.*

She sat vigilantly all night praying for her mother's recovery. Sleep deprivation didn't stop her from driving to Rotterdam and visiting the American consul the next day. Her request for a visitor's visa on humanitarian basis was denied. The story of her father's recent death and her mother's heart attack didn't move the American consul.

She called her former employer, Rubin & Stein, and asked them if they would be willing to sponsor her immigrant visa process again. The partners told her that they were planning to establish a law firm in Washington, DC, and that she would make a perfect attorney to handle the firm. She was grateful that after so many years, her former bosses hadn't forgotten her.

She next called Mr. Klein, her immigration attorney, and asked him to renew her application for a green card.

* * *

She called her mother once or twice a day during the month she stayed in the hospital. She also talked to her mother's doctor and learned that her mother's heart attack was a serious one—and it could happen again.

She realized that she had no choice but to go back to the United States. Her family was falling apart. Puri's heart attack had traumatized her children, especially Syrus and Elli, who had just emigrated to the United States and hadn't had enough time to adjust to their new home.

She didn't hear anything from Attorney Klein or Rubin & Stein. She knew that the process for her green card would take a long time. She decided to establish her permanent residency in Holland. She was truthful with Mr. Drost, the Dutch immigration director. She told him that her ultimate goal was to move permanently to the United States. "I think the American Consulate will grant me a temporary visitor visa if they know that I'm a permanent resident here. I feel guilty requesting permanent residency in Holland when my intention is to go somewhere else."

"I appreciate your honesty. Just fill out and sign these papers. I'll take care of the rest," Mr. Drost said as he handed the application forms to Roxana.

In order to strengthen her connection with Europe, Roxana also applied for a fellowship at the Max Plank Institute in Germany. The institute in Heidelberg was one of the most prestigious research establishments in Europe. She sent them a resume and a proposal to write about the Iran-US Claims Tribunal.

To her surprise, a week later the director of the Max Plank Institute sent her a letter telling her that they would be "delighted" to have her as a fellow for two years.

She showed the letter to Afshin and informed him that despite Max Plank's great offer, her ultimate goal was to go to the United States. "I've got to spend some time with my mother before something happens to her. I don't know whether you want to stay in Holland permanently or to go back to Iran. I can ask my immigration attorney to file an application for you too."

"I'm sick and tired of the weather here; and after that ten thousand guilders loss because of a one hundred guilders damage,

I'm not crazy to live with the Dutch people. Go ahead and file an application for me too."

"Are you sure you're not gonna change your mind? This is not a short trip to Berlin or other places that you can cancel at the last minute."

"I won't change my mind."

She couldn't believe her ears. For a moment she thought that maybe Afshin would change if they went to the United States. After all, he had gotten his education there. Maybe he would feel happier. Maybe he could make more money. She was dreaming about a lot of *maybes*. She didn't know that Afshin was not being truthful with her.

At the end of November, Attorney Klein called Roxana. "Your former boss, Mr. Rubin, has patiently followed all the immigration rules. He placed an ad in the newspaper and interviewed other people, as required by immigration law, and—"

"And what?" Roxana asked impatiently.

"The good news is that he has proven to immigration authorities that he can't find any attorney with your unique qualifications. We have got your Labor Department certification too. It's the State Department that's making a ridiculous demand."

Mr. Klein explained that the State Department was asking for a language test in Arabic because they were suspicious that Roxana would know seven languages.

"I haven't dealt with that language in years, but I'll take the test."

"Are you sure?"

"Yes, I am."

She bought a voluminous English-Arabic dictionary and started memorizing the words.

"Are you insane?" Lili asked her one day when she saw her studying a thick Arabic dictionary during her lunch hour. "You have never taken a test in Arabic."

"This test may be my ticket to go back to the States. I have got to see my mother before she dies. Besides, I need to settle down permanently. All these short trips that I make indicate that I'm looking for a home."

On December 1, 1986, Afshin took a four-week vacation and left The Hague for Tehran to visit his family. Roxana knew that the long separation would be hard on the kids, but she didn't object. She invited some of Darius's friends from the kindergarten to have dinner and play with him. She paid overtime to Caroline to spend more time with Kurosh.

In mid-December, she received a call from Nina. She and her family had fled Tehran and had settled in Istanbul.

"Please don't tell me you fled in a sheepskin."

"No, we didn't, but we paid a lot of bribes to get here. We still don't have any passports; we cannot get an appointment with the American Consulate because they are so busy. There's a lengthy waiting list here to see the consul. Can you please come to Istanbul? I need your help," Nina pleaded.

"Give me a few days to find a way."

She called Caroline and asked her if her mother would allow her to travel to Istanbul. The answer was yes.

Chapter 81

Nina had reserved two rooms for Roxana and Caroline at the same hotel in which she and her family stayed. After an emotional reunion with her friend, Nina noticed Roxana's children. She gave each a long hug. "I can't believe Darius has grown so much," she said. "The last time I saw him, he was only twenty months old."

Roxana realized that Caroline was watching them and hearing a language she didn't understand. "Caroline, forgive my manners. This is Nina, my best friend."

Caroline shook Nina's hands and said, "Nice to meet you."

"She is a traditional British nanny," Roxana told Nina, "but I consider her as a great mother helper."

Moments later, Nina's family joined them. Now, it was Roxana's turn to be surprised how much Ramin had grown. Nina's eighteen-year-old son was taller than his father, Bijan. Nina led Roxana, Caroline, and the kids to their hotel rooms. Bijan and Ramin helped with their suitcases.

"You see now why I was so desperate to get out of Iran," Nina said. "They could've drafted Ramin anytime and sent him to the battlefield."

"What are your plans? Are you going back to Boston?"

"I have had enough of the East Coast people and their prejudices. We'll go to LA, where my parents live."

Roxana had arrived on Sunday, so she couldn't call the American Consulate. Bijan invited everyone to a nice restaurant by the Sea of Marmara in the Adalar area. After a leisurely lunch, when everyone was waiting for their desserts, Roxana obtained the name of the

American consul and her telephone number from Nina. "Give me a dollar bill, please," she said to Nina.

"If you haven't exchanged your guilders yet, don't worry, we have a lot of dollars."

"I need one dollar to represent you. It's unethical for a lawyer to introduce herself as someone's attorney without being retained first."

Nina pulled a dollar bill out of her purse and handed it to Roxana. "I bet this is the cheapest legal fee anyone has ever paid you," she said, and laughed.

Roxana called the consulate on Monday morning. She was given an appointment to talk to the consul on Wednesday.

I can't believe this," Nina said. "We've been calling them for weeks, and they kept telling us that the consul was busy."

"Don't you ever underestimate the power of an attorney," Bijan said.

Roxana had two days to kill in Istanbul. Although she had visited the city before, she wanted to show some tourist attractions to Caroline.

"I'm so grateful you've brought me here," Caroline said. "My mother has called all our relatives in London telling them I'm visiting Istanbul. No one in my family has ever traveled to this part of the world."

To Roxana's surprise, Nina had not visited any interesting tourist areas since she had arrived. "Why not?" Roxana asked.

"I'm an Armenian. Have you forgotten about the Armenian massacre?" Nina said.

"Come on, Nina. That was under the Ottoman Empire, but this is a new generation of the Turks." She told Nina about her meeting with the Iraqi diplomat at Rik's party in The Hague. "So I should have hated the guy because the Iraqis are killing Iranians right now. As for the Armenian massacres, that was a long time ago. Did you know that one of the Ottoman rulers hired an Armenian architect to build the Dolmabahce Sary Palace in the nineteenth century?"

"No, I didn't."

"At some point, people have to stop hating each other. Instead, they should forgive and forget. Otherwise we should hate the Germans forever for what the Nazis did. This is a new generation of Germans. The same is true with the Turks."

"You're an internationalist; you see things differently. Sorry I don't. But I am grateful that they are allowing so many Iranians to come here without any visa requirements."

Roxana bought a tour package from the hotel's concierge. They were given a minibus and a driver who had some limited English. She asked the driver in Turkish to take them to the Blue Mosque and *Hagia Sophia* first.

In the afternoon, she asked Caroline to care for the kids so that she could take Nina to the Grand Bazaar. Once they entered the bazaar, Roxana got teary eyes. The bazaar was so similar to the one in Tehran. The place reminded her of her father and of the business he had built from nothing.

Caroline was so grateful for the exotic trip that she let Roxana spend more time with Nina.

The two friends found a gypsy fortune-teller who could tell their future by looking at the remains of the Turkish coffee they had drunk. The rule was to drink the coffee in a small cup, turn it upside down, leave it on the saucer, and let the remaining coffee grounds dry for a few minutes.

The fortune-teller told Roxana and Nina that each was mourning the loss of a loved one, and that both were destined to go to *Amrika*.

Roxana and Lili tried to contain themselves and to not laugh when they heard about their future trip. "Even the Turkish fortune-tellers know that every Iranian in Turkey is planning to go to *Amrika*," Nina said, laughing.

On Wednesday morning, Roxana finally had the opportunity to talk to the American consul in Ankara, by phone. She was a pleasant woman who listened to her as she explained in detail how Nina's family had misplaced their certificates of citizenship and their passports, about the tragic death of Yerem, and Nina's family who lived in California.

The consul scheduled an interview for Nina and her family sometime in late January 1987. She gave Roxana a list of documents and the components of an affidavit they needed to bring with them to the interview.

"You're going to the United States," Roxana said as soon as she hung up the phone.

Nina and Bijan cheered, as they hugged Roxana. To show their gratitude, they took her to a fancy restaurant that night. She enjoyed Istanbul, where most women wore Islamic *hejab* and no one stared at her.

* * *

When she returned to The Hague, she found a letter from the American Consulate in Amsterdam in her mailbox. She was given a date for her Arabic testing in mid-January, 1987.

Afshin returned home on the twenty-ninth of December. He was in a good mood after four weeks of visiting with his family and relatives. However, as soon as he heard about Roxana's trip to Istanbul, he went into a rage. "How could you spend thousands of dollars and travel thousands of miles to see your friend," he shouted. "It must have cost you more than $6,000."

"It was not visiting my friend. She needed my legal help. Besides, it was my money, not yours."

"Every time I talk about the way you waste your money, you keep reminding me that it's your money. It's the family money—the children's."

"Who's paying for the children's babysitters, day care, kindergarten, and even their clothes?"

She noticed that her kids were frightened because of Afshin's shouting. She quickly took them to her bedroom and tried to distract them by reading their favorite book to them.

The next morning she gave Darius breakfast sooner than usual and took him in a cab to his kindergarten. She was protecting her son from witnessing another potential ranting by his father.

When she got out of the cab in front of the bureau's building, she ran into Lili. "Please don't ask why I'm taking a cab to work. The madman is back. He had a big fight with me last night."

Lili followed Roxana to her office. She was worried. "Would you like to come and spend a few days with me until he calms down?"

"Thanks for the offer, but I can't take my kids away from their home, and I will never leave them with him."

"What was the fight all about?"

"My trip to Istanbul and the cost."

"Doesn't he care about Nina?"

"He only cares for his own suffering—losing money, my money."

"At least you had some peaceful time when he was away."

"You're right. It was wonderful. I paid Caroline overtime. When I went home from the office, I didn't have to do anything. It was like having a *wife*!"

That afternoon, Roxana asked Lili to help her get Darius from his kindergarten and take him home. After Darius was inside the house, Lili gave Roxana a ride back to the bureau. She had a deadline to file a brief with the tribunal. She said good-bye to Lili and went back to her office.

For the first time, she couldn't concentrate on her work. Every time she had found a solution for Afshin's anger, she was faced with a new one. She could've hidden the trip to Istanbul from him. Lili and Caroline would have kept quiet, and the kids were too young to differentiate between Istanbul and another city. *Why did she have to be so honest with him?* she wondered.

When she arrived at home, Kurosh was asleep. She found Darius and Afshin in the living room. Darius was showing his twenty-inch Christmas tree to his father and explaining that he had decorated it on the *Sinterclaas* Day.

"Apparently *Sinterclaas*, or Santa Claus, originated in Holland," Roxana told Afshin. "They had a big celebration here on December the sixth. Darius has learned how to sing the *Sinterclaas* song in Dutch."

As soon as Darius started singing, Afshin grabbed the little plastic Christmas tree and plucked out its ornaments. "I don't like this nonsense. You're not Christian," he told Darius.

Darius's lips quivered; he ran out of the living room. Roxana heard him crying as she gathered the small ornaments from the floor. She ran after Darius, hugged him, and took him to her bedroom. She put the ornaments back on the tree. "You see, it's fixed," she told Darius. "I'm sorry for your dad's comment. He's just come back from a long trip, and he's tired."

She read several books to Darius and sang one of his favorite bedtime songs, "*Quand Les Roses,*" before he fell asleep. She came back to the living room. Afshin was watching TV. She stood next to the TV set, positioning herself in front of Afshin, but not covering his view. She held up the little Christmas tree. "How can you smash something that your child has created," she said in a whispered tone.

"He's not Christian," Afshin shouted.

"What do you care? You don't believe in any religion."

"My parents are Moslems."

"So am I, but I don't destroy my son's creation because it's a symbol of Christianity. By the way, didn't you say that your mother was a Russian and didn't care about religion?"

"Now she's a devout Moslem. My father has always been a religious man."

"So my kids have to be Moslem because your parents are Moslem?"

"My family is right. You're making all the decisions in this marriage, not me."

"I don't have much respect for your family, which judges me thousands of miles away not knowing what a hellish life their son has created for me."

"You want a divorce; let's go to the embassy tomorrow and end this."

Afshin threw the remote control in Roxana's direction and left the room. She dodged the remote, turned the TV off, and sat on the sofa motionless. The man had raped her brain again. *Another crime in the middle of the night.*

She pictured herself and Afshin in a divorce proceeding at the embassy. All Afshin had to say to the Moslem clergy judge was, "We are Moslems, but my wife is encouraging my son to be a Christian." Even if her permanent residency was established in Holland, and she had won the custody battle in a Dutch court, Afshin still could've easily kidnapped their children and taken them to Tehran. She could not imagine a life without her two boys.

She couldn't go to sleep. Horrible consequences of a contested divorce played in her mind like a movie. She turned the TV on to get distracted. She heard a familiar song. She raised her gaze and saw Adamo on the screen. He was singing "*Quand Les Roses.*" Roxana thought she was dreaming. In all those years in Europe, she saw Adamo's concert signs everywhere, but she never dared to enter a concert hall in her Islamic *hejab.* Now Adamo had brought his concert to her living room.

She watched him dance on the large stage when he began singing "*C'est ma vie.*" He danced around the stage as if he was holding a partner. She closed her eyes and imagined for a moment that she was that partner. Adamo had invited her to the dance floor, and what a dreamy dance. The last time she had danced was more than six years ago on her wedding night.

She repeated Adamo's words in her head. "This is my life. I didn't choose this life; it chose me. *C'est ma vie.*"

Her eyes kept following him as he danced. She found herself muttering, "*Merci, Adamo.*"

Chapter 82

The next day was New Year's Eve. Roxana decided to go home early even though she didn't have any special plan for the evening.

While she finished parking the car, she saw Caroline walking away fast. She called out to her, "Where are you going in such a hurry?"

Caroline stopped and then walked a few steps back toward the car. She didn't make any eye contact with Roxana but instead stared at the curb. Her face was flushed. "Mr. Imani fired me."

"What? He can't do that."

"He told me to leave as soon as he came home. I told him I had to wait for you. He said in an angry voice that I should listen to him, and when I said that I would only take instruction from you, he told me that I was fired."

Roxana tried to convince Caroline that she probably had misinterpreted Afshin's words. She begged her to come back inside and talk with her, but she declined. "I'm not gonna come back again. I love you, and I love the kids, but I can't stand your husband."

She thought Caroline's anger would disappear in a day or two and everything would be back to normal. Her assumption proved wrong when Caroline told her, "Please find another nanny."

Roxana went inside. She had planned not to talk to Afshin because of his previous fights. She was trying to avoid a new fight, but firing Caroline was unforgivable. She was furious with him.

"How could you do this to me?" she snapped. "Do you know how difficult it is to find a good babysitter?"

"You have spoiled her," Afshin said calmly. "You've showered her with gifts, paying her twice the salary she deserves. That's why she is so arrogant and disrespectful."

"I'm paying her, not you."

"This is my house. If I don't like someone, I have a right to kick her out."

"In two days, you'll go back to the office. What am I supposed to do, sit at home and take care of Kurosh?"

"You wanted children . . . I didn't."

"They're yours. I didn't bring them to you from a previous marriage."

Roxana didn't wait for his answer. She went to her children's room. She found Darius playing with his brother. She went to the kitchen and started cooking.

* * *

When the kids fell asleep, she found her old address book. She had kept it since 1982 when she first came to Holland. The book contained the names, addresses, and telephone numbers of all the babysitters who had ever worked for her.

Afshin was watching a New Year's Eve celebration show on TV. She took the long-cord telephone, went to the dining room, and began calling her former babysitters. After receiving several disconnected lines, she decided to rest for a while, but she was too anxious to stop. She had to find a babysitter in two days.

She kept dialing more numbers. Suddenly she felt a twinge in her heart. The pain soon moved to her left arm and left ribs. She was now gasping for air. She tried to call Afshin, but she had lost her voice. She didn't know what was happening to her. Every time she breathed, she had a sharp pain in her left rib area. She managed to walk to the living room and get Afshin's attention. She wrote on a piece of paper, "Please call Dr. Jansen."

"What happened to you?" Afshin asked casually.

She tried to talk but she sounded like someone moaning with a hoarse voice.

He finally noticed the seriousness of Roxana's condition. For the first time, there was fear in his eyes. He called Dr. Jansen. "He's out of town. There is another doctor covering for him," he told Roxana.

By the time Dr. Jansen's replacement came, Roxana's left arm was partially paralyzed. She couldn't raise it or lower it. The female doctor asked Afshin to describe what had happened before Roxana started experiencing the pain. He tried to make up stories, but finally admitted that he had had a fight with his wife.

"So you did this to her?"

Afshin didn't answer and left the room. The doctor reduced the volume on the TV as Roxana took a piece of paper from the coffee table and wrote a note to her. "He came back from a trip three days ago. He has been fighting with me since. Today he fired my nanny. I am an attorney with many cases pending before an arbitration tribunal. I have to go back to work in two days. I don't have a babysitter for my kids."

Roxana noticed that the female doctor couldn't mask her disgust. "The emotional pain had been building up for three days," she said. "The shock of losing your nanny was the last straw. You've had a panic attack."

The doctor gave Roxana an injection and a prescription for some tranquilizers. She recommended bed rest for at least three days.

When the doctor left, it was midnight. Roxana heard the traditional "Auld Lang Syne" on the TV; the happy couples kissed while dancing. The "Happy New Year" sign flashed on the screen repeatedly. It was 1987; Roxana was alone and paralyzed.

* * *

The next day, she was able to talk but had a hoarse voice. She called Lili and asked for help. Lili rushed to Roxana's home, and when she heard what had happened she got so angry that she couldn't say anything except, "Bastard!" repeating it over and over. After she calmed down, she sat close to Roxana and stared at her for a while. "Look, this is me, Lili, your childhood friend. You should've called me last night."

"I didn't want to spoil your New Year's Eve."

"My celebration would've vanished if something tragic had happened to you."

When Lili left at the end of the day, Afshin came to Roxana's room for the first time. "You see, it's not only Caroline who disrespects me; your friend is as bad as she is. She didn't say a word to me."

"If I had caused you a panic attack, your family wouldn't talk to me either."

"It's your sensitivity that caused you the panic attack. If someone touches you, you get bruised. If someone talks to you loudly, you get a panic attack."

"Only in your vocabulary can physical abuse be considered as *touching*, and only you can refer to three nights of fighting as *talking loudly.*"

For several days, Roxana begged Caroline to come back, but she refused. She had found a job in a hospital. "I clean at least twenty toilets per day. I'm paid one half of what you paid me, but I'm happy here because I don't have to put up with your husband," she said.

The more she thought about Caroline's firing, the more she realized that this was Afshin's well-planned revenge because of her trip to Istanbul.

The panic attack scared Roxana more than she had expected. After six years of living with an abusive husband, she had learned how to be flexible and make speedy adjustments. She had gracefully moved and focused on what was more important in her life—her children and her career. However, the panic attack made her realize that despite her cool appearance, her brain had recorded every crisis, every disappointment, and every physical abuse she had endured. She was not invincible.

She found several temporary babysitters. Sometimes she had three different ones in one day. Scheduling became overwhelming, but she had no choice. She had to go to work every day. She also had to study for her Arabic test.

* * *

On the day of her exam, she wore her maxicoat over a business pantsuit. She looked in the mirror and for a moment she saw the beautiful Roxana she used to know, the woman who lived and practiced law in New York City. It was cold outside. She put her scarf in her coat pocket and put on a winter hat that covered every strand of her hair. She looked very European, yet Islamic—only her face was showing.

Instead of driving to Amsterdam, she took the train. She memorized more Arabic words in her head during the thirty-five-minute trip.

At the American Consulate, a female employee took her to a conference room on the second floor. After searching Roxana's briefcase to make sure that she didn't have an Arabic dictionary, she brought a booklet that contained the test. She gave her a pen and several sheets of blank white paper. "You have two hours to finish this," she said.

Roxana's heart was pounding. This was not The Hague Academy test that was conducted in English. She had never taken any test in Arabic. She opened the booklet. The subject was the Jordanian Constitution. She had to translate the Arabic text into English. Roxana relaxed, grateful that the test was law-related. She finished it in an hour and handed it to the consulate's staffer. As she gathered her coat and briefcase to leave, she was told that there was another test to come. She sat down again, wondering what was next.

The employee brought another booklet and another set of papers. "You have two hours to complete this one as well," she said. "I may be out to lunch when you finish. Just leave your papers here. I'll collect them later."

"Have a nice lunch," Roxana said, smiling. The employee left, ignoring her statement. She had gotten used to the cold and disrespectful treatment of the staff at the American consulates. *That's a price you pay for taking hostages.*

She opened the booklet. It was the Jordanian Constitution again, but this time in English. They wanted her to translate it back into Arabic. She panicked at first. But then she remembered some of the provisions of the document she had just translated minutes ago. Some attorneys who had worked with Roxana had told her that she had a photographic memory. She didn't really grasp the meaning of that remark until that day when she was faced with the second Arabic test. She had to remember the Arabic words that she had used earlier. The memory helped. It took her two hours to finish this part of the test.

She inserted the papers inside the booklet and left it on the conference table. She had been escorted to the conference room that morning, so when she left the room, she didn't know which direction to take. The female employee was gone. She walked a few feet to the right, then to the left, looking for an exit sign. She passed an office with an open door and saw a man sitting behind a desk. She decided to ask him for directions, but when she got closer to the office, the writing on the door stopped her. "Thomas Saunder" was the US consul who had sent her the letter about the exam. She decided not to ask him for direction, but as she walked away, she felt the urge to go back and talk to him. She needed to get a visa, any kind of visa, to travel to the United States and see her mother. She felt a sudden surge of courage, walked back toward the office, and knocked on the door.

"Excuse me, Mr. Saunder, may I have a few minutes of your time?" she asked while still standing in the hallway.

"Please come in," the consul said, gesturing an invitation. He motioned Roxana to sit in a chair facing him.

"My name is Roxana—"

"I know who you are. This is your file," he said, pointing to a thick file on his desk.

"That bad, huh?" Roxana smiled.

"What can I do for you?"

"Do I look like a terrorist to you?"

"I beg your pardon?" The consul looked surprised.

"During the Cold War, the US Immigration Service prevented the communists from entering the United States. These days, it's the terrorists. That's why I'm asking you whether I look like a terrorist."

"You're not a terrorist, but you're working for the enemy. We know there are many other Iranian attorneys at your bureau, but you're the one who's winning their cases."

"That's my sin? Do you know how many cases your side has won?"

"Iran agreed to the terms of the Algerian Declaration."

"True, and that's the same document the other attorneys and I are using."

"We're not concerned about the other Iranian attorneys. As far as we know, you're the only one with a US education and several international law degrees."

"With all those degrees, if I had knocked on your door and asked for a job, would you have hired me?"

"No."

"Thanks for your honesty. But your so-called enemy did. Not only did they let me have the most fascinating career for a young *female* attorney, but they also paid me well. I am here to ask you for a temporary visitor visa. I lost my father to a heart attack, and now my mother has just had a heart attack in the United States. I need to see her before she dies."

Roxana picked up her briefcase and her coat and said good-bye.

She left the American consul's office feeling relieved. She had talked to him about what had agonized her for a long time.

A week later, Roxana received a phone call from her New York immigration attorney. "Congratulations. I don't know how you did it, but you passed the Arabic test."

Chapter 83

During the first week of February, Roxana received some good news. The first was from Nina in Istanbul. She and her family had finally received their American passports and were on their way to California. Nina thanked her friend profusely. "I'll never forget that you spent thousands of dollars and traveled with two small children in wintertime to help me out," she said on the phone. "I also have another bit of good news for you."

"What good news."

"I'm three months pregnant."

"Oh my God, I can't believe it! How come you didn't tell me in Istanbul?"

"I was consumed with our problems of getting back to the United States."

Roxana had tears in her eyes when she hung up the phone. She was elated that Nina's problems were finally resolved.

The second piece of good news came in the form of a letter from Mr. Elkhouri, the Lebanese businessman. It read:

> Dear Dr. Ramsy,
>
> I heard from our friend Rik Van Rijn that you're planning to go back to the United States. I'm in the process of establishing an office in Washington. I'd like to hire your husband to manage that office for me. Of course, he has to travel to Houston a lot. I have several transactions with the oilmen in Texas.

Please let me know if he is interested.

Regards,
M. Elkhouri

Roxana couldn't believe her eyes. She read the letter twice to make sure that she wasn't dreaming. This was like a winning lottery ticket. No one had ever offered her things she desired. She had to work hard for every award and every honor she had received. Mr. Elkhouri had just handed her a gift for which she hadn't struggled.

She received the ultimate good news from Attorney Klein at dinnertime.

"Congratulations! Your green card application for the whole family is approved by the State Department."

Roxana was speechless. She sat in the nearest chair and muttered, "Thank you, Mr. Saunder."

Afshin was waiting for her to talk. "Are you going to say anything?"

"I'm trying to digest the news myself." She went to her purse and pulled out Mr. Elkhouri's letter and handed it to Afshin. "My green card application for the whole family is approved . . . and here's a job for you."

Afshin read the letter several times. Finally he got out of his chair. "Is this for real?"

"Yes."

He came around the table and gave Roxana a big hug. "Finally, we're out of this cold and damp country."

The next day, Roxana had the difficult task of breaking the news to Dr. Rohani.

Before meeting with her boss, she had prepared a detailed status report on her cases. She had also written a report summarizing all the legal issues she had researched.

As she handed him the reports, she talked about her original green card application and President Carter's deportation order. She talked about how her family was falling apart since her father's death and her mother's heart attack, and how they needed her in the United States.

"I don't believe what I'm hearing," Dr. Rohani said. "I'm shocked. I can't imagine this bureau without you."

"I've worked for the bureau for six years now and have exhausted research on all the complicated legal issues we faced. There are thousands of cases still pending before the tribunal. This arbitration can go on for at least another decade. We have a dozen good attorneys here and many more in Tehran. They'll be able to handle anything."

"Thanks to your constant coaching."

"No one needs my coaching."

"You're too modest . . . are you going to work for them?"

"Who?"

"The American companies. I've heard the American expression that 'Everyone has a price,' or, 'You can buy anyone.' They should be dying to use your expertise."

"I'll go back to private practice with my Wall Street law firm."

Dr. Rohani pulled a letter from his drawer and handed it to Roxana. "This came from Tehran International Airline. TIA is asking me whether I would allow you to work as in-house counsel in their Paris bureau. Now that you're leaving us, I'll let you answer them."

* * *

She tried to find Lili and share her good news. Lili didn't answer her phone. After several unsuccessful attempts to reach her, she finally left a message on her answering machine telling her about Nina and about her own good news.

The next day, when she entered her office, Lili was sitting by the window gazing into the park. Roxana noticed that she was wearing sunglasses. "What's with the dark shades?" she asked Lili jokingly.

"I cried a lot last night," Lili said, and lowered her glasses to show her puffy eyes.

"What happened?"

"Before I dump my problems on you, I want you to know that I'm so thrilled for you and Nina. You two deserve to be happy."

"What's going on? You're not the crying type."

"Bank Markazi has ordered me and Kayvan to go back to Tehran. They think that the significant bank-related cases are over in Holland. Kayvan will be leaving next week, but I'm going back to London. After the life we've had here, I can't work with him during the day and send him home to his wife at night."

"I think you should go back at least temporarily to show that you're not defying the bank's order; then you can resign."

"I don't care. I'm a British citizen; they cannot do a damn thing to me."

"It may look suspicious. You have had access to a lot of sensitive documents. You worked on the shah's case. If you don't go back, there may be consequences."

"I don't care."

"If you're not going to Tehran, why don't you come with me to America? They're gonna love your British accent, blue eyes, and blonde hair."

"I don't know Americans well enough to live with them."

"They're warmhearted people. Compared to the British, you'll be surprised how Middle Eastern they are."

* * *

Roxana started packing in mid-March. She gave all the furniture she had bought to charity, disregarding Afshin's objection and desire to sell. Her lease would expire in May, so she gave her house key to Lili and asked her to check her mail.

Puri had arranged for Roxana to stay with an old friend of hers in Fairfax, Virginia, until she found an apartment. Because Roxana didn't have a fixed address in the United States, she instructed everyone to send all correspondences to her old address in The Hague until the end of April. She asked Lili to call and inform her of important mail items over the phone.

Two days before her departure, Roxana remembered that she hadn't told her American friends about her green card or her plan to return to the States, so she wrote a letter to Cathy.

> Dear Cathy,
>
> Call our mutual friends and tell them that after seven years of separation, I'm returning to the United States. I feel like singing Tony Orlando's song, "I'm coming home; I'm coming home," but I don't expect you to tie a yellow ribbon around the old oak tree for me. I'm coming back, but I have to confess, it's hard to walk away from

a dreamlike career. It's also emotional to leave Holland because this country has been a home away from home for me for five years now. I know you're more fascinated by Eastern European countries, but you should come and visit Holland someday. Did you know that this small European country has protected ethnic minorities since the sixteenth century? That was when the continent of Europe was dominated by religious fervor. Refugees of all faiths came to Leiden, the "Dutch Haven." You should visit Leiden and see the rows of tulips that adorn the city streets. The lily-padded canals and bridges resemble Van Gogh's paintings.

The Dutch seem to have problems with religion. Pope John Paul's visit here in 1985 was labeled his worst experience next to the assassination attempt he experienced in 1982. We were astonished watching the footage of the riot in Utrecht on TV, where streets were filled with protesters shouting, "Pope go home."

You enjoy biking, so you would've loved it here. Bikes in Holland are treated like sacred cows in India. Some people have seen the Queen Mother biking in the streets of Den Haag.

I've gotten used to seeing my neighbor walking his dog while his wife finishes making love to her boyfriend in their bedroom. The first time he explained to me why he was standing outside on a cold day, I thought he was joking.

Amsterdam is considered a heaven for those who like to order hashish or marijuana in certain coffee shops. Euthanasia, prostitution, abortion, and gays are treated totally different here than in the United States.

I can hardly wait to see you and tell you more about this fascinating country and its people. You might wonder why I'm leaving Holland if it's this fascinating. The answer is simple. It's not home.

Love,
Roxana

* * *

After she said a tearful good-bye to Roxana at the Schipol Airport, Lili was somber. She drove to Amsterdam and walked aimlessly around the canals and over the bridges. She missed her friend, who was her *sang-e-saboor,* a patient rock. She could always rely on Roxana anytime she was in trouble. After finishing her lunch in a quiet restaurant, she drove directly to Roxana's townhouse. She had arrived just in time. The mailman handed her two envelopes.

Roxana's plane was probably thirty thousand miles over the Atlantic Ocean when Lili opened the first envelope. The first letter was from Mr. Elkhouri, informing Roxana that his oil agreement didn't go through; therefore he couldn't establish an office in Washington. "There goes Afshin's job," Lili muttered. The second letter was from Mathew Stein. It read:

> Dear Roxana,
>
> Jeffrey and I were really looking forward to working with you again. However, something has happened. Jeffrey's marriage has fallen apart. All his time is presently consumed with his divorce proceedings. We won't be able to form a partnership when his assets are under review by the divorce court. I have a good job offer to join a big Park Avenue law firm as a partner. Jeffrey is my best friend, but it's time for us to go our separate ways.
>
> I'd love to see you when you come back to the States.
>
> As always,
> Mathew

Lili stared at the letter for a long while—she was speechless. *Oh my God, how am I gonna tell her?*

PART 4

Chapter 84

The flight from Amsterdam to Dulles Airport was estimated to be eight hours. Roxana had requested four seats in the first row of the cabin's center section to allow the kids room to play. She entertained her kids during the first two hours of the flight while Afshin talked politics with a Dutchman in an aisle seat on the right side of the cabin.

When Kurosh fell asleep, Roxana went to the restroom to change her *hejab.*

She first took off the long skirt she had worn over her jeans, and then her long-sleeve loose blouse. When she took off her scarf, she felt she had removed a chain around her neck. She let her long hair down, ran her fingers through her soft auburn hair to give it a coiffure, and stood there looking at her image in the mirror. For years, she had avoided looking at her scarf-wrapped face in the mirror. She was afraid that the real Roxana would jump out and admonish her, but now she was a free woman. She could look at her image in the mirror again. At first, she felt she was looking at an old friend whom she hadn't seen for a long time, but when she smiled, she saw the Roxana she used to know—beautiful, smiling, and confident.

She put the scarf and the rest of the clothes she had shed in a bag she had carried to the restroom. When she came out, she gave the bag to the flight attendant. "This is garbage. Would you please discard it?"

"Of course," responded the attendant. She threw the bag in a large bin at her station not knowing that she had thrown away a chain that had kept a woman in captivity for six years—a painful symbol Roxana had tolerated like a thorn in her eyes. In a short few minutes, Roxana's life had changed—*Farewell to hejab, the war, and the revolution.*

When she came back to her seat, Afshin was still talking to the man seated on the aisle. He stopped talking to the passenger when the flight attendants began serving lunch. Kurosh was awake now.

"Do you remember us?" Roxana asked jokingly. "I can't feed two kids on the plane at the same time. Could you please help Darius cut his chicken?"

"Now that you've lost your nanny and a galaxy of babysitters, I hope you don't expect me to do their job," Afshin said with a warning tone in his voice.

"Don't worry, as soon as I get settled, I'll find a day care or a babysitter for them. Right now I need a little help."

"You haven't landed in your beloved country yet, but already you've started showing some attitude."

"Forget it. Somehow I'll manage to feed the kids by myself."

"No, I'm not going to forget it. You've uprooted me twice, first from Iran, now from Holland. I won't let you run my life," Afshin said, raising his voice.

"You agreed both times. Do you remember how anxious you were when you came to Holland? And how excited you were about the green cards?"

"You have ruined my life. Now your family and friends will spoil you rotten. I won't put up with this."

During the remaining four hours of the flight to Washington, she didn't talk to him. She played games with her kids or read books to them. After a long struggle, she had finally got her green card, and she was not about to let Afshin ruin her happiness.

* * *

They were taken to a room by immigration authorities at Dulles Airport. The lengthy questioning period seemed more like an interrogation. After an hour of waiting, the INS man finally gave them their stamped temporary green cards.

The next line was the customs line for non-European passengers. The customs officer looked at Roxana's Iranian passport and asked her to open her large suitcase. As she was opening the suitcase, she heard him asking Darius in a whisper, "Have you hidden any guns anywhere?"

"He's too young to be a terrorist," Roxana answered, masking her anger.

As soon as she entered the reception area, where families and relatives welcomed the arriving passengers, she couldn't help tearing up. She didn't know who took Kurosh from her arms or who took the suitcases. She didn't need to beg for Afshin's help anymore.

The next day, Puri prepared a big meal for her children. The family gathering was emotional for everyone. For the first time in a decade, every member of the Ramsy family was at the dinner table except Miremad. Roxana saw the gloomy mood of her siblings and her mother's struggle to change the mood.

"You know how much your father loved Iran," Puri said rhetorically. "He wouldn't leave Iran. He also knew that Syrus, Elli, and I were not going to leave him, so by going to heaven, he set us free."

Puri's remarks didn't help; Roxana saw the tears in everyone's eyes. While fighting tears, Puri received comfort from an unexpected source. The twenty-one-month-old Kurosh, who was on Roxana's lap sitting next to Puri, turned to her, brought his face close to hers, and said, "Mama *Poovi,* I love you." It broke Roxana's heart to see that even her child had sensed the sadness in his grandmother's face. She couldn't believe her ears. Kurosh had never spoken a complete sentence. He knew many words but was not able to use verbs.

Puri reached for her grandchild, took him in her arms, and showered him with kisses. "You see, this is the gift your father has sent us," she told her children.

Kurosh's few words changed the somber mood in the room. After that dinner, Roxana never saw her siblings sad whenever Puri was around. *They know how to hide their grief.*

She was not comfortable with the idea of staying at Shamsi's house, despite the fact that Shamsi was her mother's best friend. She found a two-story townhouse five days after her arrival in the States. The three-bedroom house was a forty-five-minute drive from Shamsi's house.

Although she enjoyed the delicious Persian meals prepared by her mother, she was eager to find an opportunity to dine in an American diner. "Every time I saw an American movie on the Dutch TV where there was a diner with red—and white-checkered tablecloths, I missed America so much," she explained.

As soon as she found a diner near Shamsi's house, she invited everyone.

She couldn't help remembering her departure from New York City. She had realized for some time now that it was not her belongings that she had sold for $500. She had sold her life away. That was the reason that the diner with red-and-white-checkered tablecloths was so important to her. She was claiming her life back, the life she had left behind hastily.

Roxana's siblings left after spending one week in Virginia. Puri stayed behind, but she was worried about Bahram, who had just received his divorce decree from the court.

Chapter 85

Roxana spent a couple of hours calling her friends in the States, telling them she was back. The cheerful reaction of everyone reassured her that she was finally at *home*.

When Cathy called her a *hero,* her response was, "Every ordinary person is a hero—too bad Steven Spielberg doesn't have time to make movies about everyone."

She promised her friends that she would visit them as soon as she could settle down.

Like someone who had a deadline, she worked hard to get her life in order. She found a kindergarten for Darius. Puri volunteered to care for Kurosh, allowing her daughter time to find a day care for him. Under Afshin's constant pressure, Roxana started looking for a house. He kept repeating the same argument until he convinced her. "The amount of rent you pay can be your mortgage payment, and that's tax deductible."

The couple viewed at least twenty houses. Afshin was the one who usually found a problem with every place that their real estate agent showed them. One day when he claimed he was too tired, Roxana took her mother along. The real estate agent showed them a three-bedroom house located in a cul-de-sac. The house was just a few minutes away from major roads and shopping areas, yet was nestled in a quiet neighborhood. Its large, fenced-off backyard was a safe playground for young children.

She bought the house feeling lucky that Afshin didn't object. She moved into the new house immediately and began furnishing the house by spending her own money. She bought a brand new car and found a nice day-care center for Kurosh. She was ready to report to work, but when she called the law firm of Baron & Rosendorf in New York to talk to her former bosses, she was told that neither worked with the firm anymore. The receptionist gave her two separate telephone numbers. She dialed each number several times, but each time she received the answering machine. During the last call, she left a detailed message for both Jeffrey and Mathew, providing them with her new address and telephone number. She waited until 3:00 p.m. to receive a call from them. When she didn't, she sensed that something was wrong. She called Lili in London.

"Sorry, it took so long to call you," she said. "I was trying to get settled down and have a fixed address before calling you."

Roxana shared her concern about the job she was offered. "I can't even find them."

There was a long pause. "Lili, are you there?"

"Yes, I am. I was just trying to find the right words to tell you that they no longer have a job for you."

"Why?"

Lili disclosed the contents of the two letters. "I didn't have the heart to tell you," she said with a sad tone of voice.

"Oh my God! What am I gonna tell Afshin?"

There was a long pause. Neither Roxana nor Lili could talk. When the reality of the situation became clear to Roxana, she wanted an explanation. "Lili, we arrived here a month ago. How could you keep this from me for this long?"

"You have every right to be mad at me. I'm sorry. I didn't tell you immediately because I was so afraid that after all the pain you had gone though, Afshin would've forced you to return to The Hague."

"I appreciate your concern, Lili, but now I have purchased a house thinking that I had a job."

"I'm sure you'll find another job."

"What am I gonna do with Afshin? He agreed to come here because he had a job offer."

"I wish I could change the situation, but I can't."

"I have to go now."

Roxana shared the bad news with her mother first. Puri assured her daughter that things would work out. "*Tavokol beh khoda kon,* trust God," she said.

As she had feared, Afshin went into a rage, accusing her of taking him out of Holland and misleading him to come to the United States.

"You saw Mr. Elkhouri's letter. I didn't write that letter."

"How do I know that you didn't ask him to offer me the phony job?"

"That's an outrageous accusation. Why didn't you contact him and ask him about the details of the job yourself?"

"I thought you would. You've been handling all of my jobs for me anyway."

"This isn't Holland. You're in America. You know the language, the culture, and the job market. Go and find yourself a job."

"What about your phony job?"

"The man is going through a nasty divorce. He has other priorities than opening a law firm in Washington, DC."

"How long do you think your savings will last here?"

"Don't worry about me. I'll work at McDonald's if I have to in order to support my children."

"With two doctoral degrees, you're gonna work in a McDonald's? Ha-ha-ha."

Roxana didn't respond to Afshin's last remark. She knew that this was just the tip of the iceberg. She knew that Afshin would fight, rant, and rave until he found a good-paying job. She had gone through his job losses many times before.

She went upstairs to her bedroom to arrange her closet. She had put all her winter clothes in a suitcase, but she also had to find room in her narrow closet for her spring and summer clothes.

As she was closing the suitcase, she noticed Afshin coming to her room.

"What have you put in that heavy suitcase?" he asked with an angry tone.

"They're all my winter clothes."

"I think you have also put some of my stuff there."

"I have no use for your clothes."

Afshin pushed Roxana away and went directly toward the suitcase lying on the floor. He opened it while kneeling on the floor. Against Roxana's plea, he pulled out many of the clothes she had neatly folded and packed. She tried to prevent him from emptying the suitcase.

"You've messed up everything. Please stop it. There's nothing in there that belongs to you."

Afshin got up from the floor, put his hand on Roxana's chest, and pushed her all the way back to the hallway. "The fact that you've designated this room for yourself doesn't mean that I cannot kick you out of here. This is my house too, and I can go to any room I want."

Roxana felt her lower back pressed against the rail near the staircase. She struggled to get back to her room, but Afshin's hand had now moved to her neck. He was chocking her and pushing her farther against the railing, as if he intended to throw her downstairs.

"Stop it. You're hurting me."

As she was pleading, she heard her mother's voice. "Roxana, what's going on?"

Puri's voice distracted Afshin. As his fingers loosened around Roxana's neck, she got a chance to release herself. She went downstairs immediately. She found her mother standing at the bottom of the staircase looking scared. Puri and the children had just returned from their morning trip to the neighborhood's playground.

"I just walked into the house with the kids. What's going on here?"

"He had a fight with me," Roxana said as she went to the kitchen. She hugged her kids and lifted Kurosh into his high chair. She fixed them each a peanut butter and jelly sandwich while Puri stood there staring at her.

"Please stop staring at me."

Puri walked closer to her daughter, gently pushed back a tress of her long hair, and pointed to a mark on her neck. "Go and look in the mirror."

She went to the bathroom and looked at herself. To her horror, she found purple bruises on the right side of her neck where Afshin's fingers had pressed. She felt devastated, but she didn't know what to do. She didn't want her mother to see Afshin's violent behavior, especially with her heart condition. She knew that her mother had not forgotten about the bruises that she had seen on her face in Tehran. She had kept the Scheveningen incident from her mother. She came back to the kitchen, where Puri was waiting, still with a question mark on her face. "What are you going to do about him?" she asked.

"It's not gonna happen again; I promise you."

She asked her mother to look after the kids. She had to drive to some remote area in Maryland to collect numerous boxes of her books and other materials she had mailed from Holland. "These are my publications, and significant international cases," she told her mother.

"Why are they in Maryland?"

"I mailed them to a friend in Maryland. But I erroneously wrote her old address on the boxes. So now the boxes are in a post office warehouse. I have to go and find them. Please ignore Afshin when I'm gone. I'm begging you."

She covered her bruises by wearing a small scarf around her neck. She took the post office's notice and drove to Maryland. As she had anticipated, she got lost several times, finding herself on narrow country roads. In some of those remote areas, she was afraid of getting out of her car. She finally found the post office and retrieved her boxes. She was exhausted when she returned home. She had been driving for more than three hours. She noticed Afshin sitting at the kitchen dining table with a grim face. "Where's everybody?" she asked.

"I told your mother not to do *fozuli,* to interfere with my life. She left with the kids."

"What did she say to deserve your mean words?"

"She expected me to drive you to Maryland 'because a young, attractive woman can get into trouble if she's lost,'" Afshin said while mocking Puri's words.

"You call that motherly advice, *fozuli*? You know what your problem is? You have been dealing with a noble family, which has treated you with decency. Look at this." Roxana pulled the scarf away from her neck and showed him her bruises.

"You have a sensitive skin and get bruised easily. I was trying to keep you away from the room."

"If my mother had not entered the house in time, you would have either choked me to death or pushed me over the railing. I have news for you. Next time you assault me, I'll call the police. I won't allow you to abuse me ever again."

"I knew it. You're back in your beloved country, and now you're ruling my life."

She put the scarf back around her neck and went after her mother. She knew where to find her. Every morning, Puri used to take her grandchildren to the playground. She enjoyed watching kids play. That was also an excuse for her to be far away from Afshin. She had witnessed too many unprovoked disputes initiated by him. She was also trying to follow her doctor's advice. After the heart attack, one of the first things her cardiologist had warned her was to avoid stress.

When Puri saw Roxana entering the playground, she ran toward her. "Please take me to Shamsi's home. I can't stand being near Afshin anymore," she pleaded.

"*Maman,* can we do this tomorrow? I have driven more than three hours. I'm exhausted."

"If you can't, please call a cab for me. One of these days, he's gonna harm you when no one's around."

"I've warned him that next time I'll call the police, but the truth is that I can't do that. Assault is a serious criminal charge. They will deport him, and he can never return to this country. What am I gonna tell my kids when they are old enough to accuse me of throwing their father out of this country?"

"I don't want him to go to jail. I don't want him to be deported either. Please try to convince him to see a marriage counselor with you."

When she couldn't convince her mother to stay with her for one more night, she drove her to Shamsi's house.

As she was driving away, she saw her mother standing at the doorstep, looking sad and blowing her a kiss.

Chapter 86

Roxana couldn't sleep that night. Afshin's choking had caused her a sore throat. She couldn't drink or swallow comfortably. She sucked on a cough lozenge, but it didn't help.

The physical pain was not the only reason that kept her awake. The images of the day's events kept dancing in her head—Afshin's shocking assault, the endless driving on strange, remote roads, and the image of her mother standing on the doorstep looking lonely and blowing her a kiss.

She was angry with Afshin for causing separation between her mother and her children. In her mind, Afshin's bigger crime was depriving Puri of the only joyful thing she had in her life—playing with her grandchildren.

The next morning, after breakfast, Roxana prepared her boys to go to the playground. She was about to leave the house when the telephone rang. It was the trembling, hesitant voice of Shamsi telling her that Puri had had a heart attack. "It happened two hours after you dropped her off."

"Oh my God, not again." Roxana ran to the kitchen and found a piece of paper. She took the name and the telephone number of the hospital.

"Roxan *Jaan*, don't worry. She is okay now. Your brothers and sisters are all here at the hospital."

Roxana's hands were shaking. She could barely hold the telephone or dial a number. She saw the ghost of death dancing in her living room. The fear of losing her mother was more than she could bear. She sent her children to their father's room. She didn't want them to see her crying. She finally called the hospital and talked to Bahram, her younger brother. "I'm trembling; I can't drive. Could you please give me a ride to the hospital?"

"Sorry, I can't. I drove all last night to be here with Mom."

Bahram had never talked to his sister in that cold, distant tone of voice. She felt she was being treated like a stranger. She left a note for Afshin about her mother's heart attack and called a cab.

The twenty-five-minute taxi ride to the hospital seemed like an eternity. She couldn't help remembering another telephone call she had received from the hospital in The Hague. She had no clue that her father would die. But this time she could feel the presence of death. After a long search in the hospital, she finally found her mother's room. Her siblings had gathered around their mother's bed—all with worried faces. She received a cold greeting from everyone except Elli, who gave her a comforting hug.

When Puri opened her eyes and saw Roxana sitting next to her bed, she teared up. "I'm sorry. I didn't mean to add to your problems." Puri tried to bring her arms around to hug her daughter.

"Please don't talk. Try to rest." Roxana kissed her mother and left the room. She found a chair outside, sat down, and covered her face. She cried quietly. Someone tapped her on the shoulder.

"Roxan *Jaan*, *Khoda bozorgeh.* God is great. She'll be fine," Shamsi said as she put her arms around her. "She didn't want you to know. She asked me to call her children in New Hampshire, but I thought you should know at least on the second day."

After some motherly advice, Shamsi went back to Puri's room, but Roxana didn't want to go back. She couldn't see her mother in pain. She knew that despite her heart attack, her mother hadn't forgotten Afshin's violence. She felt guilty for not recognizing what her marriage had done to her mother.

She was still agonizing outside her mother's room when her brother Syrus approached her. She was too tired to raise her gaze and talk to him. She kept staring at a spot on the floor.

"This is Afshin's fault," Syrus said. "Please keep him away from our mother." He had an edge to his voice, a warning tone.

Puri's doctor assured Roxana that her mother's condition was stabilized; but she couldn't help worrying about another heart attack.

She was certain that the third one would be fatal. Roxana couldn't survive another death.

When she returned home, it was dark. Her children were watching a cartoon on TV. Afshin was in the kitchen enjoying the leftovers of the meal Puri had prepared for him the day before.

Roxana was calm. She waited for Afshin to finish his supper and then approached him. "You caused my mother's heart attack. You're dangerous to me, to my mother, and to my children. Please find yourself a place and move out."

"Your family has heart attack problems. I've nothing to do with it."

"Last October in Holland, my mother came to help me out during difficult litigations in court. She witnessed all your inexcusable fights with me. She returned to the States and had a heart attack. Yesterday, she saw me abused physically again. As if that wasn't bad enough, you had a fight with her. I've started thinking that maybe you had something to do with my father's heart attack too."

"That's nonsense. Your father was the only member of your family I liked. I never had any quarrel with him."

"You're right, because he was too noble to argue with you. But he too witnessed your constant disputes with me. Please move out. You have your green card and $100,000 in your bank account. Go and enjoy your life, but get the hell out of mine."

* * *

Puri had congestive heart failure twice. She spent a total of thirty days at the hospital. Every morning after breakfast, Roxana took her children to the hospital to see their grandmother. She would return home around dinnertime. Taking care of her mother had become her new career, and going to the hospital had turned into a nine-to-five job.

After one week, Puri's children left for New Hampshire. They were all employed and had to go back to work. Neghar, the youngest, who now had a PhD in chemistry, worked for a pharmaceutical company. Elli was an office manager working for a doctor. Syrus had found a job as a computer analyst, and Bahram was promoted to the status of a senior engineer despite his young age. Everyone had a job except Roxana.

Afshin finally moved out. He had found a job managing a large electronics store. After seven years of living in constant fear, Roxana had finally found some peace—no more fights, no more shouting, and no more despair.

Puri moved in with Roxana after she was released from the hospital. Life became easier for Roxana for a while when her mother regained her health and energy.

Afshin was paid twice the salary he received in Holland, so he seemed happy. Against Roxana's advice, Puri made peace with her son-in-law. One Friday evening when he came to take the kids to his place, Puri took her grandchildren to Afshin and started talking with him as if nothing had happened between them. When she saw Roxana's worried face, she told her that Afshin had changed. "He was genuinely concerned about my health."

"Is he fooling you again, like in Tehran, pretending that he was sorry?"

"Look, I'm coming from a different culture. Divorce was a taboo in my generation. I can't encourage you to get a divorce when you have two small children and no job."

"What about Grandma Tala and eight marriages?"

"Your grandma should've been born in *Amrika*. Her case is an exception."

"I'm waiting to see how long Afshin's good mood, or maybe I should say his new job, lasts. I'm waiting for the right time to see whether he gives me an amicable divorce."

"Roxan *Jaan*, I still believe you should see a marriage counselor. He is the father of your children. Maybe this separation will change him."

"For the first time in my life, I am not scared. For seven years I felt like a student who had to report to the principal's office every day. I was an all-A student and never had to go to the principal's office. You and my father allowed me to make my own decisions since I was ten years old. But after my marriage, I always felt I was being summoned to the principal's office—I had to explain everything I did to Afshin."

"Have you noticed how your kids are missing him? Please see a marriage counselor just once, for my peace of mind."

"I will see a marriage counselor, but only to help my kids during the divorce."

Because she had promised her mother, she found a marriage counselor and had a session with her. Dr. Hafner was a highly regarded psychologist and marriage counselor in Fairfax. She was a pleasant-looking middle-aged woman who smiled a lot. When she saw Roxana for the first time she immediately asked where her husband was. "My psychotherapy involves couples only."

"I'm trying to convince him to come," Roxana said. "Could you please allow me to have this session until he joins us?"

Dr. Hafner reluctantly agreed to Roxana's request and let her talk.

She gave a summarized version of her married life to the doctor. She intentionally left Afshin's physical abuses out. As a lawyer she knew that a document recording Afshin's criminal act could be used against him in court. Instead, she emphasized Afshin's anger. Subconsciously she tried to justify it by mentioning that Afshin had followed her to support her career.

After talking for twenty minutes, Roxana saw the sign of agitation on Dr. Hafner's face. "Stop defending him. You're not his lawyer," she blurted. "Kick him out of your life."

"Excuse me?" She was surprised. This was a *déjà vu* of what she had heard from Dr. Miller, the psychologist in Holland. "Is there a chapter on *kick him out of your life* in psychology books?" she asked, trying to use humor.

"What do you mean?"

"I came here hoping you would advise me how to deal with my husband's anger. I saw another psychologist in Holland who also told me to kick him out of my life."

"Look, you're telling me that you did the cooking, but he arranged the pots and pans in a place you couldn't reach. He wanted you to work, to pay for babysitters, day care, etc. He hasn't been following you to help you with your career. He's been getting a free ride."

During her second session with Dr. Hafner, Roxana tried to emphasize the impact of the divorce on her children. "My children miss their father."

"Children adjust easily. Give them a little more entertainment. They'll forget Daddy in no time."

Roxana left Dr. Hafner's office while the doctor's words echoed in her head: "Kick him out of your life." *I already have.*

Chapter 87

After thorough research, she compiled a long list of the local law firms that specialized in international law. Every day, she sent out between twenty and twenty-five job inquiry letters and copies of her resume. She received the rejection letters at the same rate she had sent her applications. After a month of rejection, she finally had some interviews. Two big law firms showed interest in her because their clients had had transactions with Iran during the shah's regime. "As soon as the relationship improves with Iran, we'll call you."

She didn't have the heart to tell them that that would probably not happen for decades.

A partner at a medium-size law firm asked her whether she was taking birth control pills. "I was shocked when an interviewer in New York City asked me that question ten years ago. I'm astonished that a decade later that question is still being considered relevant," Roxana said, trying to conceal her disgust.

"We need someone who can be available sixty to seventy hours per week."

Another partner in a small law firm asked her about her child-care arrangement. When he heard the word *day care,* he was not pleased. "Suppose we need you at 9:00 p.m. Day cares close after 6:00 p.m."

"You just complimented me for my impressive four-page resume. Don't you think someone who has handled the jobs reflected in that resume is intelligent enough to resolve her child-care problem?"

During her last interview, with a three-man law firm, one of the partners kept asking Roxana how she had managed to practice law, participate in so many conferences, and raise two children. "When did you have time to sleep?"

After hearing so much praise, she expected a job offer, but at the end of the interview the senior partner killed her hope. "I've got to be honest with you. You're a very accomplished attorney, but it's a little intimidating for us to work with someone who has more law degrees than the three of us combined."

After reading 250 rejection letters, she recognized the problem. She was not a recent law graduate, so she couldn't be hired as an entry-level attorney. She didn't have a million-dollar client, so she couldn't join any firm as a partner. And, most importantly, she was an Iranian.

She also had realized that in a political city like Washington, DC, law and politics were two good bedfellows. The letterheads of the rejection letters she had received often included the names of some powerful former congressmen or former cabinet members who were referred to as *Counsel* or *Advisor.* She knew the background of those individuals. She couldn't compete with them because they were successful politicians, even though they were not experts in international law. She had to establish her own law firm, but how?

She began reading employment ads in the *Washington Post*. She found a research job with a large company in Washington, DC. The company was a government contractor. The subject matter was dumping waste in wetlands. The researchers were mostly recent law graduates. The pay was ten dollars an hour.

After moving out, Afshin stopped paying half of the mortgage and the utility bills as he used to. He was not paying any child support either. Roxana had to work hard and make money. She also had to establish her bar membership.

She took an intensive bar review course and was again buried in law books. In order to pass the Virginia bar exam, in addition to the general multistate test that covered specific subjects of law, she had to study twenty-six different areas of law.

Puri was a great help keeping the children entertained. However, Kurosh had just turned two and still needed his mother's attention. He was knocking on Roxana's bedroom door several times every night begging her to come out and play with him.

The night before the bar exam, Roxana was exhausted reviewing the debt-collection laws of Virginia, but she couldn't ignore Kurosh behind her door. "Sweetheart, I'm busy. Go back to Mama Puri," she said, feeling guilty.

"Mommy, if you open the door, I give you my teddy bear and all my chocolates."

She opened the door, hugged her child and took him inside. She helped him hop on the bed and showed him all her books and papers scattered on her bed. She sat on her bed, let Kurosh sit on her lap, and held him close to her while caressing his hair. She explained the books she was studying. Kurosh sat quietly for a few minutes and listened to his mother. Then he suddenly jumped off the bed and ran toward the door. "Mommy, you play with your books, and I play with my teddy bear."

The next day, she had to fly to another city in Virginia to take the bar exam. Early in the morning, as she was quietly opening the door to leave, she noticed that Darius was standing behind her rubbing his eyes. "Sweetheart, what are you doing up so early? It's 6:00 a.m."

"I know," said the sleepy Darius. "I wanted to wish you good luck."

She fought back her tears and hugged her child. "You don't have an alarm clock. How did you manage to wake up exactly at six o'clock?"

"I told my brain to wake me up at six o'clock."

She took Darius back to his bedroom, tucked him in, and left the house. During the entire taxi ride and her flight, she was not thinking about the bar exam anymore. She was wondering about the future of her children.

* * *

Nina had a baby boy in July. "I feel God has given me another Yerem," she told Roxana on the phone.

She wanted to know about her friend's new life in America. Despite Roxana's censored version of what had happened to her since their meeting in Istanbul, Nina sensed her friend's struggle. "I am on top of the world right now, but Lili is miserable in London, and you're struggling to find a job and to get your divorce," Nina said. "I pray for the day that the two of you are happy again."

"Who knows, maybe we'll see that day."

"I'll drink to that."

Roxana's peaceful life didn't last very long. Afshin lost his job and his good mood altogether. He cut the kids' visitation to one day instead of the whole weekend. He picked them up every Saturday at 10:00 a.m. and brought them back on Sunday morning. He encouraged them to play in the swimming pool in his building for hours. In the afternoon, he would take them to an indoor mall and let them hang out until dark. The kids would come home with painful sunburns, broken skin on their feet, and wrinkly skin on their hands due to long hours of being in the water. When Roxana suggested that the kids should be kept indoors during the hottest part of the day, Afshin blasted, "You can't tell me what to do when they're with me."

He had also started punishing Darius physically. One day he pulled his ear because he had run in front of Kurosh. Another day, he slapped him in the face after Darius was hit by a neighbor's kid. "I told you not to play with him," he had told him.

Roxana was furious. She sensed that Afshin was taking revenge on her by punishing her son. He couldn't abuse her physically anymore, so hitting Darius was the best way to hurt her.

She was waiting for him to get a new job and be in a better mood before asking for a divorce. One Saturday when Puri was in Shamsi's house, Afshin came to take the kids for their weekend visit. Darius was a little slow to collect his books. When Afshin blew his car's horn, Darius got scared. He dropped his books and ran out the door, but after a few minutes he came running back inside the house scratched up and dirty. Blood was running from some of the abrasions on his legs.

"Did you fall down?" Roxana asked with a panicky voice.

"Dad drove away fast before I could close the door and fasten my seat belt."

"Oh my God!" Roxana gasped.

"Don't worry, Mommy, I'm okay. Just help me wash the blood."

Roxana ran out of the house. Afshin was standing by the door looking mean and angry.

"You monster! Take him to the hospital immediately," she shouted.

"Don't make a fuss. He doesn't need any hospital."

"You'd better take him to the emergency room before I start screaming."

Afshin had never seen Roxana so angry. She had always behaved like a good silent victim, but this time, the kind, gentle wife he had known for seven years was gone. Instead, he saw a wounded tiger that was ready to attack the person who had harmed her cub.

She was trembling. She never knew she could scream that high because she had never done it before. Every time Afshin abused her, she didn't fight back. She kept asking him to stop, but this abuse was different. He was harming a child, who couldn't defend himself.

She knew that she was too distraught to drive. She kept Kurosh at home and let Afshin drive Darius to the emergency room. She kept calling the hospital until she was reassured that the result of the X-rays and other tests were normal.

It was dark when Afshin brought Darius back. He was avoiding Roxana. He sat in his car and let Darius walk to the house by himself. Roxana checked her son first to make sure he was all right. Then she approached him. "Please get yourself a lawyer. I'm filing for divorce."

"You can get a divorce, but you'll never see your kids. I'll take them back to Tehran," he warned Roxana and then drove off.

She was numb and couldn't move for a while. She walked back to her house and gave Darius a big hug. *I'll die if he kidnaps you and Kurosh.*

Chapter 88

The unexpected scream had hurt Roxana's vocal cords. She had a sore throat similar to the one she'd had after Afshin choked her. Once she lost her hoarse voice, she began looking for a divorce lawyer. She spent several thousand dollars on a well-known divorce attorney who was only interested in fighting Afshin in court. "When I'm through with him, he'll be lucky if he has a pair of pants to wear," he boasted.

"I'm not after his money," Roxana said. "He's the father of my children. I want an amicable divorce. I only want my kids. I don't want alimony or any child support."

"You're not thinking realistically."

She fired the fancy attorney and hired a nice old Irish man in Arlington. He gave her some fatherly advice. "I know it's your pride that's getting in the way, but you have to get child support. What are you going to do if you run out of your savings? Look, he has had a managerial job. I'm sure he's gonna find a similar nice job soon, but you're making only ten dollars an hour."

"I have savings that can last for six months."

Afshin ignored the proposed divorce settlement agreement he had received from Roxana's second attorney. Later, he delayed the court hearings twice by telling the judge that he hadn't found an attorney. However, when Roxana gave him a long list of divorce attorneys in Fairfax, he hired one reluctantly.

During the hearing, he took the witness stand and told the judge that he loved his wife and his children, and didn't want a divorce. "I don't have a job right now, but if I were in my country, I could've provided for my family. But here I can't," he said, trying to appeal to the judge's sympathy.

"What can I say? The poor man thinks he can be a better provider in his own country," the judge commented from the bench.

"Could you please say something about his physical abuse and his threats to kidnap my kids," Roxana whispered in her attorney's ear.

Her attorney wanted to call Elli to the witness stand. Elli had flown from New Hampshire to be with her sister during the divorce hearing, but the judge wanted to hear from Roxana. "I always let the couple come and tell their lies first before I listen to the witnesses," he said.

Roxana was about to leave the courtroom when her attorney grabbed her arm and stopped her. "Please take the witness stand," he asked.

"He doesn't know me; how dare he call me a liar?" she whispered.

She took the witness stand and described her marriage to the judge. She referred to the instances of physical abuse as well as Afshin's constant fights over money, even trivial matters. She referred to the incident where Darius was thrown out of the car due to his father's anger and negligence. When she saw the bored look on the judge's face, she finished her testimony quickly.

Elli testified that she had seen bruises on her sister's face in Tehran. She said that she had also witnessed Afshin pushing his older son and sometimes pulling his ear.

Roxana's attorney asked the judge for an order instructing Afshin not to assault or harass his client. He asked for child support and also for an order prohibiting Afshin from taking his children out of the jurisdiction.

The judge denied all the attorney's requests. "The physical abuse in Tehran and Holland are ancient history," he said. "As for the new alleged physical abuse of choking, I don't see any police report or restraining order." He then turned to Roxana's attorney and pointed his finger. "Counsel, your client is an attorney. She knows how to get a restraining order if she is assaulted. She can also bring criminal charges against him. As for the father taking his kids out of the jurisdiction, at the present time they both have custody. I have no evidence before me that he will."

"Your Honor, my client didn't want to initiate criminal charges because that would jeopardize Mr. Imani's immigration status. He would be deported," Roxana's attorney said.

The judge ignored the attorney's remarks and ordered Afshin to pay only $390 per month for the cost of Kurosh's day care.

Roxana took her briefcase and ran out of the courtroom. She couldn't believe the hostility displayed by the judge against her. For many years she had stayed in a horrible marriage to avoid the Islamic courts because she knew that they'd always favored the father. Now a judge sitting in an American court had sympathized with Afshin and acted like a Moslem judge. *All he needed was an aba and a turban.*

Roxana, comforted by Elli, sat in a chair outside the courtroom and waited for her attorney. She felt that the judge had just issued a death sentence for her. How was she supposed to prevent Afshin from kidnapping her children without a court order? she wondered.

Afshin came out of the courtroom. He walked like a wrestler who had just won a match, wearing a smirk. "You always praised the American judicial system. You thought the judges favor women. How do you like your beloved America now? In Europe, you had a prestigious job. In London you got $3,000 an hour for your legal opinion. Now you're making ten dollars an hour. Tell me what's so special about your paradise, your *Amrika*?"

She ignored his remarks. She got up and began walking fast. She couldn't listen to Afshin's victory speech anymore. Her disbelief at the judge's decision had turned into a shock now.

She spent several sleepless nights wondering about Afshin's threats. Without a court order he could use any airport in the country, kidnap the kids, and take them to Tehran.

She was relieved after a few weeks when she heard that Afshin had got a job. She knew that a good income would keep Afshin in Fairfax. She asked her attorney to negotiate with him again. "I don't trust these judges," she said. "Please try to get him to sign an out-of-court settlement. Give him anything he wants."

The attorney's negotiation failed because Afshin refused to divorce his wife. Roxana had purposefully kept her mother away from Fairfax out of the fear that she would have another heart attack. Puri was calling from New Hampshire every day. She wanted to know the details of the pending divorce. Roxana knew that she couldn't fool her mother any longer, so the last time they talked, she told her everything.

"What do you expect?" Puri asked. "The man had a beautiful wife, a cook, a babysitter, a money-making machine, and a best friend. Of course he cannot let go."

Roxana brought work home. She did many hours of overtime research in order to meet her monthly expenses. One of her worries was getting health insurance for her kids. Her temporary research job didn't provide health insurance, but Afshin's job did. She detested the idea of depending on an unreliable person like him. She knew that the minute he lost the job, her kids would lose the insurance. She remembered her contractual job with the State Department. As an interpreter, she had good health insurance. She applied to the Language Services of the State Department for her old job.

They considered her as a new applicant, so she was given a written and an oral test that took several hours. She was told that she'd be notified of the result in one week. She was pleased that she had got everything correct. After all, this was her native tongue. It was not the Arabic test that she had to study for days.

When she didn't hear from the Language Services, she called the director. "I had a test two weeks ago. My name is Roxana—"

"I know who you are," the director said. "Ms. Ramsy, I'm sorry to inform you that you didn't pass the test."

"Excuse me. Are you kidding me? I passed the test in 1971. Now, seventeen years later, my language ability has diminished?"

"I'm sorry."

Roxana had assumed that the hostage problems were over. There was no nightly reporting on the Iran crisis, but she had noticed that a lingering bias still existed against Iranians. Her struggle to find employment was the proof. People demonstrated unsettled feelings when they found out about her nationality. Whereas some Americans used a sense of humor referring to the hostage crisis, there were others who were still angry about it.

The next day her boss called her to his office. The man liked and respected Roxana. In the past, he had praised her many times because of the quality of the research she had done. She saw a sign of uneasiness in her boss. "Is there any problem?" she asked him.

"I don't know how to say this . . ." he said, pausing. "Two weeks ago we had to fill out forms to get security clearance for everybody. I'm sorry to inform you that yours failed."

"The FBI has checked me and my entire family for our green cards. Besides, I'm not dealing with classified—"

"I'm instructed to fire you."

The humiliation got worse when her boss searched her briefcase to make sure that she had not taken any research documents—materials on dumping waste in wetlands!

She sat behind the wheel of her car feeling that someone had just operated on her brain. She was numb. She couldn't think clearly. When she stopped at a red traffic light, she could see the Thomas Jefferson Memorial a short distance away. She raised her gaze and stared at the statue for a moment. *Life, liberty, and the pursuit of happiness.* She let her tears flow.

Chapter 89

Roxana began negotiating with Afshin's attorney directly. When that failed, she approached Afshin again. She enumerated the reasons that the divorce was beneficial not only for the two of them, but also for their children.

"Stop acting like a lawyer," he shouted on the phone. "Don't tell me that my kids are better off living without their father."

"Nobody's taking your kids away. You can spend as much time as you need with them. It's not healthy for them to see an angry father," she said calmly.

"Who makes me angry? You. When you're not around, I'm not angry."

"You're angry the minute you wake up. You seem to need a fight or a dispute to start your day."

"And whose fault is that?"

"If I am the cause of your anger, why don't you divorce me?"

There was a long pause before Afshin hung up.

She continued her phone conversations with Afshin several times a week until one day he agreed to divorce her. However, he imposed an unreasonable condition. "Sell the house and give me my share," he demanded.

"You paid only a $6,000 down payment. How much do you think the house has appreciated in such a short time?"

"Twenty thousand dollars."

"Don't you care about your kids? They have lived in three different places in six months. You're asking me to uproot them again?"

"If you want to keep the house, then pay me $20,000."

"You owe me thousands of dollars for the cost of the mortgage and the utilities I have paid. I don't even have the ten-dollar-an-hour research job anymore."

"I'm not living there anymore. Why should I pay for anything? As far as your job is concerned, this was your promised land, and all that nonsense. Is this how they're valuing your education?"

One day before the end of the summer when Roxana checked her mailbox, she found an envelope from the Virginia State Bar Examiners. Her heart started racing. She knew that this was the result of the two-day test she had taken in July. She couldn't open the envelope. If she had failed, she would be devastated and couldn't cook dinner for her children. Failing the exam meant another six months of waiting before she could take it again. She decided to open the envelope after the kids were asleep. She didn't want them to see their mother cry.

She went to the kitchen and started preparing spaghetti and meatballs—her children's favorite. After the dinner, she washed the dishes, bathed the kids, and read them bedtime stories.

When the kids fell asleep, she came back to the living room and opened the envelope. It was a short letter. "Oh my God, I passed," she muttered.

During the night, she woke up twice. Even though she had worked hard to pass the bar exam, she still felt that the envelope under her pillow was a treasure trove she had found. This was the most significant exam she had ever taken. She didn't need The Hague Academy's diploma; she didn't need the JSD from New York University, but she needed a bar certificate to work and support her kids.

At one point, she got out of her bed, turned the light on, and read the letter again to make sure that she wasn't dreaming. Back in bed, even with her eyes closed, she could see the smile on her face.

It was the policy of the Virginia bar not to reflect the score of the bar candidates on their letters, so the next day Roxana called and asked them for her score. She killed a joyful scream when she learned that her score was high enough to apply for membership in the bars of California, the District of Columbia, and many other jurisdictions without taking their bar exams. She hung up the telephone, raised her closed fists, and said, "Yes! Yes! Yes!"

She had another short-lived happy moment at the end of the week when she received a phone call from one of the two big law firms that had interviewed her. The senior partner on the phone offered her a job to work with a new client. Roxana's hope died away when she heard the client's name.

"I'm sorry, sir, I have to decline."

"Are you kidding me? Attorneys would give an arm and a leg to represent this company," the partner said, sounding surprised.

"You're right, but this is the company that had a huge case against several Iranian government entities before The Hague Tribunal. I represented those entities, so it would be unprofessional and unethical for me to represent the American litigant now."

When she hung up, she wished Dr. Rohani—her former boss—had heard that conversation. She had refused a $150,000 salary despite her financial need because of her ethics. Dr. Rohani didn't know that no one could put a price tag on Roxana. She had refused to demand hundreds of gold coins as her *Mehrieh* when she married. Had she accepted a multimillion-*toman* price tag, Afshin was the one who had to pay her money.

* * *

Roxana applied for membership at the DC bar. Because of her high score, all she needed was three letters of recommendation. Jeffrey Rubin and Mathew Stein, her former employers, each wrote a letter emphasizing Roxana's knowledge of various laws, professionalism, and good moral character. She was surprised when she read Attorney Keller's letter. She called him to explain why she couldn't submit his letter. "Mr. Keller, you've praised me too much," she said. "You can't tell the DC bar that they should be honored to have me as a member."

"Why not? I've worked with you on numerous difficult cases. You're a brilliant attorney, and they should know that."

"It just sounds very arrogant."

"You're not saying those words; I am. I know you're coming from a humble culture, but here in the States, being humble doesn't work. You have to let them know who you are."

"Could you please modify the letter and send it to me?"

"Too late, my dear. I've already submitted the letter to the DC bar. What you have in your hands is your courtesy copy."

It would usually take nine months to a year for the DC bar to review a bar membership application, so when Roxana received her certificate within six months, she wondered whether Attorney Keller's letter had done the magic.

Chapter 90

Keeping Darius entertained was a big challenge for Roxana. During their first summer in the States, a children's book Bahram had sent Darius—*Jesus of Nazareth*—intrigued him. He kept asking his mother to explain the difficult words. By the end of the week, he started reading the thick book by himself. The book provoked Afshin when he caught Darius reading it during a weekend visit. "It's okay with me that your brother is a Christian, but he can't impose his religion on my son," he told Roxana in anger.

"But it's okay if you're imposing your parents' religion on him?"

Afshin walked away shaking his head.

Because Darius was able to finish reading many children's books in one day, going to the public library had become a routine chore for Roxana like grocery shopping. When Darius started kindergarten, Roxana also signed him up for the after-school program. Now when he came home at 5:00 p.m., he didn't complain about being bored anymore. He was content reading two or three books after dinner.

Her daily nine-to-five freedom gave Roxana time to establish her solo practice. She found dozens of clients but ended up representing most of them *pro bono*. The clients included abused women who couldn't afford hiring an attorney to help them with their divorce, as well as people who had immigration problems but no money.

In early December, Roxana received a letter from the director of Tehran International Airline. TIA informed her that the in-house counsel job in its Paris office was still available to her. They were also offering her round-trip tickets for her entire family to travel around the world. Roxana called the director. "Are you serious?" she asked.

"Yes. You did such a wonderful job for us in our arbitration that we feel this is the least we can do for you."

"I didn't do anything. You won the case because you had a strong claim."

"You're too modest. Aren't you tempted to come and live in Paris?"

"Thanks for the offer, but I'm trying to establish my practice here, and my kids need stability. I can't uproot them again."

Roxana had always desired to visit Rio and Hong Kong, but she had to give up her dream because Darius voted for Disneyland. She thought that her little boy had suffered a lot in the hands of his angry father—he deserved to visit Disneyland.

* * *

Since she had four tickets, Roxana invited her brother Bahram to join them. He made the trip more pleasant. The kids enjoyed their visit at the Disney amusement park beyond Roxana's imagination. During the last day of their stay, while Bahram entertained his nephews, Roxana visited Nina, who lived an hour away from downtown LA.

"Last year this time, I was so unhappy, but now I have a six-month-old baby and a peaceful life," Nina said. "Sometimes I wonder why on earth I ever decided to go back to Iran."

"Have you forgotten the hostage crisis and the anti-Iranian sentiments in the United States?"

"No, I haven't, but I think we were too young and too emotional."

Nina wanted to know all the details about her friend's life. Despite her reluctance, Roxana talked about her separation from Afshin and her financial struggle to establish a one-woman law firm.

"Let me help out. I made tons of money in Iran, and I'm making money here—"

"I can't accept money from you."

"Why not? I owe you a legal fee. That one-dollar fee was a joke."

"As I told you before, you're family."

* * *

Back in Virginia, Roxana received a surprise letter from Mr. Elkhouri. She opened it immediately, hoping that he had renewed his job offer to Afshin, but the content of the letter was different. Although Mr. Elkhouri had expressed a feeling of guilt over his failure to establish the Washington office, he did not mention Afshin. Instead, he had found some clients for Roxana.

Mr. Elkhouri's friends worked at the World Bank. One needed an attorney to settle his disputes with his partners. The other two friends needed legal advice on how to form a new corporation.

It took a week for Roxana to sort out the legal issues for Mr. Elkhouri's friends regarding their new corporation, but the problem of the friend who needed a dispute settlement with his partners lasted for months.

They met at the World Bank's cafeteria. Mr. El Wafa was a pleasant Egyptian man in his midfifties. The minute he introduced himself, he said, "Elkhouri has talked so much about you that I feel I know you."

"That's very nice of him. Now how can I help you?"

"I need to have my own attorney because my partners have turned against me."

Roxana explained to Mr. El Wafa that she had just started her practice and that she had a home-based office in Fairfax. "Until I find an office in DC, we will have to meet either here or in some restaurants in town," she said.

"That's fine with me. I need your brain, not your office."

As Roxana reviewed the documents her new client had handed her, she noticed that he was staring at her with a kind smile.

"Is there something you want to tell me?"

"No. I've always admired Persian women. I followed your revolution. I saw the footage of women demonstrating against *hejab* on TV. I've also seen those who wear *chadors*. Despite their *hejab*, they're still out there in the streets expressing themselves."

"Women participated in Iran's Constitutional Revolution in the early 1900s."

"I know. You also had two queens who ruled the Persian Empire for seven years."

"How do you know that?"

"We Egyptians know a lot about the Persians and the Greeks. I have a question for you. Now that Iran has established a republic, do you think one day you'll have a powerful woman running the country like Margaret Thatcher?"

"I don't think so."

"How come?"

"Because it's very difficult to find a Mr. Thatcher in Iran." Roxana smiled.

"What do you mean?"

"A man who can stand behind his wife and enjoy her success. An Iranian woman is a Persian princess to her father, but when she marries, she has to serve a king."

* * *

Roxana's mother and her youngest sister, Neghar, traveled to Virginia to spend the Christmas holidays with her. With their help, they decorated a seven-foot-tall Christmas tree she had purchased at their neighborhood shopping center. The tree gave a new life to the house and excited her children. It also reminded her of the day Afshin tore up the little Christmas tree Darius had made in Holland.

On the last day of her family's visit, Roxana got a helping hand from Neghar to remove the heavy piles of law books from her bedroom to the storage room. She noticed that Darius was looking at her law books with fascination.

"Now that your mom has passed the bar exam, should we burn all her books?" Neghar asked Darius jokingly.

"Can I read them first?" Darius asked.

Neghar repeated that story proudly many times in many different gatherings, boasting about her nephew's love for books.

Roxana was invited to several New Year's Eve parties hosted by her friends, but she decided to spend a quiet night at home with her children. When the children fell asleep, she came back to the living room and turned the TV on. She watched the traditional Macy's ball fall, and listened to the "Auld Lang Syne" song. She couldn't help remembering the year before—her panic attack on New Year's Eve, her paralyzed left arm, and her lost voice.

She went to her children's bedroom, kissed them both, and whispered, "Happy New Year, my angels." She came back to the living room, muted the TV, and put a CD in the player. She sat in her chair and listened to Adamo singing, "*C'est ma vie.*" This is my life. I didn't choose this life; it chose me.

Chapter 91

Through Mr. El Wafa, Roxana found a few more clients. Her quick handling of El Wafa's legal issues had impressed him and his partners equally. At the end of an amicable dispute resolution, the partners retained Roxana as the partnership's attorney. The modest monthly retainer fee put some money back into Roxana's almost empty bank account, but she still worried about money. She wondered why she always had money problems whenever she lived in the United States. She got an answer a few days later when she ran into Mr. Sidell, a prominent attorney from one of Washington's large law firms. She was attending a conference about the Iran-US Claims Tribunal in Holland.

After several speakers hinted that the Iranian revolution was the result of the shah's hasty modernization of Iran, Roxana became frustrated. She had heard similar speeches and read similar arguments in the newspapers during the hostage crisis in 1979. Now, ten years later, the international law pundits still repeated the same story. She raised her hand to comment several times, but it was obvious to her that the moderator allowed comments only from people he knew.

She left the conference room and headed toward the coffee table. She didn't know that Attorney Sidell had followed her. She had known him from some conferences she had attended in the '70s.

"I saw your frustration there," Mr. Sidell said as he approached Roxana.

"Hello, Mr. Sidell, nice to see you again," Roxana said as she poured a cup of coffee for herself. "Isn't it a little odd that the topic is the Iran-US Claims Tribunal, and all you hear is the US side?"

"Well, some speakers explained the Iranians' point of view."

"Shouldn't Iran's point of view be explained by an Iranian politician or lawyer?"

"Maybe they invited them, and they refused to come."

"No one knocked on my door. I dealt with that tribunal for many years."

"What are you doing back here in Washington?"

"My mother had a heart attack. I had to leave Holland."

"Where are you working now?"

"I couldn't find a job with any international law firms, so I'm a solo practitioner now."

"The problem for you is that we have too many American experts in international law. We don't need foreign lawyers. To be honest with you, we don't take them *seriously*. When they apply to our law firm, I always tell them to go and look for a job in Australia."

"Thanks for the advice. I'll keep that in mind."

As she was looking for a place to sit and enjoy her coffee, she heard a voice, "Excuse me, do I know you from somewhere?" Roxana turned around and immediately recognized the man. He was one of the three American arbitrators from the tribunal.

"Your voice is so familiar, but I can't recognize—"

"Your Honor, I'm Roxana Ramsy. I have appeared before you several times at The Hague Tribunal."

"Ah, I couldn't recognize you without your scarf. I still remember the fascinating case you won and your argument on the continuous ownership of claim theory."

"Thanks."

"Why did you leave Den Haag?"

"For family matters."

Attorney Sidell's words echoed in Roxana's ears all night. She had to accept the fact that every successful attorney in Washington considered himself an expert in international law. After all, the city was full of foreign embassies and foreigners; that was enough to make every lawyer an international law expert!

* * *

In October 1989, Roxana was offered a part-time teaching job from a local law school. She replaced a retired professor teaching Conflict of Laws, and Ethics. The pay was low and the hours she spent preparing handouts for her students were long. But she needed to make enough money to pay Afshin and buy her freedom. The price tag was $20,000.

She drafted a new divorce settlement agreement asking for health insurance for the kids and $1,000 child support per month. She waived any alimony and agreed to pay $20,000 to Afshin. She called Afshin's attorney and asked him whether he would discuss the settlement with him.

"I'm sorry, Dr. Ramsy. Your husband has forbidden me to talk to you," the attorney said. "He believes that will create unnecessary billable hours. He hasn't paid me anything except the initial retainer fee. I believe you've spoiled him. All his married life, he had a free attorney at home, so it's difficult for him to pay attorney fees now."

She began negotiating with Afshin directly. He reluctantly agreed to the health insurance for the kids when Roxana committed herself to pay half of the insurance cost. However, he was adamant that the $390 the judge had ordered him to pay was the fair and reasonable amount of child support.

"That was only for Kurosh's day care."

In Afshin's mind, since he was not living in the marital home, he had no obligations to pay anything. She amended the divorce settlement agreement, met her own attorney, and asked him to finish the deal. Her attorney expressed his concern before Roxana left his office. "You waived everything. How can you survive without any child support?"

"I'll manage."

Using Roxana's $20,000 and some of his own money, Afshin bought a condominium. She gave him many pieces of furniture and household equipment even though she had purchased them with her own money. After the payment, she thought that her problems with Afshin would end. She didn't know that he would continue his revenge by using the weekend visits to poison their kids' minds.

One night, she was waiting for her kids to return from their father's house. She was standing on her dark porch to avoid Afshin.

When the kids came out of the car, she heard Darius whisper to his brother, "Don't say anything to Mom."

She hugged her children and brought them inside. She asked Darius to come to the living room for a while. "Sweetheart, I need to talk to you." She sat next to him, held his hands, and asked him about his father's comment.

"He told us that you're trying to put him in jail," Darius said reluctantly. "'No, Dad, that's not true,' I told him. 'My mom only wants to divorce you.'"

She hugged her son and held him for a long while. "You're right, my angel. I only want to divorce him."

After Darius fell asleep, she stared at his innocent face and felt guilty. *A seven-year-old child should not be put in a position to defend his mother.*

Chapter 92

In mid-December 1989, when Roxana was impatiently waiting for the arrival of Lili from London, she received an invitation from the American University Law School to participate in a panel discussion on "International Law and the Decade of the '80s." The seminar was scheduled for mid-January, but she wanted to do her research immediately. She had followed world events during the '80s, but until she began her research, she didn't know what a significant decade she had lived through. She had no choice but to talk about the war she had witnessed—Saddam's invasion of Iran in September 1980. She wrote how the eight-year-old war ended on August 20, 1988, leaving as many as a million dead and more than five hundred thousand injured.

She wrote about the Israeli invasion of Lebanon in 1982, the war between Argentina and the United Kingdom over the Falkland Islands, and the US invasion of Granada in 1983 and Panama in 1984.

She emphasized the two significant events of 1989—the collapse of the Soviet Union after the Soviets left Afghanistan and the fall of the Berlin Wall.

Roxana's research revealed some positive events as well. Numerous countries had become independent, and democracy had replaced some dictatorship regimes.

On the day Roxana concluded her research, she received an envelope from the court. She opened it at once, and there it was, her divorce decree. She sat in her chair, held it against her heart with both hands, and all she could hear was the voice of Dr. King, "Free at last, free at last."

She was free, but was she happy? She wondered. She felt like a soldier standing on top of the hill of victory. She had won the war but was too badly wounded to enjoy her victory. She thought about her marriage, the abuse, and how hard she had tried to save that marriage. She thought about Afshin. What was wrong with the man? He was an intelligent individual who knew how to be a revolutionary and how to be a feminist, but he didn't know how to be a good husband or a good father.

Roxana's train of thought was interrupted when she heard a familiar sound. There was a cooing coming from the large magnolia tree in her backyard. She smiled. Her mourning dove had found her again. *Does the bird know about my stormy divorce?*

She went back to her research and wrote on her notepad, "Roxana Ramsy's divorce was the most significant event in 1989." She deleted the last line and smiled.

*   *   *

When Lili's taxi arrived, the kids were asleep, but Roxana was waiting on her porch to greet her. It was a joyful reunion—the two had been apart for almost three years. Lili's first question was about her friend's long-awaited divorce. Roxana showed her the court's decree. "I never believed in Santa," she said, "but look, I got my Christmas gift a week before Christmas."

"Congratulations! You know I never liked him."

"Let's talk about you. Nina said you're going to Paris."

"Our bank is transferring me to their Paris branch. I'm planning to get my dad to come and live with me. We have relatives and lots of friends in Paris."

"But your dad didn't want to leave Iran."

"Since Aunt Narges got married and moved out, he's been feeling very lonely. He's ready now, but the government has refused to issue him an exit visa. I think it's because I left my government job; they're punishing him."

"That's why I told you to go back to Tehran and work for them for a while and then resign."

"I wish I had listened to you."

"What about Kayvan?"

"He has been visiting me in London. I suppose he'll do the same in Paris. Do you know his wife had a second miscarriage? She also lost her father. She's more suicidal than ever."

"Suicidal?"

"She has made two suicide attempts. I learned that recently myself. That was the reason he couldn't divorce her."

The next morning Roxana woke up to the smell of coffee and pancakes. She found Lili preparing breakfast in the kitchen. "It's 6:00 a.m. You should be in bed."

"It's noon in London. Besides, I want to tour the city."

"It's raining hard."

"I can visit the museums."

After breakfast, Lili helped Darius to get ready for school. Roxana dressed Kurosh to go to his day care. She covered her hair under a large navy blue rain hat and put her raincoat on. She decided to take a day off and accompany Lili to Washington.

She drove Darius to his school first. Because of the rain, she decided to drop him off closer to the entrance door. She stopped the car 150 feet away from the door. Darius ran toward the door, but a female school employee soon stopped him. Roxana waited patiently in the car while the woman was talking to Darius. But when she saw him getting soaked, she asked Lili to find out what the problem was.

Lili approached the school employee who was still talking to Darius. "Pardon me, madam, is there any problem?"

"Oh, you have a lovely British accent. Are you from London?"

"Yes, madame, but the child is soaked—"

"I asked him to explain to his mother that she cannot drop him off this close to the school's entrance."

"Couldn't you let the child go inside, and talk to his mother directly?"

"I thought she probably couldn't speak English—"

"Madame," Lili interrupted her. "That woman sitting in the car knows seven languages. You bloody Americans. You see a brown-eyed child, and you automatically assume his parents are uneducated immigrants?"

Lili took Darius inside the school, gave him a hug, and returned to the car.

"What was that all about?" Roxana asked.

"Nothing. You were right; Americans love my British accent," Lili said and smiled.

"It seemed to me that you were arguing with her."

"She was telling Darius that you couldn't drop him off near the school entrance."

* * *

Puri came to Washington to spend Christmas with Roxana and her grandchildren. She was thrilled to see Lili. While Puri was enjoying her grandchildren, Roxana took Lili everywhere. She even took her to New York City and introduced her to Judith.

At the end of her trip, Lili admitted that the United States was an amazing country. "It's a lovely place for the Americans, but people here still show prejudice against foreigners."

"Did that school employee say something to Darius on that rainy day?" Roxana asked.

"Do you always have to be so bloody smart? Okay, Ms. Know-it-all! She was explaining things to Darius because she thought you didn't speak English."

"Oh my gosh! My funny rain hat did it again." Roxana laughed.

"I wonder how you can laugh about this. One day you're on top of your profession in Europe, and then another day you're working for ten dollars an hour because you love to live in *Amrika*. I'm sorry, people in your adopted country are still racist, and they discriminate against others."

"What I love about America is that it's so vast that you can easily disappear in the crowd like a raindrop in an ocean. I'd like to disappear here for a while."

Chapter 93

In June 1990, Roxana received disturbing news from Nina. The government had imprisoned Yahya, Lili's father. Apparently he had been writing editorials for an antigovernment newspaper for a year. When they arrested the publisher, Yahya appeared in court as the publisher's attorney and defended him, but during the trial he criticized the government, the constitution, and the Islamic judicial system.

"Lili's planning to go back to Tehran and see her father," Nina said on the phone with a panicky voice.

"She just got herself settled in Paris. I talked to her last week."

"This happened two days ago. It's not safe for her to go back to Tehran. I'm going to Paris to stop her. Please come with me. You know she'll listen to you."

Roxana agreed with Nina that this was a dire situation. Lili had left a sensitive government job three years ago when she was warned about the serious consequences if she didn't return to Tehran. With no Iranian passport, she had no choice but to travel with her British passport. *She'll be arrested the minute she arrives at the airport.*

That night, Roxana kept turning and tossing in bed. The thought of Yahya, an intellectual lawyer, sitting in jail was unreal. For a moment she thought that instead of Lili, she should be the one to go to Tehran and defend Yahya, but she knew that would put her at risk of getting imprisoned herself. She had to worry about her children. Afshin would've loved to see her in jail. He would've taken their children to Tehran and would get their sole custody and keep them there forever.

She realized that this wasn't the right time for her to act heroic. She called her mother and asked her to fly to Washington and spend a few days with her children.

"Of course I'll take care of the kids," Puri said. "Please go and help Lili and her father. Yahya was so kind to us when your father passed away. For a month, he called me every day asking me if I needed anything."

* * *

Nina was thrilled when she heard that Roxana had decided to fly to Paris. "Please keep Lili occupied until I get there. I have some hospital matters to wrap up. I'll be there maybe two days after your arrival."

Nina took Roxana's hotel address and telephone number. And when Roxana asked whether she needed a hotel reservation in Paris, she replied, "Don't worry about me. I'll stay with my relatives."

Nina finished her conversation with Roxana in a hurry and then dialed another number. "I have all the information you need. But please don't show up anywhere before talking to me first," Nina said. "She's gone through hell; we have to be careful."

"I understand, but is she really okay?" a man's voice asked her.

"After the divorce, she told us that she felt like a soldier who had won the war, but she had too many wounds to enjoy her victory."

Nina placed a call to Puri and assured her that her plan was moving smoothly. "I'll see you and the kids in Washington," she said before hanging up.

* * *

Roxana's hotel on Rue St. Louis was within walking distance from Lili's place. When she entered the apartment, she saw many unopened boxes scattered around. Lili was sleeping on a small cot. Her one-bedroom apartment in Quartier Latin was typical—very small.

"I'm sorry the apartment is in such a mess," Lili said, searching for a chair for Roxana. "I haven't had a chance to unpack, much less to shop for furniture."

"I'm here to see you, not your apartment."

"If I had fixed my apartment sooner, you wouldn't have to stay in a hotel."

"My hotel is fine."

Roxana suggested that the two of them go out, find a nice sidewalk café, sit down, and talk. Lili agreed. They left the apartment and began walking. After a short walk on Boulevard St. Germain, Roxana realized that this was not the Paris of 1980 when the two friends acted like aimless *flaneurs* strolling the streets of the city and appreciating everything they observed. She was in Paris, but she felt that Paris wasn't there—the same way she had felt in 1983 when she traveled from Holland to Paris to celebrate the Persian New Year holiday.

They found a sidewalk café, and despite the nice weather outside, they chose a table by the window inside. It was more serene. Roxana followed Lili's gaze into the crowd of people walking by. When their waiter brought their café au lait, she thought the time was right to talk to Lili about her hasty decision to return to Tehran. "Your father will be freed before you know it," she said, "but his freedom doesn't mean you're gonna be free. Remember, you left a sensitive government job and stayed in Europe."

"Roxana, I have to be there. I have to visit my father and let him know that I haven't abandoned him."

"He knows that. You can be more effective getting him released here. You can write to all the European newspapers. You can get human rights groups involved and let them know he's in jail because he has criticized his government."

"There's another reason I have to go. Kayvan is divorced. Finally I'm going to be his real wife."

"When did that happen?"

"Yesterday."

"If he's free, then he can come here and live with you."

"That's true, but that doesn't change the fact that my father is in jail. I cannot be happy until he's free."

"And you think you can be happy living in Iran?"

"Look, our lives have changed so much over the past decade that I cannot really define *happiness* anymore. We were a bunch of intellectuals excited about the changes in Iran. The revolution seemed like a river running smoothly. We sat by the river and enjoyed it for a while, but all of a sudden, the river turned into a tsunami and destroyed everything."

"Maybe, we're like the *lost generation* Gertrude Stein was talking about."

"Yes, but no famous author in the West is going to write about our suffering."

"I wonder what Hemingway would've written about the Iranian revolution had he witnessed it. I wonder for which side of the war Papa would've fought, Iraq or Iran?"

"Of course he would've fought for the Iranian side. Saddam was the invader."

* * *

The Revolutionary Guard who took Lili to a small office at the Mehrabad Airport told her that she should have obtained a visa to come to Iran. He also needed to check her British passport again. After two hours of waiting, Lili felt that her friends' predictions had come true. For two days Roxana and Nina had pleaded with her not to travel to Tehran.

The Revolutionary Guard returned to the room accompanied by an airport security officer. Lili's heart was beating fast. She felt someone had put a gun to her head and was ready to pull the trigger.

"*Sarcar,* is there any problem with my passport?" she asked, her voice shaken.

"You left Tehran with a government passport eight years ago. What happened to that passport?"

"It expired. I don't have it anymore."

"Why have you come back to Iran again?"

"My father's in jail. I've come back to see him."

The officer took more information from Lili and left. Lili was alone again. She was sweating. She felt she was under arrest. Another two hours passed; the officer came back to the room, stamped her passport, and handed it to her. "If you consider yourself an Iranian, you had better travel with an Iranian passport. I have issued a temporary visa for you, but if you decide to leave, you may not get an exit visa. You also have to immediately report to your employer to face the consequences of leaving your job eight years ago."

"Thank you, *Sarcar*," Lili said, hugely relieved.

As she was leaving the room, the officer addressed her. "By the way, your father was released this afternoon."

Lili's knees buckled. She couldn't move.

"Officer, may I use your telephone? I have to make an urgent call."

The officer made a telephone available to Lili and left the room. She dialed Roxana's hotel number. It was 6:00 p.m. Paris time. When she heard Roxana's voice, she whispered, "I'm free, and my dad's free too."

"Thank God. Are you okay? I've been dying here since you left."

"This is a government telephone. I can't talk much. I'll call you from home."

Outside the terminal, Lili was lost among the crowd that was waiting for their passengers. She was shoved and pushed around many times before she found her way out. As she was approaching the taxi line, she felt a tap on her shoulder.

"Mrs. Panahi, are you looking for a ride?"

She knew that voice; she turned around and threw herself into Kayvan's open arms. She kissed him in front of astonished strangers. She had forgotten that she was in a Moslem country and couldn't display affection in public. The two lovers had tears in their eyes. They began walking toward Kayvan's car. Lili held his hand tight as if she was about to lose him again. She had traveled to The Hague, London, and Paris, but she didn't know that her happiness was waiting for her in Tehran like an unopened gift.

* * *

Meanwhile, back in Paris, Nina was trying to convince Roxana to stay a few days longer. "Now that we know Lili's safe, we can enjoy *your* Paris a little longer."

"This is not *my* Paris anymore. I miss my children. I'm gonna fly back to Washington tomorrow."

Nina took Roxana by the hand and dragged her out of her room and into the hallway. "I want to show you some people."

"Who? Where are you taking me?"

Nina knocked on the door of a room at the end of the hallway and then opened it. "There they are," she said, pointing to Puri, Darius, and Kurosh.

Roxana gasped. She couldn't believe her eyes. Her kids were sitting on a sofa next to her mother. "Oh my gosh, you flew them to Paris?" Roxana ran to her children, took them both into her arms, and showered them with kisses. "When did they come to Paris?"

"Nina thought you needed a little vacation after your divorce," Puri volunteered. "We all flew together."

"How can I ever thank you?" Roxana asked Nina.

"This is nothing compared to what you did for me in Istanbul," Nina responded. "I've bought you a gift for getting our American passports. You're gonna wear it tonight, and we'll go someplace nice to celebrate Lili and Yahya's freedom."

Nina's gift was a dress she had purchased from one of the boutiques on Rue du Faubourg. She insisted and helped Roxana to put it on. The dress was a red velvet silhouette. Its empire waist and flare skirt highlighted Roxana's body.

"This is too sexy; I can't wear it," Roxana complained.

"The last time you dressed up was for your wedding," Puri commented. "That was almost a decade ago. Enjoy the dress—go, get out, and have fun."

Grateful for Puri's remarks, Nina got the courage to fix Roxana's hair. She sat her in a chair in front of the dresser. She took the pins out and styled Roxana's shoulder-length hair. "Now you're ready for a night out in Paris."

* * *

Nina took Roxana on a riverboat tour where they played music and served buffet dinner. As soon as they were seated at their table, Nina ordered a bottle of wine. She began talking about their lives. Roxana was relaxed knowing that Lili and Yahya were both free.

Nina changed the subject of their conversation and talked about Steve Radcliff, his ex-wife's death, and his book about Iran. "Do you know that when his ex was diagnosed with lung cancer, he devoted a lot of his time taking care of her?" Nina asked. "That was the time he disappeared from Holland."

"What a kind gesture; what a decent man! Afshin would've celebrated the news if I had cancer."

"We knew all about Steve's life, mostly because of you. He wanted to know everything that was happening in your life. He wrote to us, even called us many times asking about you."

"And who gave you permission to give him the details of my miserable life?"

"I did, and Lili approved." Nina laughed. "Wouldn't it be wonderful if he came back into your life again?"

"I have two little men in my life right now. I don't need anyone else. I'm scared even thinking about another man."

"You can always have him as a friend, can't you?"

"I suppose."

Nina got up to find out when they served the buffet dinner. "I'm getting hungry. I also want to talk to the DJ. I'm tired of listening to their classic music."

When Nina left the table, Roxana looked around. For the first time she noticed that most of the tourists on the boat were married couples or lovers. There was a nice view of Paris from every window. The boat was passing through Pont Alexandre now. As she stared at the bridge's ornate candelabra-style lamps, she heard a familiar voice. "Pardon, mademoiselle, is this seat taken?"

She turned and looked up to find Steve Radcliff looking at her with his dazzling smile.

For a moment she froze, and then she felt butterflies in her stomach. "What are you doing here?" she sighed, trying to hide her joy.

"I couldn't sit back and let a beautiful person with a brilliant mind disappear in the crowd like a raindrop in an ocean."

"Oh boy, I didn't know my friends memorized every word that came out of my mouth."

"I'm glad they did."

Steve sat down and handed Roxana a gift. "This is for you."

"What is it?"

"It's my book. It'll be in the bookstores next week."

"Wow! You finally finished it," Roxana said as she opened the gift wrap. The book's title was *The Stolen Revolution.* On the first page were two words: *To Roxana.*

She turned her head around and looked outside the window. Her tears had blurred the illuminated Paris. She couldn't recognize the area the boat was passing through. She lowered her gaze and covered her face with her hands. Steve took both of her hands and kissed them repeatedly. He pulled his chair closer to her, put his right arm around her, and kissed her hair. "Let the tears out," he whispered.

"What am I supposed to say when you dedicate a book to me?" She wiped her tears.

"Don't say anything. Just let me love you."

She gazed into the window again, fighting tears. He stood up and helped her out of her chair. "No more tears. Please dance with me. They're playing your favorite song."

"I don't hear anything."

"Listen closely."

She tuned in and heard Adamo singing, "*C'est ma vie.*" She smiled.

He pulled her gently toward him and started dancing. "Do you know how many times I have dreamed of this moment—to have you in my arms—to have you in my life?"

He kissed her as they moved around the dance floor, and she surrendered. With every soft kiss and with every dance movement, she felt that Paris was becoming the heaven she used to know and the mistress she used to have. Now she owned a small piece of Paris again. She leaned her forehead on his left shoulder and closed her eyes. He held her firmly and told her how much he loved her. She knew she'd never have to listen to Adamo alone.

CPSIA information can be obtained at www.ICGtesting.com
Printed in the USA
BVOW071154290413

319385BV00001B/4/P

9 781475 980622